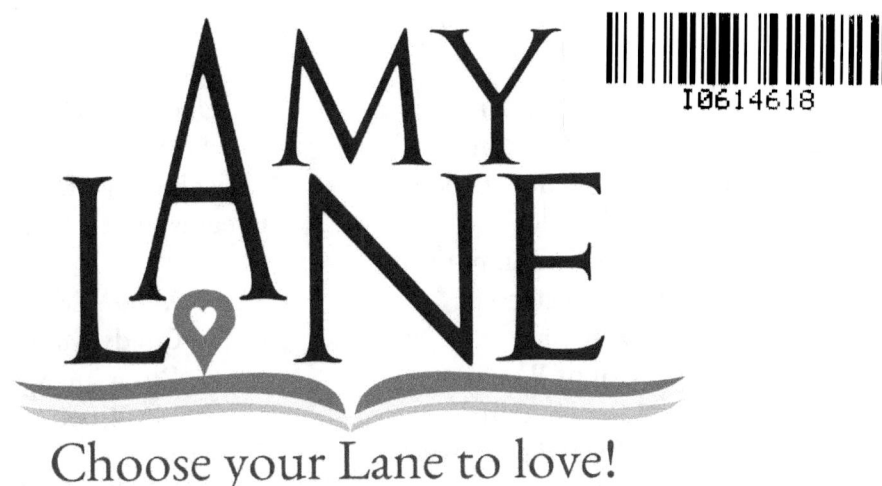

Choose your Lane to love!

Beneath the Stain

"Amy Lane at her best and yes there is lots and lots of angst!"
—Prism Book Alliance

"Lane's *Stain* is very raw and intense, showing the darker side of one young man's journey to fame."
—MM Good Book Reviews

Behind the Curtain

"…Amy can rock the socks off a blank piece of paper. The rhythm of the words, the flow of the story, her style is just brilliant. I fell as hard for the author as I fell for the characters."
—Sinfully Gay Romance Book Reviews

Bolt-hole

"…Amy Lane at her best, moving us through emotional turmoil, healing, and growth as MC Terrell emerges from his own personal bolt-hole."
—Hearts on Fire

"…another wonderful story by Amy Lane and one that I highly recommend."
—Joyfully Jay

By Amy Lane

Behind the Curtain
Beneath the Stain
Bewitched by Bella's Brother
Bolt-hole
Christmas with Danny Fit
Clear Water
Do-over
Fish Out of Water
Food for Thought
Gambling Men: The Novel
Going Up!
Grand Adventures (Dreamspinner Anthology)
Hammer & Air
If I Must
Immortal
It's Not Shakespeare
Left on St. Truth-be-Well
The Locker Room
Mourning Heaven
Phonebook
Puppy, Car, and Snow
Racing for the Sun
Raising the Stakes
Shiny!
Shirt
Sidecar
A Solid Core of Alpha
Super Sock Man
Tales of the Curious Cookbook
Three Fates (Multiple Author Anthology)
Truth in the Dark
Turkey in the Snow

Under the Rushes
Winter Ball
Wishing on a Blue Star (Dreamspinner Anthology)

CANDY MAN
Candy Man
Bitter Taffy
Lollipop

KEEPING PROMISE ROCK
Keeping Promise Rock • Making Promises • Living Promises • Forever Promised

JOHNNIES
Chase in Shadow • Dex in Blue • Ethan in Gold • Black John

GRANBY KNITTING
The Winter Courtship Rituals of Fur-Bearing Critters
How to Raise an Honest Rabbit • Knitter in His Natural Habitat
Blackbird Knitting in a Bunny's Lair

TALKER
Talker • Talker's Redemption • Talker's Graduation

ANTHOLOGIES
The Granby Knitting Menagerie
The Talker Collection

Published by
DREAMSPINNER PRESS
www.dreamspinnerpress.com

FISH
OUT OF
WATER
Amy Lane

REAMSPINNER
PRESS

Published by

DREAMSPINNER PRESS

5032 Capital Circle SW, Suite 2, PMB# 279, Tallahassee, FL 32305-7886 USA
www.dreamspinnerpress.com

Fish Out of Water
© 2016 Amy Lane.

Cover Art
© 2016 Reese Dante.
http://www.reesedante.com
Cover content is for illustrative purposes only and any person depicted on the cover is a model.

ISBN: 978-1-63477-378-2
Digital ISBN: 978-1-63477-379-9
Library of Congress Control Number: 2016902318
Published July 2016
v. 1.0

Printed in the United States of America
∞
This paper meets the requirements of
ANSI/NISO Z39.48-1992 (Permanence of Paper).

To Mary. There's not enough knitting in the world to show you how very blessed you've made me. And to Mate, because we read Lee Childs and I might get him to read Kathy Reichs. And to the kids, for being proud of me, even when I don't talk a lot about what I do.

Acknowledgments

THANK YOU *so much* to Kim Fielding, who read this and said, "Uh, they'd be having this discussion in a jail cell, not an office," and "You know, lawyers don't type up nearly so many briefs." And basically made me feel like I had a life preserver in the deep end of action/suspense fiction, because while I'm used to being neither fish nor fowl, I do like knowing how to swim.

Prologue: Good-byes in Smoke

"SHE WOULD have hated this," Jade said, pulling hard on a cigarette.

Jackson Rivers glared at his ex-girlfriend, the sister of his best friend, and one of four—no, three—people he actually cared about in the world.

Jade had promised her mother she'd quit, just like Jackson had.

"She would have hated you smoking," he muttered.

"Yeah, well, if she didn't like smoking so much, she should have quit before it gave her cancer." Jade took an angry drag and tossed him a scowl. She usually wore microbraided extensions, but her mom had been sick for a long time while all of her "children" had been dealing with college—or, in Jackson's case, the police academy. She hadn't had any fucking time to get her hair done, so it was scraped back into a severe bun on the back of her head. Jackson hoped she'd have time again. She'd always loved shaking her braids back in high school, and he'd always thought it was sexy.

"Hey," Jackson said, determined to do what Toni Cameron had asked of him. "I quit."

Jade rolled her eyes. "Yeah, well, you only started to get with me, so that's fair."

Hell of it was, she was right. Jackson would have done anything to fit in with Jade and Kaden's family. Smoking was no big deal.

"Dammit, Jackson, make her quit smoking."

Jackson turned his head and looked over the headstones in the old graveyard off Auburn Boulevard.

And smiled. "I couldn't make her stop when we were together," he said mildly, and then he went in for the hug.

Kaden Cameron, his oldest and best friend, and Kaden's wife, Rhonda, whom he'd known almost as long, stood there, and God, it was good to see them. Especially the granite presence that was Kaden. Six feet five inches of solid family man, with brown eyes so limpid and wide, Jackson used to think he could see the future in them.

And that was *before* Jackson realized he was bi.

He'd never crushed on K, though. Jade, yes, because Jackson and Jade were birds of a feather. But K represented something bigger, more important to Jackson than a potential lover.

In sixth grade, Jackson had been forging his mother's signature on the free-lunch form when Kaden had asked him to pass up his math. Jackson had accidentally passed up the form instead.

No big deal—in their school, 98 percent of the students needed that form, and the other 2 percent were too stupid to forge the signature.

But Kaden had passed the paper back and said, "Your math, idiot. And don't get too excited about lunch—they're serving mystery enchiladas today."

Jackson closed his eyes and fought a groan. "Man, last time I had the runs for a week!"

"No shit." They both looked nervously up at the teacher to see if she'd heard the profanity, but she was too busy dealing with that one kid who always freaked out and started throwing chairs.

"Well, thanks for the warning. At least I'll get some bread and milk."

Kaden grunted. "Yeah, me too. But hey—my moms is cooking a chicken tonight. Come knock on our door at six. But she's gonna make you pray. You can't get mad."

Jackson blinked. "Who gets mad at praying for food?"

"I don't know. Don't care. Just, you know. Be nice to my moms."

"Course." Even Jackson knew that when someone's moms was doing a good thing, you showed respect.

That night Jackson left his mom in a cloud of smoke—tobacco and something else that made his heart race and his eyes blur—and walked up the shaky concrete stairs to the apartment four units over. He knocked on the door and wished he could wash the smell out of his hair.

The woman who greeted him looked young—younger than his mom, and he knew his mom was way too young to have him. Her hair was up in glossy black curls, some of which spiraled down to frame her face.

And she wore a home-sewn business skirt and a sleeveless shirt, like the women in the courtroom dramas on TV.

Toni smiled at him just like TV moms too. And she fed him, and when he took too much and Kaden told him he was being a pig, they needed leftovers, she told him to go ahead and eat extra. Just this once.

It was the last time Jackson did that, because God, he was just so grateful for the food.

Toni Cameron became his savior. He didn't expect mothering, so she kept her touch light. For holidays, she bought an extra shirt and an extra pair of jeans for him so he wasn't always dressed in shit with holes. It was from the bargain bin, but so was Kaden's, and he liked that he and K dressed the same.

It made him feel like he belonged somewhere.

By the time he could emancipate himself and move in with the Camerons, he had a job, and he paid her rent as often as he could, because he didn't want to take advantage. The shame of eating too much chicken that first night never fully left him.

Toni had done her best to fix that.

He'd been almost through the academy by the time she'd gotten sick, and she'd been so proud of him. The day he'd graduated, Jade and Kaden and Rhonda had pushed her wheelchair to the front of the Memorial Auditorium so she could watch Jackson walk the stage. They were all in school, but they had about two more years to go—this was her chance to see one of her kids graduate.

Jackson had been so glad to see her there, so happy to go out to dinner and sit with her, that he hadn't told her about his misgivings. Hadn't told her that the man who'd sponsored him through the academy seemed to expect things Jackson couldn't give—things that went against every hard-earned concept of ethics Jackson had ever acquired.

He'd put on a good face for her.

He'd put on a good face for them all.

And she'd asked him, soberly, to quit smoking that night, for her. He'd told her, soberly, that he would—and omitted the fact that he'd had to quit just to get through the academy without dying of asphyxiation, because the academy was too rigorous to wreck your body. Fact was, his promise to Toni would keep him clean.

In so many ways.

"Kaden," he said, his voice thick with emotion. "God, man, I'm so sorry."

Kaden's chin quivered. "We're all sorry, Jacky. She was your mom too."

He closed his eyes. God, she was. She really was, in all the ways that counted. He hadn't been easy to mother—it was hard to cuddle with an alley cat—but damned if she hadn't tried.

"She was the best," he said gruffly. "Your mom was the best."

"I know," Kaden said, and Rhonda hip-checked him aside for her hug. "You look thin, Jacky," she said softly.

Kaden's wife was lovely. Not quite as dramatically complexioned as Jade and Kaden, she had an oval face with a strong jaw and an aquiline nose, and bold lips that smiled way more than Jade's ever had. Rhonda Cameron had only kind words for anybody, and she was going to make a fantastic teacher.

After she made a fantastic mother.

"I'll take back the weight when you're through with it," he said, patting her three-month baby bump. Dammit, Kaden, for not remembering the rubber! Rhonda was the smartest of all of them—Jackson knew she'd make it—but they just had to add the extra level of difficulty, didn't they?

"I'll hold you to that," Rhonda said softly and then stroked his cheek. "But you still don't look good. It's only been a couple of months since you graduated, Jacky. Is the job that awful?"

Jackson wanted to throw himself in her arms and sob.

Yes. Yes, dammit. The job was that awful. The things Patrick Hanover wanted him to be a part of were awful. The things he was doing to stop Patrick Hanover were awful.

Toni Cameron was going in the ground today, and it felt like the entire world was gray and putrid, because there was only so much good out there, and a big chunk of gold light had been wasted away to ash-colored skin and bone by lung cancer.

"I'll be fine," he said, his throat almost too thick to speak, and Jade grabbed his hand right then because it was time to go listen to the preacher man say words that Toni Cameron had loved.

Jackson stood still and silent during the service, not listening at all. He was too busy fighting a grand battle in his heart over the things he wanted to tell his family and the things he couldn't.

Jade needed to go back to school.

Kaden and Rhonda needed to finish and make a home for their baby.

This thing Jackson was doing—this really important, terrifying, dangerous thing—was to keep people like his family from getting hurt by people they should trust.

The Cameron family had saved Jackson when he'd been a skinny kid who'd just wanted chicken. Toni Cameron had used what precious little money she'd had to feed him and clothe him. Even before he'd moved out, he'd been able to sleep on her couch when his own apartment had been a little slice of hell.

Jackson owed them. He owed them everything, from simple survival to graduating from high school to getting through the academy. He owed them for his belief that people could be good and that good people could be happy.

He owed them the world.

Jackson would do anything to keep the Camerons away from the corruption that was eating him alive.

After the service they all went out to Hometown Buffet, because they were hungry and none of them had money for anything better. Jackson ate two helpings of chicken in Toni's honor and told Rhonda he'd be sure to remember to eat.

GOING HOME that night had been so hard.

He'd taken advantage of a union program and put money down on a duplex as soon as he got his first paycheck from the force. On his days off, he'd fixed the paint, repaired the roof, that sort of thing, and he'd just started looking for a tenant.

That night he'd gone into his still-bare little side of the house and listened, just listened, for a heartbeat somewhere within.

Valerie had broken up with him two weeks ago, right before Toni died, and he couldn't blame her. He hadn't said a word to her of what was up, why he came home shaking, why his temper was so uncertain.

There was nobody there. Not a lover, not a friend, not his family—and there couldn't be. Not until this thing was over.

Feeling more alone than he ever had in a shitty and abusive childhood, Jackson Rivers slid down the wall of his hallway until he was sitting with his legs sprawled on the floor.

And then he buried his face in his hands and cried.

Children of the Same Bowl

"OH... OH my God! Yes! Yes! Keep fucking me, asshole, don't fucking quit!"

Jackson still liked banging Jade like a screen door in a hurricane, but the woman was *loud*. And bossy. But oh God, could she work her inner muscles like a *champ*.

Best do what the lady says!

Jackson rabbited his hips until his six-pack ached, relieved when Jade screamed, "Holy fucking hell *yes*!" and gushed fluid around his cock, which was her signal for him to come.

Thank. God.

Well, she'd been screaming His name enough—maybe He was in the room.

Jackson orgasmed neatly, like flipping a switch, and collapsed on top of her, breathing heavily into the hollow between her ear and her shoulder.

"Good for you?" he asked.

"You know it, baby," she purred, running a french manicure through his hair.

He panted for another moment before propping himself up on his elbows. "Don't take this the wrong way, J, but you know, even when I'm in bed with a guy, I usually top."

"Get your sweaty ass off me," Jade muttered, pushing at his shoulder. "And stop talking about your icky gay habit. I need a cigarette."

Jackson rolled over to his back and pulled the rubber off, then threw it in the trash next to the bed. "No smoking in the house—you know that."

She pulled her lips away from her teeth and rolled her eyes. "You just got a free pity bang and you're going to be picky about the smokes?"

Jackson let out a throaty laugh and grabbed a wet wipe from the bed stand, then cleaned the smell of sex off his body. Jade had soaked the sheets—he'd change them once she got up.

"Pity bang was mutual," he said, shaking his head. Same old Jade. She'd actually come on to *him* that night. They'd been hanging around the office, shooting the shit, talking about the old days. He and Jade had lost their virginity together and weathered exes and next-exes together. Since Jackson wasn't looking for a long-term thing *ever*, sleeping together when the opportunity arose was habit. The fact that Jade was a legal secretary at the defense firm Jackson did PI work for just ensured that they'd run into each other at opportune times in their libido/attachment cycle.

Jackson's libido had, in fact, been jonesing for someone else tonight. That day he'd seen a certain counselor—tall, pale, slender, cold as a fish in the courtroom—take apart a dirty witness. He'd watched from the corner of the courtroom while nursing an aching erection. He and Ellery Cramer had been glaring at each other for six years, and Jackson was more than ready to stop being his fetch-and-carry boy and start being his fuck-and-suck-me boy, but Jackson had needed to grab a file for another lawyer at the firm, and by the time he'd returned, Cramer had already left.

Damn.

Well, it wasn't like Jackson had a reputation for being a faithful lover—or even for honoring a crush. Jade had been ready, willing, and available, and she was better than sex alone.

And the woman was sexy and shameless. With a grunt and a sigh, she swung her legs over the bed and grabbed one of his T-shirts from the clean pile by the side of the bed. It hung past her thighs but clung tightly to her ample chest making her nipples stick out like pencil erasers, and she didn't give a shit. Wearing that and nothing else, she strode to his tiny patio, pink microbraids swaying down her back. She stopped at the leather purse she'd left on the floor by her business suit to get her cigarettes.

Jackson stood up and started stripping sheets. Unlike Jade, he didn't bother covering up a damned thing. Jade knew where all his scars were, and he'd long since given up keeping them covered.

For a moment the silence was punctuated by the rustle of linen and Jade's deep exhalations sounding through the gap in the sliding glass door. About the time Jackson had tossed the dirty sheets in the hamper and pulled the comforter back on the bed, Jade ground out the cigarette and came back in, closing the door to keep the cool air in. She pretended not to see the rumple-haired shadow sliding in at her ankles.

"All Zenned out now?" Jackson asked dryly, throwing himself naked on top of the comforter.

"That is the ugliest cat I've seen in my life," Jade told him, disdain twisting that full mouth.

"You say that every time you see him. Billy Bob is going to get a complex." Billy Bob might have been a well-groomed Siamese in another life—one that didn't involve going out into the neighborhood and fucking or fighting every other animal for a four-block radius. Jackson had started feeding him a year ago, when he'd been a gangly, sexed-out adolescent. He'd been missing an eye and half an ear, and had a big divot in the middle of his nose. Jackson could swear he'd seen the motherfucker dry-humping the neighbor's German shepherd once, but if the poor animal had given birth to freakishly mutated catdogs, nobody had told Jackson.

"That cat...." Jade shook her head and made a mm-mm sound. "That cat is bad news."

Jackson scratched Billy Bob under the chin, delighted when ol' Billy purred for him. "For other cats," he said affectionately, and Billy Bob began to drool shamelessly.

"Jackson?" Jade said thoughtfully. "Can I ask you something?"

"Anything."

"Who were you waiting for tonight?"

Oh God. How embarrassing. He hadn't thought she'd known. "You, darlin'—you know that."

She gave him a sideways eye roll while pressing against the sliding glass door, still looking into the clear sky, and he felt suitably chastened. "I know you got a thing for him."

Jackson grunted. "Out of our league," he said softly. "You and me are street tacos and hamburgers. He's filet mignon and caviar."

She shook her head, looking away. "I'm caviar and salmon, you presumptuous motherfucker. Take me out on a date once in a while and you'd know."

Oh. He'd hurt her—that was never his intention! "Sure, Jade. Name the place. We'll kick back a bottle of wine and—"

"Why him?" She turned around and leaned back against the door.

He sighed. "'Cause he's good. He really fights. It's not just show."

"You sure it's not just the whole nasty gay thing?"

Jackson laughed and stretched. "I ever get soft with you?" he taunted. Because no. He played for both teams with gleeful abandon.

She shook her head and sighed, coming to the bed and stretching out next to him. The smell of cigarettes clung to her, reminding him of when they'd both snuck smokes as a kid. "You ever think we're getting too old for this?"

Jackson grunted. Thirty—he'd already turned, but for Jade it was just around the corner. "Pity sex?" he asked, grinning dryly. "No one's too old for pity sex."

She grimaced. "No," she said, her voice dropping quietly. "This thing we do where we know the other one will be around if we're between special friends we fuck."

Oh hell. "You thinking of breaking up with me, J?"

She rested her head on hand, propping up on her elbow. "My brother already has two kids," she said soberly.

"Your brother knocked up Rhonda in college," Jackson said, smiling. God, Rhonda was meant to be a mother—and Kaden was a father like none of them had ever had. Responsibility sat on Kaden's shoulders so easily, it was hard to believe they'd grown up together.

A house, businesses, beautiful kids—things had turned out for K and Rhonda, hadn't they? They were going strong. K might have needed two jobs to help support his family, but his family loved him. Every time K had a double shift, Rhonda greeted him at the door with dinner and a beer, and every time Rhonda stayed up late grading papers, K got the kids up for school.

Domestic as hell—they made Jackson wish for happy endings.

"Yeah," Jade said. Her full mouth pulled tight in the corners. "I used to feel sorry for them, right? Because you and me, we got to go out and do big things." She sighed. "But I'm lonely, Jacky, you know?"

Oh hell. "J—"

"Yeah," she said, her face relaxing into disappointment. "It's not me. I get that. You got your big exciting life, and you get to fuck anything that moves—"

"Hey," he said, touching her cheek gently. "You and me—I love that we can do this."

She sighed. "It's… it's too easy. I had a chance to go out the other night, and I thought, 'I should just call Jacky up. I know he doesn't have anything going.' And it's not that this guy was bad—it's just that with you, I knew what I was going to get."

Oh.

"No strings," he said softly.

"Yeah," she said. "I think we need to cut them."

He sighed. "Yeah, fine. But…." He hated to ask. But J knew—knew why he'd rather have anyone, even a bad date, here some nights.

"I'll stay the night," she said quietly. "And any other night you need me. Just from now on…."

"You'll sleep on the couch," he said. Or the guest room bed. Hey, it was comfy. The entire little duplex was comfy. Not paradise, but he kept it neat, made sure the furniture didn't screw up your back, kept the beds clean. He wasn't there a lot, but the place didn't suck.

"Yeah."

She looked so sad. He grabbed his boxers from the pile of clothes on the floor, then slid them on in a quick movement. It was still hot, in spite of the little AC unit cranking away, so after he turned off the light, he kept his spot on top of the comforter. He lay back down facing her, and in whispers, like the teenagers they had been, they talked about their childhood, growing up off Del Paso Heights, going to MLK Junior High, where the prostitution and drug trade had happened on campus, in full view of the public, before school.

The place had been cleaned up since then. It still wasn't a great district, but at least the kids didn't have to wade through drug deals to get to class. That didn't change the fact that Jackson and K had fought their way through school, back-to-back sometimes, to keep themselves and the girls safe.

They had a lot of stories, Jackson and Jade. It was good to get them out in the dark of the night so they could say good-bye.

AT SIX o'clock in the morning, Jackson's phone rang, and Kaden cracked their little world wide apart.

The New Fish Objects

ELLERY CRAMER knew his tie was perfect, but he checked it anyway as he got off the elevator on the fourth floor. Pfeist, Langdon, Harrelson & Cooper was one of the best criminal defense firms in Sacramento, and it didn't get that way because its employees neglected details.

And Ellery wanted his name on that list of partners so bad.

When he'd first gotten his degree, he'd dreamed of opening his own practice, but no. His sister had run numbers on that—she was an actuary—and had determined that his best chance for financial success lay with hooking up as a junior associate and working his way up to partner.

Six years after signing on with Pfeist, Langdon, Harrelson & Cooper, he was one of their most trusted trial lawyers, and he was conscious of the honor.

He was also conscious of his suit.

Today he wore the silver pinstripe, which, although it didn't complement his dark hair and eyes at all, *did* make him look severe and imposing, and he was all for that. He'd spent two hours cross-examining a witness that day and had enjoyed making the guy—a police officer, no less—crumble like a cookie.

Ellery did so enjoy his petty torments.

But as much as he enjoyed destroying police officers on the stand, he wouldn't ever mess with Leonard Pfeist's secretary. Nope—Ellery was *very* good at knowing who to toady, and the secretary was the heart of the firm.

"Good afternoon, Jade," he said pleasantly and was greeted with a heavy-eyed scowl in return. Ellery gaped at her, uncertain of how to respond. Granted, he and the firm's legal secretary weren't close. Jade was a little too rough around the edges for Ellery to really warm up to. He got that Leonard Pfeist, the most junior of the partners, did the hiring, and *he* seemed to rely on Jade's street-smart, tart-mouthed presence, but Ellery had been brought up conservatively. Between Jade's unapologetically vibrant appearance and the female sexuality that rolled off her like perfume, her whole presence made him *very* uneasy.

But he'd never seen her look like she could rip someone's head off with her bare hands, and that was the way she was looking at him now.

"Took you long enough," she snapped. "Did or did your schedule *not* say you were supposed to be in the office an hour ago?"

"I was in court!" Ellery objected. "It went—"

"I know when it went to. And I know you stopped for coffee and probably to schmooze that judge you're always trying to flirt with. What you *needed* to do was to be *here* because you've got someone here who needs your fucking help!"

Ellery stared at her, his mouth opening and closing in surprise. Smart-mouthed, yes, but never insubordinate—never *rude*. "Uh—"

"Take it easy on him, J—he didn't know."

Oh great. *Him.*

Ellery stared at Jackson Rivers with a distaste that had nothing to do with the man's looks. Dark blond hair, green eyes, and a square jaw—if the remains of an adolescent acne problem hadn't roughened his skin, he'd look like a movie star. As it was, he appeared weathered and capable—stringy, no-bullshit muscle and an uncompromising glare. Jackson was the law firm's head PI, and while the job was not supposed to be as glamorous as television made it look, Ellery had always wondered if maybe Jackson Rivers didn't break a few rules to be so goddamned good at what he did.

Need a witness background? Yeah, sure, he was there. But he was there with the *dirt*—the stuff that made the witness unreliable, the stuff that Ellery could use to keep a client out of prison.

But it was just not fair that he was so goddamned *beautiful*. That broke a rule or two that Ellery really loathed. Jackson was good-looking and personable. He and Jade had history and kinship; they seemed to speak a different language sometimes. Jackson would swagger into the office and shake hands with Leonard Pfeist and flirt with the other secretaries and face the clients, confident and unafraid....

It made Ellery feel like he had in school. Exceptionally singular, unexceptionally alone.

"He don't know and he wouldn't care if the problem didn't end up on his lap," Jade snarled, making Ellery wince. Well, he'd always thought she harbored sort of a dislike for him, and she certainly wasn't bothering to hide it now. "Are you *sure* this is the guy we want?"

Jackson's gaze raked Ellery up and down, and Ellery had to remind himself that Jackson was a *PI*—he had no say in how the firm was run or who got which cases. Leonard Pfeist might think he walked on water, but there were three other partners who had a say in things, and Ellery was in good standing with all of them too.

"He's not afraid of the cops," Jackson said, pinning Ellery hard with a green-eyed glare. "Everyone else worked at the DA's for a few years—they've got ties. This guy doesn't give a fuck about anything but winning."

"Yeah, for *himself.*"

Jackson's shrug rankled. He apparently thought that was fair.

"J, does it matter why he wants to win as long as he wins for K?"

"Yeah," she muttered. "Unless he thinks it's better to cut and run. He'd better not bail on my brother—he needs us, Jacky!"

Jackson's jaw tightened and his glare intensified. Ellery's hands were sweating, and he hated himself desperately for wanting this man's approval. He drew himself to his full six foot two and pulled his lips back in disdain. "Whatever your little family matter is," he sneered, "I'm sure you can deal without me. What makes you think I even *want* this case?"

Jackson snorted and rolled his eyes. "Don't stress yourself, Pinstripes. If you've got the guts for it, you're going to want it. No self-respecting shark would turn this one down."

"Let me be the judge of that. Do I even get an explanation?"

"I'll tell you on the way to the jail."

ELLERY'S FAMILY considered themselves liberal, but that didn't mean they wouldn't have pressed the locks on their doors for reassurance if a man who looked like Kaden Cameron had approached their car.

Easily six foot five with skin of darkest brown and a head shaved bald, Kaden dominated the small bare conference room of the county jail. The bandage taped behind his ear didn't make him look the slightest bit vulnerable either. He had craggy, ageless features, a scowl that could shake mountains, and shoulders that looked like they wouldn't fit through a door. He appeared to be every inch a badass, from his Lakers sweatshirt to his black Converse, but his file told another story.

That didn't mean Ellery's hand didn't shake as he took a quick sip of water and set his cup back down on the plain steel table.

"So you can put your house down for collateral," he said, because the first order of business was *always* making bail.

"My house," Jackson said promptly. "Not his. It's a duplex. I have a renter on the other side—"

"That racist asshole still live next door?" Kaden interrupted, but the look Jackson shot him wasn't annoyed.

"He's not racist, K, just old."

"Yeah, he's an old *racist*," Kaden grumbled. "Seriously, Jacky, did you *hear* him arguing against Kobe Bryant being one of the greatest ever?"

"It was at my house over Thanksgiving, dumbass," Jackson said, rolling his eyes. "You two had to be threatened with a potato gun—and your own wife did the threatening. You remember that?"

Kaden flashed a nostalgic smile. "Heh. Yeah. Rhonda was *pissed*."

"She should have been. You were all up in his face when he was trying hard to be your friend. He was playing with your children—he won't even talk to his *own* kids. Just because he doesn't like your pick of basketball players doesn't make him a racist. And you have a *daughter*, K—do you really want Kobe Bryant to be a hero? Mike's a good guy."

"He's not going to be so good when he gets evicted because you gambled his home on me," Kaden said, and Ellery made a quick reassessment.

He'd assumed that Kaden had gotten distracted because—like a lot of Ellery's clients—he was in denial of how much trouble he was in, but that wasn't the case at all.

"Not a gamble, K, 'cause you're not going to run. And you know what? Even if you *did* run, I'd rather get an apartment than know Rhonda and the kids were out on the street."

The man who looked Jackson Rivers in the eyes was obviously capable of meeting reality. "They're going to be on the street anyway," he said. "If I can't work during this bullshit, we can't make payments."

Ellery didn't blurt out "Pro bono?"—but he wanted to. He must have made some sort of noise, though, because Jackson sent him a glare that was probably meant to shrivel Ellery's manhood, root, stalk, and berries. Ha! Little did the man know he put on Kevlar undershorts in the morning.

Figuratively, of course.

"Your sister's moving in," Jackson said, pulling Ellery back from the shoring up of his self-esteem. "She'll help Rhonda with the payments until you can. Don't worry, K, your people gotchu." Jackson glanced back at Ellery. "You got anything else to say?" he demanded.

Ellery glared at him. "You know I do. The bail hearing is tomorrow, first thing in the morning. I need something to give the judge besides just who's going to help with the payments."

"I'm not going to run," Kaden said. "I've got a wife and two kids and a fuckin' dog who thinks I invented the morning crap. I own a house and part of a business. I've lived my whole life in this city. I'm not a flight risk, and I didn't kill no fucking cop!"

Ellery sucked air in through his teeth and looked at the anemic file, which featured the single crime-scene photo. That alone was weird, because there shouldn't have been a photo in the file at this juncture anyway. Even if he normally *did* have photos at this point, the fact that there *was* only one bothered the crap out of Ellery. Jesus, a hundred CSIs in Sacramento, and they get one lousy photo and some even blurrier pics of fingerprints? Something horribly wrong was going on here.

But the image bothered him more than the lack of evidence. The image was of Kaden slouched down against the counter of the gas station franchise he owned a piece of. His eyes were closed, and a trickle of blood leaked from under the black stocking cap he'd been wearing.

A SIG Sauer P229 handgun lay near his outstretched hand, pointed in the direction of the police officer who lay sprawled dead with a hole the size of Texas in his chest. A blood pool spread luridly over the floor.

"Now see," Ellery said delicately, "we may be able to get you out on bail, but I think it's that last part that we're going to have trouble with."

When he looked up from the brief, it was not Kaden's hard look of resignation that punched him with the most grit. No—it was Jackson Rivers's blistering look of accusatory fury that made him think that Kevlar undies just weren't going to be enough.

"I think maybe you need to tell me what happened," he said deliberately. "And don't leave anything out."

Kaden Cameron met his gaze straight on, and Ellery wasn't imagining the hostility there. "There isn't much to leave out," he said, voice flat. "Because I don't remember *crap*."

Yeah. And if that was true, that was going to make things *so* much more difficult.

"Well." Ellery resisted the urge to shove his chair back and fidget. "This is going to be a real short meeting."

From the twin looks of disgust he got, he figured that was the wrong thing to say.

TWO HOURS later he wished he could take it back. It wasn't a short meeting, but what it lacked in brevity, it made up in supremely painful frustration.

He'd given into impulse during the first hour and had stood up to pace. In the middle of the second hour, he'd taken off his jacket and loosened his tie. Jackson, who normally wore jeans and a sport coat, had shed his sport coat and—to Ellery's mortification—toed off his dress shoes.

Kaden had given him a ration of crap about it too—the first *non*business thing he'd said since he'd started to tell the sketchy, thin story that was making Ellery grind his teeth.

"I'm trusting you with my life, son, and you can't even keep your shoes on for me?"

"Not for you, not for your sister—"

"You'd keep them on for Rhonda," Kaden joked weakly.

Jackson rubbed Kaden's bald head. "I respect Rhonda. I saw you throw up in the fifth grade. The mystery's gone."

Kaden yawned and stretched then, and he probably would have tried to stand up, but his ankles were cuffed to a ring in the floor. "Yeah, well, that would bother me more if I was looking for a blow job, but since I'm all straight, I think I'll live."

"You are all talk. Fact is, you never moved on me 'cause I was dating your sister and, you know, awkward."

"Yeah, Jacky. That's it. That's why I never changed teams."

Jackson smiled fondly at him and then met Ellery's eyes. "Is there any way we can let him stand? His knees have got to be killing him."

Kaden's grunt told them both that was the truth.

"Yeah, sure," Ellery heard himself saying. Normally, no. Not with the violence he'd seen in the picture at the beginning. But for two hours he'd grilled Kaden Cameron on the events of August 12, and all Kaden had admitted to was stealing a Red Bull from his own store.

He'd been pissed during the interview, yeah. But Ellery couldn't blame him.

"I'll be right back," he said, and he summoned the guard outside the door to come in and unlock Kaden's chains, citing physical discomfort. When the guard had left—after taking the ankle chain out of the loop but leaving Kaden's ankles with a minimum amount of play between them—Ellery sat back down and nodded at him. "Okay, Mr. Cameron. You walk and stretch, I'll sit and talk. I'm going to summarize this as I understand it, and if you think I've gotten anything wrong, you need to stop me as I'm talking, because otherwise that's the story I'm building your case on, do you understand?"

"Got it," Kaden said, pushing heavily to his feet.

"So, at eleven o'clock you were working behind the window at your gas station—now is that a time you usually work?"

"No," Kaden said, pausing as he clasped his hands in front of him and, with a clank of chains, lifted to work out his shoulders. "I'm usually out of there at nine, but our night guy—"

"Connie Coulson—that's the guy?"

"Short for Conrad, yeah. Anyway, Connie, he calls up in the last five minutes of my shift and says he can't make it. Doesn't say why, and I'm like—"

Ellery consulted with the notes and moved his lips in time to what Kaden would say next.

"*Fuuuuck.*" Kaden and Jackson met eyes then, probably in understanding of Kaden's wife, Rhonda. She didn't seem to be the type who would take her husband's overtime away from the family in stride.

"Okay, I've got that," Ellery continued. "So he called and you stayed." He frowned. "Were you going to stay the entire night?"

Kaden shook his head. "Naw—I mean, we would have lost some sales, but there's no law that says a gas station has to be open all night. I was gonna put a Closed for the Night sign out, and Denny—"

"That's your partner—"

"Yeah. He would have opened up in the morning."

"Okay, so you were working the counter at around 11:00 p.m. when two policemen entered."

Kaden nodded. "Yeah."

"Officer C. Miles and Officer S. Bridger. Right?"

Kaden's shrug was sort of awful, considering the dead rookie and his own uncertain fate. "I don't know their names. They came in and I was drinking my Red Bull, right? 'Cause I'd hit *the wall*, you feel me?"

"I feel you," Ellery said with reluctant sympathy. He remembered studying for the bar exam between jobs. "You needed to stay awake."

"You know it. And one of the cops, the younger one, walked in front of the counter. I turned to look at him and he started talking to me about a call they'd gotten."

"They said you'd reported a robbery." Ellery knew this detail, but he wanted to see if Kaden stayed consistent.

"But I hadn't," Kaden insisted. "Man, I probably wouldn't have reported a robbery if there'd *been* a robbery. Everybody knows the cops out there are dirty."

Ellery had been circling things on his pad. Jackson had been pacing alongside Kaden, both of them radiating sympathetic nervous energy.

With Kaden's offhanded declaration, all motion in the room stopped.

"K?" Jackson said tentatively.

"I'm sorry," Ellery said through a suddenly dry throat, "could you repeat that?"

Kaden cast a tortured glare at Jackson. "They're dirty, Jacky— they've been dirty since they got rid of you."

Jackson swallowed. "But… you… you've gone to that gas station five times a week for six years. The cops were shaking you down during that time? You couldn't have told—"

Kaden shook his head. "Jacky… I didn't want… man." Kaden's voice broke a little. "Me and J and Rhonda—we watched you *die*. Twice. They almost didn't bring you back. The room looked like a slaughterhouse. And you still got the scars. You're gonna have them for fucking ever. And we knew—and even if they didn't kill *you*, Jacky, they'd kill me, or Rhonda. So I didn't call the cops. I wouldn't have called them in. And there I was, watching the blond one—the young one, looked like you when you were a kid, but with whiter hair and a softer chin. He was talking to me, sounding so fucking sincere asking me about the robbery, and why would they have gotten a call if I hadn't reported it—it was like listening to a corrupt puppy. And my mouth was dry—I swear, my mouth was dry, because… *dirty cops*. In *my gas station*, and it was eleven at night. I took another swig of my drink, and…."

Kaden's pacing of the small room had brought him back to the table. All of the anger, the nervous energy that seemed to have driven him, just drained out like water, and he collapsed onto the chair, his body heavy enough to make it squeak in protest.

"My vision started blurring," he muttered. "And then there was a pain in my head and I blacked out. When I came to, I was handcuffed to the gurney and someone was reading me my fucking rights."

The room fell suddenly silent. Ellery kept his eyes fixed on Kaden Cameron's face. Partly to see if his client was telling the truth, but partly because....

Because Jackson Rivers was shock white, and perspiration had popped out on that high, fair forehead. He'd heard Kaden—there was no doubt—but Ellery was sure he'd had the story memorized the first time Kaden had gone through it, before Ellery had even arrived on the scene.

The detail about the dirty cops had thrown him and thrown him hard, and Ellery was suddenly burning to know more.

But not before he cleared one or two things up.

"Wait a minute," he said, studying the crime-scene photo. "Wait—didn't you say your video was disabled?"

"Yeah," Kaden grunted. "And it shouldn't have been. Denny and I, we work hard to keep that thing in repair."

Ellery looked at the picture again. "I knew it—this is too clear to be a video picture. It looks like a camera phone. But... but Officer Bridger—the older officer, the one with the gun—he was calling it in, right? The one who snuck up on you and—"

"He snuck up on me because I was *drugged*!" Kaden snarled.

"I know that!" Ellery snapped. "I'm just saying. I don't have any actual *crime-scene photos*. It should be too early for them at all. But now—I've just got *this* one trying to pass itself off as something official. If Bridger was in such an all-fired hurry to get the ambulance for his buddy and get backup for you, who took the damned picture?"

Kaden stopped short and looked automatically at Jackson. Jackson took one last hard breath—and stepped forward. Ellery wasn't sure what the man's demons were, but he could be *very* sure of one thing.

Jackson wasn't stupid either.

"Let me see that photo," he demanded.

Ellery handed it over without conscious thought. He *should* dig in his heels a little, just so Jackson knew whom he could and could not fuck with, but damn, that guy had a *way* about him. Ellery was pretty sure his mother would cave to whatever Jackson Rivers asked for, and that woman didn't cave to *anything*.

He heard Jackson's swallow across the room, and Ellery's curiosity about what could shake him up this badly began to burn a hole in his belly. Ex–law enforcement showed its mark all over him, but he obviously didn't like cops, and what Kaden had described was…

Horrific. Something horrific had happened to him. Something so bad his friend had protected him from an ugly—and apparently accepted—fact of his everyday life.

"You were lucky, K." Jackson's gruff voice shocked the silence that had fallen. "I don't know why he didn't kill you."

Kaden agreed. "It's a fuckin' miracle right there."

Suddenly Jackson looked over his shoulder. "Hey, do you *have* a gun in the store?"

Kaden nodded, looking puzzled. "We do, but we keep it in the safe because we hate it. And it's a .22, because who needs a fucking cannon. What the hell kind of gun *is* that?"

"SIG Sauer P229," Jackson said absently. "It's not standard police issue, but it's one of the most popular handguns in the world, and I'll bet it's got a filed-down serial number—or a suspicious history." He glanced from the picture he was studying to Ellery. "We need an independent ballistics match—can you request that?"

Ellery nodded and grabbed his pen to add it to the list of things he'd written there as Kaden spoke.

"Wait." Jackson jerked Ellery over with his chin. "Look here—the edge of the photo. What do you see?"

Ellery left the table and peered over his shoulder. Jackson was actually shorter than he was, not that he carried himself that way. And he smelled… well, like sex. Like sex and faintly of tobacco and a little like sweat. A man who had been called out of bed early, perhaps? Whose bed was anybody's guess—his reputation, from what Ellery could see, was well-founded.

An impatient rustle in front of him brought Ellery's attention back to the photo, and he saw the border Jackson was outlining with a blunt finger. "I don't know. It's sort of red and blurry—"

"K, get over here. What does this remind you of?"

"My head *hurts*, Jacky—can you maybe come over here for the man with a concussion?"

Jackson gave an apologetic grunt. "Yeah. Sorry about that." He circled around the back and held the photo out so they could both see.

"Oh… Jesus. Looks like one of Rhonda's pictures. Her damned…." Jackson met his gaze and nodded. "Her damned cell phone cover overlaps the frame."

Jackson met Ellery's eyes with a gaze that could pierce steel. "We need to find out where this came from. See here?" Ellery had no choice but to look over his shoulder to see. "The reflection here? Those are jeans—this wasn't taken by a cop, and certainly not by a forensics expert. This was taken by someone else. Why don't we have regular crime-scene photos here?"

Ellery frowned and pawed through the brief like it would suddenly sprout legitimacy. "I don't know—I mean, we shouldn't have *anything* yet."

"Yeah? Who was the tech?" Jackson thrust the brief at Ellery and paced, energy burning off his body like a lightning charge.

"It doesn't say," Ellery muttered. "I've been looking for a signature, a chain of evidence, but I've got nothing. I mean, this is a *cop*, and I don't even have a preliminary forensics report."

Kaden stared at him hard. "So doesn't that mean no more case?"

Ellery grimaced at him. "That's what it *should* mean, Kaden, but we've got two things here that might screw that up."

Jackson and Kaden sighed in tandem and shook their heads.

"A cop and a black man," Kaden muttered.

"A cop and a black man," Ellery confirmed.

Jackson's jaw clenched, and Ellery spoke quickly to keep him from grinding his teeth.

"Okay, we've got some places to start here. We've got Connie— because it's awfully damned convenient that your guy calls in sick the night two cops come in for a shakedown."

"But they weren't trying to shake me down!" Kaden objected. "I'm not stupid. A cop asks for money and you hand it over!"

"Cops don't ask for money," Ellery said, feeling dumb. He felt even dumber when the other two men in the room grunted and rolled their eyes. "I mean I know there are dirty cops," he defended. "But there's not even any investigations into this area of the city. General consensus is corruption isn't a problem here. I mean these guys don't always follow procedure, but what you're talking about is blatant—and widespread.

How could they get away with this?" Oh God. Could he *sound* any more like an idealistic fifth grader?

Kaden started to laugh, and it wasn't a pleasant sound. "Hey, Jacky, think this guy's neighborhood can be seen from space?"

"Yup, K—it's just *so* white." They bumped their fists together then, like it was an old joke between them, and Ellery was no longer part of the Hardy Boys.

"I'm serious," he said stonily. "I don't know what happened here, but we cannot go into this thinking every cop is out to get us, or we'll never get to the bottom of this."

Kaden looked bored, but Jackson didn't—he looked *furious.* With deliberate steps, he strode into Ellery's space, backing him up until he hit solid metal.

"You listen to me," he hissed, just as Ellery's head made a painful thump against the door. "This man is my *family*, and if you can't get him out on bail, he's walking into a killing field, do you understand me? Prison is no good for Kaden—half our neighborhood went to prison, and they know he's the friend of an ex-cop and they hate him. And if you *can* get him out on bail...." Jackson looked behind him, and he and Kaden communicated wordlessly. Jackson shook his head and turned that disturbing crystal-green gaze back on Ellery. "He's going to be in more danger than ever. His bail hearing is tomorrow, and then we've got what? Three months? Four? Before the prelim?"

Murder? Of a cop? "It could be a year or more," Ellery admitted.

"So if they go for a capital crime and there's no bail allowed, that's a year or more with him in a cell and his family out here trying to survive. If they *do* let him out on bail, that's *months* for every crooked cop in Northern California to find a reason to stop him and beat the holy Mother of God out of him—"

"You're exaggerating," Ellery rasped. Those things didn't happen in Sacramento. It was one of the most diverse cities in the country—people *had* to learn to live together or the place would be a war zone.

"Just because it *hasn't* happened here doesn't mean it *won't*," Jackson snarled. "And if it *does* happen and shows up on YouTube going viral, wouldn't it be convenient if the cop we see beating my *brother to death* is actually a dirty cop covering a murder."

Oh God. Yes. It was entirely possible. The penalties for policemen accused of racial bias were notoriously light. But—

"Not here," Ellery said, praying he was right. "We have a black mayor—"

"We have a black *president*," Jackson retorted. "If the last two years since Ferguson have proved anything, it's that old prejudices don't go away just because liberals like to hope a lot. Kaden can't go to prison—he'll never make it. And he can't go free unless—"

"Unless we find out why this happened and all the bad guys are put away first," Ellery said, his stomach knotting. Oh God. Jackson hadn't been kidding—this was the case that could make a lawyer's career.

Or it could shatter it into a thousand teeny tiny pieces.

Ellery could hear the three of them breathing in the silence that followed, and very quietly, Kaden make a soft groan of pain.

Jackson backed out of Ellery's space immediately, and Ellery had just a little more air to breathe.

"K," Jackson said softly, "we could let you go now to processing or—"

"I'll get him into the infirmary," Ellery said, surprising himself. "Has he seen his family yet?"

"In the hospital," Jackson said. "Before they shipped him here and I got him into the interrogation room."

Ellery looked at him sharply, and Jackson shrugged. "You're right—not every cop is crooked, and I've got some contacts. He's seen his wife and kids—and if you can get him out on bail, he'll see them again."

Ellery nodded. "I'll see what I can do about getting him an overnight pass to the infirmary—to keep him out of general population. I can stay with him in there for a couple of hours." Ellery glanced reflexively toward the door, where a guard waited patiently outside to take Kaden to his cell when his time with his lawyer was up.

Jackson backed up another step, giving Ellery some more space to breathe, and perversely, he missed that body, throwing off heat.

"So," Jackson said after a moment that left Ellery adjusting his suit and looking surreptitiously at Kaden to see if *he* saw any… tension… in the way Ellery and Jackson were behaving.

It was probably all in Ellery's fevered imagination anyway.

"So," Jackson said again, taking a few steps toward the middle of the room. "We've got some leads. We need to trace the gun and the picture in the brief. We need to talk to Connie first; then someone needs to spend an afternoon analyzing that picture."

"And I need to get hold of the *real* crime-scene photos." Ellery tried not to harbor dark suspicions of being left to swing in the breeze by the DA's office.

Jackson looked at him and swallowed, then closed his eyes. He turned to Kaden and said, "K?"

K shrugged. "You need to let him know how bad it could get."

Jackson scrubbed his face with his hands. "Ellery, you need to type up your notes for your brief and let me see them—"

"I don't need to—"

"We're not doing this again, do you understand? Not with another lawyer. You need to type up your notes and let me see them, and then we can discuss whether you *really* want this case or whether you want to fucking bail."

"Why does—"

"Because." Jackson swung his arms wide, probably to relieve some of the tension. "You get your name on a request for another lawyer and everyone knows you saw it, everybody knows you elected to stay the fuck away. It's your get-out-of-dead-free card."

"You're being dramatic—"

Jackson's oxford was unbuttoned to the second button, a white tank exposed in the V at his throat. The sleeves were rolled up and it was—per usual, even when he wore a sport coat—untucked, which was why he could reach behind him, grab the back of the neck, and haul both shirts over his head.

Ellery's mouth dried up, then his throat, then his eyeballs.

A giant flower of scar tissue bloomed right below Jackson's collarbone, and another one at his midsection. Each bloom was accompanied by fissures, deep lines of stitching, layered, a thousand different ways to put a man back together one flap of muscle, fascia, and skin at a time.

"Those are...." Ellery managed to rasp, and Jackson raised his eyebrows. "Big," Ellery said at last. "Those—usually bullets—" Usually a bullet scar looked smaller from the front.

"Hollow point, Teflon coated, went straight through the back of my Kevlar," Jackson ground out. "See? You want to type up your notes. You want to review this case really good. And then, before you take Kaden back to the infirmary, you want to make really sure you want to stick around."

Jackson pulled his shirt back on without self-consciousness and turned toward Kaden.

And broke. "I...." He scrubbed his face with his hands. "K, I swear to God, if you hadn't been in the hospital, I would have smuggled you the hell out of town."

"That's illegal," Ellery said and then felt stupid.

"Nobody's going to mess with me," Kaden said, voice easy.

"Not in the infirmary," Ellery interjected. "Kaden...." He grimaced. "So... you have a concussion?"

"Yeah."

"Great." Ellery could manage the infirmary thing if nothing else. "Can you have a stomachache a little later?"

"I could, but, you know, been there, done that."

Oh hell—he didn't *look* like a man about to throw up. "Wait, do you need to get sick *now*?"

Kaden looked at him blankly. "No, not now. I woke up barfing, but the doctor shot me full of something—"

And just like that, plans of having Kaden fake nausea to ensure an infirmary stay flew out the window.

"Mother*fucker*!" Jackson bit out. "Goddammit, son of a—"

Ellery had to agree with him. "You were going to the hospital for tox-screen results, weren't you?"

"Right after I hit up Connie—I've got some connections. But if the doctor gave him something *before* the tests—"

"That means the tests will be tainted." Ellery whirled on one foot and dented the fucking wall. He looked up and saw Jackson and Kaden staring at him like he'd grown another head. "God*dammit*, Jackson Rivers. Why me? That's all I want to know. There are ten associates and four partners in this firm, and you had to walk up to me and say, 'He! He is the one! I shall ruin his life in the name of truth and fucking justice!'"

Jackson regarded him with no pity whatsoever. "Because I've seen you in the courtroom," he said. "You had Lofgren on the stand today again, didn't you?"

Ellery nodded, surprised by how much Jackson knew about stuff that wasn't his business.

"You make him cry?" Jackson asked slyly.

Ellery's toe was starting to hurt from his largely ignored outburst of temper, and it made fidgeting more difficult, so he stayed still. "How'd you know?"

"Because Liv Getchell was a friend of mine." Jackson's full mouth turned up at the corners like he was enjoying a particularly cruel joke. "She was a sweet kid trying to take care of her own sweet kid, and her boss made her mule coke from her place in Del Paso to his place in West Natomas. And when the cops came down on that little shindig, she was the one who got burned. And you kept her out of jail, and she didn't lose custody of her kid, and she may be on welfare and living with her mother now, but you went after the right guy to break. And she was pro bono. I was there for the whole trial, because her mother made me promise, and you didn't let up once. You may not have believed she was innocent—hell, you may not even have cared. But you got her out of that, and you did it without a plea, and I *know* the pressure must have been huge to plead out. So I know you can do it, Cramer. I know you're capable. But I know you need to commit."

"I'll do it," Ellery said, hating himself. It was stupid—he knew it was stupid. Stupid and juvenile and dumb. But his own mother had never come to see him in court. His sister the actuary had never come to see him in court. Not one damned boyfriend had ever come to see him in court.

But this man—this arrogant, irritating, bossy, smug, superior asshole—had come to see him in court.

And he'd liked what he'd seen.

God, Ellery would *die* for that sort of praise.

He might very well have to. The thought drew him up short—as did the memory of the scars on Jackson's chest.

He looked straight into those piercing green eyes, green as beer bottles, green as spring grass, and said it again. "I'll do it. Go to the hospital anyway—the nurses know what the doctors don't tell."

"Got it," Jackson said dryly, and Ellery had no doubt that had already been on his list.

"Go interview Connie immediately afterward, and do you use our computer specialist, or do you have a contractor?"

"I got Crystal her job at the firm," Jackson said flatly. "She'll do fine."

"Jesus!" Ellery burst out. "Is there anybody here you *haven't* slept with?" He'd seen him—Jackson Rivers, God's gift to every lonely horny single person for a ten-block radius, had all the scruples of a tomcat. Ellery had seen him walking in with junior associates in the morning and walking out with the witnesses in the evening. Ellery *knew* he was sleeping with Kaden's sister in the same way he *knew* Jackson was responsible for the debauching—and happy coming out—of the intern they'd had working there the summer before. Rich, poor, black, white, or brown, male or female, cis or trans—discrimination was *not* in Jackson's vocabulary.

But he was apparently surprised that Ellery had noticed.

"Anyone here I haven't slept with?" he repeated. "Yeah. I haven't slept with Kaden." Kaden gave him a fist bump, even as he carried on. "And I haven't slept with *you*."

Ellery let out a frustrated growl. "Excellent. We know where you draw the line."

Jackson rolled his eyes. "Yeah, well you're not bad-looking, but you've got that stick up your ass and I always top. It'd get crowded, trust me. Now can we get back on task? You get Kaden to some peace and quiet, and I'll run to the office and see Crystal. It would be *awesome* if we knew where that not-crime-scene photo came from. If you lose your nerve before you send K back, you buzz me and let me know who you're giving the file to, in case anybody asks." He whirled on his heel and, to Ellery's surprise, sank to his knees in front of Kaden like a supplicant, touching his knee with the familiarity of a family member—or a child. "K, you hang in there, okay?"

Kaden nodded and palmed the back of Jackson's head, bending practically in half so they were touching forehead to forehead. "Jacky, I know you'll do your best, okay? So even if this goes south, I don't want you to—"

"Shut up." Jackson's voice was thick and cracked, and Ellery had the uncomfortable realization that this was a family meeting in the middle of a criminal case interview, and he was not prepared. "You're going to be fine," Jackson muttered, and Ellery felt the lie in the pit of his stomach. Ellery knew the dangers of Kaden going into prison if law enforcement wanted him dead. Or if he had enemies in there from high school. Or if he was just a young street tough who'd stepped wrong.

"I am," Kaden said, with confidence Ellery didn't feel. "Because I know you and Jade'll take care of Rhonda and the kids. I'm going to be peachy—I've got all the faith in the world."

Jackson nodded and scooted back far enough to leverage up on Kaden's knees. "I'll see you at the bail hearing tomorrow."

"I'll wear my good orange jumpsuit," Kaden cracked, but even Ellery could see the tightness in the corners of his mouth and the way the sweat beaded on his shaved head. Kaden knew what Jackson had known when he'd grabbed Ellery by the scruff of the neck and hauled him into Interview Room 4: that they had a limited amount of time to prove Kaden had been set up by Officer Scott Bridger for the murder of Officer Collin Miles before Kaden was killed by the cops who'd put him in jail or the people he'd meet when he got to prison.

"Rivers," Ellery said as Jackson neared the door. "Look, I know this should go without saying, but… you know. If you talk to anyone from law enforcement, try to figure out why Bridger would want his partner dead. And why frame Kaden—or Connie for that matter—to do it."

Jackson regarded him blankly. "Yeah, Cramer, and I'll be sure to wipe my ass the next time I cop a squat on the john. Would you like me to report back on *that* too?"

Ellery's face heated. "This just…." He shook his head. "I need those crime-scene photos. I don't even have a signature here from a CSI, just the police report and this damned picture. I've got a crime scene *release* signed by some guy named Owens, and I've got to tell you, I have *never* heard of him. And I need the interview with Connie. And the interview with whoever took that picture. And *five minutes* of alone time with Scott Bridger. So the sooner you can get back to me with information, the better chance we've got of getting the case against Kaden dismissed, you understand?"

"Like I said. Not stupid. In fact, I think I see the bigger picture better than you do. But you let me know when the catch occurs to you, okay? In the meantime, let's get K cleared and home safe." He turned and looked over his shoulder. "I'll check in on them for you, so don't worry, K." And then he was gone.

The door closed, and Ellery took a moment to lean against the doorframe and breathe a sigh of relief. Kaden's solid chuckle from across the room forced him to open his eyes.

"Feel like a tornado picked you up from a picnic and spit you out in a tsunami?"

Ellery felt a reluctant smile curving at his lips. "Something like that. Why?"

"Because that's our Jacky. He coaches my son's soccer team—the kids call him Captain Crazy."

"I don't think he'd respond too well if *I* called him that," he admitted and then made his way to the center of the room and sank into the chair next to Kaden. "How's your head?"

"Hurts like a motherfucker. Why?"

"Why'd they let you out of the hospital so quickly if you're still hurt?" Ellery asked, suddenly curious.

Kaden shot him an amused look. "Because Jackson is loud, persistent, and doesn't take bullshit for an answer. I told him my story once, and he had me on the jail transpo outta there within thirty minutes."

"Ah." Ellery swallowed against the irritation. "He's very quick," he said weakly. "He didn't need me for direction at all."

"Yeah, well, he could probably take—and pass—the bar exam tomorrow if you forced him to," Kaden said, not surprising Ellery.

"Why doesn't he do that?" Ellery didn't know what Jackson's accounts looked like, but he was pretty sure Jackson's mortgage payment could fit inside Ellery's Lexus payment. Why wouldn't he try to advance himself?

"Because Jackson didn't want to be a lawyer when he grew up," Kaden said.

Ellery wished these people would stop making him feel stupid with just a tilt of their head and a few emphasized words. "Let me guess—"

"You don't have to guess. You know what he wanted to be because he *was* one. Local po-po, homegrown on his home turf. He was good at his job. Fast track, in line to becoming a detective—Rhonda and Jade stayed up for a week helping him take his lieutenant's exam. I'm betting after a couple of years, they would have rec'd him for Quantico because that boy—that boy worked *hard*."

"Until…." Ellery wanted the story, but he didn't want to beg.

Kaden knew it. "Until you ask him yourself. Or find someone who wants to dish dirt on my brother. But I've got too much to say for *myself* to want to spend time satisfying your little crush there."

"It's not a crush," Ellery said weakly. "I'm potentially putting my—"

"Life," Kaden supplied, his voice hard.

"Career," Ellery corrected, because God help him, he couldn't imagine it another way. "I'm potentially putting my job and my career on the line for him. It would be nice to know—"

"Let him give the orders," Kaden said. "Let him make the decisions. You're a good lawyer—I mean, he wouldn't have shanghaied you if you weren't—but whatever skills you think you have in the courtroom?" He nodded so Ellery would nod too. "You've got to forget the hell out of those, you hear me?"

"Yeah," Ellery said, acid turning in his stomach. A part of him wanted to know what kind of Kool-Aid Jackson was giving people in their water bottles, but most of him had been damned impressed by Jackson's reasoning—and his ability to make lightning-quick decisions. "I hear you. Jackson's calling the shots for this one."

Kaden gave another one of those unexpected barks of humor. "Yeah. And I'm telling you, my sister is a shameless, shameless woman, and she swears by the guy in bed. If you ever feel like taking that stick out of your ass, you may want to rethink your stand on him. I understand he's like a religious experience."

Ellery had no comeback for that. "How about we concentrate on saving your life," he said, feeling like an asshole for dodging that whole subject. "And you know, maybe my career while we're at it."

"And not getting Jackson hurt again," Kaden said, like this was a deal breaker.

Ellery understood that maybe, for this little family he'd seen in action, it really was.

Street-Fighting Fish

JACKSON REALLY hated the system sometimes.

He'd run to the offices, which sat square in the blocks of downtown that housed the courthouse and the jail, and gotten Connie's address from Crystal. She promised to spend the rest of the afternoon rendering the photograph into something larger and more detailed and looking for clues to see if they could find the eyewitness to their very convoluted crime.

Unfortunately Connie's house was down by Del Paso Heights, and they'd taken Kaden to where they took *all* the criminals, whether they were from Folsom Prison or a local gang throwdown, and that was UCD Medical Center.

Jackson figured he'd do the med center first, Connie second, and then end up with a chance to catch the police station while they were changing shifts. He still had some contacts there, and he'd like *very* much to know what was going on.

It was funny that Ellery had cautioned him to question the nurses and not the doctors—Jackson hadn't been very excited about authority *before* it had tried to kill him.

This section of Stockton Boulevard had been cleaned up considerably in the past fifteen years—Jackson remembered, because he'd been part of the cleaning crew. He'd been a patrol officer when a city councilman had been busted having a crack-and-whore party a little down the road at Johnson's Greenbrier Hotel, and he'd also been the first on scene for a murder in the little convenience store across from the hospital.

But then gentrification had truly taken hold, and the Stop-and-Rob had been gussied up by a uniform store next door, and the hospital had been expanded. And Jackson's favorite part, the Cancer Survivors' Park, had been added. The bronze statues of the happy family holding hands in the corner had always given Jackson hope.

It was like Kaden and Rhonda's house—happy families won sometimes. They just did.

And speaking of happy families....

He found Dave and Alex out by the parking garage behind the ambulance entrance, sharing a cigarette break. That was pretty much where he expected to find them this time of day, because they would have screwed each other silly in Alex's car for the first part of their lunch, and this was their comedown.

You learned a lot about the nurses who took care of you on a daily basis. Dave had given him his twelve-o'clock painkillers and had talked about taking his break with his boyfriend. Alex had changed his catheter bag at two, and he'd always looked freshly laid. It hadn't been that hard to put together.

"Hey, handsome—you taking care of our property?" Alex asked as Jackson trotted out of the parking garage to greet them. Alex—tiny, perky, and blond as a cheerleader—smoked like he was about to hide the cigarette from his mother.

"It's not yours anymore," Jackson said, smiling. "The hospital gave me a full lease on the equipment when I left. You remember the paperwork?"

"Oh no, honey." Dave was taller, wider, darker in hair and skin, and built like a tank; he wielded his cigarette like a magic wand and camped like a Boy Scout. "We don't *do* paperwork."

Jackson rolled his eyes. "Who needs paperwork when you bitches put out in person, right?"

"You know it, baby," Alex purred. He drew hard on the cig and then crushed it out in the sand pit. After he'd exhaled smoke, he stepped forward and shook Jackson's hand. Some of the cheerleader fell away and he gave a genuine smile. "How you doing, hon?" he asked seriously. "The whole hospital is talking about your friend this morning—apparently you stepped on Dr. Snidenhower's toes." The boys knew Kaden, Rhonda, and Jade—they'd been his only visitors over those months of recovery. Jackson had seen Alex and Dave working as he'd been pulling the strings that got K out of the hospital and into the jail—and he'd been grateful.

"Yeah, well, that guy was a jerk when I was here," Jackson muttered. Hence the nickname Snidenhower. Jackson had it on good authority that Alex and Dave were the only reason he wasn't walking around with a colostomy bag under his belt. Scheideman was a little overzealous with requesting surgery, and apparently both of Jackson's boys—as he'd called them by the end—had lobbied fiercely to let Jackson's body try to heal first.

It was a thing for which Jackson would forever be grateful.

"The guy's a jerk anyway." Dave flicked his ash into the sand pit, dark fingers curving gracefully. "But that's not what you're here to talk about, is it."

Jackson shook his head. "You know what I'm here to talk about?"

Dave looked over his shoulder to see if anyone else was coming out to the back bay to nurture their filthy habit. Nobody so far, so he gestured Jackson in with a jerk of his chin. "Your boy? The friend who caught the po-po bus? So, Scheideman got pulled off that poor dead kid in the cop's uni—he was trying to resuscitate him because he didn't have the balls to call TOD."

Nobody wanted to call TOD on a cop. *Nobody.*

"So…."

Dave tsked his impatience but kept going. "So Doc Memphis called TOD, but Scheideman got sicced on Kaden, the hot guy with the cute kids."

"There was a wife too," Jackson supplied dryly, mostly to see Dave roll his eyes.

"Right. Anyway, so a guy—not in uniform, but smelled like bacon if you know what I mean—he grabs Scheideman's arm on the way down the hall, and he's talking like they're planning a terrorist attack. Anyway, I got into the room about two steps after them. You were at reception raising six sorts of hell—baby, I just stayed out of your way. Anyway, Scheideman didn't even look at the chart when he called for the Haldol. He didn't know your friend had been throwing up—"

"Like a *champion,*" Alex confirmed. "It's not that the meds weren't appreciated, just that, you know, makes it that much harder to figure out if he'd been roofied."

"Did they run a tox screen?" He'd asked for one—had asked every doctor within shouting distance for one—but that didn't always mean what he hoped for.

"Honey," Dave cooed, "would we *do* you that way?"

Jackson blinked. "Yeah?"

"Yeah, we ran you one—*before* the Haldol—and no, the doctor didn't ask for it. We had the blood work in before ol' Shiny Man opened his mouth." Dave dropped his camp for a second. "You were in our unit for months, Jackson. And we saw the marshals there for protective custody until the case got out of court. Honey, if you were there battling for Kaden, screaming for a tox screen, you knew what you were doing."

Jackson let loose a sigh of relief and managed a smile. "You know, some people don't believe in guardian angels anymore, but you two give me faith."

Dave exhaled the last puff and ground his cig in the sand. "Yeah, you say that, bitch, but you never put out." He winked and nodded to Alex. "Baby, our break's up. I'll cover for you if you go get the results from the car."

Jackson gasped a little, but Dave looked at him meaningfully.

"Go," he said, his voice dropping. "We made copies. We did the same for you, although I know you don't remember. The minute the po-po came asking for your charts, Alex and I felt a tingle in our short hairs."

"Wait!" Jackson called, hoping for a break—or a familiar name, at least. "Do you know the name of the cop who was putting weight on Scheideman?"

Dave shrugged, but Alex nodded. "Yeah—name was Owens. Short guy, dark hair, sort of greasy. Wore a uniform. Totally fucking average—I couldn't have picked him out of a lineup if he was sucking Scheideman's dick."

"Well, baby, if Scheideman was getting his dick sucked, I say let it happen—it can *only* mean good things for us." With that Dave flopped his wrist at them and turned and flounced off.

Jackson and Alex started walking toward the garage, and Jackson was sure that to anybody watching, it would look like Alex and Dave had a spat of some sort and Jackson got to calm Alex down.

Jackson waited until they had disappeared from sight of the hospital to ask, "You were afraid someone was going to fix the tox screen results?"

Alex shrugged. "Shiny Man isn't the only guy who welcomes kickbacks. Usually they're from drug companies, but… well, you were the first. But after you started to use us as a resource, Dave and I, we sort of started to keep an eye out for that kind of thing, right? I mean, Scheideman wanted to give you a crap bag, and somebody—I'm not sure who—was trying to convince us that you took a .22 in the chest and not a hollow point in the back."

Jackson squinted at him in the dark of the garage. "I never knew that—who was it?"

Alex shrugged. "It was eight years ago—you know that. I didn't even see him. I heard him talking to Scheideman, and Dave and I made copies of all your charts. When the DA's office came and asked for medical records, *that's* what we gave them. And like I said, you started to PI for your firm, and we started to… let's just say we're very, very careful when we see an officer-involved shooting."

"You could have told me." Jackson felt a chill snake through his bowels. "I mean I…." He thought of Kaden. "Alex," he hissed, wishing he could say this telepathically. "You guys could put yourself in danger—"

"Dave gets frisked at least twice a month walking home from the liquor store with cigarettes and wine," Alex said matter-of-factly. "It's our neighborhood—we've lived there for twelve years."

"You guys have been together since—"

"Nursing school, yes, since the dawn of fucking time—pay attention here, Jackson. They get away with it because he's black and he wears Converse and pedal pushers on his off hours, and you know Dave, he says it's a crime against fashion—"

Alex was trying to make light of it, but Jackson could hear the bitterness. "Is it because of this, you think?"

Alex nodded quietly. "Yeah. I think it's because of this. Most of the nurses—and I know you get this—we fight the good fight together, Jackson. But me and Dave—I mean, it only takes one cop with a grudge and Dave's kissing a brick wall when he just wanted some fucking cigarettes."

"Why didn't you say anything?" Jackson asked, a sort of fury burning in his gut. All of the things he hadn't known….

"We gave you info when you needed it," Alex said mildly. "Look, we're all for doing what's right, but you can't protect the world."

"I can't even protect my family," Jackson muttered.

"Yeah, well, the next time you come asking for info, you could always bring us smokes and wine."

Jackson made a mental note to do just that. He thought of Dave— sassy, bitchy, easygoing Dave—who did the softest blood draw of anyone on his floor and could talk someone down from a shitty-assed night of pain with a matter-of-fact kindness that warmed Jackson's soul.

"Cases of it for Christmas," he said.

Alex winked at him and pointed. "Kk—there's our fabulous fuckmobile!" He reached out with his remote and clicked while they were about three cars away.

It did not blow up—and for half a second, Jackson's heart stopped because he thought that was what had happened.

But it *did* catch fire, quickly, like an accelerant had been poured all over the interior.

He and Alex stopped flat-footed, staring at the old Ford SUV as flames raced along the interior. A horrific crack popped through the air as the back window burst, and another one as the side window exploded.

"Mother*fucker*!" Alex snapped as the roaring sound hit them both. "I had three pairs of designer scrubs in there. And *shoes*, Jackson—a new pair of nice cushy nurse tennies and…." His voice caught, and Jackson threw an arm around his shoulders while he fished for his phone and called the fire department.

Oh yeah. He wanted them first. No cops on the scene until the last possible moment.

"You got insurance?" he asked as the two of them backed up a couple of steps. The heat was getting intense near the car, and Jackson felt a little pang—the car was about ten years old. He'd bet it was one of their first big purchases together.

"Not for a fucking arson fire!" Alex snarled, running his fingers through his hair. "God*dammit*, Jackson. You know what was in there, don't you?"

Jackson paused as dispatch connected him. "Of course I do," he said. God, somebody let this fucking day end.

"WHAT DO you mean the company owes them a car?" Even over the phone, Ellery sounded puzzled, which was funny, but he also sounded like the stick was easing slowly out of his sweet ass, which was sexy.

If Jackson hadn't been watching Dave and Alex remind themselves in a quiet bubble that they were glad to be alive and it was only the fucking car, he could almost have been distracted by Cramer's voice on the phone.

"I'm saying they had copies of Kaden's tox screen in their car— and it was rigged to catch fire when Alex hit the clicker."

"Not blow up?" Ellery asked, but he sounded confused and not skeptical.

"Because a bomb has casualties," Jackson muttered. "A bomb draws attention to itself. A car fire means a short—if this is a short in the wiring, they're at fault, nobody cares. But I'm telling you, I watched that fire spread as we were walking toward the car. It didn't just start to smoke and then spout flames—"

"It burned fast and hot from the beginning?"

"Oh yeah," Jackson confirmed. The black smoke roiling off the vehicle had driven him and Alex outside, but he was watching the firemen coat it in foam and call towing for the carcass. God.

"Why not just steal them?" Ellery asked, but not like he doubted Jackson's assessment.

Jackson thought about poor Dave, harassed for being a nurse, for being Jackson's friend. For being black. "Because this sends a definite message," he said grimly. "They don't want these guys on our side."

"Well, that's not going to happen. I'd say they're a valuable resource." Jackson could hear clicking on the other end, and it sounded like Ellery was furiously double-tasking.

"Yeah—they were doing me a solid and this was the result. I get that we're not made out of money—"

"An early-model SUV?" Ellery said, and it sounded like he was clicking buttons.

"Yeah, about ten years old."

"Well, the replacement is five years old, and it should be there at the end of their shift. Keys will be delivered to the information desk by the main entrance."

"Yeah?" Jackson was shocked. This was movie money, right here. "How'd you get the partners to agree so fast?"

"The partners don't know yet," Ellery said grimly. "But I'll make a case for reimbursement. How many cases have they helped you out on?"

"Ten, twelve—ask Jade to look them up in my work laptop. It's under the reception counter. It's documented."

"Good. This will be compensation—tell them they're officially on retainer as professional consultants, which, by the way, makes fucking with them a bigger crime than it already is."

Oh God. Jackson hated being indebted to this guy—he really did. But this was solid. Truly fucking solid. "It's fucking hard to hate you when you're being a decent person. Ask Jade for the paperwork and tell her what happened—she knows these guys, she'll make it a priority."

"You still going to Connie's house?" Ellery asked, apprehension in his voice.

"You can't keep me away," Jackson growled. "What the hell did Kaden wander into?"

"You, sir, need to move your ass and find out."

Ellery hung up crisply, and Jackson was left staring at his phone. God, he'd been pissed that morning—not even so much at Ellery but at having to make himself naked, show his scars, just to get this guy, this guy who held Kaden's future in his hands, to stop looking like he'd stepped through the looking glass and start working like this was a real fucking case and their lives depended on keeping Kaden alive and out of jail. Forever.

Well, apparently Ellery was doing that. Jackson could almost forgive him for being an uptight prick who looked at Jackson—and Jade—like they were trash.

Besides, Ellery Cramer wasn't bad-looking—and he had that sort of ice-blue-blood thing going on in his ramrod posture and his defiantly clenched jaw. Sexy. Power, strong will—those things had always attracted Jackson. He was not above comfort sex or a playful romp, but the person who made Jackson work for it was the lover Jackson wanted in his bed.

Yeah, that crush was still going strong, but Jackson had too many people looking to him right now—and somebody did *not* want him to have too much information.

He sighed. And if he was fronting the money to help out Dave and Alex, Ellery had a bank account to stand on in the "not an asshole" department.

And if that bank account was helping out his friends, Jackson was obliged to knock the chip off his shoulder so he could stand with them.

He approached them slowly but with purpose, and he got there in time to see them cup each other's cheeks and smile absurdly through tears they probably wished they hadn't shed.

Dave saw him first, and they dropped their hands to their sides—and then clasped them.

"So… you want anything else? A pint of blood, perhaps? We got chocolate and vanilla—let me open up a fucking vein."

Jackson winced. "Not necessary," he said, feeling the guilt-shiv twist in his stomach again. "But here—" He handed Alex his card, with Ellery's number and extension written hurriedly on the back of it. "This guy here is having an SUV delivered to the hospital to get you home. The delivery guy is going to leave the keys at the info desk in the front. By the way, you're now official consultants to the defense firm, so if anybody gives you shit about hanging with me, tell them they're interfering with a crime investigation and that's a fucking crime, you hear me?"

Jackson nodded and watched as the two of them, stunned, nodded back.

"Good. And now, as just a personal favor to me, could you do me something?"

"You got us a car?" Dave asked. "Hell—I'll blow you and Lex'll get your rims."

And *that* made Jackson laugh. "Uhm, kind of you but not necessary. No. Stay away from this case. They set your car on fire—you're consultants, not spies." He swallowed and tried not to look to where the smoke had eased up, but the stench of hot metal and melted upholstery remained. "And you're friends. Guys, you're smart, and you're so fucking helpful, but most importantly, you're alive, got it?"

They both nodded, and Alex came in for the hug. Jackson squeezed him tight, wishing he could do more, and Dave went over both their shoulders and squeezed tighter.

The hug eased up and Alex said disconsolately, "You know, we didn't even have sex in it anymore. We just mostly sat and talked and…."

"Yeah, baby." Dave squeezed his shoulder. "He gets it."

Jackson did.

JACKSON CONSULTED with the fire chief before he left—with mixed results. The chief, one Abe McKenzie, was a thick-chested, buzz-cut veteran of the department, with gray shooting through the stubble on his head and goatee; he lived and died law and order. Jackson asked for a copy of the arson report on the down low and was told it would be made available to the firm when it was available to the DA's office and not a moment before.

"What about the police department?" Jackson asked, frustrated.

"They'll get it if it's pertinent to an open investigation," McKenzie said, his voice gruff from too much smoke and too many fires. His team was busy cleaning up, and the forensics team had moved in to photograph the scene. He turned from his scrutiny of the busy, almost scavenger-like proceedings to regard Jackson fiercely. "Is there a *problem* with the police having that report?" he asked evenly.

Jackson returned his stare. The guy had a shallow line of scarring along his jaw, and white, even teeth, which, so far, Jackson had only seen when McKenzie's lean lips had been pulled back in a snarl. *Now* this *guy could keep you safe at night*, his inner alley cat whispered, but Jackson ignored that voice for the business at hand.

"I think the car was torched to cover up evidence exonerating a guy who was arrested this morning," Jackson said, keeping the root of that evil out of his voice. "I'm leery of *anybody* getting their hands on it."

McKenzie's eyes darted to the upper right and then back to Jackson's face. On a lesser person it would have been an eye roll. "Nice dodge, Mr. Rivers, but we know your name and we know your story and we know that you've got an axe to grind. We're not your fuckin' axe, you understand me?"

Jackson snorted. "Just don't be the fuckin' three-ton whetstone in my way, and I've got no problem with that," he muttered. He fished a card from his cell phone case and handed it to McKenzie. "Any help you got, I'll take. Any shit you got, you can dish that somewhere else."

McKenzie let out a bark of laughter and raked Jackson up and down with his eyes. "You? You need them both at the same time. Now get out of my face and let me secure my scene."

"Yes*sir*!" Jackson backed up and gave the guy a two-fingered salute before turning away to his car.

He'd left his old Toyota illegally parked, thinking he was just going to hit Dave and Alex up for info, not witness an arson fire.

It had a ticket on it.

He crumpled the ticket up into a tight and tiny ball and chucked it into the back, where it joined its litter of brethren and sandwich wrappers, rolled up identically. Once a month, he rather enjoyed sweeping them out like little recyclable ping-pong balls when he cleaned his car. Usually he saved one or two for Billy Bob to play with—he thought of it as a circle-of-life sort of thing.

What he did *not* enjoy was cruising all the way down 5 to 80 to take the Northgate off-ramp to the little knot of dirtied suburb where Connie lived. Jackson hated this part of town. Sure, his duplex on Elvas wasn't in an *awesome* neighborhood, but he'd grown up here, in North Sacramento. The apartment complex where he'd lived through high school was still there, crumbling concrete stairs and all. God, the day his mom'd kicked him out so her boyfriend could move in had been the best day of his life, because Kaden's mom had taken him in and let him sleep on their couch—even though he was pretty sure she knew he was sleeping with her daughter at the time.

But he'd gotten a job ASAP, and after high school, when K was in college and Jackson had been taking preliminary criminal justice courses and applying for the academy, he and K had roomed together for a while in an even shittier apartment. He'd thought his life would be chocolate once he got in.

Not so much.

Connie Coulson lived right in the middle of the real estate that used to represent the center of Jackson's life. Jackson could have hated the guy for that alone.

South Avenue was an oddly rural collection of tiny houses on plots with actual yards. Some of the yards were well-kept behind wrought iron or hurricane fences, and some were trashed, and all of them were brown and dusty in the final days of summer during a drought. Before she'd passed away, Kaden's mom used to say the neighborhood was like the neighborhood she'd grown up in as a little girl in the South—only without the green to make it pretty.

And with too many fences.

Connie Coulson's cottage-style house was not one of the ones with the wrought iron or hurricane fencing. His lawn was dirt, and his dirt was full of trash. It looked like the back of Jackson's car, only without the military precision of the rolled-up balls of paper.

This would have been in keeping with the décor of the rest of the neighborhood, but when Jackson parked, he noted the Navigator-style SUV in front of the house—hell, it was almost as big as the house itself.

Black, chrome rims, tinted windows—nice, Connie. Unobtrusive. Way to show you were *definitely* living on the salary of a gas station clerk.

Idiot.

Jackson knocked sharply at the door, unsurprised when it didn't open. He heard ratlike scuttling throughout the house—also unsurprising. The scuttling grew louder, and after pausing, just a moment, to see which direction the pounding footsteps were going, he took off at a dead sprint for the backyard.

And got there just in time to see a scrawny guy with shockingly red hair and greenish freckles against pale skin burst out the back door.

Jackson took three full strides, hitting the middle step of the porch with the ball of his foot and using his momentum to vault over the railing. He caught Connie midair, and together they crashed through the other side of the rail, landing with a solid thump on the hardpan dirt below the porch. Connie lay on his back, mouth opening and closing like a landed fish, and Jackson had *his* fall cushioned by about a hundred pounds of stringy flesh and pointy bone. He felt some bruises starting on his knees and at his ribs, but he was doing well enough to sit up on his knees, straddling Connie's thighs. He took a second to wish that of all the men he'd interacted with this day, he'd been able to sit like this on anyone but this one.

Connie raised his arms weakly to try to fend Jackson off, and Jackson grabbed his wrists before the fending could work its way up to a full-on flail.

"Nah-nah-nah," he managed, slamming Connie's hands down above his head. "You've been a bad boy, Connie—you don't get to go anywhere until you tell me what you did."

"I don't gotta tell you *shit*!" Connie really hammered that last word, and spit flew out of his mouth.

Jackson grimaced and wiped his chin on his shoulder but didn't loosen his hold. "You took last night off," Jackson said and watched him flinch—pretty hard to miss from this close up. "You called your boss, who'd been working all day, and told him you were sick, and now he's in jail for something he didn't do. Now I was coming to see if you were really sick—if you'd been smart, I would have found you with a shit-ton of Kleenex and in your bathrobe, but *no*. You've got to be blowing out of your own house like a bright-eyed fucking squirrel and force me to bring you down. So we know you're not smart, and we know you're not *sick*—what we *don't* know is why you called in and left your boss swinging in the breeze."

Connie closed his eyes. "Didn't want to hurt Kaden," he said, his breath coming in forced pants, probably because hey! Jackson was lying on his ribs. "But... but see...." He grimaced and bit his lip. "I was supposed to be there. I was supposed to be the fall guy. Because they said if I didn't, they'd...." To Jackson's disgust, Connie began to cry, big hiccupy sobs, with snot running down his nose into the creases by his mouth and everything. "See," he wheezed, "I play the ponies at Expo—"

"Gambling?" Jackson asked, scrambling up. He kept Connie's wrists clasped together and reached into his pocket for a handy zip tie. He wasn't a cop anymore, but old habits died hard.

"Yeah—I was in deep, they knew it. One of them came in for his payoff and passed me a tip."

Jackson grunted. "And what a nice car you bought with it!" He wrapped the zip tie with professional speed and pulled tight.

"What the fuck?" Connie demanded, shaking his bound wrists. "You're not even a fucking cop!"

"Nope. But I need you to answer my questions, and I don't feel like tackling you again." In fact, Jackson's knee—which was already a miracle of modern engineering and daily collagen boosters—was singing the opening number from *Les Mis*. His chest, which still showed the lumps of scarring under the skin, ached from the exertion, and he longed for his Pilates ball so he could stretch out his torso.

And he wasn't about to tell this shithead *any* of that.

"Yeah," Connie muttered. "If you were a cop, I'd be fucking *dead*. Those assholes...." He shook his head and turned miserable green eyes to Jackson. "You've got to understand, they were already shaking us down. First it was free coffee, then it was free food, and that wasn't so bad, right? Treat the guys right and they get the perps before they hit your front door. But I got in deep with my bookie—"

"Name?" Jackson had his phone out and was making notes furiously.

"Hendrix."

Jackson frowned. He had a line on most of the big names in town—Sacramento had a lot of small sports action, some high rollers betting on basketball and the football teams in the Bay Area and, of course, the ponies. But most gamblers in the area went to Cache Creek out by Stanford Ranch. Indian gaming—big casinos, lots of action.

Hendrix was *not* on his list of contacts for gambling.

A car backfired, and Jackson looked down the gap between the house and the fence to see a black SUV with tinted windows cruise down the street, taking its time. Out of instinct, Jackson backed up a little so he was covered by the house and asked, "Who in the hell is—"

"Sergeant Ross Hendrix," Connie said guiltily. "He runs a 'friendly' game of poker out of the back of one of the restaurants on Del Paso."

"Friendly?" Oh, there were all sorts of ways cops could be friendly. Jackson hadn't trusted any of them as a kid, not as an adult, not as a cop, and definitely not as a "retired" officer.

"He's good," Connie muttered, shaking his head. "You come out ahead a couple of times, and then you lose, just a little. Then you lose just a little more. And then you do just a little favor—"

"Which was…?"

Connie looked away. "I… I looked the other way. That cop that came into the station—Bridger? Saw him with a working girl in the back of his car. She was… working. On him."

Jackson groaned. "Seriously? Can they not come up with anything more original? Just once I want to see a bad cop trying to take over the fucking world. But no—money, gambling, sex—"

"Drugs—"

"Fucking lovely. Jesus, I want some new fucking vices."

"Just once," Connie sneered, struggling awkwardly to his feet, "I want to see a *good* cop with *no* fucking vices. Wouldn't that be fucking lovely?"

"There are good cops out there," Jackson said fiercely. God, he'd known some—some dyed-in-the-wool, true-blue fucking heroes. There just weren't enough of them—with or without the bad cops, there just weren't enough people anywhere Jackson had ever felt he could trust.

"Yeah?" Connie asked bitterly. "Well, where were your good cops when I was told I had to be there to take the fall for Collin Miles? There was supposed to be a ruckus—someone was supposed to make like they were raising hell and then *I* was supposed to shoot…." His voice broke. "Shoot…."

That damned black SUV ambled by again, and in the silence left after its dirty engine moved on, Connie started to cry. "Man, my dog got sick last year. I had to pay the vet to put her down. She was just… so trusting, you know? I can't shoot no fucking cop!"

Jackson turned around and took a few steps toward the middle of the yard, fingers locked behind his head. "So you called in sick," he said, seeing it fall into place.

"Yeah. Yeah."

Jackson pushed against his locked fingers, twisting his torso so he could stretch out his chest. He glanced over his shoulder to smile gamely at Connie and wondered what to do with him. God, he was a witness. He was a witness against *cops*. But turning him over to the DA right *now* would get him killed, because the DA wasn't going to start a case based on the hearsay of a guy with a gambling problem who worked in a gas station.

Jackson pivoted on his left foot, because his right knee was starting to swell, and took a step toward Connie, and the SUV engine blatted into the silence.

And a slug tore through Connie Coulson's jaw, and another one hit his arm, and another one hit his chest before the sharp report of the Uzi hit Jackson's eardrums.

Jackson threw himself down face-first, breathing the hardscrabble dust left by the drought, and listened as the Uzi tore the house above him to shreds.

Ten rounds per second, Jackson recited, the details of his gun manual coming to haunt him like it had during his long stay in the hospital. *Israeli made, telescoping muzzle, ten rounds per second, three seconds to pass the house, thirty, maybe forty rounds, just wait, Jackson, wait and they'll drive on, 'cause they're cowards and they think Connie's the only person here....*

Ten rounds per second. When forty-five shell casings were found in the street, Jackson would know that it had taken less than five seconds. During the entire five seconds, he relived the bullets ripping his lungs, cracking his ribs, tearing a hole out of his chest—maybe ten times a second? Maybe fifty times a second? Maybe a hundred?

Maybe too goddamned many times for a guy who'd survived and knew what bullets could do to flesh.

The shooting stopped, the car rattled into the distance, and Jackson stayed on the ground taking inventory, counting bruises, bumps, his swelling knee, the fire along his cheek that meant he'd been grazed, his own breath harshed by panic. *Fine. Fine. You're fine. No hits.*

Oh fuck.

Connie.

Jackson looked at what remained of Connie Coulson, a shredded pile of flesh and bone bleeding into the dust.

The stupid gambler who couldn't shoot his dying dog and who had called in sick because the only way to get out of the hole he'd dug himself was to go to ground.

Poor kid. He couldn't have been older than twenty-five.

With an oath, Jackson pulled his phone out and called 911. He asked for the fire department and a paramedic.

They'd get there first.

He thought briefly about running out to his car and taking off, but even if he wouldn't have been fingered for the crime, he knew without looking that his car had been parked *right* in front of the fucking house.

Oh holy shitballs. When he was done cleaning what was left of the shit and the fan, he was going to need a ride home.

A Most Unusual Habitat

THE LAW offices were a few blocks away from the county jail. After leaving Kaden in the infirmary, a guard by his bedside, Ellery had braved the baking heat to walk back, mostly so he could talk to the thin thirtyish woman who had looked so much more comfortable sitting alone in front of her keyboard than she did talking to Ellery.

"I'm sorry, Mr. Cramer, but it's not as easy to render as they show it on television."

Ellery took a deep breath and very, very carefully adjusted his tie. "I understand that," he said, although he really didn't on an emotional level. People said that all the time, that what took months in real life was often shown to take an afternoon or half an episode on television. Intellectually, he got it. In the television shows, he was supposed to be busy and cutthroat at work and then play golf on the weekends and get scads of ass on the side—but no, not happening.

Instead he was an asshole at work because he had to be, and on his great nights, he got an hour and a half on the elliptical machine while studying motions. On not-so-great nights, he fell asleep over his coffee—while writing motions.

"I'm not asking for this person's life story and third-grade photo or anything. I would settle for some sort of identification or proof that he or she—"

"She," Crystal said with confidence. With brief keystrokes, she pulled up a photo in the process of rendering. "See?"

Ellery squinted at the reflection of the would-be photographer in the shiny stainless steel edge of the counter. He was reluctantly impressed—she'd said it wasn't finished; she hadn't said it was so far along.

"Christ, it's still not that clear," he muttered.

"Yeah. You can tell it's not a crime-scene photo—those are much higher definition and taken from several angles. This one is just head-on. But you can see her, right? Jeans, high heels—"

"Turquoise glitter polish," Ellery noted. "Yeah. Girl." The feet were tiny, the toes almost absurdly plump and sausage shaped, pale as eggs. "Little girl, little girl… what were you doing in that scary place?"

"Why didn't anybody see her?" Crystal asked, and Ellery glanced at her, frowning. She was actually a pretty woman—dirty-blonde hair, straight, pulled from a heart-shaped face in a careless ponytail. And she'd already justified Jackson's faith in her tenfold.

"That is a good question," Ellery mumbled. "And why isn't she mentioned in the police reports…."

"Yeah—I mean, they used her picture. Shouldn't they know about her?"

Ellery resisted the urge to bang his head against Crystal's giant computer. "You know, usually when you see a guy with a gun near his hand, the guy did it. I mean, it may have been self-defense, it may have been drug rage—but he usually did it. Straight as an ice pick—not a question to be asked. *This* is a goddamned Gordian knot."

Crystal grunted. "Yeah, well, you maybe wanna stop trying to knit and start looking to see if anyone's filed a missing persons report on a white girl with pink hair, young—maybe fifteen to twenty—and…." Crystal grimaced. "Track marks."

Ellery frowned and squinted at the rendering. "Are you sure—"

"Look right there."

The picture was blurry, but sure enough, Crystal had caught the tiny detail.

"Shit," Ellery muttered. "How did you—"

Crystal met his eyes and pushed up the sleeve of her summer-weight cardigan. And showed him the scars on the inside of her elbow. "I know, Mr. Cramer. Which is why I turn all my evidence over to Trish at the end of the day so she can be the one to testify."

Trish was a solid-looking mother of three—you'd trust Trish with your life, your dinner, and your best suit at the dry cleaner.

Ellery nodded and tried not to pass judgment—and then remembered that Jackson had gotten her the job.

"So, uh—Jackson?" Ellery asked tentatively.

She looked at him with suspicion. "You want to hit that?"

"I don't do crowd scenes," he snapped, and she rolled her eyes at him.

"Neither does he. He just…." She grimaced. "He just *none of your business*. If you ever end up at his place, you keep his business his."

"Look, I don't want to compare dick size—"

"Pretty fuckin' big—"

"I just want to know what happened to him. Why'd he leave the force?"

She raised her eyebrows, her gray eyes wide behind her thick glasses. "You're not from Sacramento, are you?"

"No—"

"Let me guess. Somewhere back East."

"Boston," he said, again impressed.

"You went to school in the West—"

"Stanford," he said. The computer tech was winning at *This is Ellery Cramer's Life*—it was a little humiliating.

"Parents have money," she said thoughtfully, and he ground his teeth. "Still together—one of them, probably Mom, has completely unrealistic expectations. You're on the quick track—want to be partner so you can show Mommy what you're made of. And because whether or not she approves of the gay, you want to prove that you're just as good as the brother or sister who came before you and is gleefully producing spawn with a vetted partner."

Ellery swallowed. "Have you been running my personal information?" he asked, horrified.

Crystal snorted. "Dude, I'd get fired for that. No, I read your aura. You're like, all cream and pink and dashes of maroon. Some navy. I mean, it's a handsome aura, really strong, but sort of predictable, you know?"

"I have pink in my aura," Ellery said numbly. "You know my life history and I have pink in my aura and none of this tells me who tried to kill Jackson Rivers and why he hates cops."

Crystal snorted. "Well he *hates* them because they tried to *kill* him. *Duh.* But that's why I asked about where you came from. Eight years ago this was front-page news for a year. The trial lasted ten weeks, and Jackson was in protective custody until it was over. Which was easy, because, you know, he was in the hospital for another four months after that. I mean, I think they had to grow him a new goddamned lung or something."

"But I thought he *was* a cop," Ellery said. There was no mistaking ex–law enforcement.

Crystal met his eyes seriously, all trace of mockery gone. "Well yeah, Mr. Cramer. But you turn in a dirty cop and your career is pretty much over. It's over even more quickly if you'll never be back to 100 percent."

Ellery was gritting his teeth again. He wanted details, but Kaden had been right: if this had been front-page news eight years earlier, he needed to read up on the front page. Just not when he was trying to save Kaden's life.

"You're probably right," he said, trying desperately to relax his jaw. "And if you could print out the rendering as far as you've got it, I'd be really grateful."

"No, you won't," Crystal said wisely, looking at him through her glasses with knowing eyes. "But it really is kind of you to try to mask your impatience. Look Jackson up—and if you have any questions beyond that, let me know."

Why are people content to go home with him if they know it's going to be a one-night stand?

"Thank you," he said—sincerely this time. "I will."

"Because he's a good guy," she answered out of the blue. "Anyone who's gone home with him has a story to tell about how he helped them out—even if it was just saving them from being alone on a really shitty night." Her voice dropped, and she looked down at her computer keyboard, her expression embarrassed. "Or from using after five years of being clean and off the streets."

Oh. "Oh." He could barely swallow, his throat was so dry. "I'm sorry—"

"Don't be," she said, and her full-lipped smile was winsome and pretty and wise beyond her years. "I didn't use, and I felt better, and that's really all that sex has to be sometimes."

"True," he said, trying to remember the last time that was all sex had been for *him*.

"Until it's not," she said.

That was it. He was done. "I have stuff to do at my desk," he muttered. But God, anything other than having his entrails read by Grunhilde the computer tech witch woman here.

"Sure, Mr. Cramer. And I prefer Madame Arcati—I played her in high school."

"Good-bye, Crystal."

"Bye, Mr. Cramer." She waved cheerfully and he fled.

KADEN WAS snoring softly on the infirmary bed when Ellery got back to the jail. So was the guard, a paperback dangling limply from his hand.

In a way it was comforting—at least Ellery knew he wasn't the only one who was pretty sure Kaden wasn't a ruthless killer who had shot a policeman in cold blood.

On the other hand, if Kaden *had* been a ruthless killer, he would have escaped by now, and Ellery's career would have been over.

Awesome.

With a deep breath, Ellery sat down near the medical counter and started pulling shit out of his briefcase. First things first: he reread the notes on his legal pad, trying to figure out what he needed to do next. Hm... star *render picture*, add *heroin-addicted teenager* next to that, underline it. Put *missing persons and DBs* in the margins.

Witnesses. They needed—

Well, they *had* a witness—someone bearing *false* witness, but it was always entertaining and informative to watch someone lie.

With the impetus of direction, he took out his phone and called ADA Arizona Brooks.

"Zona?"

"Ellery," she said with genuine happiness. "Good to hear from you—which case are we talking about today?"

"*The People v. Kaden Cameron*," he said, and he could hear the sunshine turn cold on the other end of the line.

"Tell me you didn't catch that one," she said tensely. "Ellery, I like you—I do. But this is... this is bad."

"It's particularly bad if the guy doesn't have a defense attorney on his side," Ellery said, his voice hard. He could admit it—he was channeling his inner Jackson Rivers, because the fear in Arizona's voice disturbed him. Arizona was a fiftyish amazonian woman with cropped gray hair who faced down criminals with little more than a fierce glare and a shrug.

"Yeah, but you don't get it. I'm getting pressure from all sorts of places to put this guy away—"

"But it's fishy—I mean, can you not *smell* the fish? It's like someone threw a brace of trout in your car in the morning and let them cook on your backseat!"

There was a pause.

"Uh, Ellery, that was a really involved metaphor. Tell me that didn't happen to you."

"I wasn't liked in high school," he said grumpily. God. His mother had had to replace the car. "But that's okay. I'm not well-liked now. And I still smell fish—particularly with this case."

"What can I say? His tox screen came back—"

"Faked," Ellery said starkly. "With a timestamp *way* beyond the expiration date of any sort of drug in his system. The real results were burned up in a car fire—but that's not the point. The point is, I haven't gotten the real crime-scene photos yet, have you?"

"Well, it's a little early for the official forensic evidence, isn't it? Don't we usually wait for arraignment for that?" She sounded amused, because yes, the state had forty-eight hours after the bail hearing to arraign the suspect, and that was usually when the state released its evidence.

"Yes, yes, it is—but I still got a picture that's trying to pass itself off as an official crime-scene photo. Did you get it?"

Her voice got suspicious. "Cameron in front of the counter, gun near his hand—"

"Does it have a red blur on the top left edge?"

"Yeah—that's not like Lutz."

"Do you see his name on your files?"

"Yes, but the signature doesn't look like his."

"Well, I have a totally different name altogether. And it's not a crime-scene photo. The resolution is too low, and you can see the reflection of the photographer in the chrome on the counter—it's a girl, white, pink hair, late teens, possible drug user."

"Shit." Zona's muffled oath told Ellery she'd seen the same thing he had—and that he'd given her some information she hadn't had before. "You're right—where in the *fuck* are our real crime-scene photos? This… god*damm*it!"

Oh yeah. He looked at Kaden and hoped he might have just found his ticket home.

"Your evidence is tainted, Counselor."

"We're *not* dropping the case against a cop killer because of this," Zona snarled. "We *will* get Lutz's photos, and *then* we'll build a case."

"Zona, why would they taint the evidence like this—"

"I got no idea."

"Have you even *talked* to Scott Bridger?"

Arizona's sigh was pure frustration. "No. IA has him locked up tight. We may have to depose him together, with all three lawyers present."

"Does that not *tell* you there's more fish here than in my car?"

She laughed a little. "I have no idea why you weren't well-liked. *Everybody* loves the guy who's right all the time."

"This is dirty, Zona. We're supposed to believe it happened just like that picture—but that picture wasn't taken by an accredited forensics team member, and the tox screen *you* have isn't the one that was taken before the patient was given Haldol for his nausea."

"What the—how do you—"

"Motivation. My client is innocent and I don't want to see him suffer, so my people are moving like the fucking wind. What do you have on your side?"

Her voice sank. "Money," she hissed. "There is a *load* of fucking money here. You have no idea who's sending me e-mail telling me I need to get this guy under wraps."

Oh hell. "No, but I'd *love* to know!" he sang.

"No." He must have reached her threshold of cooperation, because he didn't hear any compromise in that tone. "Look, pull the tainted-evidence card tomorrow—I won't stop you. Maybe they'll drop the case and your client can go…."

"*Where?*" he demanded. "Where in the hell are my guy—*and* his wife and his children and his sister—supposed to go if we don't have someone else to pin this on? Where do you think he's going to be safe?"

"Canada?"

"This is wrong, Arizona. This is not why you're working at the DA's office." She legitimately wanted to put bad guys in jail. Countless lunches, a few late-night drinks, and the one thing he knew about her was that she was legit.

"I've got the law, and I've got who my office wants to prosecute—you know that. If you can get your guy off, do it. If you can even get him out on bail, do it. But I can't help you, Ellery—not if I want to keep putting bad guys away."

"Look," he said, reduced to begging for crumbs, "call me when IA calls you—"

"They're not going to *not* invite you—"

"Just like we're both going to get legit crime-scene photos, right?"

Her silence was gratifying. It meant she was thinking.

"Yeah, no harm in that."

"I need an invite to that party, Zona—it's not fair *or* legal if I don't get to depose the witness for the prosecution."

"I'm not stupid. I'll call you."

"Thanks."

Her sigh gusted through the mouthpiece, and he had the sudden thought that maybe Zona wasn't well-liked either—that maybe she'd treasured their lunch dates and their late nights at the bar as much as he had, because they were equals, and because they had to be assholes to do their jobs right, but they were doing their jobs because they wanted to do the right thing.

"Be careful, Ellery. This should have been a no-brainer—the way this guy looks?"

"You mean the whole black thing?" he asked, forgetting that he liked her.

"You know it's easier to convict a black defendant than a white one. I didn't make the system—"

"But you're telling me I should cave to it. Well, I'm not."

"Well, somebody expected you to—"

"Not me," he said, feeling again the satisfaction of knowing that Jackson Rivers had picked *him* to defend his friend. "I was specially requested by the defendant—I have no idea who he was *supposed* to get."

"Huh." In the background he could hear her pulling hard on a straw. Well, she loved her sodas at the end of the day. "Not that I can't see you've got your hands full, but maybe, you know, next time you're taking a dump with your laptop, you should look up and see who was *supposed* to draw this case."

Ellery blinked. "Why—"

"Because whoever at the public defender's office was *supposed* to draw this case, *that person* might know who was hoping for a quick indictment and a plea of life without parole instead of the death penalty."

"Is that what you're supposed to offer?"

"Yup. Almost verbatim."

"So my client is working the night shift for a sick employee—"

"He was what?"

"Do your own goddamned work, Arizona. You want to put a guy away using tainted evidence and money from the capitol, you figure out how and why he did it. I'm not feeding you *jack*!"

Ellery pounded End Call and rested his face in his hands. At that moment there was a knock on the door, and a guard stepped aside to let Jade Cameron—wielding her office ID—into the infirmary.

"Come in?"

"Mr. Cramer?"

Just that morning he would have been afraid of her—she *still* looked like she could bite off his head in one snap of her even, white teeth. But she also looked tired, and worried, and near tears.

"Should you even be here?" he asked. "I was sure they were going to kick *me* out."

"Yessir," she said softly. "To both of us leaving. But it's more than that. I've got to go stay with Rhonda and the kids—they're scared and they're freaking out and they need reassurance." Gently she reached out to the bed and palmed the back of her brother's head.

"Jade?" He captured her hand and brought it to his cheek, and she stroked it with her thumb.

"No worries, K," she whispered, bending down to kiss his forehead. "I'll take care of them, okay?"

"How's Jackson?" he asked, and Jade looked up, meeting Ellery's eyes and grimacing.

"He needs a fucking ride," she muttered. "Apparently his car got shot to shit when he was interviewing Connie."

Kaden frowned and pushed himself up, the cuffs around his wrists making it awkward and the paper on top of the green vinyl crackling. "Someone shot at Connie?"

She sighed and sank to her knees in front of her brother. "Not *at*, K. Somebody *shot* him. Jackson hit the dirt first. He won't say it, but if his car is completely totaled, I think it was pretty close."

"Oh my God," Kaden whispered. "J, they're going to get Jacky!"

"He swears nobody saw him there," she said, looking at Ellery and nodding. "But he's got to give his statement at the scene, and he said he'd better stay away from me and the kids until this is all wrapped up. He said he'd see you tomorrow at the bail hearing, okay?"

Kaden nodded, visibly upset. "Connie—Jade, he was just a stupid kid. I can't believe—"

"Believe it," she said flatly. "And be on your toes. You get as much sleep as you can right now, K, because you need to keep your eyes open tonight."

"You're sleeping in the infirmary," Ellery said, because that much he *had* accomplished. "But she's right."

Kaden half laughed. "That's just awesome. So when someone rips my ass open with a toothbrush, at least I'll be in a good place to get it stitched up."

Jade harrumphed. "That's no way to look at the good side. Now shut up and give me a hug so I can tell Rhonda you're okay."

Ellery looked away from this hug like he'd looked away from Jackson's good-bye, focusing instead on his notes and on reassigning a few of his other cases since this one was obviously going to take a lot of his time. He looked up when Jade approached his makeshift desk at the dispensary counter.

"Jackson's going to need a ride home," she said quietly. "But he won't ask you for one because he's got his manly pride or some shit like that. And if you could call me and tell me he's okay, I'd be much obliged."

She said it humbly, as though she was not the same woman who'd hated him almost on sight that morning. Ellery should have been annoyed, but instead he felt like he'd won a small skirmish with an old, respected enemy.

"I hear you. I'll pick him up." Why not? They had a lot to discuss. "Text me the address," he said. "I'll call Jackson."

Jade nodded and left, after giving her brother one last anxious hug.

Instead of going back to sleep, Kaden yawned and sat up, rolling his shoulders and trying to stretch in spite of the cuffs and the leg irons.

"Mr. Cameron?" The guard spoke up for the first time, and Kaden looked over and smiled.

"You ready to kick me out so this man can be left unmolested?" Ellery asked. Something in his stomach twisted. Good man. This was a good man.

The guard winked. "Not that I'm complaining," he said, yawning into his paperback. "I got a chance to read, and a nap, and some quiet— telling you, it's better than a vacation." He stood up and moved toward the door. "But it's time for my replacement to take over, which means visiting hours are almost over."

"He'll stay here," Ellery confirmed. "Butch, if you could make sure?"

Butch nodded. "Yeah, no problem, Mr. Cramer. We'll keep him here and out of general population—he'll be safe for tonight."

Ellery nodded, and for no reason at all, that moment when Jackson had stood in the conference room, teeth bared, *chest* bared, his scars on display to teach Ellery about consequences, flashed before his eyes.

"Butch?"

"Yessir?"

"Could you make sure the person who's assigned to watch him is someone you know?"

Butch was in his late fifties, a grizzled bulldog of a man without a lot of hair left but with some of the bluest eyes Ellery had ever seen. He squinted those eyes at Ellery and blew out a breath. "Yessir," he said thoughtfully. "I'll make sure it's someone square."

Ellery met Kaden's eyes, and Kaden shrugged. It was the best they could do.

"I'll see you tomorrow at your bail hearing. Jade knows to bring your suit to county so you can—"

"Look like a fine upstanding citizen," Kaden said, smiling a little. "Tell our boy to stay safe."

Ellery grimaced. "Looks like I'll have to—I'm apparently his taxi until he gets himself some wheels."

Kaden jerked his chin, shooing Ellery toward the door. "Maybe he'll get something better than that shitty Toyota this time."

Ellery laughed a little as he exited. Ellery'd seen Jackson's shitty Toyota too—he'd even gotten close enough to see the psychotically round little balls of trash that popped on the floor in the back like ping-pong balls.

His laugh faded, the echo down the white-tiled corridor of the jail sounding a little eerie.

He was never going to see that car again. And from the sound of it, Ellery was lucky he was going to see Jackson Rivers at *all*. That image—Jackson, green eyes flashing, muscled body heaving with emotion—would not fucking leave him *alone*.

Jade had said he wouldn't ask—too much pride. Well, that didn't surprise Ellery either. He checked out of the jail, nodded thanks to his escort, and then stepped into the swelter of the late-August afternoon. He hit the speed dial for PI with a little twinge of guilt. Maybe he should put a name there.

"I just gotta take this—" Jackson had obviously answered the call before his conversation was over. "Yeah," he muttered into the phone.

"Need a ride?"

"Shit."

"I'll take that as a yes," Ellery said dryly. Pride. Yup. Jackson Rivers had it. "You at Coulson's place still?"

"Ugh."

"Is that a *word*?" Instead of turning toward the firm's offices on L Street, he headed back toward the levee and the courthouse parking, where he'd left his car earlier.

"I'm sorry—I just haven't had a chance to call the towing company yet. Look, Cramer, I'm going to be an hour or two, so I might as well just call a cab and you can—"

"I'll call the towing company when I get there, and I'll be right out." He hung up before Jackson could object. "So there," he muttered to the nearly empty sidewalk and the concrete buildings to his right. God, what in the hell? Your car got shot up while you were doing your job, your best friend is in jail, your support system is all involved in *that* mess, and you won't take a ride? Fuck that!

For hell's sake—Ellery Cramer didn't need an engraved invitation.

He didn't even need to examine his motives too closely.

HE PULLED up to Connie Coulson's house and tried to smooth the wrinkle out of his nose. The neighborhood was terrifying—Ellery was glad there were cops out front, no matter how dirty, just so his damned car didn't get destroyed. Or stolen. Or stolen *and* destroyed.

The summer heat seemed to beat down especially hard on this stretch of road, and every lawn was a desert of dead grass and dirt. And trash. One of the houses he'd passed had a burst bag of dirty diapers strewn across the front yard, complete with scavenging dogs.

The house next door had expensive wrought iron and dogs the size of Hyundais. And a couple of scrawny, nervous smokers jittering in the far corner from the garage.

And a cop car around the corner.

Ellery didn't want to think about what that meant. Were the cops staking out the place to close down the shop? Or, given the can of worms Jackson and Kaden had opened for him that morning, were they waiting for their take?

He hated this feeling. He'd always believed in law and order, and even though he defended people—and not always the innocent—he'd believed the system was designed so that when people *were* innocent, they had a voice.

To find out, to be shown in lurid color and twisted flesh, that part of this system was flawed—was *soiled*—was the ultimate in losing faith.

He was driving his Lexus through the shadow of crime, and his gods of law and order had deserted him. And the people wearing their uniform were swarming over Connie Coulson's house like maggots.

Ellery parked on the shoulder of the road in front of the house next door to Coulson's, in front of the coroner's van. Even as he got out of his car and walked around the van, the coroners were shoving the gurney and its burden, the body-sized zippered black bag, into the refrigerated back of the bus.

He resisted the urge to gawk morbidly, well aware he would see crime-scene photos in exceptional detail, hopefully bright and early the next morning. And hopefully taken by one of the CSIs swarming this particular scene and not a random bystander with a camera phone.

In the meantime, his attention was caught by the dirty, banged-up man standing, hip cocked, with all his weight on the ball of one foot, as though favoring the other leg.

He'd bled through a bandage on the outside of his arm, and he had a bruise and a cut under one eye. His clothes looked as though he'd rolled around in the dirt, and the knee of his jeans was torn, showing a bad scrape and swollen joint under the fabric.

He had his arms crossed and was staring with a stony sort of fury at the five policemen surrounding him.

Ellery had taken three steps toward him, the better to get on his high horse and be the sort of defense lawyer cops abhorred, when he saw the car.

The car with no windows and a peppering of holes through the hood, and a spill of ping-pong-ball-shaped trash littering the ground by the back door, which had apparently opened in the onslaught.

Ellery's mouth went dry, and he looked from the car to the house, which was torn apart like paper. Behind him, the coroner's van started up and drove away at a sedate pace, no siren.

He looked at Jackson again, in better shape than the house and the car—and in *much* better shape than the man in the back of the coroner's van—and took a deep breath, trying to still the retroactive flood of panic rushing through his veins.

The stride he resumed toward the figures on the lawn was a little less high-and-mighty and a little more determined.

"Again," Jackson was saying, voice flat, "I was in the backyard. Connie took the rounds because they had a clear line of sight down the side yard. I saw him go down, and hit the mud myself."

"Not fast enough, huh, Rivers?" asked the thirtyish cop with gray-shot black hair and deep lines by his eyes and mouth.

"Am I *dead*?" Jackson snapped. "If I'm not dead, then it was fast enough."

"Yeah, well, too bad you didn't give Coulson some warning," another officer said. This one had plain brown hair and one of those faces that would remain young for a very long time. And gray eyes that looked like they had *never* been young.

Jackson's face went hard, like granite and nails. "Yeah. That's why Connie is dead, because I didn't know someone was shooting at us until I *saw him get shot*!" Jackson scrubbed his face. "You know who Connie Coulson was, don't you?" he asked conversationally.

"Two-bit hood?" That guy with the deep crow's-feet had a smart mouth on him. Ellery wanted to smack it off.

Jackson looked at the guy with eyes as flat and cold as a soulless sea.

Ellery would have said that look wouldn't have worked, but the cop—all of them, in fact—started to shift around, fidgeting as Ellery had wanted to that morning.

"Who was he, Jackson?" Crow's-feet said after a moment.

"He was the guy who called in sick to Kaden Cameron's quickie-mart last night. He's the guy who was *supposed* to be there when Bridger and Miles came in."

Silence. Nothing but silence.

Jackson shook his head in disgust. "Yeah—and not one of you has anything to say to *that*, do you?" He spotted Ellery and turned away from the interrogation circle, only to be stopped by a shove to the shoulder from one cop and a kick to the swollen knee from another.

He almost went down but stopped himself with his hand. "We're done here," he growled.

"I thought you IA rats were tough," Crow's-feet sneered. "C'mon, Jackson, can't you hang around with your brothers long enough to keep your story straight?"

"Yeah," Dead-eyes sneered, clearly enjoying Jackson's little grunt of pain. "From what I hear, the story's not the only thing he can't keep straight."

"Yeah, Rivers—I thought you were supposed to screw the *female* nurses. The guys you just let blow you!"

Oh God, that must have been a reference to the guys with the immolated Ford. Whatever it was, it had apparently snapped the very last of Jackson's reserves, because his arm cocked back in the unmistakable precursor to what was about to be an epic beating of ex-cop ass.

"Hold up there," Ellery called, hustling across the yard as though he'd never paused. "Do you have any reason to detain Mr. Rivers?"

He pulled up short in front of Jackson, buttoning the front of his sadly wrinkled jacket and fixing the officers with a dispassionate eye. "I'm Ellery Cramer from Pfeist, Langdon, Harrelson & Cooper," he said, pulling out a business card and dropping it on Crow's-feet's clipboard. "Jackson Rivers is here on our behalf investigating the arrest of Kaden Cameron. Do *you* have an excuse for not letting him attend to his damaged property or seek medical attention?"

"He declined medical attention," Crow's-feet said, throwing the card on the ground like trash. "Apparently he thinks rats heal themselves."

"Or maybe he was afraid you people would poison his bandages, and he prefers to live?" Ellery insinuated with a saccharine smile.

"We're not dirty," Dead-eyes snarled.

Ellery rolled his eyes. "Do you know that nearly a third of the women who get abortions in the United States belong to those radical religions that picket the Planned Parenthood locations?"

The policemen looked at him blankly. For that matter, so did Jackson.

"So your point would be…," Dead-eyes said slowly. He seemed to be the leader, and Crow's-feet seemed to be the most aggressive. They'd been the ones to try to knock Jackson to the ground.

"That some of those women walk into the abortion clinic, get abortions, and then walk out of the clinic and join the people in the sidelines screaming at the people going inside for mammograms and pap smears. Just because someone's screaming about evil in their loudest voice doesn't mean they're not participating in what could get them in the most trouble."

Jackson let out a reluctant chuckle. "You all have been schooled by a man in a suit," he said with cheerful rancor. "And he's right. I've been humoring you bozos, but you've got my official statement—several times. Now either take me in or let me go—but I need some water, and a Band-Aid, and a fucking chair. If you're not willing to offer me any of that shit, you've met my lawyer. He just made you all look like assholes."

Jackson turned his back on them, damned near kicking the grass backward like a cat pleased with the dump he'd just taken.

"You ready to go, Mr. Cramer?" he asked, heading for Ellery's car.

"I am indeed. Which towing service do you use?"

Jackson looked at him with a truly ferocious grin. "Don't need one. Saunders over there"—he jerked his chin toward Dead-eyes—"ran my plates and realized they were obligated to tow the thing anyway, on account of too many parking tickets."

Ellery groaned. Of course. Of *course* Jackson would land on his feet.

Except he really wasn't walking too well.

Ellery clicked his remote so Jackson could get in and then swung into the driver's seat while Jackson orgasmed over the all-leather interior.

"Oh man," the guy purred. "This is… mmmm…." He made kneading motions with his fingers and everything. "Is this sort of thing even *legal*?"

"You should feel it in the winter, when the seats heat," Ellery said dryly. "Do you need medical attention for your knee?"

That opened Jackson's eyes right up. "Do you got any ibuprofen, Princess? I don't want a doctor, but I could *seriously* use a painkiller and some ice." His voice sank to a grumble. "Of course I have *both* a bottle of Motrin *and* an ice pack in the damned car, but was I allowed to touch it? No-ooo!"

"Part of the evidence too?" Ellery asked, not without sympathy.

"Yeah—all sorts of stuff from my car that they decided they needed. My sports jacket, water, my painkillers, my fuckin' Taser…."

Jackson was starting to sound loopy, and Ellery asked, "Your insulin?"

He got a grunt in return. "I'm not diabetic," Jackson muttered.

"Hypoglycemic?"

"Not diagnosed," he admitted grudgingly. "I just need a fuckin' granola bar or something. God, *that* would be awesome. And some ice. And some Motrin. And some—"

"Jack in the Box," Ellery muttered with distaste. "We'll have to settle for that."

Jackson grunted and threw himself back against the seat. "Chipotle?" he asked plaintively. "I'll buy."

"If you walked into a Chipotle right now, you'd scare the customers," Ellery said. "I'll buy. Where do you live, and where's the one nearest your house?"

Jackson groaned. "Ugh…. Okay, where the fuck are we again?"

"Well, we just passed a junior high—"

"*Fuck*—can you find Northgate? Take a right on San Juan and a right on Truxel. There's probably one closer to my house, but—"

"Yeah, thinking's a problem right now."

"It's been a day!" Jackson snapped. He took a breath. "How's K?"

"A lot calmer than I would be," Ellery admitted. "His sister got a chance to visit. They're sweet together."

Jackson gave a half laugh and tilted his head back. "Yeah. J and K—always had each other's backs. Good people."

"How long—"

"Grade school," Jackson said, his voice going sour. "We just passed it. I'm going to close my eyes for the rest of the tour if that's okay."

Ellery swallowed. He should just stay quiet. He and Jackson had a lot of business to take care of that night. Once Jackson got some food and some first aid, Ellery needed to run a *lot* of shit by him, because his conversation with Arizona made no goddamned sense and Jackson might have some insight. So yeah. Long night. Leave the guy a—

"This is sort of a rough neighborhood." Apparently keeping your mouth shut was not the hallmark of a great defense attorney.

"This is a garden spot right here," Jackson snorted, eyes still closed. "You should have seen it in the nineties."

"Tell me." Because the neighborhood had shaped them, hadn't it? Jade, Kaden, and Jackson. Had made them the tight-knit little band of musketeers they were.

"What's to tell? Bad neighborhood is bad. The nineties were… well, drugs, gangs, guns—that was the nineties. I mean, they've cleaned it up some. The schools started working with the parents who started working with their kids—there's a whole new thing going on. But back then the good parents were just, you know, *good parents*. Jade and Kaden's mom was one of the best. Me and Kaden had each other's six all through school, so she was good for me too."

"What about your own—"

Jackson grunted. "Cramer, you know, I got shit for sleep last night, okay? Do I have to tell you about my day? And you and me got shit to sort. I have basic needs right now. I've got to fucking eat or I'm going to fucking kill you right fucking now. Some water would be *perfect*. Motrin would be better. Ice would be icing. And I need to feed my fucking cat, because he got left inside this morning, and if he hasn't crapped on my bed, he's probably eaten something I cherish."

"You have a cat?"

"*Arrrrgh!*"

"I'm turning right—are we a grown-up now?"

"Fuck you."

And that, apparently, was that.

Ellery left him to bleed in the car while he got them food, sodas, and a couple of bottles of water. When he stopped at the gas station for painkillers, Jackson handed him his takeout wrappers, neatly and psychotically rolled into the little round balls, and asked him nicely to put them in the trash.

He came out with a cup of ice, a towel, and Motrin, and was greeted with a genuine—if tired—smile. One that had teeth and made the little crinkles in the corners of those green eyes bunch up. It was just wide enough to show off a slightly crooked front tooth and a quirk to Jackson's upper lip.

"Thank you," Jackson breathed, downing about six painkillers before wrapping the ice in a napkin and resting it on his knee. "This is amazing—you're a totally decent human being and I owe you."

"You're very welcome," Ellery said dryly, starting his car and trying not to fuss too much about the blood and water stains on the gray leather upholstery. "Where to now?"

Jackson grunted. "Do you have a creature or anything? Dog? Cat? Fish? Plant?"

"I have a fish tank with a fake fish and plastic plants. It looks lovely."

"Well it can feed its goddamned self and it won't crap on the rug. My place, then—don't worry, it's not a shithole. Anyway—get on 80, take 5 to J Street, and I'll walk you from there."

"Which street do you live on?"

"Elvas—if it wasn't so late, I'd say take Power Inn, but traffic should be not horrible."

"Yeah. I know where it is." A decent neighborhood—not great. Close to the college but not too close. It was the sort of place a guy could live on a cop's salary if he was just starting out. Ellery wondered if that was where he lived when he'd been shot.

And those questions reared their ugly heads again.

A few minutes passed, and Ellery waded through traffic. It was nearing eight o'clock, and the sun was going down. Traffic was thinning a bit, which was a blessing. Although his AC was cranked full blast, he could smell the heat still radiating from Jackson's body and the sweat of a long day.

"I've got cookies," Jackson said, eyes still closed. "And milk. And beer if you want it. And chips if you like to nosh."

"You sound all prepared," Ellery noted.

"Cereal and instant oatmeal too," Jackson told him. "And a comfortable couch."

"It's going to be a long night." It went without saying.

"You can even borrow some of my sleep shorts," Jackson confirmed.

"That's kind, but I've got some in my gym bag. Got Internet?"

"Yup."

"It'll be just like college." Except Ellery couldn't recall ever having a study group with someone who looked dangerous and muscular, reclined and half-somnolent in the front of his car. His mouth went dry, and he took a deep drag of his own soda before setting it back in the cup holder. "Or maybe law school."

Jackson let out a short, bitter bark of a laugh. "As long as we're both still learning, I'll take that."

Ellery's heart beat hard in his throat. Jackson's house. In his sleep shorts. With his cat. Yeah, sure, he'd be sleeping on the couch, but it was like having membership to an exclusive club. Ellery hadn't been in a lot of clubs through school. Chess, debate, science—most of the membership requirements for those were that you had to want to use your brain for something besides flirting with your classmates.

This club was sort of the opposite of that. Except Jackson was counting on his big brain to do more than win the chess tournament.

THE HOUSE turned out to be a duplex—painted blue-gray on the outside, with white trim and a neatly kept postage stamp of a yard. As Ellery pulled into the driveway, he had to be very careful to avoid a scruffy guy wearing a grease-stained T-shirt and assless jeans tinkering under the giant black F-250 in the space next to Jackson's.

Jackson grunted. "Wonderful. Mike's working on the damned truck."

They opened the doors and the heat of summer roared in, along with country music being played at top volume.

"Mike," Jackson hollered as he exited the car. He came down hard on his knee and yelped and then soldiered around the front anyway. "Mike, goddammit, can you just not play Billy Ray at top volume tonight?"

Mike shoved himself out from under the truck with the muscular, easy movements of a man in his thirties or forties, but his hair was white. His face was relatively unlined, though, so Ellery couldn't make a guess at his age—something about the crinkles at his eyes and the absolute capability in his bearing made Ellery think of Sean Bean. Mike pushed up from his dolly quick as a jackrabbit and eyed Jackson up and down before turning his gimlet blue-eyed gaze to Ellery and his smoky-truffle Lexus.

"Another guy?" he asked, squinting in disbelief. "You have got a parade of *fine*-looking women in and out of here, and you still have to bring home *another* guy?"

Jackson squared his jaw and lowered his head. If Ellery didn't know better, he'd say it was his *own* expression when he had to deal with his mother.

"My women—"

"And men!"

"Are none of your business—"

"But you had *Jade* here, Jackson. She is *smokin'* hot, and funny, and a damned sight more than you deserve. Why this bozo with the Lexus when you can have *Jade*?"

The look that crossed Jackson's face was both patient and sad. "Because Jade and I don't fit that way," he said gently. "And she's only ever going to sleep on the couch from now on. And this guy is here to help keep Kaden out of prison, so be nice."

Mike's half-badgering, half-exasperated expression changed just that fast. "What in the hell did your people do to Kaden!"

Jackson grimaced. "Not my people anymore, Mike—and it's bad. Ellery here is his defense attorney—we've got some work to do."

Mike took off his baseball hat—Deere tractors—and scratched the back of his snowy-white head. Maybe all the white was premature, because the man's face, while a little weathered, really was quite young. "Yeah, I hear ya. Let me know what I can do." He frowned. "And you fucked yourself up again. God almighty, kid—you have to stay healthy, or who's going to manage your wild animal?"

Jackson laughed and spun around on his good leg, waving behind him as he limped toward the front door on the right side of the duplex. "It's a *cat*, Mike. I think they were a thing in the 1800s—when you were *born*!"

"Not that kind of cat," Mike said sourly. "I swear that thing was fucking my dog the other day, and he doesn't swing that way."

Jackson smiled fondly. "Well, if Paulie starts squirting out mutant catdog assbabies, you let me know—I'm good for palimony."

"Screw child support!" Mike retorted. "He hurt my damned dog's feelings! That fucker better be over here with flowers and Milk-Bones or my dog's going to grieve himself to death!"

Jackson tossed a winning smile over his shoulder. "Well, Mike, that's up to your dog. As long as Paulie didn't kick him out of bed, Billy Bob'll be sweet to him after. You know that—he's a tomcat, not a cad!"

Mike shook his head and sank down to a squat, checking on something underneath the truck. "Fucking queerass tomcat, sticking his wiener where no wiener belongs." As Ellery neared the front door, Mike raised his voice in order to be heard unmistakably. "And I'm not talking about Billy Bob!"

Jackson took a step backward right into Ellery's chest, but like with most athletic men, the contact didn't seem to register. "You got a problem with where I put my pecker, Mike?" His voice was still laced with humor, but the good nature was balanced on an edge.

Mike stood up again and shook his head. "Just take care of our family," he said, and Ellery heard a true note of upset. "No pecker poking until your people are out of jail, okay?"

"Our people, Mike," Jackson said gently. "They're your people too." The heat from his back seared Ellery right through his dress shirt and tank. For a moment it was hard to catch his breath.

Mike shrugged, and Ellery watched his mouth work. He swallowed after a few deep breaths. "Just tell Rhonda and the kids that Uncle Mike'll get them anything they need," he said humbly.

"Yeah. I'll do that. Jade's there now, but I'll call Denny at the gas station and see if they need any help, if you got time."

"Yeah. Not getting much work at the shop—tell him I got time."

"Thanks, Mike—that's a stand-up thing to do." When Jackson *finally* took a step forward, Ellery became aware that he'd been supporting some of Jackson's weight. His limp was getting worse.

But he didn't even grunt. Just opened the door and began calling for the cat. "Billy Bob—Billy Bob, you old fucker, where the hell did you crap?"

What followed was a very vocal, very articulate harangue from a cat who obviously *thought* he was a human when, in fact, he looked like a car wreck.

"Oh my God," Ellery muttered, taking in the tattered ear, the scars, the thick chest and neck, and Lord almighty, the *sneer* over one crooked tooth as the cat thug-walked up to Jackson, bitching the entire way.

"Yeah," Jackson muttered. "Meow meow meow—all you do is bitch at me and crap. Pay some rent, motherfucker, just pay some goddamned rent, it's all I fuckin' ask. I mean, I'd ask you to use a rubber, but you'd bankrupt me, yes you would. And you got no thumbs, motherfucker— you'd rip the goddamned Trojans, don't lie. I know you'd do it. I'd have a truckload of clawed-up rubbers in the backyard and you'd still be knocking up everything on the fucking planet. Don't meow at me, asshole, you know I'm right."

During the monologue, Jackson rubbed the cat's ears, scratched the sweet spot at the base of his tail, and finally hefted what looked to be fifteen pounds of pure feline muscle into his arms so he could touch his nose to the cat's and smooth back its ragged whiskers.

That cat stopped bitching long enough to purr until drool trickled down under its chin, and Ellery got to see the thing up close, since they were *blocking the hallway* in front of the now-closed door.

Yeah. Proximity didn't make that cat any prettier. The cat's balls were big enough to be seen swinging from its backside as Jackson held him, and Ellery thought maybe both man and cat would be a little happier if those things hadn't been so fucking large.

"Uh, hello, pussycat," Ellery said. He tentatively stretched out a finger to stroke a scarred nose, and the cat hissed and spat. Ellery withdrew the finger in a hurry.

"That's no pussycat," Jackson said smugly, his green eyes glinting happily over the cat's head. "That's a cock-kitty."

Ellery gave him a narrow-eyed glare. "Isn't that sort of, you know, sexist? Like the, uh"—he blushed just saying it—"the assbabies thing. That's not really a valid representation of the gay and bisexual community—"

The crinkles in the corners of Jackson's eyes disappeared, as did his scorching warmth.

Ellery fought the temptation to shiver.

"I'm going to go put my politically incorrect cat out now," he said, and Ellery could delude himself into thinking there was some hurt in that censure. "I'm surprised you haven't asked me to get him fixed."

"I'm sorry," he said, following Jackson as he hefted the drooling bulldog of a cat down the hall. "I mean, it would probably be better for the—"

Jackson paused midwalk and fixed him with that scary glacier of a gaze, and Ellery swallowed, keeping his eyes level. Jackson swung his head back around and kept walking.

They passed a kitchen to the left and a living room to the right, a bathroom, a spare bedroom, and were heading toward what was probably the main bedroom. Everything looked… neat. Clean. Uncluttered but not bare. Framed photos graced the hall at sparing intervals, and framed prints adorned the living room and guest room. Some were bright, some dark, some classic, and one from a movie that had come out the year before. The hardwood floors had some dust in the corners, but there weren't any beer cans on the floor.

Ellery tried hard not to be impressed—and to mend what he'd obviously broken. "I didn't mean to sound like a—"

"An insensitive liberal?" Jackson said dryly. He pushed into the bedroom and limped past the bed to the sliding glass door. Ellery wrinkled his nose—he smelled cigarettes here, and he loathed smoking. Looking to the small porch that led to the backyard, he saw a paint can full of sand and a couple of butts—different brands.

Oh. So not a smoker, but courteous to those with the habit.
Interesting.

"A prude with a stick up his ass," Ellery supplied. "I just—"

"Have a stick up your ass," Jackson replied, the smugness in his voice almost intolerable.

"Look, I just think that, since you are apparently out and proud and bi, maybe you should—"

"I am *not* representing a cause," Jackson growled. "And let's get one thing straight." The cat squirmed in his arms, and he slid the door open and unceremoniously dumped it on the ground. "You'd better take a shit out there!" he hollered as the cat darted away. He closed the door and turned back to Ellery. "You and I don't have to like each other," he said, pulling his shirts over his head and throwing them into a hamper by the headboard. His hands went to his belt and Ellery found himself looking anywhere—the green-and-gray comforter, the Lautrec print on the wall, the strip of navy blue painted near the ceiling that gave the room some solid character—*anywhere* besides Jackson as he stripped down.

"I don't dislike you," he said tentatively. "Oh, you have a television."

"Well, right now it's tuned to het porn, so don't turn it on!"

Ellery flinched from his snarl. "I'm… I don't know how to be around you," he admitted, hating that he was backing down from this ex-cop, in his bedroom, in a way he backed down from *nobody* in the courtroom.

"*Be* around me?" He heard the thump and rattle as Jackson's belt and jeans hit the ground, and a pair of boxers sailed into the hamper. And Ellery kept his eyes directed *right there*. "What does that even *mean*?"

Ellery swallowed. "You… you are two steps ahead of me," he said. "And you have seen and done things today that I don't know if I could deal with. And I'm in your…."

"Bedroom?" Oh God—his voice was close, and suggestive, and he hadn't reached for a towel or a sheet or underwear or anything.

"House," Ellery corrected, risking a look at him.

Jackson's green eyes loomed closer than he'd thought, and that glacial cold he'd snapped on had completely reversed polarity. Ellery's breath caught, and he couldn't look away.

"Mr. Cramer, are you afraid to look at me naked?" Jackson asked, purring.

"N-no," Ellery lied.

Jackson took a step back, ice-cold again. "The scars freak you out," he said flatly, and *that* of all things forced Ellery to look at him again.

"No," he repeated, but this time it was the truth. He could see Jackson's chest, and it appeared muscular and well worked, just like his abdomen. The scars just *were*, bare and inglorious but not ugly. Simply flesh—painful keloid flesh, but flesh. Ellery reached out a shaking hand, the urge to touch overwhelming him. Very carefully, he stroked his fingers down the whole of that amazing chest, sweaty and strong and covered faintly with dark blond hair—because no, Jackson Rivers wouldn't give a fuck about grooming.

Jackson's indrawn breath, sharp and surprised, pulled Ellery back. Jackson's hand—dusty, battered, bloody at the knuckles and tough—cupped under Ellery's chin, and Ellery was forced to make eye contact again.

"Oh," Jackson said, and he nodded as though surprised. "Okay. I… I need to shower. And we have work to do. And if you're here too late, you can sleep on the couch."

"The couch?" Ellery gasped, absurdly hurt. He'd just made a *pass* at the guy and he was exiled to the couch when even the neighbor knew Jackson slept with everything that moved.

"Yeah." Oh, yay, the sarcasm was back. "Because *you* are not a one-night fuck, Cramer. *You* are a complication." Jackson's jaw lost some of its hardness, and his lower lip quivered, just once, before he had his game face on again. "My brother's in jail tonight. I'm not getting laid when my brother's in jail."

Oh God. Jackson had needed to remind *Ellery* about professional behavior. There was not a hole deep enough in the world, much less in Sacramento, for him to hide in.

But Jackson didn't castigate him or humiliate him—any further than he'd humiliated himself, at any rate. "Let me shower," he said abruptly, turning his back and stalking—well, limping, but limping with *power*—toward the bathroom in the hall. "You boot up our computers. My network is *Homerange*, I use my work e-mail for ID, and my password is *raging4rivers*, no caps, no spaces, four is a number, not a word. We good?"

"Got it!" Ellery followed him out of the intimacy of the bedroom, yearning for his laptop and maybe a beer.

It wasn't until Jackson took an abrupt right into the bathroom for his shower that Ellery realized he'd been staring at the man's bare, muscular ass since he turned around and walked away.

Don't get too excited about that. It's probably the last time you'll ever see it.

But as Ellery sat down, microbrew in hand, and started to log on to the Internet, he thought, *That right there would be a crying shame.*

He also thought that he had a half an hour, *maybe*, to finally research one Jackson Quinn Rivers and find out what in the hell had happened before Ellery moved to Sacramento.

Fish Afraid to Jump

JACKSON LEANED back against the wall as the water sluiced down, and closed his eyes against his day.

His body ached, his knee throbbed, and the water stung the myriad scrapes and bruises he'd acquired struggling with Connie.

And then he remembered the look of misery on Connie Coulson's face right before he confessed to being unable to put his dog down, and how *that* was the guy who'd ended up blown to pieces in his own backyard.

God.

And none of that—*none* of it—could keep him from feeling the burn of Ellery Cramer's tentative touches on his chest.

Jackson had read the guy all wrong.

Or a little wrong.

He was still a bit of a prig, and he still had a stick up his ass, but maybe he had the stick up his ass because a better alternative hadn't presented itself.

Maybe, just *maybe*, Jackson would be the better alternative.

But Jackson really couldn't *do* that right now.

His knee ached fiercely, and he spent a moment hating his former colleagues. God, bitter, jaded cops were bitter and jaded. They hated an IA rat with a dead-eyed passion. But they weren't dirty. The officers who had cornered him after Connie's death had been as eager as the next cop to give Jackson shit, but none of them had been in on it.

Jackson had spent enough time with Hanover, God damn his soul, to know what a dirty-cop smirk looked like. He'd spent enough time with himself, wearing a wire, to know the grimace that shame bile brought to a cop's face.

So they were dealing with dirty cops, yes—but not the ones who'd given Jackson his ration of crap.

In fact, Jackson knew exactly two dirty cops at this point. One was dead and the other was hidden behind a union lawyer.

With a grunt, he turned off the water and toweled dry, then hobbled to his room to get dressed. He came out in two minutes, hair combed, wearing basketball shorts and what Kaden used to call a *beater* until the eighth grade. That was when Jade had pointed out the term was short for *wifebeater*, because that was the uniform worn by the guys in the show *Cops* when they got arrested for domestic abuse. Rhonda had put an end to *that* term right quick, but Jackson still heard it in his head whenever he wore a ribbed tank.

He could deal with the Mikes of this world—the old guys who tried really hard to give change a chance but who were dismayed to find that political awareness had passed them right by while they were scratching a blue-collar life out of an information age. If Jackson had stayed a cop—and hadn't had a year with little to do but surf the Internet and try not to become a troll—he might have become Mike. Confused about how all the best intentions turned into saying all the wrong things.

Pondering that, he got to the kitchen and saw Ellery glance up from his laptop almost guiltily. Great. Somebody had been looking up Jackson's past.

Jackson sighed and plodded to the refrigerator to get himself a beer. He came out with a carton of hummus and some veggies, as well as some pita chips from the top of the fridge. He set it all down on the table, then settled down to his own computer, which lived in the kitchen already.

Ellery looked up from where he was clicking madly—probably to disguise his search history—and made a grunt of disbelief. "You're still hungry?"

"It was a fuckin' *day*," he defended through a mouthful of carrots. "Anyway, I figured I'd give you time to either finish up your porn or ask me a question." He swallowed and looked at Ellery with meaning. "Either one is good with me."

Ellery flushed. "You were a cop for six months," he said, and Jackson was a little disappointed. Honestly, he'd been hoping for porn.

"I was," he acknowledged.

"Does that include academy training?"

"Nope—and it doesn't include my year in the hospital and rehabilitation."

Ellery pursed his lips and looked Jackson over very carefully. "You were really young," he said after a moment.

Well, not as young as he felt *now*, with those perceptive brown eyes focused on his face and that remote, handsome face engaged in some sort of human emotion interface. "And your point is…."

"Why'd you do it?"

Jackson tried not to choke on his snap pea. "I'm sorry?"

"You were young, you were broke, you came from a disadvantaged background. Every profile in the world would point to you becoming the kind of cop your partner wa—"

"Dirty," Jackson said darkly, trying not to think about that first horrible realization. "You're talking about what makes a dirty cop."

"Yeah," Ellery acknowledged. "Why wasn't it you?"

Oh, like Jackson hadn't asked himself this question. He'd spent a year on his back, in pain, wondering if the sniper from the force who'd gotten him was going to come back and take another shot. Yeah, they'd caught the guy. Yeah, he'd been shipped out of state, some military prison where he might survive in general population. But that hadn't stopped the fucking dreams.

Ellery was looking at him like this was a nostalgic stroll down childhood memory lane.

Jackson glared. "Do you remember eighth grade?" he asked, not at random, although it probably felt like that.

Ellery's eyes unfocused and then moved to the left, as though he were accessing information in a particular database. "Yes," he said after a moment. "My acne showed up, I was thirty pounds overweight, and my mom made me take her best friend's daughter to the school dance."

He had to laugh at that. "Sounds…."

"Pathetic?" Ellery asked bitterly.

"I was going to say bucolic. Eighth grade for Kaden and Jade Cameron, Rhonda Adams, and Jackson Rivers, day two. Rhonda got to school a few minutes ahead of us and was hanging out across the street. She watched a few drug deals go down and saw the girls she used to play dolls with agree to sneak behind the school to give blow jobs for money. She was so busy watching—and hoping nobody noticed her from her spot under a tree—that she didn't notice the Drek."

"Drek?" Ellery was staring at him, entranced, like a little kid hearing a story.

"Short for DeAndre Ricky. Drek. Anyway, Drek saw Rhonda, recognized that she was a 'good girl,' and decided he was going to pull her around behind the Jiffy Lube and make her not a good girl anymore. She was kicking and screaming when K and J and me walked up, but Drek was a six-foot gorilla who had flunked the eighth grade three times. So Rhonda was ours, right? We launch ourselves at Drek and are in the process of getting the holy mother of shit beat out of us when a cop shows up. And God, nobody in our neighborhood loved cops. Cops were going to take you from your moms when she got high, they were going to bust you for having a beer—cops were the fucking boogieman in Grant Union District in 1995, you feel me?"

Ellery nodded, and Jackson tried to put away the nausea thinking about that day brought up.

"So the cop shows up and Drek's not giving up—he's got Rhonda, and her clothes are torn and she's crying, and the cop pulls out a Taser and takes him down. Now, today, I know he did it all wrong—he fucking did. Broke about ten kinds of rules, including Tasing a minor without announcing his affiliation with the police department, but back then? Drek went down, shitting his own pants, and we went to get Rhonda up and help her home. We were all beat to shit—J too, because she fights mean—and we weren't going to school after that. Anyway, the cop takes one look at us and shakes his head and says, 'You keep your bitch dressed and she won't cause no trouble, you hear me?'"

Ellery gasped.

"Yeah." Jackson took a heavy pull off his beer. "See, the lot of us—black, white, whatever—we were all thugs and whores to this guy. He sincerely didn't give a shit who we were just as long as we didn't cause trouble. But...."

"But he saved your friend."

Jackson nodded. "Yeah. He saved my friend. And then walked away. And that was... *fascinating* to me. I started watching the cops after that. I started seeing who was there to help, and a few were. When they started the whole urban cleanup thing at that district, I watched to see who abused the hell out of their power, and there were a few of those too. And there were a few who weren't great and weren't awful. They just *were*—just guys doing a job, but they didn't know enough about human nature to do it any better than that. And they didn't give enough of a shit to learn."

"So when you became a cop—"

"You say that like it's easy. Training they give you, if you make it, but room and board and tuition? No. I had to work for two years to save up enough money to get me through six months. When I was in, K and I worked night shifts at a gas station just like the one he owns, because he was going to business school and I was taking criminal justice classes to prepare for the police academy. We roomed together, and the girls stayed with his moms—*mom*." So easy, sometimes, to slip back to being in the sixth grade, when the kids said *moms* because it was cool. "And it was hard. I volunteered for nearly every cop function I could find, including wiping their asses so I could get someone to sponsor me and hire me when I was done, but it was worth it, I thought."

"Yeah? Who sponsored you?"

"Hanover." Jackson watched as Ellery choked on his last swallow of beer. "You recognize the name."

"You got partnered with him," Ellery said, and the look of horror was eloquent.

"Yup. And within the first month, I watched him take bribes, I watched him take drugs from one dealer and have another front them, and I watched him take favors from the working girls so he'd let them continue to work."

"I'm so sor—"

"I did it because I'd just worked most of my life not to be that guy. Not to be the cop who didn't care about the good from the bad. I wasn't going to let *that* guy's shitty character define *my* life."

Ellery nodded. "That's… well, it's sort of fucking noble. I'm really impressed."

Jackson rolled his eyes. "I'm glad it impresses you. I don't guarantee I'd make the same choices ten years later, but I'm glad that one impressed you."

"You wouldn't?" He sounded hurt.

"I wouldn't go dirty," Jackson said, surprised how much he wanted Ellery to know that.

"Then what would you do?"

Oh, the what-if game? Jackson was a master at it. "I don't know. Quit the force, maybe. Say I wasn't cut out for it and then move the fuck away. Where'd you grow up?"

"Boston."

Jackson thought about it. "Yeah, I could live there. But you don't sound like a Kennedy."

"Elocution lessons, and no, I only wish I was kidding."

Jackson snorted. "The proverbial silver spoon?"

Ellery leaned back in his chair, and the expression that crossed his face was curiously filled with self-loathing. "My mother picked out the silverware before my sister and I were conceived. We had to pick a career that both provided a service and made a decent living. She had veto power on what our tuition money went to. Coming home for winter break was like being a duck and getting deboned—every part of your life as a college student on display at the dinner table." He shuddered.

"Must have made your first sexual experience a *hoot*!" Jackson commiserated in spite of himself. Apparently Norman Rockwell paintings were made of hardcore political movements and inflated expectations.

"Oh, it was," Ellery said darkly. "For all involved."

Jackson snorted. "How many was that?"

"Well, me, my sister, our mother and father, and the friend I brought home from college to introduce to my parents. *He* was surprised to find that the Kinsey scale worked in fractions and that my family *would* have him pinned to the nearest tenth of a degree before the first course was over."

Oh for crap's sake. Ellery was trying to put up a good front like this didn't bother him, but Jackson had been a good cop because he could empathize. "I'd never sport wood again."

"It took me a human sexuality class and a shrink," Ellery said, and it didn't sound like he was kidding even a little. "But that's a perfect life compared to getting shot on duty while you were wearing a wire. I couldn't figure out how they knew. It wasn't in any of the papers."

Jackson closed his eyes. "Yeah, see, *that's* the sixty-four-thousand-dollar question right there. I was working with two IA rats and two members of the DA's office to collect data. And… it was a nightmare. For three months I got up, put on my wire, and went into work and hoped I didn't have to blow my cover to keep Hanover from fucking blowing someone away. He was using by that time. He liked to spin the barrel of his revolver and fake Russian roulette. Me, him, the poor kid in the back of the fucking squad car, it didn't matter who he pointed that thing at. Anyway, so we had a case—"

"You had hundreds of hours of audio!" Ellery leaned forward, hands clasped, his body language that of a suppliant. "How could you have hundreds of hours and still be going back in there?"

Jackson shrugged. "I don't know. I mean, you said it yourself, I was young and dumb. The lawyers, they had all the goddamned answers.

My gods the cops had fallen, but the lawyers were still up on high, you know? So I'd ask every day, can we stop now?" His stomach roiled just thinking about it. "I lost fifty pounds. Hanover kept telling me to lay off the fucking crank, but it was all fucking nerves. And then one day I get out of the car to check out a complaint, and Hanover stays behind the wheel, and suddenly—" He shook his head. "By the time I heard the shots, I was on the ground trying to breathe. And Hanover's brains were splattered all over the driver's-side door."

He paused for a moment, freezing in his eighty-degree kitchen. That was the kicker right there. Not that *he'd* been gunned down but that Patrick Hanover had too. Whoever had done it—

"They were trying to shut him up," Ellery said, meeting his eyes.

Jackson nodded, still cold. "Mission fucking accomplished."

"But... but you, you were the message."

"Don't rat on your people." Jackson could say that now, because he had eight years between the hospital and the present.

"Yeah. Hanover was—"

"He wasn't working all by himself," Jackson confirmed. "But all departmental resources went toward finding the guy who fired the shots, and I was not in any position to complain that only five people were supposed to know." He scrubbed his hands through his hair. "But this— this is old fucking news—"

"No," Ellery said thoughtfully. He straightened up at the table. "I mean, I wanted to know. Who's not curious? And the old press releases don't say what really happened. But... but something weird happened today, and I've got...."

He stood up and started to—well, not pace. He wasn't pacing, because that implied rhythm and urgency. This was more of a meander. He started to *meander* around Jackson's kitchen, shirtsleeves rolled up, linen suit pants rumpled. His hair was usually slicked back and pristine, but now it was falling down from his brow in straight clumps, and every now and then he'd shove them back from his forehead and more locks would break free.

Jackson liked it. Ellery looked human that way. Vulnerable and approachable. This wasn't the Ellery who won cases, this was the Ellery who'd lost his first boyfriend because his parents were apparently social nightmares who couldn't let a boy get laid without an interrogation.

"What?" Jackson asked, shaking himself back to the task on hand. "What do you have?"

Ellery let out a whoosh of breath. "I am *dying.* How hot is it in this kitchen?"

"Eighty. I turned the AC on higher, but it usually takes another minute or two. Do you want to shower?"

"I've got some clothes in my gym bag," Ellery admitted. He sounded distracted. "It's out in the car."

He was obviously working something through. Jackson held out his hand. "Give me the keys. I'll get the gym bag and put it in the guest room. You go take a cool shower and it'll make the eighty degrees tolerable. Deal?"

Ellery nodded, still in his figuring zone. Jackson knew about this zone—he lived there sometimes when he was working on a puzzle. He forced himself up from the table and walked into Ellery's space. Ellery didn't seem to notice as Jackson reached into his left pocket—the man was left-handed; it only made sense. The jingle of the keys startled him out of his trance, and he jerked back.

"What are you—"

Oh yeah. Tactical error. Ellery smelled like sweat and aftershave, and *this* time Jackson wasn't distracted by pain. In fact, he felt shocked open by the intimacy of the old story, the old life he'd lived, and when Ellery focused on him, mouth softly open, pink tongue darting out to wet his lips, he felt that intimacy pressing on his chest and ribs.

"Getting your keys," he said gruffly, feeling the flush of arousal wash his body. "So you can go shower and we can get to work."

"I...." Ellery closed his eyes and tilted his head. Lightly, he inhaled, his nose pointed at the hollow of Jackson's neck. "You smell really good."

"Body wash." Oh no. No, this couldn't happen. No no no no. Jackson took a step back. "I... we have a plan, Cramer. We need to... we need to save this...." He waved his hand in front of them and between. "This *thing* for after Kaden's safe."

Ellery nodded. "Yeah," he rasped. "After Kaden's out of jail." And just like that, all distraction snapped away. "I will hold you to that, Jackson Rivers," he threatened. "This—if you won't do it now because it's a complication, you'd damned well better not walk away, because *that* would make things—"

"Really fucking complicated," Jackson admitted. Hell, if he and Ellery had been on a date, they would have been fucking already. Jackson would have bent him over the table and taken him and fed him, let him shower, and then… let him sleep in the guest bedroom.

Because Jackson in no way wanted Ellery Cramer to see him any more naked than he'd already been.

A droplet of sweat traveled from under Ellery's hairline down his temple and along his jaw. For a moment Jackson watched it, fascinated, while he avoided those dark, perceptive eyes.

"It's hot," he said at last and whirled away before he could reach out and taste it.

MIKE WAS still out there, his side of the garage open, the cage lights on and bright. He'd turned the music down but not off completely, and Jackson reminded himself to call Denny when he went back in. Jackson opened the trunk and grabbed Ellery's neatly packed gym bag, smiling because in *his* car, the gym bag would have been hard to differentiate from the bag of rags he used for the soccer team car wash.

Then he remembered that gym bag, rag bag, and piece-of-shit car were all pretty much destroyed.

He pulled back and slammed the trunk shut, sighing.

"That didn't sound good," Mike said, walking around the truck and wiping his fingers fruitlessly on a truly irredeemable grease-stained rag. Shit. He'd been the one to donate most of his rags to the fucking car wash.

"I have to get a new car," Jackson said, because somehow that was the least awful thing about this day.

"What happened to your old one?" Very carefully, so the rivets in his assless jeans wouldn't scratch the shiny black paint on his baby, Mike leaned back against the truck.

"It's in Toyota heaven." Jackson's soft nylon basketball shorts would mostly just buff the Lexus, so he leaned slowly back too.

Mike's eyebrows shot up. "What in the hell is it doing there?"

"I don't know. Probably giving rides to those little anime girls with the gigantic eyes." Jackson half laughed and swung Ellery's black Puma bag a little more comfortably. Anything so he didn't have to think about the drop of sweat near Ellery's ear and about how the stuck-up fucker with the stick up his ass was their best hope to keep Kaden out of jail and alive.

"Now see, when I say things like that, you people say I'm sexist," Mike muttered, and Jackson had to stop and think about it.

"You know, you got me," he said after a moment. "But I'm pretty sure that's on the approved list. I think it's because I didn't objectify them."

Mike wrinkled his nose. "You mean all I have to do to stay out of hot water is not talk about *tits*? I mean, I could do it, but I'm saying, it would take some of the fun out of life."

Hell. Jackson couldn't process that. He couldn't even quantify it. "Man, I don't know what my car is doing in Toyota heaven, but if you can think of it doing something sexy that doesn't break any rules, be my guest."

Mike thought about it for a minute. "I got nothin'—but I'm telling you, when this baby finally goes, he's going to be in Ford country with big, buxom farm girls who've got *ginormous* tits. I'm not going to apologize for that either. This truck works its ass off for me—if he wants tits and ass, that's what he's gonna get. And if he wants *balls* and ass, there's gotta be a truck in the lot that's still got those chrome ones dangling from the tow ball."

Jackson stared at him, a twisted version of Pixar's *Cars* playing behind his eyes, with horny trucks humping sexy little Volkswagens and producing midsize sedans in the process.

Would he be humping another truck or a Volkswagen?

And *bam*! There was Ellery, a little sport truck with a brown paint job to match his hair and eyes, and a large set of brass balls.

Jackson's laugh was a little hysterical, but it was a laugh. "I'm glad nobody can see what's running behind my eyes right now," he admitted, chuckling. "They'd have me committed."

Mike sobered. "You said it was bad."

"I've got no words for how bad it is," Jackson told him, sobering just as quickly. "But Ellery might have some words to fix it."

Mike shook his head, pursing his lips consideringly. "He's not bad. I mean, if I was a truck-humper, I wouldn't mind jumping his flatbed."

Jackson couldn't help it. He collapsed, his elbows resting on his knees, his stomach heaving. "Aw, fuck you," he managed to wheeze before losing his shit completely.

He was still laughing when he walked back into the house and heard the shower going. He dropped the bag just inside the bathroom and went back into the kitchen for a big glass of ice water.

The AC had finally kicked in. It was livable at the table, and Jackson sat down and gave thanks for air-conditioning and ice cubes and guys who kept trying to be decent when the world was a confusing fucking place to be decent *in*.

TWO HOURS later he and Ellery were taking turns pacing in Jackson's tiny kitchen. The tile was old, and every time one of them hit the place three feet from the refrigerator, the crackle of broken tile and a squeaky floorboard could be heard throughout the house. Billy Bob had come back in and kept trying to sneak up onto Jackson's laptop, and Jackson was so scared he could swear he felt ice crystallizing in his intestines.

What Ellery had put together in his head made a lot of sense, and it was terrifying.

"See, it's where the e-mails came from," Ellery had explained as he'd walked out of the shower wearing a black T-shirt and white nylon shorts. Not sexy, no, but it did weird things to Jackson to know they had similar leisure clothes. He would have predicted Ellery Cramer slept in linen pajamas, something flowy and prissy and girly.

This was just so clean, so masculine, that Jackson's truck-humping engine kicked into gear. He suddenly wanted a crack at Ellery's tailpipe and his low-hanging chrome balls. It was an insidious thought, funny and hot at the same time, and it took some serious shit to break it loose from Jackson's cortex.

Unfortunately Ellery was dealing this hand, and it was all business.

"The DA's e-mails?" Jackson asked, to clarify.

"Yes. Arizona said they were coming from the capitol, but she was afraid to tell me from where. But it got me thinking. You've got to be around for a while if you're working there—you need to form connections, be trusted. You don't just spring up in the capitol without some backstory. And that shit that went down with you—"

"That was eight years ago," Jackson said, nodding. "I see where you're going."

"Right? So you need to tell me the names of the four other people who knew you were walking in with a wire. You said you went in for three months, but if Hanover was as dirty as you say he was—"

"God, he was worse." Jackson closed his eyes against the sounds of Hanover banging a prostitute behind a shitty apartment complex in

Oak Park while the girl practically sobbed because he was so rough. He'd been told—again and again he'd been told—that if Hanover wasn't killing anyone or putting them in the hospital, then Jackson was a recording device, and that was all.

But he'd had to stand there, sick and nauseated, and hear that—and feel like the evil of it had seeped through his pores, infecting his bones and marrow with the grotesquerie of corruption.

"A week," Ellery snarled, his intensity shocking. "A *week*—that's the longest you should have been there. You were trying to catch one guy, and if they were trying to get someone bigger, they should have *told* you."

He was glaring at Jackson so hotly Jackson could feel his shoulders twitch.

"Yeah," he muttered defensively. "Well, I know that *now*."

Ellery grunted and shoved his hair back from his face. Since he'd come out of the shower with no product in it whatsoever, Jackson had begun to see the kid who'd been bullied by his parents at Christmas. His jaw looked strong when he was wearing a suit, but in the harsh light of the kitchen, as he sat there in what amounted to pajamas, it looked bony and obtrusive. The scowl he leveled so effectively at people on the stand became a squint, and he had a tendency to blink when he was baffled or irritated about something.

These things should have put Jackson off, but no. Instead, they made the guy look a little bit dear.

Jackson liked the man behind the curtain. He was human. Jackson just hoped he could put his armor back on when it was time to keep Kaden out of danger.

"I don't understand," Ellery muttered, wandering some more. "You have the copies of your case files, but there's shit missing. Did you even *look* at this when they gave it to you?"

"No," Jackson admitted. "I was breathing through a tube at the time. Kaden said my IA lawyer sent them to my house. Mike was getting my mail, and apparently they kept me from getting evicted and shit, so, you know, I got home, there they were."

"So." Ellery checked the list in front of him. "We've got Walt Hanline, the ADA; Paul Emory, *his* assistant; Bess Carillo, your IA liaison; and Leo Finch, your IA lawyer—those were the other four people."

"Yeah." Idly, Jackson leafed through his file, although he could have sworn he'd read it a million times already.

Ellery said the name just as Jackson saw it in the file.

"Then who in the fuck is Bill Chisholm?"

Jackson slow-blinked and pulled out the documents he'd just spotted. "You mean this motherfucker here with his signature all over the papers closing the case? I've got no fucking idea."

"Esquire," Ellery muttered. "He's a lawyer. Who in the hell is he working for? It doesn't say, he's just—there should be a document here, one that specifically tells us who all the parties are, named in the process, and it's *not here*."

Jackson squinted at the paper. "Okay. So tomorrow, after Kaden's hearing, I look up these people and we have ourselves a reunion. I figure out who the hell Bill Chisholm is and I ask him what his fingerprints are doing all over my fucking file. But none of this helps *Kaden* tomorrow. I mean, our gut hunch that the dirty cops now are connected to the dirty cops then is *great*, but what do we do for K?"

"No—no, this helps. It does," Ellery insisted. "Because…." He closed his eyes. "Shit."

"Shit?"

"Shit, all we have is your word for it that the cops were shaking Connie down."

"Ya think?" Oh Lord. There went Connie's face, miserable and terrified, scrolling in front of Jackson's eyes before the red matter and bone followed. "We might have had some proof that K was roofied, but—"

"Got burned up."

"I was fuckin' *there*," Jackson snarled. He took six deep breaths. Then four more. Something. There was something here. This had dirty written all over it, but *proof—*

"How'd you do on the picture?" He met Ellery's eyes hopefully.

Ellery nodded but not with the assurance he'd been hoping for. "I've already got a motion to dismiss the case based on contamination of the chain of evidence."

"But even if they dismiss the case—"

"Which I can't guarantee." Ellery had been wandering aimlessly, and suddenly he let out the equivalent of a roar and launched into a series of jumping jacks. He startled Jackson so badly he jerked and toppled the chair, ending up on the floor looking up.

Right at Ellery's flopping chrome balls.

Ellery stopped and looked down at him, squinting. For the first time, it occurred to Jackson that he must have contact lenses—he might have taken them off when he'd showered. "What in the hell are you doing?"

Jackson couldn't stop the semihysterical laugh. "Would you believe I was watching your junk flap? *Jesus*!" With a groan, he pushed himself up and righted the chair, pretending not to see how Ellery Cramer, badass attorney, put both hands in front of his crotch and blushed.

"I was trying to get the blood flowing," Ellery said with dignity.

"Yeah, yeah—I figured." Jackson closed his eyes and stretched, feeling the pull in his bullet scars and glutes and thighs, in his back and shoulder muscles, and finally in his neck. "I just have a dirty mind. But back to Kaden—"

"Did you two ever—"

Jackson looked at him sharply. "What? No! Kaden doesn't work that way."

"Okay." Ellery bit his lip. "Just checking."

"Can we keep him out of prison now?" Jackson wasn't really *mad* at the question; he was mostly embarrassed. It was embarrassing to be the guy who had reflexes like a cat when he was the cat who fell off the television.

"Okay, I've got it." Ellery mimicked Jackson's stretching movements, pulling his T-shirt tight against his surprisingly muscled chest. The whole inappropriate-junk moment was forgotten in the flash of hope.

"What? What do you have?"

"Okay, so here's the thing. Whether or not they drop the charges, the doctored photograph means we need time. And it throws suspicion on the police, which means that maybe we can ask for protective custody for your friend and his family. He'll still be under arrest and awaiting trial, but—"

"He won't be in jail. I hear you. Okay, it can buy us some time."

A giant spring uncoiled in Jackson's stomach. Okay. Kaden and his family—he was doing something. He had a plan.

He glanced at the clock and moaned. It was past eleven. "Shit. I've got to call Rhonda and the kids—"

"Tell them to be there at the courthouse and have stuff packed. Give their pets to the neighbors—"

"Jade will stay and take the house," Jackson said with some confidence. "Don't worry, we have their backs. I'll call Denny too and give him Mike's number."

"Yeah, I've got to type up my memoranda and notes." He paused. "Look, this whole thing might be stronger if I ask for protective custody and don't even discuss bail—"

Jackson nodded. "Yes. Yes to that." Connie. Just… just *standing* in his yard. "Do you think I want him or his wife and kids hanging out at home where anyone can get them?"

"What about Jade?" Ellery asked softly.

Jackson thought about it. "I think her job with the firm makes her too much of a risk to take out." His heart beat in his throat as he said it. Jade. He couldn't even think… but they needed her to pick up the pieces of Kaden's life. God, what could a stupid, fucked-up, broken system do to a family without someone to watch its back? "I'll leave it up to her, though." He grimaced. "And I've got to make that phone call right now."

He'd turned his body, but he and Ellery were still looking at each other in the electric pause between actions.

Ellery's intensity had returned, and his eyes darkened, hooded and sharp, focusing on Jackson's face.

For the first time in years, Jackson fought the urge to fidget.

Lost.

"What?" he asked explosively, pulling his hand through his hair. It had dried wild, a thousand different directions, and he hadn't cared, but now, for the first time in… well, ever, he was aware that he was… unimpressive.

Ellery looked away, biting his lip. "So… the couch?"

"Guest bedroom's fine if you don't mind tripping over the weight sets." Jackson shrugged. "There's some blankets in the closet, and pillows too—make self comfy."

"We'll have to get up really early—I need a clean suit."

D'oh! "God, yeah. I'll bring my skateboard and tag along to the courthouse. I can catch a bus to a car lot after that." God. He had money—the Toyota had been paid off, and he'd received a settlement after he'd been injured—but… a car. He'd not been planning on buying a car right now. He swallowed that and remembered that he had a debt. "I'm grateful," he admitted. "You picking me up. Hanging out here so we could go over this. It's… you know. Above and beyond."

"Well, I guess Ms. Cameron said it best—I'm only doing it for myself." His mouth twisted bitterly.

"I don't believe that," Jackson said softly, and then he turned to go, breaking eye contact, breaking the moment. And goddammit, he owed this man a little bit of truth.

He turned back. "Uh...." He rubbed the back of his neck. "You shouldn't hear... okay, not gonna lie. You're going to hear me... sleeping. I don't sleep great. Just—you know, when I start to make noises, do me a favor and just call out to me, okay? Knowing someone's here usually grounds me."

A body in the bed did it, 99.999 percent of the time. Only Jade ever really knew how bad it got, and that was because when he'd known it was going to be really bad, he'd asked her to stay over. He'd needed someone to shake him awake because he couldn't stop screaming. *Most* of the time just having someone in the house did it, which was why his guest room and his couch were clean and prepped for visitors. Whether he managed to convince someone to sleep in his bed or not, when he felt the bad shit coming, he could almost always talk someone into the couch.

It was cute that Ellery assumed he was hot enough to get lucky every night. Why would Jackson disabuse him of that notion? Sometimes it was true. Hell, a *lot* of the time it was true.

But just as often it was Jackson asking unashamedly if someone could sleep on his couch in case the bad dreams came. He spread it out—nobody got put upon more than once a year or so.

He used Mike as a last resort, because Mike would hear through the walls if Jackson didn't get someone else to come sit with him through his stupid neurosis.

But it just wasn't honest not to tell Ellery it was coming. He'd been damned human.

Right now he was gaping at Jackson like he'd done something heinous—picked his nose and flicked the boogers in his soup, maybe?

"You... you have nightmares *every night*?"

"No!" He felt affronted. "I... I just know," he said with dignity. "Once, maybe twice a week. I can feel it coming. When it's bad, a friend in bed usually stops it." He scowled. "I said we're not doing that yet."

Ellery nodded, looking suddenly embarrassed. "Yeah. Okay. Go do your stuff. I'll make myself at home. Don't mind the screaming in the bedroom, got it."

Jackson forced himself to roll his eyes. "Don't be dramatic. Don't you think, if it was *really* bad, I'd have gone and gotten help by now?"

A strange sort of rictus contorted Ellery's face. "You," he said after an awkward moment, "are the most exasperating man I have ever met. The fact that we are even *remotely* attracted to each other terrifies me in the pit of my *balls*. Have a good night, Jackson, because I'm going to sleep like a fucking *baby*."

He turned then and picked his cell phone up from the charger. Jackson used that as his cue to go make his own calls.

HE'D KNOWN they were coming, though. At twelve thirty, after talking to Jade, Rhonda, Denny, Mike, and then Jade again, and *then* Rhonda again, he'd shut off the light in his room and shut the door. Billy Bob hopped up on the pillow next to his, and he let the fucker because the damned cat had no manners and didn't give a shit.

He buried his hands in Billy Bob's ragged fur and closed his eyes, trying to picture anything—open blue sky, a field of flowers, a fish tank, snow in July—*anything* to ward off what was coming.

But it was no good.

Patrick Hanover had never touched him—wasn't bi or gay and hadn't hated gay men in any way, shape, or form.

But maybe it was because he'd told Ellery the story of the day Rhonda had almost been raped, her pretty yellow shirt torn off her slender body, wrecked so badly that Jackson had walked home shirtless to cover her up, because K's shirt had been destroyed in the fight. He hated reliving that day, the helplessness, that terrifying knowledge that the three of them were giving that fight their *all* and it still wasn't going to make any difference.

So maybe it was the helplessness.

Maybe it was the memory of Hanover banging the girl behind the hotel. That sick dread, that soiled sexuality—the invasiveness of corruption that Jackson had been forced to swim in. It had been like swimming in a pool of maggots. It didn't matter how he sealed all the entrances and exits, that sickness was going to find its way in.

So as he fell asleep, he could feel Hanover's hands on his body, unwanted, crawling, probing, and then the hands became tentacles, painful, sucking bits of his flesh into their grip. One stuffed itself into his mouth, and one bound him across the thighs, caressing his flaccid, hiding cock. One probed between his thighs, into his asshole, with knowing little wriggles. *You like this. Don't you wanna? Don't you wanna be? Don't you want me in you? You can be a dirty cop.... Don't you want that to fill you up? Let me in, let me fuck you, I'll take over your skin....*

And he didn't scream. Not yet. Because he was strong, and he knew he was strong, and the dream didn't batter itself against his strength anymore.

No, the dream knew where to go to level Jackson Rivers.

Sometimes it was Jade being beaten, being raped. Sometimes it was Kaden being gunned down, his brains painting the pavement, a grinning gunman with a badge standing behind him. Rhonda being raped as a child. Their children being desecrated and harmed—Jackson's dreams were merciless, and he thought he was ready for them all.

But he wasn't ready for a stranger—a pale, proud-jawed, brown-eyed stranger—regarding him quizzically, that challenging squint making him look skeptical and irritated but not scared.

God, you need to be scared!

And then, while Ellery stared at Jackson in wonder, the thing, the insidiousness, began to crawl along his pale skin, tinge it gray, scaly, gelatinous, crusty garbage green, and he didn't see, he just stared in disbelief as the same thing embraced Jackson, drew him deeper into foul, stenched darkness.

Fuck! Ellery, run!

But he couldn't talk, couldn't scream, could only watch as the filth crawled up the pale skin, as those bright eyes, dark and curious, went flat and dead, like those of the young cop who'd given Jackson shit today. That kid had let his heart die already. Ellery hadn't, but Jackson couldn't stop it, and he could only watch it happen. Could only struggle, his cries trapped by the putrid *thing* forcing its way down Jackson's throat. Could only kick when the thing invaded him, forcing him to stay because of pain, the intrusive pain of a bullet through flesh or a missile up his ass. It didn't matter; something was forcing his flesh wide open, and Jackson was bound and gagged and scared and—

Boom!

Ellery!

Jackson saw Ellery's blood, bones, and gray matter spattered across his eyeballs as the dream fucking *won* and all he could hear was screams.

Fish in the Bed

THE BEDROOM light had gone out about an hour before Ellery was done working, and he silently blessed the fact that Jackson was getting some sleep.

Ellery had seen the rings of exhaustion under his eyes.

For the first time, he wondered if they were there because of more than a night of catting around.

God, the asshole had been so unassuming about it too. "Hey, I know you put yourself out to be in my house tonight, but since you're here, if you hear me in some fucking psychic pain, maybe just call my name and chill me out, okay?"

All casual, nothing scary to see here folks, just a guy who'd had his life ripped away and forged a harder, more dangerous life in its wake.

Ellery felt both proud and ashamed of his attempts to seduce Jackson Rivers.

Proud because he usually wasn't the aggressor. No, he was no longer the sad, awkward college boy who had to let his mother in on his every decision. But he wasn't the alley cat either, making an effort to shake his ass to attract a likely tom. He'd been damned near suave this night, and the fact that Jackson had looked tempted was something of a personal victory.

But he was ashamed because Jackson, whose morals Ellery would have said didn't exist, had needed to remind him *repeatedly* that they had more going on than just two guys and their libidos.

It was clear to see that Jackson's family—in the truly bonded sense of the word—was at work here, and Ellery, the interloper, had no right to distract Jackson from his job.

Ellery was more of a professional than this.

Which was what he told himself as he typed up his notes for the next day's bail hearing. He was a good lawyer. He had the potential to be a *great* lawyer, and if he could protect Kaden Cameron from all the demons lying in wait for him in this pit of corruption and serpents, then he'd consider himself well on his way.

So he'd almost regained his equilibrium—and his secret sort of relief that not *all* of Jackson's exploits were sexual—when he heard the first stirrings of the dreams that "weren't that bad."

"Jackson?" he called, not sure how loud he'd need to be. The muffled screaming and the pounding on the bed continued. "Jackson!"

And they only got louder.

Ellery hit Save on his finished brief and closed his laptop. Cautiously he stood up and padded down the hall, turning the lights off as he went.

He'd never had cause to be afraid of the dark.

He knocked tentatively on Jackson's door, hoping that might interrupt the dream. "Jackson? You said call your—"

"*Nooooo!*"

Oh *fuck* this shit!

Ellery charged through the unlocked door and, in the light from the sliding glass door, saw Jackson sitting up in bed and screaming. The cat was cowering in the corner, and even in the dimness, Ellery saw the sweat pouring from Jackson's face.

"*Jackson!*" he shouted. His knees sank into the bedding, and he grabbed the sleeping man by his shoulders and shook him hard.

Jackson flailed, all muscle and bone. Ellery dodged—and didn't dodge—a couple of blows, but aside from a solid clock to his shoulder, nothing landed with enough force to bruise. Holding on to Jackson proved the most difficult. He twisted and lunged and screamed until Ellery was forced to wrap his arms around those wide shoulders and throw them both on their sides.

There was no instant awakening, just a gradual reduction of the struggle. They stayed there, Ellery's chest to Jackson's back, until Jackson's breathing slowed and the flailing arms became a simple tightening in the chest.

"Jackson?" Ellery's voice sounded frightened, there in the dark, and his heart was pounding hard enough that he felt it in his stomach. That had been… horrible. Terrifying. Jackson did that a few times a *week*?

"It's not—" Jackson took a breath. "—usually that bad."

Ellery wanted to hit him—and he wanted to cry. "What in the hell? Not usually that bad? Is it *ever* that bad?"

The sound Jackson let out might conceivably have been a whimper, if it hadn't issued from Jackson Rivers's throat.

"You're okay?" Jackson asked, like the words were forced out. "Just… you're okay. Tell me you're okay and you can go back to—"

"I'm here," Ellery murmured, rubbing his cheek against Jackson's hair. "I'm here. I don't know what you saw in the dream, but I'm here."

This time it really *was* a whimper. "Okay. Okay, good. Thank you."

"I'm going to straighten out the covers, okay?" They were rumpled underneath Ellery's shoulder, and he hated that. A little bit of struggling and some tugging and then Ellery had them both under the thin comforter, grateful that Jackson's air-conditioning had finally started working. He wrapped Jackson up tight in the blankets and then added his arms across Jackson's chest again, rocking him softly.

"Sorry," Jackson whispered, not rejecting the comfort. "Sorry. So sorry. It was bad this time."

"Want to talk about it?" Wasn't that what they said? You talked about the dream and it got better?

"No." Jackson burrowed more deeply into the covers and back into Ellery's chest, grinding his ass up against Ellery's groin. Ellery grunted and thrust back against him, half in arousal and half in irritation. Even *he* knew this wasn't the time.

Jackson's strangled laugh told him Jackson knew it too. "Really?"

"It's been a while," Ellery mumbled.

"Stop flirting with judges," Jackson chided back, his voice sleepy and slurred.

"He's a *friend*!" Ellery protested, half laughing himself. The Honorable Todd Lang, fortyish, buff, with silvering blond hair and a liberal bent, had been Ellery's racquetball partner and lunch date for the past three years. As far as Ellery knew, Todd was straight, and as far as Todd knew, Ellery was a shitty racquetball player.

And that was all.

"You flirt," Jackson mumbled. "Your eyes get all glowy and you smile. Don't smile at the office—just look all badass." Jackson's shiver was the only thing that kept Ellery from taking offense.

"I'm trying to keep up with *you*," he said truthfully. "You've got the bad-boy thing going, and the ex-cop thing going, and the PI thing going—"

"Most boring job in the world. I've done more fucking sudoku than should be allowed by law."

Ellery chuckled, glad that some of the lost-and-scared was fading from his voice. "Well, you swagger. You swagger into the office and flirt with… *everybody*, and walk out with people on your arm. Playing racquetball with a judge is small potatoes."

Jackson's chuckle bordered on a sob. "Anything," he confessed brokenly. "Anybody." He pulled in a ragged breath. "Human shields. Keeping the monsters away."

"Sh… sh…." Because it was clear that just mentioning the monsters made them big and strong and real-life again. "I'll be your human shield tonight, okay?"

Jackson nodded miserably, face half-buried in the comforter. "Just need to know you're all right. Kaden's in jail—someone's got to be all right."

His voice was thick, syrupy, jagged, and Ellery's heart gave a giant painful thump.

He was crying like a child, and he didn't want Ellery to see.

"C'mere," Ellery whispered, shoving at Jackson's shoulder until they were facing each other. He seized Jackson's hand, clammy and clenched, and brought it up until the battered knuckles dragged against Ellery's cheek. "Feel? I'm fine."

Jackson nodded, green eyes closed, lush playboy mouth pursed. Even in the darkness, Ellery could see his lashes were spiky, and the light from outside reflected off the shiny parts of his cheeks.

"Yeah," he whispered. He took a deep breath but kept his eyes closed. "I used to have girlfriends," he said. "And boyfriends. And relationships." He took another breath. "I miss those."

"Why'd they stop?"

"'Cause I almost died. Was seeing a girl when I started wearing the wire… broke up with her because…."

"Because undercover is hard." Ellery had represented a couple of people who had done that—gone in, recorded the bigger crime, got out of jail. One day. Maybe two. An hour. Not three months. Almost in spite of himself, he wiped the dampness from Jackson's cheek with his thumb.

"Yeah." Jackson sighed. His breathing deepened, grew a little steadier. "When I got shot, the only people there for me…."

"Were the Camerons."

Jackson's voice was even, nearly asleep. "I miss their mom." One more breath, and a shudder, and he was out.

Ellery was tired. He'd finished what he needed for the courtroom. He just needed to print it out, but he could do that at the courthouse. His phone was set in the kitchen at top volume, and he assumed Jackson had set an alarm of his own. Screw the couch—or getting up, for that matter.

He closed his eyes and wrapped his arm a little tighter around Jackson's shoulders.

A human shield to keep the monsters away.

IN SPITE of the lateness of the hour when they fell asleep—and the exhaustion—Ellery woke up a few minutes before either of the alarms went off. Jackson was still tight up against his body, and he was backed up against the wall.

For a moment he just lay there with his eyes closed and took stock.

He had a bruise on his shoulder. That was uncomfortable. The temperature had dropped in the night, and that made the heat Jackson's body threw off bearable. And Ellery Cramer, who hadn't gotten laid in a *year*, was in bed with an insanely hot man—who had an unashamedly broken soul.

And there was a cat sprawled on his hip, laid like a casual scarf on a shoulder.

Oh yeah.

And Ellery needed to save Kaden Cameron's life that morning.

Reluctantly he opened his eyes. And found Jackson's gaze fastened hungrily on his face. He hoped his morning smile was a good one, because Jackson got it up close and personal.

Jackson didn't smile back. "I'm sorry," he said, his eyes darkening. "This was not... you were never supposed to see that."

Ellery felt a flush of mortification heat his throat and cheeks. "Well, I'm no one-night stand, but I think I did okay."

Jackson grunted and rolled away. "One-night stands never see that," he said gruffly, standing up. "*Jade* has never seen that. I'll shower first."

He started stripping, his back to Ellery, shoulders rippling as he pulled off his tank and shoved his shorts down. Ellery got a glimpse of Jackson's ass—taut, heavily muscled—as he stalked out of the room.

Huh.

So *Jade* had never seen that. Ellery could actually get out of bed on that one—which he had to do anyway because, well, clothes.

He scowled and swung over to Jackson's closet. They were roughly the same size, and Ellery seemed to remember Jackson wearing… where were they… he knew they were in there….

Hm. Old service uniform, wedding suit, an astounding array of sport coats, some jeans in the hanging wire shelves. Oh, come on! Ellery had seen him wear them to court himself!

Ah, there they were. Two basic suits, European cut, one with pinstripes on charcoal and one in navy.

Woot! Ellery would far rather use the extra time they had that morning getting his case together than going to his house for clothes.

He made the bed and laid the suit out, hoping for approval, and was in the process of raiding Jackson's underwear drawer when Jackson emerged from the shower, towel over his hips, looking barely more awake than he had when he'd gone in.

"Why am I wearing a suit?" he grumbled, looking puzzled.

"You're not—*I* am. This way we'll have time to print out the brief now and we won't have to rely on finding a printer at the courthouse."

"Oh." Jackson scowled at the suits on the bed. "Why don't you wear olive or brown?"

Ellery squinted back at him. "Because you don't *have* olive or brown?"

"No, moron—*your* suits. You keep picking my colors. Navy, by the way. Gray pinstripes look okay on you, but navy or olive or brown look much better."

"Because gray pinstripes are serious suits," Ellery said with dignity. He wasn't aware a man could look *bad* in a gray pinstripe suit.

"You have dark hair and dark eyes and pale skin. Just no. But anyway, aren't you afraid your judge friends will think we're sleeping together?"

Ellery tried to pretend he didn't get a gut-punch of thrill at the thought that someday that might just be true. "It will probably make me look sexier," he said glumly. "It may even improve my chances the next time I'm out on the—ungh—"

Jackson still had one hand on the towel around his waist, but he wrapped the other arm around Ellery's hips, flattening his palm against Ellery's stomach and yanking him back so Ellery was flush against his body. "You listen to me," he growled. "If you are in *my* bed, you are there until I say you're not—you understand?"

Ellery gasped and his temper spiked—and so did his passion.

He turned so they were chest to chest, and the heat Jackson threw off enveloped him. He tried not to get lost in it. "Then *you* understand," he growled. "Nobody but me gets to see your nightmares. You're going to play the caveman thing with me, then we're both in the same goddamned cave."

Those eyes bored into his, fiery ice, and then Jackson took a forced step back and looked away. "May never happen," he muttered. "Go take a shower."

And Ellery had *had* it with the "we can't right now" excuse. He followed Jackson, grasping his chin, forcing those eyes to meet his.

"I mean it," he said, his best courtroom gaze locked. "Until we *both* walk away from this, I got dibs."

Jackson's mouth quirked up at the corner. "What are we, ten—"

Ellery hauled him forward and kissed him hard, tongue sweeping in. Jackson's gasp of surprise filled something aching in his stomach. He'd felt so… so *limited* next to this man, so lost in a world he barely skated over. But Jackson let out a needy little moan, and Ellery could fill it, *Ellery* could give something more than just a wickedly written brief.

Jackson grabbed Ellery's ass with both hands and ground up, humping and frotting with a blatant urgency, and Ellery had to push both hands against Jackson's chest to break away.

They both panted, staring at each other for a moment, and Jackson looked as lost and as stunned as Ellery felt.

"Not until—" Jackson threatened.

"Your brother is safe," Ellery acknowledged, chest heaving. "But nobody else until it's out of our systems, you hear me?"

Jackson cocked his head, contemplating Ellery like a cat eyeing a mouse. "Why?"

Ellery frowned and backed up, watching as Jackson got a better grip on his *tented* towel. "Because *I* do relationships, and whether we even *have* sex, that's what this just became."

Jackson looked like one of those cat videos when the cat got water on its nose. "Since *when*?"

Ellery knew his smile was smug, and he didn't give a shit. "Since you gave me fashion advice," he said, sweeping off to the bathroom. "Not even *Mother* tells me what to wear."

In the shower, he beat frantically at himself so he could achieve that barely satisfying three-minute hand-date he'd become so adept at in college. As he leaned against the white tile, panting and watching his jizz wash down the drain, he was forced to admit that had been a great line—but fashion advice wasn't really the reason.

No, the reason they were in a relationship was no more and no less than that Ellery *said* so. He'd fallen asleep with that man in his arms, allowing Ellery to see him so naked after a day of being badass and fearless he'd been shaking with it. Jackson had let *Ellery* do that when he didn't even let Jade. There had been a curious source of power in those hours, a sense of fulfillment that Ellery had not ever imagined when holding someone you thought you barely liked.

Ellery wanted that. He wanted *Jackson*. If he had to bait the guy with sex to get him to curl up on Ellery's bed for some basic comfort stroking, then so be it. Ellery was defending Kaden pro bono—and putting his reputation and even his safety on the line to do it.

Kaden was a great guy and all, but Ellery didn't even defend innocent men unless there was something in it for him—at least a notch on his belt.

Ellery had found his payment for this case, and its currency was Jackson Rivers.

"Do you have evidence to support this?" The Honorable Charles Bentley was a rumbly, weathered sort of man, hunched over his bench like a dragon hunched over his gold. He'd long ago lost more than a few threads of his comb-over, and he peered at the case notes in front of him like he was translating the Rosetta Stone into an undiscovered language.

"Yes, Your Honor. May I approach the bench?"

Ellery had managed his notes and copies for Arizona, and he handed them over as they huddled at the bench.

Judge Bentley scowled at Ellery in irritation. "This case was going to suck enough—you realize that, don't you?"

Ellery grimaced. "Yes, sir. But instead of waiting for the real evidence to come in, we were given what was supposed to be a legal document with an *un*documented photo in it, and that's grounds for dismissal. Mr. Cameron's friend Mr. Coulson—who was supposed to have been in the minimart when the crime took place—was shot and killed in a drive-by incident only hours after the crime. We might have had proof that the suspect was drugged and rendered unconscious when the crime took place, but the paperwork—the *original* paperwork, not the paperwork with the timestamp *hours* after evidence of drugs would have disappeared—was burned up in a mysterious car fire. This file verifies all of it. And if there's even the slightest chance this is true—"

Bentley nodded. He wasn't the easy judge, or even the flamingly liberal judge, but if you dotted your i's and crossed your t's, and had your memoranda, briefs, and your police reports in meticulous order, he was actually better than either of those things. He was absolutely consistent about maintaining order and procedures.

Ellery couldn't have picked a better court official out of a lineup of them, and Bentley didn't let him down.

"Is the DA intent on prosecuting *this* man for the murder of Officer Collin Miles?"

Arizona nodded coolly. "He is our suspect at the moment, Your Honor."

"Well, then, given that making him your suspect also puts him in *immediate* danger if Mr. Cramer's theory is correct, I have no choice but to remand Mr. Cameron and his family into court custody. Is the man's family ready?"

Ellery looked to where Jackson and Jade sat flanking an elegant African American woman wearing a cream-colored suit dress, and two children, a boy and a girl, both dressed neatly in school uniforms.

Jade was dressed in her best chocolate-colored suit, and Ellery thought he'd never seen a family look more composed or more legitimately innocent in his life.

Jackson sat on Rhonda Cameron's right, and he was wearing jeans and a sport coat. He leaned forward, elbows on knees, and those clever green eyes didn't miss a single detail of the hearing. Ellery got the feeling he was searching out the faces of everybody in the courtroom as well. Jackson saw Ellery's questioning look and nodded. He turned and spoke quietly to Kaden's wife, who in turn spoke to the children.

"Yes, sir." Ellery turned back to the judge. "The family is ready."

"Pretty cocky, weren't you?" Bentley asked dryly, but Ellery's poise never wavered.

"I had to be, Your Honor," he said soberly. "These are good people and their lives depend on us."

Bentley's eyes went wide before his usual stoic mask of objectivity slipped back into place. "I'm glad you're taking this seriously, young man. A peace officer has been killed, and protecting his killer is *not* going to make us popular."

"It will if he's innocent," Ellery said without blinking. He'd defended a lot of people in the past six years, both as lead counsel and co-counsel, and had been passionate about his place in the court system, even for the guilty.

But maybe because he'd *met* Kaden Cameron, he felt more strongly about this case than any other. Maybe it was that he'd known part of Cameron's family before the crime in question that made him more passionate, or maybe it was that he'd become more and more immersed in a world where people didn't trust the police and had to deal with crime on their own. He'd never felt quite so invested in seeing a client protected, in personally seeing justice done, so that the people caught in the cogs came out unhurt.

Of course, maybe it was because he'd held Kaden Cameron's best friend in his arms through a rough and painful night too.

But no. Ellery was too much of a professional to let that affect his job, right?

Jackson caught his eye again and winked grimly. For the first time in his life, Ellery felt like he belonged to the cool-kids' club. An intense and frightening club, maybe, one in which the members weren't going to be popular and might even be in danger—but Jackson had given him chances to back out, and he'd said no. At first, it was because this really *could* be the case of his career. But after that first phone call from Jackson, angry and disheartened and self-recriminating, Ellery had—maybe for the first time—seen what sort of stakes his clients played for.

When Jade had come in, worried for her brother but worried for Jackson too, he had wanted to be in the game *so* badly.

Now, after the night before? After their kiss that morning? He'd have to be flattened with a stun gun to let anybody drag him away.

Ellery and Arizona walked back to their seats, and the judge had everyone rise. As he pronounced the defendant remanded to protective custody along with his family, trial to be determined later, a collective sigh went up on Kaden's side of the courtroom.

And an angry murmur went up on the side of the state.

"Cop killer!" someone shouted, and the cry was taken up—along with the ugly racial epithet Ellery had so dreaded. The court officials showed up, two competent, frightening men with big shoulders, lean faces, and MIB suits, and Jackson herded the family along with them and out.

Ellery finished packing his briefs into his case, and Arizona came up to talk to him.

"You'd better be right about this," she said grimly. "My office is tracking down Kaden Cameron's every last traffic ticket, his hospital bills, every time he even *breathed* wrong, and you know the first thing that came up, don't you?"

It was unavoidable. "Hit me with it—I will not be surprised."

"Your PI is sleeping with your defendant's sister!" she hissed.

"Nope. Not surprised. And not 'is sleeping'—'*was* sleeping.' They grew up together." He thought of that story, the three of them banding together to save Kaden's wife-to-be. "You spin this into a family conspiracy and I'll show you this family for real, Zona. Jackson Rivers coaches Kaden's kid's soccer team. You saw those kids in uniforms? I listened to Kaden Cameron brag about his kids in dance and sports, his wife the teacher—you try to make this family dirty and I'll show the world what racial bias really looks like. And *then* I'll show the world what it's like to live with the dirt on the wrong side of the law. You know so much about my PI, Arizona, you tell *me* why they had him wear a wire for *three months* to indict a cop who was dirty when he only needed to wear it for *one day.*"

Arizona looked at him like he'd grown another head. "He did what? Why would he need to indict a cop? He was shot by one—wasn't that enough?"

Ellery squinted at her. "Arizona, I'm going to do you a solid. You need to go look up the IA investigation Jackson was participating in *before* he got shot by someone from his own force. I know you probably think you saw the whole thing on video eight years ago, but that file—it's interesting reading."

"Why would I even have that file?" she asked, frowning.

Ellery's internal alarm started pinging. "Because it was a joint initiative between the DA's office and Sac PD," Ellery said, watching her wide, square-jawed face harden to concrete. On a hunch, he said, "Bill Chisholm had his signature all over it. Did he work for the DA's office back then?"

Arizona's head snapped back like she'd been slugged in the chin. "How did you know?" she hissed, grabbing Ellery's bicep. Her manicured nails were leaving dents—or bruises.

"Because I have access to the original files," he said, and his warning bell dinged a little louder. "Jackson showed me, thinking they might help."

"I had no idea that investigation was happening," she said, her voice a foul, murderous grumble. She thrust out her jaw like a boxer. "What does this have to do with Kaden Cameron's case, anyway?"

"Jackson was investigating police corruption—he had his partner dead to rights. It should have been an end to the investigation. But they kept sending him in and not telling him why. What does that tell *you*?"

Her eyes narrowed. "It went a lot deeper than one guy taking payoffs."

"How cute and naïve that you think that's all he did," Ellery said, disgusted. He *liked* the way Arizona looked outraged when he said the word *naïve*. It made him feel like he was on the right track. "But yeah, that's exactly why they kept doing it. And then Jackson was shot—and he was supposed to be dead, trust me. His partner *did* get dead, and they hunted down the sniper, and that was the *end*. No investigating deeper, no more IA, and Bill Chisholm's got his fingerprints all over the case, right down to Jackson's commendation and his release from active duty. Eight years later, same neighborhood, where everybody *knows* the cops are dirty but everyone's terrified to tell, a cop gets shot in a quickie-mart—allegedly by a guy who claims to have been drugged. We've got no legal crime-scene photos, no explanation, and a civilian photo taken by a girl with track marks who apparently had the surviving cop's permission to be there. You tell me nobody's dirty, I'll call you a filthy stinking liar."

Arizona was staring at him, her lips compressed so tightly her red lipstick had rubbed off and Ellery could see a blue tinge around the outside.

"You stepped in a big steaming pile of shit," she said after a moment, her voice hoarse.

"Yes," he conceded. "Yes, I did. But you know what's not in that pile of shit?"

Arizona swallowed. "Solid proof."

"A-fucking-men. So you keep taking your pressure from the capitol, but you let me know when you have a chance to do some real law work on your own, okay?"

"Don't be smug," she snapped. "I need to see that file!"

"I'll have copies made and send one to your office. But do me a favor—let me talk to Chisholm first." Ellery still had no idea who Bill Chisholm was, but he had a feeling he knew where he worked.

"You're welcome to," she said sourly. "If you want to commit career suicide, you have to do it alone."

She turned and stalked away, and Ellery looked around the mostly cleared courtroom. The audience members had been escorted out, most of them grumbling loudly but so far nobody threatening to get violent. Ellery was very aware that could change at any moment.

He made his way into the hallway and to the antechamber, and saw that Jackson was still there, but Kaden and his family had been taken away already.

Jackson startled when Ellery walked in, and then he looked relieved.

"Did the marshals get them away okay?"

Jackson nodded. "Jade's gone to get their stuff out of the car. They have their neighbor's kid watching the animals. I promised I'd check every day until I knew they were going to be okay." His expression softened then, wavered, before he shored it up. "You'll need to make appointments to see him—me too."

He swallowed, and Ellery quickly realized what was wrong.

"That's your family," Ellery said, thinking that if his mother's voice disappeared from the other end of the phone for an unspecified amount of time, it would freak him out. Yeah, she was overbearing, manipulative, and obnoxious in the extreme… but she was his mother.

"You'll see them," Ellery consoled, and for the first time, he actually saw the impact of what Jackson was losing. Jackson was a grown man, but those people he was fighting for, they were all he had.

Well, them and the cat.

"I'd rather make it safe for them." Jackson's voice grew crisp and active, and he paused for a moment and checked his phone, then texted. "I'm telling Jade to go into the office—"

"Tell her to find out where Bill Chisholm works in the capitol while you're at it," Ellery said, not minding the smug bastard in his voice when he said it.

Jackson's sardonic look was worth it. "Proud of yourself?"

"Ellery can play too," he said with dignity, and the tenseness, the defeated set to Jackson's shoulders, relaxed.

"Ellery likes to play top," Jackson said dryly.

Oh God—he was referring to that morning. Ellery flushed. "I top," he said, because he couldn't help himself.

There was a knock at the door, and Jackson sauntered past him to answer it. "Ellery?" he whispered when he drew even. "I always top."

Jackson opened the door, and Jade rushed into his arms for an uncomfortably long hug. Ellery cleared his throat and glared over Jade's head, and Jackson raised an eyebrow and hugged her for just a heartbeat more.

Jade pulled back and gave them both a watery smile. "Okay, boys, we've seen them to safety. Now we need to figure out what the hell happened. What next?"

Jackson narrowed his eyes and started issuing orders.

Ellery narrowed his right back and started issuing his own.

Swimming Upstream

JACKSON MUST have been losing his touch. He leaned against the passenger door and glared at Ellery as they cruised up 80 toward Roseville.

"I can get my own car," he muttered.

"Stop being a child. I got the firm to give you a down payment, but you need me there to expense it."

"We don't have time for this. We have—"

"Cool your jets, Jackson. I brought the laptop. I'll be working while you get a functioning vehicle. It's not a hardship."

"I put the board in the back of your car. I could have *skateboarded* to a dealership in town."

"But we don't have the discount with the dealers in town." Ellery pitched his voice like a mother talking to a fractious child. "And if you keep bitching, I'll suspect you don't want to spend time with me."

A slow moment passed, and Jackson tried to catch his breath. It was *embarrassing* how much he wanted to spend time with Ellery.

Ellery didn't hear the thickness in Jackson's chest, though, and for a moment his guard dropped and he became the somewhat nerdy social outcast Jackson had never suspected lurked behind the guy in the expensive suits.

"So you *don't* want to spend time with me," he said, sounding sad.

"Don't be dramatic," Jackson muttered. "We just have shit to do."

Ellery perked up like he heard the neediness behind the snarl. "Well, consider this on your list, and we're getting it done," he said primly.

Jackson laughed in spite of his funk. The kids had looked so scared. He wasn't sure how to process that. Kaden and Rhonda had been, well, K and Rhonda. They'd fussed about extra clothes and hair ties and enough shorts and at least one sweater and a swimsuit in case there was a pool. Jackson had watched the two of them switch into team mode ever since they'd started actually dating in their junior year of high school, and it had always impressed him. He and Jade could play second fiddle to their leadership, but they'd never be first seat.

Jackson had still been touch-and-go when Rhonda had delivered their oldest, a girl named River. Jade had talked up being jealous—mostly, Jackson suspected, to keep him from crying when he woke up and realized he'd missed a part of his friends' lives that he'd been looking forward to. Rhonda had named their little boy Diamond, so Jade'd shut up.

River and Diamond. Jade and Jackson had once talked about getting married just so they could be auntie and uncle together, because those kids were bright spots in their lives. But that had just been talk. Jade was still waiting for someone she hadn't grown up with, and Jackson had been so… afraid. Afraid of nightmares, afraid of getting close, afraid of letting anyone actually see what his nightmares looked like. He'd bring people over, fuck them if they wanted or talk to them until they fell asleep on his couch, because he *knew* that with another person—living, breathing, warm—in his house, in his bed, he could keep it together.

But the night before…

He hadn't.

And this asshole who had mostly been fun to mess with or lust after—privately—had been the one person to see the frightened child Jackson hid so very well.

Jackson wasn't sure how to deal.

So he dominated. That was what he did.

And Ellery was doing it right back.

Jackson wasn't sure what to do with that. His first instinct was to bolt. Why else would he put the board in the back of the Lexus? But Ellery had a contingency for *that* too. Jackson's second instinct was to curl up in a corner and hiss until he came up with a plan.

Yeah, Jackson. How's that working out for you?

"So after I get the car, you're going back to the office and I'm going to interview—"

"We'll have it delivered to your house, and the two of us can go to the precinct and talk to the IA liaison." Smug bastard.

"Why do you need—"

"But after that, we're going to stop and make, like, thirty copies of your damned file, and we're going to leave one in your house and one in the office and send one to my mother and one to each of the partners of the damned firm," Ellery said darkly.

"We're going to *what*?" Jackson asked, horrified. "Why in the hell would we want to—"

"Because the DA's office doesn't have the file we do," Ellery told him, still scowling. "And they should, because you had an ADA and his assistant working on your shit. There is no fucking reason for that shit to disappear unless people up top decided to *make* it disappear. So yeah. We're going to make a zillion copies and make sure everybody has one and send a couple of them to unrelated third parties and a safety deposit box as well. That shit is going to get some *play*."

Jackson sighed and leaned against his fist. "Wonderful. Maybe we can dredge up some of the footage. I'm sure they've got some shots of the EMTs working on me, or me in the hospital. Department milked that shit for months."

"You're lucky they did," Ellery told him. "As far as I can see, that might be the only reason someone else in the department didn't take a crack at you. When you finally came out of the ICU—"

"Sniper captured, trial done with, news over," Jackson filled in. "Yeah, I get it."

"But seriously, why risk another shot at you when—"

"When I had my file and I had to pull my shit back together." Jackson sighed again. "Why? Why Kaden? Why Kaden's gas station? Seriously?"

"Maybe it was the luck of the draw," Ellery said. "They were running that area already, and Kaden was bound to have a dust-up. Or maybe it was… lucky," he said after a moment.

"*Lucky!*"

Ellery nodded. "Look, Jackson, I know Kaden is your friend, but that's the point. If this had happened to anybody else, *any* small business in that section of the city, that person would have been screwed. Nobody would have believed them, they would have gotten a public defender with two hundred cases, and it would have been pled out. I looked up the guy Kaden would have drawn if you hadn't intervened? He would have sold Kaden down the river just to get him off his roster. And the problem would have gone on and some poor innocent person's life would have been ruined and they would have been clueless as to why."

"But Kaden—"

"Kaden has you and Jade, and not only do you work at a law firm, *you* have dealt with dirty cops, and you've got info nobody else does. So maybe if everything happens for a reason, the reason for *this* happening is that you're in a position to stop it. I mean, that's what we're really going after, right? Not just the person who's trying to frame Kaden and why, but to root out the corruption, get rid of the same people who almost killed you, right?"

Jackson scrubbed at his face. "Sure. Why not. Hop on that donkey and go fight that windmill. I hear you."

"I thought you might," Ellery said, and he was so goddamned smug Jackson wanted to smack him.

"But what's *your* excuse?" Jackson asked.

He was surprised when Ellery gave a lying shrug. "Like you said, this case could completely make my career."

"Yeah? That the only reason?" Jackson needled, irritated because Ellery had seen so cleanly into his own motives.

"Sure," Ellery said, eyes directly on the road. They'd reached Roseville, and he took the Sunrise exit, which opened pretty much onto a giant intersection.

Jackson just kept staring at him until he cut a sideways look toward the passenger's side.

Jackson forced a laugh. "You're not doing this for me!" he insisted. "You hardly *know* me. No, no, no—like you said, your career, your chance to defend someone innocent, my—"

"Six years," Ellery said, voice brittle. "Do you remember the first time we met?"

Jackson grunted. "I was leaving the building with Jade and the... yeah, the waitress who works in the sandwich shop around the corner." He chuckled in reminiscence. "She was sweet. We used to pity fuck about once a month before she met her husband—nice kid."

Ellery growled. "Yeah. Pfeist introduced you to me and you took your arm from around that girl and shook my hand. And if you were straight, that would have been fine. You were hot, I couldn't have you, so the fuck what. We didn't have to like each other to work together and boo-fucking-hoo."

Jackson remembered that, remembered seeing Ellery looking remote and unapproachable, rich and unembarrassed. He remembered that icy sweep of Ellery's brown eyes down his body and how he hadn't been *nearly* as okay with his scars then as he was now. He'd become defensive, had assumed that Ellery's disdain would be solely based on appearances and that nothing he could do would impress the new guy at the office.

"I looked you over," he said, remembering it now. A blatantly sexual, body-stripping gaze, one he'd used on a couple of people to get them naked in seconds.

"You made me hard," Ellery confessed, sounding pissed as hell. "Just one look. And you turned away. And that was it—you had your exclusive little club of everyone who *wasn't* me, and I got dry reports and sarcastic retorts when I asked for more. The end. Ellery Cramer, off the fucking island."

Jackson let out a half laugh. "So… that's what this is? A chance to be part of the group?"

The light turned green, but not before Ellery cast him a smoldering, half-resentful, half-lustful glare from under hooded lids. "A chance for you to see me as worthy," he said, and it should have sounded corny, but he was angry and vulnerable and defensive.

Jackson shook his head and stared blindly out the window. "You were a rich guy right out of college, Ellery. I was a disgraced—"

"You were *not* disgraced!" Ellery objected hotly.

"Well, as far as the department goes, someone leaked the IA thing when I was in the hospital, and no. Not a lot of visitors. So yeah, you looked at me all cool and shit, I was going to shake you off my back feet. Better that than give you a chance to…."

Shit.

"I won't hurt you."

Damn him. Damn Ellery anyway for seeing it when Jackson didn't want him to.

"We're not in a relationship." Jackson could swear they weren't.

"I'll be at your house tonight. I'll bring takeout."

Jackson grunted. "You're psychotic."

"Yeah," Ellery said, a shit-eating grin taking over his face, "but at least you're taking me seriously."

"You're going to bat for K. I have to," Jackson retorted. But his voice sounded weak in his own ears.

THE DEALERSHIP was a struggle as well. Jackson wanted an old Toyota sedan—he had insurance and the expense money, and he was hoping to break even when all was said and done.

Ellery had actually *called ahead* so he could test-drive a new Honda CR-V.

"What in the hell?" he asked as they were escorted to the car. "I wanted—"

But Ellery had sort of… well, there was this thing he did in the courtroom. Jackson had seen it himself. He just stood, tall and remote, and the world parted around him to his specifications. Jackson was used to getting his way, it was true, but he was used to *fighting* for his way.

That wasn't what happened here. What happened was Jackson ended up with his ass in the damned CR-V, with Ellery on the passenger's side, giving directions for the test drive.

"I'm not getting this," Jackson said moodily.

"Do you feel that?" Ellery asked excitedly. "See how easy it steers?"

"This sticks out like a sore thumb—"

"Well, sir," said the eager salesman, "studies have shown that white and silver cars are practically invisible these days. The majority of the cars on the road have a similar color and body type—older vehicles are really more noticeable."

Jackson pulled to a halt at Lead Hill Boulevard—and oh, yes, the brakes were wonderfully responsive compared to his old car—and glared at Ellery. Not the salesman. Ellery.

"I liked my old Toyota," he said grimly, not wanting to think about having to reclaim his stuff from the damned thing in the junkyard. "I've had that car since I graduated from high school."

Ellery's bored look indicated this didn't surprise him in the least. "Well, yes, but now you have your adult card, Jackson. You can drink and *everything*. Now tell me you hate the damned car and I'll let you go cruise the old clunkers—"

"But this one's on *sale*," the rep practically wailed. "And it's got a *warranty*—"

"Against bullet holes?" Jackson snapped, swinging the thing in a *sweet* little U-turn that threw the guy up against the back window. Ellery remained upright, and Jackson thought foully that he probably sat on a Pilates ball for part of his workday. There was no other explanation.

"Well, no," the sales rep said, sounding depressed. He was a decent guy, really. Had talked about his wife and how much she wanted this car, but they had three kids, so she had to go with the Odyssey instead. "But I mean, life doesn't come with guarantees, and this is one sweet ride!"

Jackson grunted.

"Admit it," Ellery said, nodding. "You like it."

He opened his mouth and started gesturing with one hand, but before he could frame the refusal he *really needed* to voice, Ellery turned to the sales rep and started negotiations.

Aw, fuck.

This was the part Jackson sucked at anyway.

Fucking hell.

"I'm not getting silver."

TWO HOURS later Jackson fumed in the passenger seat of Ellery's Lexus again as Ellery parked at Tahoe Joe's.

"We have things to do," he muttered.

"'Gee, Ellery, thank you for the car. I'm hungry, aren't you?' 'Why yes, Jackson, I'm hungry too, and since the world isn't coming to an end *this instant*, I think it's safe for us to eat, don't you?' 'Absolutely, Ellery. I think we should eat.'"

Must. Not. Laugh. "There's a Wendy's down the street," Jackson muttered.

Ellery gave an elegant snort. "Nobody eats fast food in this car."

"We ate Chipotle last night," Jackson parried.

"That's not fast food—and it's an exception."

"You're mighty smooth for a guy wearing an off-the-rack suit from Penney's." He didn't look bad in it, actually. Although Ellery had one of those slender builds—he could have worn an American box suit and made it look good.

"I used to look up your court dates," Ellery said as he parked the car.

Jackson stared at him. "Because…."

"Because I'd see you in a suit or a tie—it was like watching a cage match wrestler dress up like a stockbroker. Sexiest fucking thing I've ever seen."

Jackson's tongue cleaved to the top of his mouth. There wasn't another goddamned thing he could say. In a daze, he got out of the car, following Ellery like a puppy into the damned restaurant. What else was he going to do? Someone else was driving.

Lunch was surprisingly productive. Ellery brought his laptop, and he had Jackson sit next to him at the booth so they could create a timeline and make a list of threads to pull.

The air-conditioning was pretty intense, and Jackson didn't notice how close they were sitting—or how much it was affecting him   until Ellery hit him with an irritated elbow.

"What is that… that *thing* you're doing?" he muttered. "It's making the seat buckle."

Jackson stared at him and, quite unconsciously, flexed his asscheeks tight and then relaxed them.

"Yeah! *That!*"

The rush of heat that hit his face shocked him. "Just, uhm… glutes… stretching…," he mumbled. Oh God. He was *hard* from sitting next to Ellery. He'd been flexing his ass to make his cock rub against his jeans. Jesus fucking Christ, he had no more self-control than Billy Bob. It was just that the guy had said something… sweet. Totally sweet and, well, *courtly*. Looking to see when Jackson was going to be wearing a suit? Who *did* that?

The slicker-than-snot lawyer picking daintily at his salad so he didn't eat any croutons—*that's* who.

"Well, stretch some other way," Ellery said in annoyance. "Did you have anything to add?"

Jackson nodded. "Yeah. Do we have a blown-up resolution of the girl who took the picture? I've got some places I can check to find her. If she's a street kid, they've got limited hangouts in that area."

Ellery nodded, expression inscrutable. "Any other ideas?"

"Yeah." Oh, this part was unpleasant. "We should also check the hospitals and the morgue. Unless she was someone special, Bridger had no reason to keep her around."

Ellery grunted. Well, he'd defended guilty clients—he knew the horrible things people could do to each other. But nobody liked to think of how bad it could get.

"I'll do that tomorrow," Jackson said, because that sort of thing was his job, and the Ellery Cramers of the world didn't need to be fishing around morgues and seeing the dirt beneath the city's fingernails.

"I'll come with you." Ellery met his eyes with a level gaze, and Jackson was mortified to drop his eyes first.

"Please don't," he said after a moment. Very consciously, he scooted away. "If she's in the morgue, it's hard to see."

"I'm not made of glass." Ellery turned toward the computer and made a notation with an unnecessary flourish.

"But it's not needed," Jackson told him. "You're more important doing… you know. Lawyerly things. If we can't get in to see Bridger today or at least talk to his lawyer, you need to do that. And I know you got rid of some of your cases, but not all of them. You need to keep up with your—"

Ellery just looked at him, head cocked.

Oh God. He was out of excuses, and Ellery could see right through him. "I've got to go to the bathroom."

He fled and huddled in the corner of the one stall, checking his watch, wondering how long he had to hide in there without looking like a total freak and trying hard to figure out *why* he was freaking out.

You are stronger than this.

He was. Eight years of one-night stands, and Jade when he was needy, and he had managed to avoid the sex-and-emotion tangle with ease and aplomb. He *had* no angry exes. Everybody he'd ever slept with had greeted him with a smile and a handshake or a hug when he'd seen them the next day, or week, or month.

And as time passed and people found relationships and moved away, or moved on, if the smiles were tinged with pity and concern?

Well, Jackson was fine.

He'd been an emancipated minor at sixteen. Had woken up on his birthday, grabbed the trash bag he'd packed his clothes into the night before, and moved into J and K's front room. He'd had a part-time job, had helped with the rent, and hadn't given Toni Cameron a day's worth of worry.

As long as he and J and K had one another's backs, he didn't need another soul.

And he was definitely not an asset in Ellery Cramer's well-ordered world.

He opened the stall door at the same time Cramer came in.

"All done," he said brightly, checking his zipper for show. "You know, too much breakfast. Had to make room."

"We didn't eat breakfast," Ellery said quietly. "You are really panicking."

"I'm fine." Jackson clenched his jaw. "Whatever you need me for, boss—let's eat and hit the road."

He hit the sink and plunged his hands under icy water, glad for the distraction.

Ellery met his eyes in the mirror and, in two strides, wedged himself up against Jackson's backside. "I only bite if you need me to," he whispered.

"Please." Jackson's voice cracked, and to his shame, he closed his eyes. "Ellery," he begged, voice husky, "you know how cats are famous for killing mice?"

"Yeah."

"Sometimes I think they just want someone to play with. 'Cause you should see the look on Billy Bob's face when I catch him with a little brown mouse. A vole. Once it was…." Oh man. "It was a half-grown rabbit. And he was just so damned sad. So just… just remember. The cat doesn't always *mean* to hurt the mouse, but sometimes that's what happens."

He dropped his gaze to his hands, which were growing numb in the cold. Fuck. They were in a drought. He turned off the water and reached for a towel, Ellery's body lighting him up along his back the entire time. He felt soft lips at the nape of his neck, and when he looked into the mirror, Ellery's eyes were closed.

"This is sort of a redneck town," Jackson said after a moment.

Ellery wasn't stupid. He took a step back and toward the sink just as someone else entered, and Jackson dried his hands. The two of them made their subdued way out to the table, where the food was waiting, and they made polite work-related conversation while they ate. Jackson's panic subsided, and he thought that maybe Ellery had forgotten the whole cat-and-mouse game they were playing—had maybe even forgotten that Jackson was apparently ruled by his cock and too weak to say no when Ellery Cramer touched him.

Until they got into the car. Ellery hit the ignition and the AC kicked on, thank God, because outside it was hotter than the bowels of hell after the devil ate curried fish. Then Ellery caught Jackson's gaze.

Jackson's breath stopped, and he thought he was going to have to jump outside the car and into the curried hell again. Idly, he looked across the street and saw kids sliding down water rides on big inner tubes. Now *that* was the way to spend an August afternoon, wasn't it!

"Jackson?"

"Yeah?"

"In your little analogy about the cat and the dead mouse, which one of us is Billy Bob and which one of us is the dead mouse?"

Jackson swallowed. "I'm Billy Bob, you asshole. Why would I compare anyone else to my damned cat?"

Ellery shook his head. "You know, I defended a junkie once. He swore up and down that he couldn't remember killing the middle-aged woman for her credit cards. *Swore* it was a bunch of bad drugs and he'd been too high to even know what he was doing. I didn't believe him, but I defended him. And so did one of the big guns—I think it was Harrelson—"

"The bald one who likes bow ties?" Jackson asked, because the partners of the firm really *did* stay high above the hoi polloi.

"Yeah!" Ellery smiled warmly, like they were friends. "Anyway, Harrelson wanted me to put him on the stand. He was this sweet little hamster of a guy, big brown eyes and this *really* convincing schtick. But I wouldn't do it. I just...."

"Had a feeling?" Jackson couldn't help it. He was hooked. The car idled and they cooled off, and Ellery kept eye contact.

Jackson couldn't get away.

"Yeah." Ellery nodded. "Exactly. So we lost the case because the evidence was overwhelming, you know? And the guy was getting hauled away by the bailiff, and he starts shouting. And he says, 'I'm going to get you, you fucking eel—I'm going to do you like I did the old cunt, and I'm going to slam your head against the wall until your eyeballs spit blood.'"

Jackson cringed in spite of himself. Yeah. It was great when the firm was defending the innocent, but not everybody was innocent. "Sweet."

"Mm-hm." Ellery reached out and, very slowly, stroked Jackson's lower lip with his thumb. "I'm really good at knowing when someone's lying." He cupped Jackson's jaw then, with a gentleness Jackson was not sure he'd ever felt from a lover.

"I'm not lying." At least he didn't *think* he was lying. "I—work long hours. I'm not great at being there for people. I haven't had a relationship for eight years. Why would you think I wasn't going to break you—"

"Because you haven't broken another soul in your life." Ellery smiled. "You're not going to break me. Don't panic."

"I'm *not* panicking," Jackson gritted. "Now move it. Your carbon emissions are warming the fucking planet, and it's hot enough."

At that point Ellery's pocket buzzed, and he pulled out his phone. Jackson watched as he arched one eyebrow sardonically. Without another word, Ellery put his phone away, backed the car up, and started toward Sacramento.

"Don't panic," he said again. "Spend all your time figuring out what to say when we interview Scott Bridger."

Jackson let out a gasp of air, feeling gut-punched.

The dirty cop who'd set up Kaden? Yeah—*that's* where he needed to be spending his emotion.

THE SACRAMENTO Police Department had been remodeled in this century, but an interview room was an interview room.

This one had padded seats and beige walls, and instead of a criminal on the other side of the table, it was a cop.

But Jackson could detect no discernable difference between this room and the county jail.

He wouldn't mind spraying the walls with Bridger's blood, just to change it up a little.

Scott Bridger hadn't served on the force when Jackson had been there. He'd served in the military before the academy, and for some reason, for Jackson, that made things worse. He'd seen chaos in the rest of the world and he wanted to come spread it *here*? It was like he'd betrayed two faiths and had corrupted all the religions in the world.

And it was hard enough for Jackson to come to the precinct.

Burnt coffee, scuffed tile, the hum of computer banks in the squad room—Jackson remembered how proud he'd been when he graduated from the academy. He'd thought that this place was going to be his home.

He hadn't realized that his roommates had already shit themselves there and trying to clean up the mess could get him killed.

This bland, featureless room felt like the precinct's toilet getting ready to flush all the wrongs away.

If they could flush a turd like Bridger, Jackson would be happy to be in the bowl when it happened. Unfortunately Bridger wasn't the only turd in the bowl.

"Wait—I'm getting interviewed by the *defense* lawyer? That fucker killed Miles and you're making me talk to the shitpiles defending him?" he growled at Bess Carillo, who had apparently gotten her law degree and was serving as IA counsel now. She wore her tightly ringletted orange hair in a ponytail just like she had eight years ago, but now she wore a flowing, boldly printed dress to go with her bangly earrings and bracelets.

Jackson usually didn't mind this look on a woman, but given what this particular woman had put him through, seeing her dressed like she was going to a party at the beach set his teeth on edge.

Ellery's fingers digging into Jackson's bicep were the only thing that kept him on his side of the table.

"The DA didn't want to see you," Ellery said to Bridger. This was true—he'd gotten a text on their way to the precinct, and ADA Brooks had said she would interview Bridger the next day. "She seemed to think everything out of your mouth would be bullshit."

Jackson kept his face straight. As far as he knew, this was *not* true.

"As far as I know," Ellery continued, "you wouldn't know bullshit from fish poop, so how about you talk to me and I can tell her if you're worth her time."

"But... but... she's the *DA!*" Bridger was a square-built fortyish man with dark hair and really nice blue eyes. Physically, he was good-looking—even the kind of guy who could turn Jackson's key in the right moment—but knowing what Jackson knew? It made him more than repellent.

"Yes," Ellery said, nodding. "But you know who the DA *really* doesn't like?"

"Cop killers?" Bridger sounded like, for the first time, he was considering an alternative.

"Dirty cops."

Bridger blinked.

And then, in the middle of the stellar air-conditioning, he began to sweat.

"I'm not a dirty cop," he graveled.

Then he blinked sweat out of his eyes.

Ellery smiled, all pointy teeth, and proceeded to eviscerate him like a hunted deer. After the first few volleys, Ellery let go of Jackson's arm and Jackson relaxed back into his chair, watching as Bess Carillo, once the IA liaison, now IA counsel, tried to get her client to shut the fuck up while she avoided any eye contact with Jackson whatsoever.

Interesting.

Jackson remembered her from his time working with Internal Affairs, and she'd been bright-eyed and eager. It had been her idea to keep sending Jackson out into the field with the wire, and she'd been… *fervent* was the word Jackson would use. She was *fervent* in her pursuit of corruption.

Apparently she was not so *fervent* in her willingness to protect the people under her care. She sat, one hand in her corkscrewed orange hair, blocking Jackson—and her client—out of her vision, and the other hand scratching what could have been penises on her legal pad. Jackson was pretty damned sure it wasn't actual notes.

It wasn't until Bridger let out a wounded moan and said her name that she and Jackson were called back into the fray.

"You're going to let him talk to me like that?" Bridger asked, sounding petulant.

"I simply asked how much money you and Miles had extorted from that particular service station in the past year." Ellery stared at him as though this wasn't a leading question.

"Miles wasn't even with me the past year," Bridger burst out. "We'd been partnered up about four months. Sweet kid. Sucked he had to go out like that."

"Sweet kid?" Jackson said, perking up attentively. "Really? Because I was a sweet kid once. I seem to remember something about being that kind of sweet kid and having people want me dead."

"You were a *rat* and everybody knew it," Bridger snarled. "Oh yeah—you think I haven't heard of you, Rivers? The whole fucking *world* has heard of you, and now you're keeping the scum out of jail—"

"Or keeping the scum from putting the innocent people there," Jackson replied, mind whirling. Yeah. Miles would have been there long enough to smell the dead fish sitting next to him in the squad car. And Bess Carillo—*fervent* Bess Carillo, Miles's supposed advocate—might have had a hand in getting the damned kid killed. "But we're not going to talk about that. What we're going to talk about is who took the crime-scene photo."

He saw Bess frown and then turned his attention to Bridger. Who was looking anywhere but at his lawyer.

"I don't know. Lutz, I guess. Isn't his name on the picture?"

"But Lutz wasn't called to the crime scene," Jackson lied smoothly. He had no idea if Kevin Lutz had been called in to take pictures or not. But Bridger's demeanor—and the sweat that had not let up—told him Bridger knew *exactly* who had taken the picture, and that it wasn't a fiftyish black man with gray hair at the temples.

"In fact," Jackson continued, "we'd *really* like to know the name of this girl." He reached into Ellery's file and pulled out the rendering Crystal had done of their mystery photographer. He slapped it in front of Bridger and watched the man flinch as though punched.

"I have no idea," Bridger muttered. "How in the fuck am I supposed to know about some sleazy fucking whore hanging out in the quickie-mart?"

Jackson looked at the picture. A young woman in bright clothing and a tight shirt in August did not automatically spell *whore*. "How do you know she's a working girl?" he asked.

"Jeans are painted on," the guy sneered.

"Lots of girls wear tight jeans when they've got nice legs. I don't see clown makeup, don't see bangles, don't see a lot of spandex. Nothing to market her livelihood, Bridger, just a T-shirt with the sleeves cut and skinny jeans. What makes you assume she's on the payroll?"

Bridger glared at Jackson with loathing. "'Cause she *looks* like a skanky junkie whore," he said, his brows drawn in, ugly.

"Well, even if she was," Jackson said thoughtfully, "can you tell me what she was doing taking pictures of a crime scene?"

"How in the hell would I know that!" Bridger snarled. "You'll have to ask Owens. He was the first flatfoot who answered the call."

Jackson and Ellery shared a look. "But wait a minute," Jackson said, something that had been bothering him finally curling up and making a home in his brain. "We've got this picture of Kaden Cameron knocked out, a gun by his hand, and a dead body. Why isn't Mr. Cameron in cuffs?"

Bridger froze.

"I mean, this was supposed to be—it was supposed to pass for—a legitimate crime-scene photo, but your suspect is unconscious and not cuffed. And a civilian is taking the picture. And none of the people who are supposed to be at the scene are at the scene yet. *Explain* this to us, Bridger. We want to understand."

Jackson had begun to lean forward more and more and more, until he was glaring into Bridger's face, an ugly rage settling into his bones.

"Fucking explain this!" he shouted.

Bridger spat at him, and it caught him squarely on the cheek.

Jackson didn't move. "Carillo?"

"Yes," she husked, as though surprised she could find her voice.

"I'd like this man charged with assault. Spitting on someone in public is still a misdemeanor, isn't it?"

"Jackson…." But her voice fell, and he knew he'd won. "Yeah. My client is aware of the charges. If Mr. Cramer will fill out his paperwork, I'll file it."

"You'll *what*?" Bridger turned to her, outraged. "You stupid fucking cow! It's your job to keep me out of—"

"It's my job to make sure my cops behave like cops," she hissed. "That's my job. You just crossed that line, and he's right. Your bad. Next time keep your temper."

"Fuckin' bitch rat cunt," Bridger growled.

"You don't want to spend a night in lockup?" Jackson said sweetly. "Then you tell me the girl's name."

"Hey—" Carillo made a halfhearted effort to protest, but Jackson slammed her with full-boiling fury in his look and shut her down.

"Hey what?"

"Nothing," she said. She closed her eyes for a moment, and Jackson saw the remorse there—and didn't give a shit.

"Luanne," Bridger said into the sudden silence. "Luanne Chisholm."

Jackson couldn't stop his gasp of breath, and behind him he heard Ellery mutter, "Holy fucking Jesus."

Oh yeah. *This* was a lead.

"One more thing," Jackson said. "And then we'll be on our way."

"I can hardly wait." Bridger was looking at Carillo like he was going to *eat* her, and Jackson hoped she'd be calling for another lawyer for him and some protection for herself. He really hoped these things arrived before he and Ellery left, but he wasn't invested enough to offer a friendly word of advice.

Fervent Bess Carillo, who liked to rope rookies into spilling their guts. And then, apparently, didn't have the power to protect them once they had.

"Why that gas station? What were you doing there? Did you have a thing against Mr. Cameron?" He needed this. He needed it said in front of Bess Carillo and in front of Ellery.

"I didn't know Kaden Cameron from a rock in the road," Bridger muttered. "But Connie, he used to play poker with us. He'd always let us have our fuckin' coffee and candy bars for free."

"Was that why you were there?" Jackson asked. "Is that why you picked Connie to shoot Miles and frame him for murder?"

Bess Carillo gasped, but Bridger just regarded him with disgust.

"I got nothing more to say to you. And I want another fucking lawyer." He leered. "Think I can get a pricey one from the firm you work at?"

"No," Ellery said before Jackson could lunge across the table and shatter his hyoid bone while strangling him. "I'm afraid our firm couldn't defend you, Mr. Bridger. It would be a conflict of interest. But I shall certainly give our information to the ADA. She will have much to say to whomever you decide to hire."

With that, Ellery packed up his briefcase, and he and Jackson stood. There were officers at the door as they left, and Jackson looked over his shoulder. He should be able to pity them—the dirty cop and the IA lawyer who wanted to put him away but ended up defending him instead.

He couldn't.

His stomach felt like it was made of fucking bile. He'd have to vomit all that out before he had any room there for compassion.

Fish in the Current

"So," ELLERY SAID when they got back in the car. "Bess Carillo."

"Yeah."

It was the first word Jackson had spoken since they'd left the interview room, and Ellery wondered which one of them would hit something first.

"I didn't know she'd be representing him."

"We've had a lot of balls in the air." Jackson's voice was affectless, and Ellery's stomach clenched. Oh, this was so bad.

"From IA liaison to IA counsel. That's sort of an unusual move."

"She probably got tired of people hating her." Jackson's arms were folded, and he stared straight ahead as Ellery turned down J Street and headed for the nearest FedEx. He had Jackson's file in his briefcase, and his stomach was *itching* to get copies made and mailed. He couldn't explain, even to himself, why this had become an imperative—and why he wasn't willing to leave the file in his office and have Jade run the copies.

It would just take too long, and that was no reflection on Jade.

"No," Ellery said, "seriously. That's like… like switching sides. I mean, she didn't have her law degree when she was working with you. I wonder what happened."

"She made a rookie wear a wire for three months and he nearly ended up dead," Jackson said bitterly. "And now she wants… I don't know. Absolution? Wants to help from the other side? I've got no clue. And you know what? I don't give a ripe shit, because as far as I can figure, she didn't learn a damned thing. That woman had guilt just pouring off her like Bridger had sweat—I'll give you *odds* that Miles went to her about Bridger. Stupid fucking rookie, thinking, 'Hey! I don't want to be an IA rat, so how about I talk to my union lawyer and see what I'm liable for if my crooked partner gets caught.'"

Ellery frowned. "So, what? Do you think she told someone?" He grimaced. "I'd say that would be a violation of ethics, except everything she did with you was a violation of ethics. Fuck. God, this gets worse every time we pull a thread."

"Augh!" Jackson pounded the roof of the car with his fist. "God, I need to fucking hit something."

Ellery felt a surge of satisfaction. Nailed it! "Well, we have—"

"Yeah, I know. We have fucking things to do. Where are we going, anyway? Shouldn't we be running down Chisholm?"

Ellery shook his head. "We need to *research* Chisholm first, not go charging down the halls of the capitol shouting his name."

Through the upholstery, he felt Jackson's deep breath shuddering as he bled out some of his tension. "We need to research female relatives—probably his daughter—too." Another breath. "Please. *Please*, Ellery. Let me do that alone."

"No," Ellery said unequivocally. "And not just for the reason you think. I was busy talking to Bridger, and I got exactly what I expected."

"A coarse, loud-mouthed bigot who is divided from criminals only by his badge and not another fucking thing?"

"Yes. And by the way, nice move with the pressing charges."

Jackson grunted, and Ellery wished he could risk a look at his face. "You think that was on purpose?" He scrubbed some more at his cheek.

"There are wipes in the glove compartment," Ellery told him sympathetically. Yeah. He'd want a full Silkwood after that too. "And it's gross and I'm sorry, but it was a good move. And while I was doing my job with Bridger, you were getting a bead on Carillo. I mean...." He flushed. "I always knew you were good, Jackson. *Always* knew you were good at your job. But working with you? That's a rush. You and me together? We can get shit *done*."

Jackson's reluctant chuckle warmed him. "The firm isn't going to pay for you to have your own private private. You know that, right?"

Ellery paused and thought about it. "I don't know. I mean, this case—it's going to be *big*."

The thoughtful pause was welcome, because it meant Jackson was thinking—and he was clever as hell. "You want to open your own firm," he said after a moment.

Hearing it said out loud? Was terrifying. "That wasn't why I took the job at the firm." He could remember: him, his mother, and his sister, Eileen, sitting at the table and running numbers for which career path would yield the most success and the biggest opportunity to make an impact. He hadn't wanted to run for office—he'd just wanted to be the big dog at what he did.

"Yeah? Why did you take this job?"

"I wanted maximum impact." It sounded self-righteous and priggish to his own ears.

"That's exciting."

And judging by the dryness of his tone, it didn't do much for Jackson either.

"I mean, I was supposed to become a partner. This case, if we're successful, that would practically guarantee a partnership." And even as he said it, he knew it wouldn't be enough.

"Why the change in plans?"

They reached a stop sign, and Ellery turned to meet his eyes. "Because I don't want to ever have to defend a guy like Bridger. Or that scum weasel who killed the schoolteacher for drug money. I *like* advocating for people like Kaden—"

"You don't always get innocent people," Jackson said, one of his eyebrows going up. "Green light."

Ellery checked the light and hit the gas.

And then hit the brake, barely avoiding the speeding black Dodge Durango hurtling through the intersection with a loud backfire.

Ellery put his hand to his chest, adrenaline thundering through his system at the near miss, and when he looked to check on Jackson—

He wasn't doing so good.

"Jesus. Jackson—"

"Just drive," Jackson said through gritted teeth. "I'm going to send Jade that license number."

"You got the license number?" Ellery was impressed—and not reluctantly anymore. Now that he was on the same side, he wanted to root for Jackson like a slutty cheerleader.

"Yeah," Jackson said through a gasp of air. "Just keep… just head for where you were headed, okay?"

Ellery looked at him. He was dripping with sweat, face a clammy white. "What's wrong with you?"

"I know that car." He was making an effort to breathe shallowly. "It's the same car that drove by when Connie Coulson was shot. I'd recognize that backfire anywhere."

Oh God.

Suddenly *Ellery* wasn't doing so good. "That was on purpose," he said, horrified. "They were trying to ram us—"

"And probably shoot us while we were figuring our ass from our end," Jackson said, nodding. "C'mon, Jade. Text me back."

Ellery's hands were sweating by the time he found FedEx Office, and he was relieved when Jackson got out of the car and went inside with him. He was trying really hard not to fall apart.

Jackson must have seen, though, because his hand—hot and moist, no doubt—rested briefly in the small of his back as they went through the door. It was a small touch, impersonal perhaps, but it hadn't been necessary. Jackson was taking care of him.

Ellery's stomach calmed down a tad, and he remembered that he could breathe in the air-conditioning. He nodded at the guy working the bigger machines, who nodded back as he grabbed the counter key from the rack. Then he steered Jackson to a color copier and got to work.

Jackson tapped madly on his phone, head down, peering up every now and then to take in his surroundings, and Ellery made and collated ten copies of Jackson's pillaged file. When he was done, he bought mailers and sent a copy to each of the firm's partners, the DA, Arizona, a contact he had at the DOJ, and his mother.

Jackson had come out of his phone coma by then, and as he watched Ellery copy the addresses, he let out a strained chuckle.

"Mrs. Taylor Cramer, Esq.?"

"My mother," Ellery replied, not smiling. "She may be a colossal pain in the ass as far as my love life is concerned, but if you and I get taken out the next time we get in the car, this will make sure she has my back."

Jackson grunted. "Hunh."

"Hunh?" Ellery glanced over his shoulder. "You don't have a contingency plan?" he asked, feeling as though, given the life Jackson had lived, this would be a given. "You know, in case?"

Jackson shrugged. "Yeah. If I'm taken out, J, K, Rhonda, the kids, they get all the money I have in the bank and they get the hell out of Sacramento. Mike gets the duplex. I had it drawn up in a will about two years after I got out of the hospital."

"Hunh." Ellery finished addressing the envelope and started to gather the pile of them on the counter.

"Hunh what?"

"I don't know. I would have thought something more… vengeful. Like 'get the assholes who took me out.'"

"Yeah, well…." Jackson pursed his lips. "Thing with that is, we had that plan in place right up until the kids were born. And I woke up and there was this… you know. I mean, she was Kaden and Rhonda's, but she was named after *me*, and Jade was in her life too. We had one of those late-night beer-and-whine sessions right after I got the job at the firm, and I said I didn't want them… *doing* anything if something bad happened to me. If something bad happened to K, Jade and I would gather in and help Rhonda out. And if something bad happened to me, they would love me best by getting the fuck out of this town and never looking back."

Noble. How very… noble.

Ellery was having trouble swallowing his anger at how very fucking *noble* that was.

"If I got killed because of a case," Ellery said thoughtfully, "my mother would mobilize the Department of Justice, the FBI, Homeland Security, and the National Guard. No stone would remain unturned, and several people would be imprisoned or killed before the rain of hell stopped falling."

"Well, yeah." Jackson nodded. "Forget about it. One of the kids? Rhonda would be shipped to Canada or something, and J, K, and I would be an assassins' platoon."

Ellery couldn't swallow the anger anymore. Six years they'd been working together. He'd seen Jackson come in looking bruised, banged up, and occasionally bloodied, and he could admit it now: he'd worried.

Jackson Rivers, tomcat, who always seemed to hold his own. Well, tomcats sometimes got run over by semis, and Ellery had held his breath, just praying the semi never came.

The promise was rash, but he had to make it anyway. "I'd do something."

"Do you even own a gun?" Jackson asked dubiously.

"It wouldn't matter." Ellery swallowed and nodded, promising himself too. "I'd do something. I'd call my mother and ask for pointers if I had to—"

Jackson grimaced, as though trying to keep the moment light. "Wow, you really *do* care!"

"I do." He'd been given an out, but he couldn't seem to make the moment less intense. "I'd hurt someone," he said, his chest and throat aching with the tautness of his certainty. "I'd... I'd make them pay."

Jackson looked away, taking a step forward in line as the next customer finished shipping what looked to be an entire linen closet to her nephew in Michigan. "I have guns at home in the safe," he said casually. "I'm not afraid to use them."

"Them?" Oh God. He couldn't seem to catch his breath. "Multiple guns?"

Jackson met his eyes for a searing moment. "Do you think there would be enough left of your killer to walk away?"

Ellery smiled, warmed by threats of violence, and then it was his turn at the counter.

Nope. Jackson would leave no prisoners and no wounded if Ellery was harmed. That was Ellery's tomcat: scars, guns, and claws.

MAIL DONE, and it was nearly seven o'clock. Ellery checked his e-mail, determined there wasn't anything he couldn't work on from Jackson's kitchen, and headed off down J Street. Instead of making the snaking left at Elvas, though, he kept going to Power Inn and got off on American River Drive.

Jackson looked around at the *Better Homes and Gardens*–style suburbs, clearly uncomfortable. "You live *here*?"

"Yup." Ellery *loved* his house. It was about the size of Jackson's duplex, both halves put together—both bedrooms and the living room were vast and spacious. His mother had flown out to decorate, and she had exquisite taste. She also, for all her overbearing nightmare social skills, loved her baby boy.

It looked like a tasteful showplace, with dark burgundy walls, oxblood paneling on the floors and olive throw rugs. Masculine and understated, the furniture all matched—Italian leather in black, with ebony coffee table and end tables, it was all top-of-the-line and comfortable. If Ellery had actually had enough of a social life to have people over, they'd have been suitably impressed.

Hell, his last boyfriend had offered to live in the guest bedroom even after they broke up, but since Ellery suspected Clint had cheated on him in there, he'd declined.

Ellery wanted Jackson to see his house. He didn't think the elegance would impress him, but maybe the *permanence* would. This was not where you took one-night stands. The bedrooms were too far apart for anyone to hear you if you called out in your dreams—you'd have to sleep in the same bed for comfort.

Ellery *really* wanted them to sleep in the same bed.

With a certain reluctance, Jackson followed him in through the front door.

"You should have just dropped me off at my place," he said, prowling into the sunken living room and sniffing reluctantly at the potpourri the housekeeper left out. "We both have work to do tonight—"

"And it will be easier if we're in the same room," Ellery said cheerfully. "C'mon. I'll let you pick out my suit for tomorrow."

Jackson sent him a glare that could have boiled diamonds, and Ellery smiled pleasantly into the face of it.

"Besides," Ellery continued like that glare had been an actual sentence, "I like your company."

Jackson gave a short bark of disbelief. "My company could get you *killed*."

Oh yeah. That. Ellery had managed to forget for an entire fifteen minutes that they'd had a near miss not two hours ago. Apparently Jackson wasn't going to let him forget for a longer stretch.

"What did Jade say?" he asked soberly, gesturing for Jackson to follow him at the same time.

Jackson sighed and followed, but Ellery could swear he heard a rumble on the way up the stairs. "She said the plates belonged to an SUV that was supposedly junked two years ago after a collision—so they stole them from the trashed vehicle, which is pretty canny, actually, but starting to piss me off. Damn. You really do need more traffic in here, Ellery. It's pretty swank."

Ellery preened. "See? Yeah, my mother decorated. I'm not ashamed."

The comforter was cream and neutral beige, and the bed frame was ebony inlay, like the furniture in the living room. The throw rug under their feet was a plush neutral with burgundy flecks, and the window behind the bed let the sun in during the afternoon but was positioned so you could sleep in a *long time* before it streamed into your eyes like a flaming sword of justice.

Ellery opened his closet, taking satisfaction in the neat row of suits inside, and then he remembered Jackson's words that morning. "Really? Olive and chocolate?"

"Holy God, you have got more suits in there than I've ever worn in my entire life. Have you thought about taking a vacation?"

Ellery lifted a shoulder. He knew he was privileged; he wasn't going to be embarrassed about it. Much.

"Birthdays and Chanukah, Mother buys me a suit. By the time I'd served my first internship, I'd come to sort of treasure them. I started asking for socks and underwear too."

"Hunh."

Ellery was starting to both love and loathe that sound. It usually meant Jackson had assessed yet another way in which they didn't fit. "Hunh what?"

"Chanukah. That's one of the few ethnic minorities we *didn't* see in my high school."

Ellery turned to him, head cocked. "White people were the minority at your high school," he pointed out reasonably.

"Ninety percent of our teachers were white," Jackson said, surprising him. "Our administration was almost entirely white. If K and I got sent up to the principal's office together, K would get two weeks' detention and I'd get let off with a warning. Not really the minority when that happens, you know?"

Wow. "I… I never thought of it like that." Ellery's private school had been a combination of Jewish, Catholic, and wealthy Middle Eastern students. Yeah, they'd split into factions, but usually their disputes were settled on the debate floor.

"Kaden was *so* behind me becoming a cop." Jackson's eyes went blind to the glory of Ellery's bedroom, and although Ellery couldn't resent him for it, he could wonder—would he ever measure up? "He wanted somebody in there who wanted to be part of the community. I mean, you've got the cops who harass the kids in front of their homes and the cops who play catch with them if the kids'll let them. We wanted one of *those* cops in the system."

"What about when you became a PI?"

He had to ask it, even if it made Jackson startle and take stock of his surroundings like he was coming back from a particularly vivid vision.

"He was glad it was for a defense firm." Jackson gave him a quick grin. "He said the people we knew in school were more likely to end up needing a defense attorney anyway, so I could still give some back."

Ellery let out a pained laugh. "So? Have you seen any?"

Jackson shook his head. "From our neighborhood? They can't afford our firm. But the partners have let us do some pro bono work that I'm really proud of."

"The Getchell case," Ellery remembered. Jackson had seen him in court.

"Yeah." Jackson let out a breath and started to massage his neck as he sat down on the bed. "Well, grab your suit and your pj's, Cramer. If you're going to sleep in my guest room—"

Ellery sighed and toed off his shoes. Jackson's suit was relatively stain-free, but he was still going to have it dry-cleaned just to be courteous, and it was still hot enough to crisp a man's eyebrows outside. He turned his back as he undressed, from general habit more than anything else. "I told you," he said, looking at Jackson in his closet mirror, "I'm spending the night in your bed."

Jackson scowled. And got up and walked out of the room.

In bemusement, Ellery watched him go, wondering if maybe he was pushing too hard.

But Jackson could overpower him with a flick of the wrist. And right now, he hadn't said no.

ELLERY CHANGED into some walking shorts and a microfiber T-shirt, and they had dinner at a little brewpub on J Street. Jackson flirted with the tiny brunette waitress, a girl whose plainness was practically forgotten after her first smile. She helped him scrounge up some takeout for his ugly ferocious cat, whom she knew by name. Jackson left a generous tip, and as they were walking out of the pub, she said, "Jackson! You going to keep this one?"

Jackson cast a furtive look at Ellery under his brows. "This one's sleeping on the couch," he muttered.

The girl's happy gurgle of laughter warmed Ellery's heart. "Sure he is. I'll take that as a maybe. See you both later!"

They stepped out into the early evening city swelter for the two-block walk to the parking lot. Ellery was careful to avoid the giant sidewalk cracks caused by the many fruitless mulberry trees, but once he found his footing, he bumped Jackson's shoulder purposefully.

"I take it she's stayed at your house?"

"Yup." He cast Ellery a sideways look. "You even going to ask?"

"The couch or your bed? No."

"You don't care?"

Ellery thought about it as they finished their walk. "Well, I *do* care," he said after a five-minute pause during which neither of them spoke. "I mean, you've slept with half the city. It's a lot to live up to. But it's not going to matter."

"Because you're sleeping on the couch?"

"It's cute how you keep bringing that up like it's a real possibility. No." He clicked the remote.

Jackson growled to himself and then swung into the car. Ellery waited for him to say something, using every instinct he'd honed in seven years as a practicing attorney to remain patient. Jackson wanted to say something—he *did*—but if Ellery prompted him now, he'd be shut tight forever more. *C'mon, Jackson... c'mon... opening up isn't that hard. C'mon, buddy... five, four, three, two....*

"Then why?" Jackson asked just as they made the turn to Elvas.

Ellery let out a breath he hadn't known he'd been holding. "Why what?" God—he'd forgotten the question!

"Why won't it matter?"

Oh! Suddenly Ellery's uncertainty evaporated like their sweat as they'd been walking. "Because I'm going to be the only one you remember," he said, voice hard. "And if you shake me off, everybody you fuck afterward is going to be a pale imitation."

Jackson made a weak laughing sound, but Ellery paused at a stoplight and looked at him. He wasn't really laughing at all. Instead he was staring out into space, brows knit, like he was trying to decide the truth of the words.

To Ellery, who was used to assessing people, their motives, what they would say or do next, this was a *very* good sign.

Mike wasn't working outside, and his truck wasn't parked out front either. Jackson grunted, nodding at the empty space. "He's working at the station tonight. Jade texted me—she was glad to have him."

Ellery thought about the older man, salty and blunt and terrifyingly capable. "Yeah, well, God help anyone who tries to fuck with him. He'd probably beat a bad cop into submission with a crescent wrench."

That startled a guffaw out of Jackson, and he was laughing as he got to the front door—and then stopped.

His entire spine went rigid, and Ellery could see him quivering in anger.

"What?" he asked softly.

"Someone's been here," Jackson said, voice throaty with anger. "The door's been jimmied, see? Scratch marks—fresh."

He tried the knob gingerly and then unlocked it before giving Ellery an impatient look over his shoulder. "Really? We're going to have sex on the porch?"

Ellery took a step back so their bodies were no longer touching and grimaced. "Not a plan."

"Just wait here," he muttered and pushed in. Ellery followed, because he was done taking orders that required more distance between them than necessary.

The house wasn't trashed, but Ellery thought Jackson was definitely right. There was something wrong. The chill of the air-conditioning hit them with their first breath—and Ellery clearly remembered Jackson turning it off as they'd left.

"They cleaned up your table," Ellery said, stating the obvious.

"Yeah. Okay. The coffee cups are in the sink and—" He looked at Ellery like this should have been obvious. "They went through the paperwork stacked on the table and probably tried to look at my computer files." He chuckled lowly, sounding decidedly unfriendly.

"Encrypted?" Ellery asked.

"I had Crystal do the security. She worked for an identity-theft ring for a while when she was using—she could teach Homeland a thing or two." Jackson's grimness returned. "Fuck. Do you think they let the fucking cat out? Billy? Billy Bob? C'mon, you little fucker, let me know you're here!"

He wandered off, calling more and more frantically for Billy Bob, and Ellery swallowed hard against the feeling of invasion. Someone had been here. *Here.* Granted, Jackson's house was pretty much Grand Central for one-night lovers, but still, there was something personal about it. The squeaky place on the tile, the pictures of the Cameron family, including a few of Jade and Jackson, on the hallway walls. The purple afghan over the back of the brown corduroy couch and the scrap quilt on the matching recliner—these were personal things. Whether they'd been made for Jackson or he'd picked them up at a consignment store, this was Jackson's personal space in a way that Ellery's house was not.

Ellery resented the fuck out of whoever had been there.

And it would hit him later—and hard—that he didn't even think of calling the cops.

"Billy!" The relief throbbing in Jackson's voice tore at Ellery's chest a little. The cat. The cat was the one thing in his life that was his and his alone.

Jackson came into the kitchen holding an overly affectionate Billy Bob, and Ellery had time to admire, yet again, the animal's truly battered appearance. But Billy Bob was repeatedly rubbing his whiskers against Jackson's nose, so being battered and scarred apparently didn't mean he was incapable of love.

And Jackson was clearly his home.

"Did you see anything else?" Ellery asked, walking over to scratch the cat under the chin. Billy Bob accepted the gesture warily but didn't growl—a definite win!

"Yeah. Someone went through the boxes in the guest room closet. Mostly pictures and yearbooks and stuff, but they'd sifted through it. There were blurry handprints in the dust. Gloves—you could tell." Jackson shook his head, jaw clenched. "They were looking for something but—"

"Didn't want you to know what it was," Ellery said, nodding. "Yeah. And something paperwork related. I'll bet you anything it was—"

"My file." Jackson took a deep breath, and then another, until Billy Bob squirmed out of his arms because of the discomfort. Jackson closed his eyes and pinched the bridge of his nose and shook, just trembled from the effort of controlling himself, from keeping it all together. His home—his sanctuary—and his brutal past, all of it, violated. He was so proud.

Ellery ached for him.

Carefully, knowing he was risking anything from a scathing comment to a crack in the jaw, he stepped into Jackson's space and gently brushed his lips across a sweaty blond temple.

Jackson took a deep breath and let it out slowly, but didn't back away.

Ellery put a hand on each shoulder and kissed his cheekbone.

And another slow, simmering breath, and this time—Ellery could swear to it in a court of law—Jackson leaned forward, just a hair, just a heartbeat closer, just a—

Ellery kissed the corner of his mouth, allowing his tongue to come out and trace the seam of his lips.

Jackson clasped his face in both hands, crashing his mouth on Ellery's and plundering with irresistible force.

Ellery gasped and dropped his hands to Jackson's hips as Jackson backed him up against the refrigerator, magnets and papers flying. He kissed—*devoured*—taking with a fierceness that should have frightened a sex-in-the-dark guy like Ellery Cramer.

It exhilarated him.

He returned the kiss, shoving his hands down the waistband of Jackson's jeans, kneading his taut, muscled ass and grinding them together through their clothes. Jackson growled and ground back, hard and unmistakable.

Ellery's hands shook as he took advantage of ease in the fit and shoved the jeans down Jackson's thighs. Jackson grunted in surprise and then plummeted back into the kiss some more, leaving Ellery to play. He kept one hand kneading a taut asscheek, fingers slipping closer and closer to Jackson's crease.

With the other he gripped Jackson's cock without apology, squeezing and trying hard to stroke in the limited space between them. He skated the edge of his thumb around the cockhead, sliding in the slit, and Jackson ripped his mouth away.

"My bedroom," he ordered. "Condoms. Lube. Now."

Ellery dropped to his knees instead. He wanted time to admire, to tease and torment, but this was not that time. He opened his mouth and engulfed, lips stretched, throat abused, and he was barely halfway down. He wrapped his fist around the bottom of Jackson's cock to make up the difference, and Jackson's hands slapped the refrigerator above them. Ellery pulled back for a moment without letting go and realized that Jackson was supporting his weight against his arms and that there was a definite tremble to his knees.

Ellery dove forward again, swallowing, tasting soap and sweat and man. Jackson let out a gasp, and he tasted bitter salt, and that was good too.

He craved more, shoving his head farther, swallowing, wanting *everything*, wanting his mouth full of come, overflowing, wanting it down his throat and down his face and neck. He wanted Jackson on his skin.

Jackson knotted his fingers in Ellery's hair, pulling him back. Ellery went reluctantly and looked up at him, eyes narrowed as he licked the spit from around his lips in blatant invitation.

"Bed," Jackson repeated. "Condoms. Lube. *Now*."

"Sure," Ellery told him and then went down one more time, pulling back before Jackson could haul him up by the armpits. Jackson gave him a hand up and kissed him again, back against the refrigerator. Ellery pushed him, and he whirled, walking Ellery backward as they bumped against the table, the doorway, the walls, kissing, grabbing, biting each other's lips and yanking at each other's clothes in their tumble down the hall.

Ellery lost himself for a moment, Jackson's hands everywhere: stomach, flank, thighs, backside, neck, chest—nipples, oh dear God, his nipples! He regained control naked on the stripped bed as an equally naked Jackson rifled through the bedstand for the jumbo box of rubbers and giant bottle of lubricant.

"Could you *be* any more seventies porn star," Ellery snarked, breathless.

Jackson pinned him with a glare as he sheathed up. "Yeah—my sheets are fuckin' clean."

Ellery glared back, aware that Jackson had taken the issue of who topped into his own well-filled hand.

"Spread 'em," Jackson growled.

Ellery did, thinking this was wrong. He could feel it. Not the sex—his blood pounded fiercely inside his skin, stretching it, threatening to explode outward unless he got some relief from the terrible pressure. The sex was inevitable, necessary, *cataclysmic*—but how....

Jackson needed. He needed.

"Condom." He held out a hand, thinking Jackson would assume he was just too fastidious, or even positive, but not caring.

Jackson threw one at him without question, and Ellery slicked it on before his hands shook too hard. Then he lifted his thighs, holding them with his arms, baring himself wantonly—even comically so—but making his asshole target zero in Jackson's mission to lose himself.

He was prepared for pain, for roughness, impatience.

He was *not* prepared for Jackson's gentle touch on his thighs, his palms warming, massaging, loosening. Jackson moved closer, supporting Ellery's legs against his torso, and kissed the insides of his knees, smoothed his hands up Ellery's stomach, and tickled the crown of his sheathed cock.

Ellery groaned and tilted his head back, forcing himself to relax and not to scream, begging under Jackson's gentleness, the reverence this rough man was showing his body.

Jackson dropped his thighs and settled between them, kissing his way up the planes of Ellery's abdomen, underneath his pecs, then between them. When he got to Ellery's throat, Ellery's eyes were squeezed shut, and every brush of Jackson's lips roared through him like sound.

Jackson traced a slow line from Ellery's chin to his ear and then whispered, "Please tell me you like it. Tell me you're begging to be fucked."

"Augh!" Truth was, Ellery loved a good fucking—he just hadn't really gotten one yet. But something told him he wasn't supposed to just yield and close his eyes and be made love to like a *gift*. He'd gotten plenty of gifts in his life—he was tired of *gifts*. He wanted to fucking *give*, and give to this man, but Jackson was in control right now, and Ellery wouldn't take that from him for the world.

Jackson reached between them and stroked him hard, until Ellery saw stars in the effort not to come.

"*Yes!*" he begged, angry at himself for giving in. "God, yes, take me, dammit! C'mon, Jackson, *fuck me!*"

Jackson fumbled with the lube briefly, and again that terrible, terrible controlled gentleness, the slow circles around his sphincter, and gentle one-finger penetration after.

Ellery groaned and pushed forward some more, impaling himself and allowing that finger to saw back and forth, pushing gently, opening him up for the bigger intrusion to come.

One finger. That was all, and Ellery was gibbering, all intentions of holding out forgotten. He started to shake with orgasm, and Jackson squeezed the head of his cock through the condom.

Which was so thin it didn't feel like it was there at all.

Ellery let out a sound that wasn't human as what should have been his orgasm rolled through him, surging under his skin, washing him hot and cold. When it was over, sweat sheened his skin and Jackson had three fingers in his ass, and Ellery was done.

He arched his torso off the bed and screamed, "Fuck me, motherfucker! I fucking need! Fuck me!"

Jackson yanked his fingers out so fast Ellery keened at the ache, and then… oh God, it was huge, painful by its very existence, and it battered into his body like the mast of a giant sailing ship.

Ellery howled and shoved his pelvis down so he could take more of that thing up his ass.

"Want it want it want it," he chanted, until Jackson gave a last little thrust and grunted, lodged all the way in. Ellery's muscles contracted and released in a wave, radiating from his asshole out, leaving him to scrabble helplessly at Jackson's shoulders as he moaned and begged for more.

"Oh God. Jackson… please… for fuck's sake, move. Please move… please… I need you to… *yesssss*!"

Jackson began to rock back and forth rhythmically, hard and slow, each thrust punctuated by the slapping together of their skin.

Every thrust was another revelation of stars behind Ellery's eyelids. He could have come already, with Jackson's fingers, with the first penetration of his cock, and with every thrust to the hilt. He could have exploded, filling the condom with come—but he didn't.

He held on, held on to his orgasm, controlled it with every last ounce of power he had.

Because Jackson wasn't just fucking him, he was kissing him, showering his face with kisses, with gentle blessings, with reassurance.

"You're awesome, God, so sweet. Could fuck you forever…. It's okay, let go…."

So sweet.

Ellery opened his eyes and saw Jackson, his jaw locked, his shoulders shaking and sweating with control. Oh God. Look at them locked in this dance to see who would be in charge. Ellery wanted to give in—with all his flesh, he did.

Instead he reached up and cupped Jackson's cheeks with both hands and hauled him down for a kiss, so filthily intimate that the steady power-fuck stalled out and Jackson melted into him, muscular arms buckling as his practiced dance became a sweaty grapple.

Jackson moaned into his mouth, the effort that had kept him in control suddenly destroyed by a simple kiss.

Ellery kept kissing, raising his heels up to force Jackson as deep as he could go. God, so close.

With an effort, he ripped his mouth away and whispered in Jackson's ear. "Come."

Jackson lost it, rutting inside him mindlessly, making rabid, feral snarling noises in the hollow of Ellery's shoulder.

"*Come!*" Ellery cried, and oh God, *yes*, he felt it, a mighty pulse inside his ass as Jackson mewled in pleasure and pain and gave in, ceded the reins to Ellery's hands as he came, vulnerable and needing, inside Ellery's body.

Ellery nuzzled his ear, whispering, "I've got you. It's okay, I've got you. Come. I've got you. I'll protect you. Don't worry. Just come."

The spasms finally stopped, and Jackson collapsed against him, shuddering. His abdomen squashed Ellery's cock, still swollen from arousal, still on the cusp of orgasm, against his own stomach, and Ellery squeezed, pushing Jackson out.

"But...." Jackson pulled back, chest heaving, and regarded Ellery from puzzled, nearly crossed eyes. "But you didn't—"

His muscles were slack and soft, which was the only reason Ellery could flip them over with a few quick heaves of his legs and stomach. And then he lay, hands on Jackson's biceps, groins mashing together. Jackson's come was running out of the condom, and Ellery sat up and pulled it off. It hit the trash can next to the bed when he tossed it.

"But...."

Ellery bent his head and kissed him again, hard, and then pulled up and kissed down his throat. Jackson groaned, tilting his head back, and gave Ellery complete access. Ellery pulled hard on the skin, hard enough to mark, and Jackson bucked his hips, his dick filling slowly with blood again.

"My turn," Ellery murmured, licking a soft line down Jackson's collarbone. He wrapped his lips delicately around a tulip-pink nipple, and the low moan that followed told him he'd done that just right. He pulled a little harder and Jackson moaned a little deeper, and again, until Jackson was grinding and thrusting up and Ellery was pinning him down. He kissed across that muscular chest, stopping to graze the tender pinkness of the scarring there with his lips. Jackson pushed gently at his head, and Ellery met his eyes and shook his head.

And kissed it again—gently, in case there was still pain, but purposefully—because this was important. Ellery knew the scars were there, and he knew what caused them, and they were part and parcel of the man.

Jackson looked away, and Ellery kissed his scars one last time and moved to the other nipple. He licked it first and then pulled, and harder, before he fumbled with the lubricant without stopping his tormenting suckle.

He managed a healthy dollop on his fingers and then reached into Jackson's crevice, hoping Jackson wasn't too tender for this to feel good. He slid his slicked fingers respectfully between Jackson's cheeks, shifting to get his hand in to work. Gently, he slid a little bit of lube across Jackson's pucker, and the whine of arousal gratified him *very* much.

"You like that?" he asked. *C'mon, man, tell the truth. If you say no, I have to stop.*

"Nnngh… ahhh…."

Ellery slid just his fingertip in at that second syllable, and he studied Jackson's face, closed eyes, slack expression, and hoped—*oh God, let this work.*

He slid it in deeper, and Jackson braced his feet against the bed, spread his knees, and bore down, swallowing his finger in one lunge.

"Mm," Ellery murmured, pulling it out a little and sliding it back in. "You like this?"

"Nungh…."

"Come on, Jackson. I've got to come like a motherfucker, and I need you to use your words." He slid it in again and added a second finger.

"Oh… oh… oh my God," Jackson moaned. "Oh—*yes!*"

Oh yes!

Ellery scissored his fingers, stretching, while he nuzzled Jackson's chest and sucked on his nipples. He damned the fact they didn't have a washcloth. He wanted to suck that amazing cock some more. They didn't, and Jackson needed to be tested, but it would happen.

Instead, he pulled his fingers out and scooted up again, positioning himself at Jackson's entrance.

His cock ached fiercely.

"Jackson, man, you need to ask me for this."

Jackson's eyes opened reluctantly, and his mouth dropped, lower lip wobbling. He was lost, so lost. Ellery nudged him gently, but hard enough to let him know that he wanted it.

"You need to ask."

Jackson closed his eyes. "Please," he begged softly. "But… slow."

"Yeah."

Ah… slow. So slow. Sweat dropped from Ellery's forehead to Jackson's cheek as he pushed in gently, and with every millimeter, tight flesh snapped around him, holding him like a velvet vise.

"Good?" he asked, holding on to himself desperately.

"Yesss," Jackson breathed, closing his eyes. "Faster. Harder. Now." "*Yes!*"

Ellery shoved his hips forward, and Jackson's joyful scream rewarded him. Oh *yes*, faster and harder, pushing into that delirious heat. Jackson started a low, stuttered moan of pleading, and Ellery didn't let him down.

"You need this, you fucking need it, and I'm gonna fucking give it to you!"

"Yes," Jackson conceded. His eyes were closed, his thighs were spread, and he was melted, pliable as butter against Ellery's body, and all Ellery wanted was for him to be lost in what Ellery could provide.

"Fucking *mine*, you hear me? *Mine*—no one else's, you're fucking *mine* and I fucking want you. I want you, and I'm taking you, and I'm never giving you back!"

Oh yeah, he meant it. Six years watching this body rough-and-tumble into his life, his workplace, his *dreams*?

"Oh," Jackson breathed, and then, just when Ellery thought he was going to *die* from deferred orgasm, an amazing thing happened.

Jackson let out another moan, this one low, guttural, ripped from his pelvic floor, and blessed heavens, he *came*, another climax wrung out of him, seed jetting out in a hard spurt, limbs twitching feebly and going limp as the last bit of his energy and will was spent with his come.

Ellery took one look at Jackson, slack-jawed, bemused, vulnerable, and sexed out, and his orgasm steamrolled through him, starting with his toes and working its way up to his groin, where it exploded outward.

He screamed, entire body twitching, no more control over his limbs than a piece of spaghetti had in a boiling pot. Climax rocked him. He poured come into the condom in Jackson's ass and collapsed, sobbing, face buried in the hollow of Jackson's shoulder.

He couldn't have moved if someone had put a gun to his head.

After several moments of harsh breathing, sweating bodies stuck together unable to move, he became aware of a few things at once.

One was that his eyes were burning, slow tears leaking from the corners. Another was that Jackson was still giving fractured little moans with every tenth breath, almost like sobs.

The last thing was that Jackson had raised a shaking, clammy hand to Ellery's hair and was gently, so gently, stroking it back off his forehead.

Ellery pulled away just enough to see his expression, and he looked… haunted. A little frightened. Alone. Ellery lowered his head for a kiss, and then another, and another. He pulled away and whispered in Jackson's ear.

"It's okay, you know? I'm here."

Jackson nodded and looked away, and Ellery turned his head so his cheek was on a muscled shoulder. His softening cock slid reluctantly from Jackson's ass, and he swallowed.

It was okay. Jackson wouldn't believe it just yet. Why should he? As far as Ellery could see, the world hadn't done Jackson Rivers many favors. Good friends he'd fought to keep—that was one.

And now Ellery Cramer was another.

But how would he know that with just one fuck? He'd learn.

ELLERY HAD rolled to the side so they could cool off in the air-conditioning, and their breathing returned to normal before he heard the knock at the door.

Ellery shot up, muttering, "Shit! That's probably your car. I'll go sign for it."

"I can sign for it," Jackson said, casting him a look of annoyance. "Stay there." His smile broke up the irritation. "I like looking at you naked."

Ellery felt the color flush up his throat, and he smiled shyly from under the fall of hair at his brow. "Nice to hear," he said softly. Jackson winked and slid into his jeans commando-style, then strode to the front door in a hurry.

Ellery lay back on the bed and listened to the muffled sound of voices, and when Jackson returned, he was skeptically jingling the keys to the SUV. "You really think nobody's going to notice that car?"

Ellery smiled a little. "Only if they look at your obsessive-compulsive litter in the back."

Jackson frowned and shoved the keys into his pocket. "How do you know about that?"

"Did you ever have a crush on someone, Jackson?"

Jackson narrowed his eyes. "Not of the stalking kind," he said. "I mean… I thought you were hot, but I didn't care what you ate for lunch."

"No?" Oh, of all things, how was this not a human touchstone? "How do you not have a crush in school?"

"Well," Jackson said, throwing himself across the bed jeans and all, "you spend your first years worried about getting beat the hell up or getting food. Then you lose your virginity at fourteen to your buddy's twin sister, and vice versa, and you pretty much fill in the empty places that way until you split up after high school. And *then* you're a grown-up, and if you see someone you like, you ask them out, and if they say yes, you go out, and if they say no, you ask the person next to them and see."

Ellery laughed like he was supposed to and ran his hands through the haphazard tumble of Jackson's dark blond hair. "And then you get scared and hurt and you become a walking condom commercial," he said softly. "I think I see."

Jackson's eyes darkened, and he swallowed angrily. "Don't feel sorry for—"

"I don't." Ellery closed his eyes and then looked at Jackson head-on. "I… I want you to know where I'm coming from. For the last six years, you've been sardonic and dangerous and… and fucking *hot*. And I had a crush, you understand? So when we actually make it into bed together, it's not going to go away. It's going to get deeper. It's going to mean something. I may not be your high-school sweetheart—"

Jackson snorted.

"—*but* that doesn't mean what we just did isn't important to me."

Jackson let out a sigh and turned his head away, resting his cheek on his outstretched arm. "Can't we just go back to fucking?" he said plaintively. "It's always so much easier when it's just—"

"Making love." Ellery cupped his cheek and scooted so they were lying face to face. "It doesn't have to be important, Jackson, but c'mon. Talk to me."

"'Bout what?" And it wasn't Ellery's imagination—he was *trying* to sound like a pouty schoolboy.

"I don't know. What's your favorite movie?"

"Easy. *Full Metal Jacket*. What's yours?"

"*The King's Speech*." Ellery sighed. "That is *not* promising."

Jackson rolled to his stomach. "Favorite kids' cartoon?" he said cautiously.

"*Darkwing Duck*!" Ellery said excitedly.

"Let's get dangerous?" He wrinkled his nose.

"Well, I was a neurotic kid from the suburbs. A comic duck was as dangerous as I was going to get!" Ellery defended, laughing. "Your turn."

"*Transformers*," Jackson gave up reluctantly.

"More than meets the eye!" Ellery did his best robot impersonation and surprised a laugh from Jackson. "You know, like you."

"You are making me really uncomfortable in my masculinity," Jackson said, drawing his dignity about him like a cloak. "I have had about enough pillow talk, thank you." He stood up and rummaged through his dresser to come up with a tank top. "Okay, I don't know about you, but I want something cold and sweet, and I've got nothing in my freezer. And I've got a… a… *Honda* in my driveway that is *not* feeling any more real with me sitting in here. Grab your notes and let's go for a drive."

Ellery grinned at him. "I might want to grab my pants first."

"You're just excited someone took them off you," Jackson muttered, but Ellery could see two red crescents appearing at his cheekbones.

"Absolutely," Ellery agreed. "And I hope you plan to take them off again."

Jackson scrupulously avoided eye contact and started looking on the floor for Ellery's clothes. "Yeah, whatever," he mumbled.

But Ellery's enthusiasm was undimmed. Ellery Cramer *was* dangerous, and Jackson Rivers *was* more than met the eye, and his optimism knew no bounds.

Fish Under the Bridge

THE PIERCING light of justice knifed through Jackson's eyeballs like an ice pick, and someone was hammering Armageddon down on his head with every thud at the door.

"*Jackson, open up, you asshole! I need some fucking money!*"

"Oh God," Jackson muttered, burying his head under the pillow. "No. Fuck no. Not today."

Ellery shoved at his arm. "Jackson, who is that and why is she doing this to us?"

Oh hell. Ellery was there. Ellery was *still* there, and they were naked, and his sheets smelled like sex, because they'd had it *twice* more last night. The first time was right after they'd gotten back from their drive to the park for ice cream and cold soda, and that time Ellery had let Jackson top. Not like he was humoring him—no. Just like he *enjoyed* that position and didn't mind getting his ass plowed.

They'd gotten up and done some more work after that. Ellery had drawn up briefs, and Jackson had made lists of contacts and researched all the key players in the game until he was done.

Then Ellery had stood up and stretched and gone in to brush his teeth. Jackson had turned out the lights and locked the door and gone to do the same—

And found Ellery in his bed when he stepped out.

He'd been wearing his boxers and smiling sleepily at the door, and Jackson couldn't decide which was stronger: the urge to bolt, or the urge to climb in with him and maybe plunder his mouth some more, or glide his palms over the smooth skin of his ribcage.

Ellery had seen him hesitate and had just… lain there, eyebrows up, the knowledge that he wasn't getting out of the bed unless Jackson asked him to lying heavy between them.

He had made his position loud and clear. Jackson had to tell him, or he wouldn't change his course.

Which meant that if Jackson turned around and went to sleep on the couch, Ellery would know him for the coward he really was.

Mortifying but true—and still almost not enough to get Jackson in that bed, where a man who knew his secrets and didn't care waited. A man who was willing to fight for his family and who seemed willing to take Jackson, baggage and all.

Because God, if Ellery was willing to deal with all of *that* shit, what would happen to Jackson when he *couldn't* deal anymore and Jackson was left alone? He'd fought so hard to not *need* anybody.

What would happen if he let himself need?

Ellery seemed to see inside him, though. "Don't worry, Jackson. I'll still be here in the morning."

"Everyone's here in the morning," Jackson muttered. "They just don't come back the next night."

"Because you don't let them." Ellery's dark eyes bored into Jackson's skull like he was daring Jackson to deny it. "But I think we've already established that you don't 'let' me do anything. I can decide for myself."

And that was the crux of the matter, wasn't it? Ellery *was* strong enough to decide for himself. He *did* know what he was getting into.

And Jackson didn't know what to do with that.

So he turned off the light, let the cat in for the final time, and crawled into bed.

And was surprised by Ellery's mouth on his own in the dark and how sweet their fingers felt on each other's skin. They used their hands, stroking each other off to a sleepy climax, and for once Jackson was too tired—and too sated—to make the person in his bed get up so he could change the sheets.

The dream tried to creep up on him in the wee hours, but Ellery rolled over and spooned him, rubbing his shoulders, pulling him back against Ellery's front, and the dream went away.

The next day was Saturday, and Jackson had been pretty sure they'd get to sleep in before he started making his investigative rounds, and that had given him some peace too.

Until now.

"Oh God," he groaned again and then rolled out of bed and put his jeans on, not even wanting to *look* at Ellery, who was as naked as he'd been and probably rumpled and sexy and dear. "Hell. Fuck. Shit. Cock.

Bugger. *Ass*." He stumbled to the doorway and then turned to Ellery in naked supplication. "Look, if you respect me even a little at *all*, you will just hang out in here and pretend you never heard the following conversation, okay?"

Ellery raised his eyebrows and was probably just about to say "Fuck no!" when Jackson whirled on one heel and took off for the front door.

Shit. Mike had worked late at the station the night before, and the *last* time she'd visited, he'd threatened to shoot her in the head. Jackson really did not want to have to look for another tenant while he visited his friend in prison.

"All right!" he called. "I'm coming, I'm coming—Jesus *fuck*, bitch, can we fucking *not* wake up the entire fucking neighborhood?"

He tore the door open and glared at the woman on the other side.

She was exactly forty-five this year, but it was a hard-lived forty-five. The lines in her thin face were etched deep, and her upper arms and shoulders, exposed by the tight white tank top she wore, were crepey and sun weathered. Her hair was bleached blonde, her face was freckled with too much sun, and her denim miniskirt clung tightly to an ass that had been slender when she'd been a new mother at fifteen but was now emaciated and bony.

Her blue eyes were hooded, obscured by lines in the corners, none of them laugh lines, and her fingers as they rose up to knock at the door were yellow, stained so badly by nicotine that it crusted under her nails.

There was a cigarette smoldering in her other hand, held carelessly between her first two fingers, and the smoke rose up in a choking cloud.

"Is that what you greet me with, you high-and-mighty bastard? Did you just call me a fucking bitch?"

"Yes. And I'm going to slam the door in your face if you don't put the cigarette out—*not* on my lawn, bitch. I've told you before, Celia, you can't smoke in my house."

She sniffed disdainfully and shook her bony ass down the lawn to the sidewalk, where she flicked the butt and ground it out under her thin-soled sandal, and then sauntered back. Jackson crossed his arms and leaned against the doorframe, praying to God that Ellery had stayed in the bedroom like he'd asked.

Oh Jesus. Of all the reasons Jackson didn't want people to see how he lived, this one right here was right at the top of the list.

"You're *still* not going to let me in?" she whined when she got back up to the door. "I just—"

"What do you want, Celia?"

"A new tattoo," she said promptly, and he grimaced. She'd gotten a few over the years. The ink was still visible on her breastbone and her back, especially since the spaghetti tank she wore covered not much of her flat chest. With the amount of time she spent in the sun—and the number of times she'd chosen drugs or liquor over food—that ink had all turned purple and bled, leaving behind only faint, discolored memories of the images she'd originally wanted.

He was pretty sure the one on her neck was a butterfly, but it had looked like a Rorschach test since he was ten.

"I'm not going to fund your next tattoo," he muttered. "Try again."

"Rehab?" she said, what should have been an impish grin creasing her features. It made her look like an evil gnome.

"If I believed *that*, I would have sent you years ago," he said, bored. "One more try and I can legally *kick you* off my porch. And if you won't go without holy water, I'll see if Mike's home and he can wave his .45 around and see if *that* scares you."

"Jackson!" she whined. "I'm hungry! Can't you even give your own mother some food?"

A memory swamped him, a childhood he'd tried hard to forget. Jackson, five or six, hungry—hunger beyond hunger, the kind of gnawing in your belly that won't let you think. Watching Celia—younger, prettier, up-for-anything Celia—snorting coke she'd paid for with food stamps. Jackson had come in asking for some food, and her dealer had thrown him a granola bar just to make him go away.

He took a deep breath, a controlled one, to keep the violence at bay.

Remembered when he was twelve and Kaden's mom had divided a lasagna that was supposed to last them two days—and eked out a portion for Jackson, who hadn't eaten in that long either.

"You're not my mother," he said coldly. And saw, clear as day, Kaden's mom in a wheelchair when he graduated from the academy, skin an ash-colored parody of the comforting dark brown he remembered from his school days, her body wasted with cancer she couldn't afford to fight. He owed Toni and J and K better.

"Wait," he said before she could retort. "I'll give you food—and money for whatever—if you stay right there and answer a question or two."

He took a step back, closed the door, and started down the hallway for his phone, which was in the charger by the bed.

Ellery was in the kitchen by the sink, where he could have seen the whole exchange on the landing. Jackson glared at him and headed right past him and down the hall.

"Wait, where are you going?" Ellery called.

"I need the picture of Luanne Chisholm," he muttered, grabbing his phone. He hustled back, bare feet making hollow slaps on the hardwood. He swung open the door again, and Celia was still there, glaring resentfully at the doorway.

"Here," he said imperiously, pulling up the picture. "Her. You seen her?"

"I don't know every chickie in the old neighborhood," she retorted.

Jackson grabbed her shoulder and made her actually look. "Have. You. Seen. Her?" he growled.

Celia didn't do what he expected. "I thought you were out of that, Jacky." Her voice lowered, and the look she sent him was almost tender. "I mean… I know you were… you were hurt last time. I thought you'd be staying away from this sort of thing after that?"

Jackson's stomach gave a triumphant *kazing!* while his heart… tried really hard not to engage. "This is for a case, Celia. Her name is Luanne Chisholm and—"

"I didn't have anything to do with it, Jacky," Celia said, backing away from him. "I swear. I—I wasn't there. I just heard from Jimmy—you know Jimmy? Guy used to feed you when you were a kid. Well, he's lookin' for more girls, yanno, and he said the cops… well, this one ain't workin' no more."

Hell. Mentally, Jackson put *check morgue* on the top of his list.

In real time, he pulled a twenty out of the wallet in his pocket and held it out to her. From mother to confidential informant. Well, she'd never been great at motherhood.

"Here," he said, shoving the money into her greedy hand.

"Aw, Jacky, that won't buy me—"

He added another twenty. "Wait right here. I'll get you some food."

Ellery was still in the kitchen, wearing his boxer shorts and making coffee, and Jackson felt the strangest sense of longing. He'd had a fantasy—a stupid normal fantasy—of the two of them drinking coffee in his kitchen that morning.

He thought of the woman outside who'd spawned him, and how she'd contaminated his day with her nicotine-stained fingers, and he wanted to flee. Without looking at Ellery, he grabbed a plastic bag from the drawer and shoved most of a loaf of bread in it, as well as half a jar of peanut butter and an unopened bag of store-brand Cheerios. He sprinted back to the door and hauled it open just in time to see Celia hit the sidewalk and turn right, the money probably already shoved in her purse. She lit a cigarette as she went.

He stopped, chest heaving, and spent a fruitless breath hating himself fiercely. Stupid. Stupid, stupid, stupid—he knew it when he was six. You'd think he'd learn.

He turned back around and threw the bag on top of the refrigerator, where the plastic jar of peanut butter thumped loudly. Shower. Next on the agenda. Turning away and heading for the shower was his best bet for not having to look at Ellery, not having to see the pity or the acknowledgment there or even answer any questions.

"Shower," he mumbled. "Back in ten."

He was out of the kitchen before Ellery had a chance to answer.

He was careful with his jeans—they had his phone and his wallet in them still—but he didn't wait until the water heated up to step under. For a few moments, he shivered under the spray, numb and trying desperately to get his sense of self back in place. College. The police academy. A year in the hospital. Eight years putting himself back together. *This* was who he was, not the child mewling for a granola bar from a drug dealer.

This.

He barely startled when the curtain pulled aside and Ellery stepped in. "I'll be out in a sec," he mumbled, eyes focused on the corner of the tub.

"Jade's in the kitchen," Ellery said, sliding behind him and wrapping an arm around his waist.

Jackson took a breath and straightened his spine. "Damn. I *really* have to—"

"She's borrowing coffee for Mike's coffeemaker. She'll let herself out. I guess she brought him home last night."

Jackson frowned, trying to remember if he'd seen Jade's car on the curb or not. He must have, right? "Why didn't she come in and sleep on my couch?" he asked, grateful for something to think about.

"I guess because she was happier sleeping in his bed," Ellery said, laughing a little.

Jackson took a moment to absorb that. "I think my head just exploded."

"Yes, well, she said the same thing about us, so you're even. I *would* posit the fact that he's not bad-looking, and leave it at that."

"You think?" Because Mike had never pinged him that way—not even a little.

"Yeah. He's like a redneck Sean Bean."

Jackson took a minute to absorb that. For some reason it made the whole weirdness better. "Well, he's only forty-five—I mean, stranger things."

"Yeah."

The soberness in Ellery's voice took him by surprise.

"I could have… I could have done without you ever meeting her," he said after a moment. "Or seeing her. Or hearing her. Or knowing she was alive." He wasn't talking about Jade.

"How'd you get out?" Ellery pumped some soap into his hand and lathered it against Jackson's chest. Jackson leaned into the comfort and tried not to admit he needed it.

"Celia got pregnant," he said, hating this story. "I told her she had a new source of welfare the day I turned sixteen, and her boyfriend was happy to see me leave."

"You have a brother or sister?" Ellery sounded stunned.

"Yes and no." Jackson made a bitter sound—not a laugh, but not much else. "Celia brought her home and, after a month, got bored and tired of not getting high. She left the baby alone in the apartment all night, and Kaden and I called CPS. Welfare came and got her, and Celia had to move. The baby was finally just put into foster care for life." Jackson hated himself so much for this. "I always felt…. You know, kids in the movies, they would have taken care of the baby."

"You were sixteen," Ellery said, lathering up Jackson's thighs and then his back.

"Yeah. And Celia was fifteen when she had *me*. Which was why I didn't. 'Cause if she could fuck up that bad with *me*, there was no fucking telling what I would do."

Ellery's hand stopped, and he plastered himself along Jackson's back while the water sluiced off the suds. "Jackson?"

"What?"

"You're a good man."

"Shut up."

"I mean it."

"No, you don't. You're saying it because you think it's something I need to hear. I'm an asshole."

"Shut up," Ellery ordered. He stepped back and soaped up his hands again and started lathering up along Jackson's crease, under his balls, along his cock.

The fierce arousal of the night before began to gnaw at Jackson's innards.

"Ellery," he tried breathlessly, "we've got to... *ohhhh....*"

Ellery breached him with two fingers, and Jackson's vision washed dark as he tried to remember why he didn't let anybody do this. Anybody.

He couldn't remember. Something about intimacy and being in control. Something about knowing he could do the job right but not trusting anyone else to be able to do the same. Something about being tired of pain and not willing to risk it.

Something that didn't matter now that Ellery was stroking him from the inside out, fingers stretching, the delirious pressure in his ass increasing, his cock swelling and aching along his thigh.

"This," he gasped as Ellery thrust fingers into him again, "needs condoms!"

Ellery swore. "*You* are getting tested. Today. Now turn off the water!"

"No," Jackson muttered. Ellery pulled his fingers out, and Jackson threw a bad-tempered look over his shoulder. "Shower sex is awkward anyway."

Ellery covered Jackson's abdomen with his palm and rutted up against his thigh, his cock hard and leaking. Jackson moaned, bracing his weight with one hand and grabbing his own cock with the other, and Ellery continued to thrust, their skin growing slippery with precome because they were too close for the water to rinse it off. Jackson's own hand wasn't as *good* as Ellery's touch, and he beat furiously, trying to make up with speed and roughness what he was missing in touch.

Ellery groaned and bit his shoulder, and that twinge of pain, *that* sent him over. He gave a strangled cry, and Ellery groaned again into his back. The heat of Ellery's come painted his backside, and Jackson's semen shot whitely against the shower wall.

Now he reached down and turned off the water, and their breathing echoed in the small space.

And his ass ached with wanting. A peculiar feeling—he couldn't recall ever *needing* this act, but the memory of Ellery inside him and his own lack of control… haunted him.

It would have been one thing if he'd hated it, or if Ellery had rutted and come, leaving him high and dry. But that wasn't what happened at all, was it? Just once, someone had made Jackson's needs important.

Jackson thought wistfully that it would feel really good not to have to use condoms, even if it was just until this thing with Ellery had run its course.

"Testing?" he said into the silence.

Ellery skated an exquisitely gentle hand across his shoulder blades. "We can both go, but, well, I got tested after my last boyfriend, and it was negative. But yeah. Both of us. You'll feel safe."

Jackson reached across his shoulder, ignoring the way his muscles and scar tissue pulled when he made moves like that. He seized Ellery's hand and gently kissed the fingertips. Their bodies were drying in the air, but since it was already going to be another scorcher, he didn't think either of them cared. Of course they *might* care at the end of the day when they realized that they hadn't shampooed their hair, so he figured he should get his act together.

"Sure," he said, grateful that this, of all things, allowed him to shove Celia and the awfulness of her morning visit back in its hidden drawer in his brain. "But first I need to turn the water back on. You got my creases, but I don't think either one of us soaped up our hair."

Ellery groaned. "Ugh. Yeah. Okay. But go quick. I don't care what you say, shower sex isn't awkward enough to keep me from trying it again."

Jackson turned then, wrapped his arms around Ellery's hips, and held him for a moment before moving his lips next to a small, slightly awkward ear. "*You* are a good man," he said softly.

Then he turned away and turned the water on and got back to what had the potential to be a really shit day.

HE DROVE. Didn't say a word, just grabbed his keys and his wallet and thumped out the door in a button-down and jeans, and Ellery followed him. The night before, he'd pronounced the CR-V decent—the moonroof had been his favorite part. This morning his favorite part was that the air-conditioning system could freeze the balls off a brass monkey in the middle of an inferno.

Ah… *that* was the stuff.

As he pulled away from the curb, he saw Jade's car parked on the other side of Mike's duplex. Oh.

He grunted. "Sean Bean?"

"Yeah," Ellery said. "Sean Bean. You've seen him in *Legends*, right?"

Jackson nodded, surprised. "Yeah, I watch that one."

"Hot, right?"

"Of course!" Jade, his first lover—his best friend. "She deserves Sean Bean. She deserves better, but, you know, I've only got one tenant that she apparently slept with."

"As long as she doesn't get you." Ellery sniffed prissily.

Jackson guffawed. "It's been an intense couple of days," he said when he had breath. "Give it a week and you'll be ready to pitch me into a pit of lions, trust me."

"No. Besides, you were born in a pit of lions. I think you're quite comfortable there. And then when I wanted you back, *I'd* be at risk." Ellery had one corner of his mouth drawn up in irritation, and Jackson had to shake his head.

"It's touching that you assume anybody would want me back," he said. "Or even at all. I know what I am, and I know what I'm not. So please, let's just—"

"Stop talking," Ellery responded. "I'm bored. Where are we going?"

"Morgue at UC Davis." Jackson's voice hardened. "I know when Celia's lying and I know when she's scared. She saw the picture of Luanne, and she was scared. And she said, 'I thought you weren't a part of that' and talked about me getting hurt, which tells us…." He waited for Ellery to pick up the thread.

"That the dirty cops are well-known in *all* parts of the city," Ellery deduced. "And that something bad happened to our girl with the pink hair."

"And not just any girl," Jackson said, proud of this bit of information. They'd sat at the table for three hours, and he'd been scrubbing the lists of employees for *anyone* by the name of Bill Chisholm who worked at the capitol building. "The daughter of the chief aid to Gary Hallenbeck, Assemblyman District Ten."

"Huh," Ellery mumbled to himself. "So big, influential, but close enough to Sacramento to grab himself a bit of local talent at the capitol. Nice."

"Whatever," Jackson grunted. "I had to look up District Ten to see where it was, you know that, right? I had no idea we were District Four."

"You never had a mother who wanted you to run for office," Ellery said dryly.

"Celia," Jackson retorted darkly.

"I didn't say you had it *better* than I did!" Ellery sounded horrified at the thought. "And in this case, it's helpful. My mother lobbies for fair-trade agreements, many of which involve the port cities. So she may very well know your Assemblyman Hallenbeck, and if just making an appointment with Chisholm doesn't work, it might get us an invite to the capitol to ask some questions."

"Very swank." Awesome. Just fucking awesome. *Jesus*, what was this guy doing in his front seat, much less his bed?

"But first—"

"The morgue. I called ahead. Toe Tag has a couple for us to see."

Ellery made a sound of pained nausea, and Jackson grimaced.

"You don't have to," he said, feeling like he was about to throw a kitten into the middle of a tractor pull. "It's not necessary."

"I'm not going there to *prove* anything to you," Ellery snapped. "I'm going there so you don't have to do it alone."

"And I'm telling you I've done it before—"

"You don't have to do it *now*—"

"And what good is it going to do me the next time I have to go?" Jackson roared. "*Jesus*, Ellery! You're a sweet guy—"

"No, I'm not."

"But it's not necessary to protect me from the big bad world. I'm obviously okay!"

Ellery let out a long, wordless noise that Jackson took to be a negative on the "I'm okay!" theory, and Jackson was done.

"Do you want anything?" he asked, swinging into a fast-food drive-through before he could second-guess himself. Ellery had dressed in slacks and a polo shirt today—Saturday working clothes, apparently— and Jackson figured if the guy was as hot as he was, a soda would be welcome before they ended up charging through the concrete-and-steel bowels of the hospital.

"Diet Coke, extra-large," Ellery said promptly. "And God, you're a pain in the ass."

"You're fucking welcome." Jackson laughed evilly, because hey, he'd topped too.

"Shut up." Ellery crossed his arms and scowled. "I'm not sweet. You know that, right? I spent time between internships volunteering *in prisons* so I could deal with about anyone on the fucking planet. I'm not sweet."

"You're not Scott Bridger!" But Jackson was reluctantly impressed. "That was really smart."

"Thank you," Ellery said humbly. "I wanted to do it right."

That phrase sat there between them as Jackson ordered an extra-large soda for himself and a couple of breakfast sandwiches. The silence of eating and thinking took over the car, not unpleasant, and Jackson was almost startled when they paused at a light and Ellery spoke again.

"Why do you do that?"

Jackson looked at the crumpled ball of wax paper in his hand. "Do what? This?" He held up the sphere, roughly an inch in diameter.

"They're always so perfect. Why do you do that?"

Jackson snorted and shrugged. "Not enough toys as a child."

"Hunh." He punched the *n* in that word, probably so Jackson would know it was his sound. Asshole.

They'd reached Stockton Boulevard by this time, and Jackson took a left into the parking garage. He circled around back again and was almost glad when he didn't spot Dave and Alex taking their smoke break. He loved them, but he was there on grim business. He'd ruined their lives enough for the time being.

Toby Tagliare was the clerk down in the morgue—he kept the bodies from escaping, as he liked to say. He was in his midfifties, a sweet, happy little round man who reminded Jackson of a hobbit or a gnome or something. He had pictures of his very happy, very vibrant, very *large* family on the desk behind him, and Jackson often wondered if he liked working in the morgue for the peace he found there or if he was just *extremely* well-adjusted.

Because there was no doubt about it. Toe Tag was never crass about his patients, but he was rarely morose about them either.

Rarely.

"Jane Does?" he asked hesitantly when Jackson enquired. "And what did you do to your arm?"

Jackson grimaced and ripped the cotton ball off the crease of his elbow. "Routine blood test," he muttered, not wanting to think about that. Ellery had just sort of steered him to the lab on their way in. It had been that easy. His results would be available online the next day. Ellery had gotten a vial of blood taken too, but Jackson would almost rather he hadn't. Please. The guy could probably *donate* blood, he was so close to fucking virginal.

Or, well, he couldn't donate blood *now*. The thought was the only thing that kept Jackson from cringing in mortification all the way down from the lab to the morgue.

Yeah, Ellery Cramer was rich, polished, and out of Jackson Rivers's league, but he was *now* in Jackson's bed. So okay. They could get blood tests together. He couldn't fall apart over that.

But he didn't want to share the info with Toe Tag either.

"Well, here's the trash can. You may want to bring that with you, by the way. I've got three Jane Does, and none of them are pretty." Toe Tag cast an apologetic look over Jackson's shoulder, and Jackson checked to see which face Ellery had put on for this.

Ah. The austere mask-of-stone look. Jackson approved.

"I'll bring the trash can," Jackson conceded, "but he might be tougher than he looks."

"They never are." Toe Tag shrugged, because yeah, Jackson was holding the trash can, so now it was all on him.

Or, hopefully, in the can.

The first Jane Doe was in her fifties, homeless, and extremely decomposed. Jackson grunted, said, "No, Toby, not this one," and Toe Tag nodded and slammed the drawer.

Ellery let loose a pained heaving sound that made Jackson stick close to his side for the next drawer.

This one was younger, in her twenties, and she'd overdosed in a public restroom with no ID. Unfortunately she looked nothing like the girl in the photo render. For one thing, her hair was a rich, glossy black instead of pink, and for another, whereas the other girl had delicate, doll-like features, this girl had been a bold, stunning beauty.

Not now, though. Now she was pallid and frozen, wasted potential, wasted life, a slab of meat in a freezer drawer. Sad, yes, but not horrifying.

Jackson made himself ready for the next potential candidate.

It was every bit as bad as Toe Tag had hinted. The face had been demolished until bone showed through at the cheeks and chin, and the body was so broken, shoulders, upper arms, and ribs jutted out and through skin at odd angles, poking up against the white sheet that shielded the rest of the body, making it look like she had surrendered again and again but the destruction had kept on coming.

About the only thing recognizable about the piece of human hamburger on the table was the vivid pink hair lying lankly around the head.

"Time of death?" Jackson asked, because suddenly that was crucial.

"Thursday night between midnight and 4:00 a.m.," Toby replied promptly. "Does that mean something to you?"

Jackson took a deep breath of refrigeration and blood. "Yeah." It meant that she'd lived long enough to take the picture and for someone—Bridger?—to see it and use it. And not much longer.

Next to him Ellery made an unfortunate—and unfortunately recognizable—sound.

Jackson shoved the trash can at him just in time.

Ellery wrapped his arm around it and proceeded to toss his breakfast with admirable velocity. Jackson stood back until he was done. Toby had shut the drawer by then, and he took the trash can from Ellery without comment and handed him a bottle of water.

While Toby went to dispose of the can in medical waste, Jackson grabbed a handful of wipes from Toby's desk and tried to clean Ellery up. He wiped his mouth first and then his chin, making sure he got his neck and any spots on his collar. Ellery avoided his eyes the whole time.

"What?" Jackson asked after he'd gotten rid of the wipes and washed his hands thoroughly at Toby's sink.

"I feel stupid," Ellery said at last.

Jackson pulled some mints out of his pocket—he'd brought them along just in case. Then he stepped aside and let Ellery finish his own washing and freshening.

"You see these?" he said, holding them up and shaking the Tic Tac box.

"Yeah?"

"You can have a couple, but you gotta know, I didn't put them in my pocket just for you."

Ellery's mouth quirked, his usual dry self-deprecation peeking out. "Thanks."

Jackson nodded. "That? What happened in that box? That wasn't just a murder. That was an…."

"Abomination."

Jackson nodded slowly. "Yeah. And I think…."

"What?"

"Nobody can recognize her. Nobody. If she was young enough and never got arrested, there'd be no reason for her to ever be fingerprinted."

"Wouldn't matter," Toby said, returning from the room that had the big hoses and the drains on the floor. The trash can was clean and still a little damp, and he grabbed some paper towels and started wiping it down.

"Yeah? Why not?" Jackson asked, stepping aside to let him in.

"Because her hands were soaked in drain cleaner—like, wrapped in cloths, soaked in Drano. No useable prints."

"That's… horrible," Ellery said, the word coming from deep in his body. "That's—they didn't just *kill* her, they tried to erase her entire being."

"Yeah," Jackson said, thinking. "And you know, people never try to do that to people who are nobodies."

Ellery met his eyes, and his hands were still shaking and his eyes still red rimmed, but his chin had that same resolve Jackson had seen when he was making some poor policeman cry. "And we know who this somebody is."

For a moment they were in perfect accord.

"Go find a toothbrush—there's one at the gift store," said Jackson. "I'm going to take some pictures. If this *is* who we think it is, we know someone who needs to see them."

TEN MINUTES later, as they trudged to the car, not so much in the agreement department.

"We didn't tell him!" Ellery protested for maybe the thousandth time.

"I told him we *may* know," Jackson retorted for maybe the thousand-and-first time. "But if he knows, he's *obligated* to notify next of kin."

"Which is a good thing!" Ellery shouted. "It's a good thing—because if maybe her father knows—"

"You're sure he's her father?" Jackson asked, powering down for a moment. He'd made the assumption, but Ellery had been the one to check the facts.

"Yes." Ellery nodded. "Eight years ago, when he left the DA's office to work for Hallenbeck, there was a modest announcement in the paper. It mentioned a wife, a son Charles, and a daughter Luanne. The perfect political family."

Jackson grunted. "Well, back when Chisholm had his dirty fingers all over my paperwork, she would have been a baby. So… think of this. He's working at the DA's office and he wants… out. Better. He has *aspirations*."

"Right. So in order to get out, you need to either run for office or back someone who's running." Ellery sounded like he knew.

"Okay. So Chisholm wants money, but all he knows is cops and lawyers, and the DA's office makes squat over a chainsaw, and cops make worse." Oh, this felt good. The heat was smacking them like a wet woolen blanket, but that was okay. His car had *air-conditioning* now, and finally, *finally* they were making progress.

"Squat over a chainsaw?" Ellery's voice wavered between puzzled and horrified.

"Yeah, you know. If you're not careful how you spend it, you're gonna lose your bits. Anyway, so he needs green." They entered the parking garage, which felt cool only because it was out of the sun but also innately more dangerous. Jackson steered Ellery toward the stairwell, because he didn't trust the elevators in this particular garage.

"Yes," Ellery agreed, seemingly oblivious to the strategy. "Definitely green. And maybe he starts noticing that your friend Hanover is driving a little better car than everybody else."

"Right," Jackson agreed, liking this theory. "So he starts to cover for Hanover—for a price."

"Maybe he starts planning some of the graft." Ellery paused just long enough to bump Jackson's hand with a certain intimacy. "From the sound of it, he was probably too out of control to go unnoticed for too long."

Jackson paused on the stairwell. "Oh God. All those hours." He closed his eyes. "Hell. Shit fuck motherfucking *hell*."

Ellery's fingers curled around Jackson's, but his voice stayed just as crisp as it had been. "Yes. So Chisholm starts picking up Hanover's business, and he's the final signature. Bess Carillo was probably not dirty—"

"But she was easily steered." Jackson's stomach roiled at the thought of it. "Like a certain stupid rookie who just kept walking into the cauldron of fucking doom because people told him to."

"Right," Ellery said. His fingers tightened, and Jackson pulled himself out of his anger and self-hatred for a moment.

They'd had sex the night before. Maybe, just maybe, it had been more. He was not the same guy. He might even be stronger than the guy who had kept walking into a shooting gallery and finally gotten shot.

"You didn't let it destroy you," Ellery said softly. "I think she did. Why else flip to being a union advocate?"

Jackson blinked slowly. "More money," he muttered. "Oh *God*. Oh God, oh God, can you see it? Because I can see it!"

Ellery nodded, just as slowly. "Yes. I do. Chisholm became the kingpin, but he's moved to a higher office. Hanover is dead, but Chisolm still likes the income. He hires the sniper—who professes a personal vendetta so he doesn't get the chair—and pays Carillo off. Eventually, when the heat dies down...."

"He starts again." Jackson was shaking by now. Anger and sweat cranked him tight like a plucked string, so tight that the giant backfire of a big SUV practically gutted him with fear.

And then he caught his breath and knew what *real* fear was like.

"Get *down*!" he hissed, dragging Ellery to his knees as he crouched.

For once Ellery didn't argue with him. For a moment they crouched in the stairwell while Jackson strained his ears for the sound of a car in desperate need of a tune-up. God. Yes. It sounded familiar, but nobody ever won a case based on the *sound* of a backfiring car.

Very carefully, he pushed up and looked over the edge of the well.

And watched as Scott Bridger, tinted window rolled down in the darkened garage, drove by in a very familiar Dodge Durango.

Jackson ducked so quickly he banged his elbow on the cement wall. "God*dammit*."

"What?"

"*Bridger*," he hissed. "Bridger is driving that stupid fucking car!"

Ellery closed his eyes. "How is that possible? He couldn't have been driving when we almost got rammed, and it would have been hard for him to get away from lawyers when Coulson got shot."

Jackson took a moment to admire how quickly his brain worked. "Wow. I didn't even go there. You're right. Totally. So he must have an accomplice."

"Right. But what is he doing here *now*?" Ellery glared at him, his brown eyes snapping and furious, and Jackson, who had never equated sex and danger, was suddenly so hot for him that he found himself leaning forward for a kiss.

He pulled back—and to his senses—long enough to think. "Shit. I've got to call Toe Tag."

He pulled the phone out and nodded at Ellery. "Look over the edge for me." Quickly, he punched in the number. "Toby!" he hissed. "I need your help."

"Jackson? Didn't you just—"

"Look, a cop might be coming by. Scott Bridger. If he comes down to you and asks to see your Jane Does, could you do me a *huge* favor?"

"Don't show him the one with the pink hair?" Toby asked grimly.

"How'd you—"

"You can't lie for shit, Jackson, and your buddy the lawyer was pissed. You know who she is."

"Yeah, and we need that knowledge to stay among us for a minute." He grimaced, remembering why he hadn't just told Toby in the first place. "I'm sorry. I didn't want to make you a part of this."

"Jackson, you know, we have Dave and Alex over for dinner once a month. My wife adores them. Seems to think Alex is the gay son she never had."

Jackson fought the temptation to bang his head against the side of the stairwell. "I owe you all so fucking much."

"It's nothing. Just don't show up here in a body bag and we're even. Later."

Jackson nodded and checked with Ellery before standing up. Just as they started back up the stairs, they heard a clatter in the landing above them and looked up just in time to see Bridger clattering down.

"Mother*fucker*." Jackson pushed in front of Ellery and took the stairs up in a power run, trying to make it look like they'd never paused and couldn't give a fat rat's ass if they saw Bridger.

For a moment it looked like it might work. Bridger was focusing on his own feet and muttering to himself, and Jackson and Ellery pretended they were doing the same thing. Ten steps, five, two—

"Jesus, what are you doing here?"

"Visiting friends," Jackson retorted, looking him in the face since the pretense was over. "Since you don't have any, I assume you've got hemorrhoids."

"So cute," Ellery muttered behind him. "And so stupid."

Up close, Bridger looked dangerous. In the heat, his ruddy face blotched unhealthily red, and his mirrored sunglasses took away any humanity he'd retained. His arms and chest bulged with muscles, and his knuckles were raw and battered. Jackson's stomach twisted when he thought about how they had probably gotten that way.

"Are you saying I'm stupid?" Bridger growled, trying to pass Jackson in an effort to get to Ellery. Jackson blocked him, and again, and again, Bridger's chest bumps getting aggressive and insistent.

"I'm saying *he's* stupid," Ellery said clearly, "because you're too insignificant to antagonize."

"I'm *what*?" Bridger roared, and Jackson scraped his elbow on the concrete of the stairwell as he grappled with the leviathan. Fuck, the guy was big, and now he was pissed, kind of at Ellery, but mostly at Jackson for getting in his way.

Fortunately he was also dumb.

He cocked his arm back and howled when he banged it on the handrail, and then tried a punch that had no aim and no follow-through. Jackson ducked it and then went in for the hug, hauling the guy close and personal so he could reverse their positions in the cramped stairwell.

"Get *off* me!" Bridger snarled.

"My *pleasure*!" Jackson snapped before catching one of Bridger's knees with his foot and shoving at his hard, muscled torso with all his might.

Bridger went over, landing on his back and shoulders as he slid down the stairwell, yelling the whole way.

Jackson grabbed Ellery and started charging up to their level before Bridger hit the landing.

"But what if he's hurt?"

"Do you hear him yelling?" Jackson asked, thanking God he kept himself in shape and apparently Ellery could run.

"Get back here, you fucking coward! Traitor! Pussy!"

"Yes I hear him yelling!" Ellery panted. "The whole world hears him! Which level are we on?"

"One more!" Jackson risked a look behind them and saw Bridger hoisting himself painfully to his feet—and getting ready to charge up the stairs and at *them*.

Which was actually a pretty good idea.

With his next step, he heard the jingle of his key fob, one of the new types that unlocked the door by its very proximity. He sighted their landing and turned, letting Ellery pass him.

"Bridger!" he yelled, looking down the two landings and hoping the guy wasn't cranked up enough to fly.

"I'm—" Pant pant pant. "—gonna kill you!" Bridger gasped.

"What's stopping you, you fucking murderer!" Jackson called back.

Bridger stopped for a moment, horrified. "You can't—you fucking *traitor*!"

"Yeah, I tell IA about a dirty cop and I'm a traitor—you *kill* a cop and you're a murderer!" Jackson called back. Very carefully, one step at a time, he edged up to where Ellery stood.

Bridger hesitated then, mired in a surprising grief. "He... he was a good kid, Miles," he said, like it had just occurred to him. "A wife, a kid—"

"And you deliberately roofied your witness and shot him," Jackson snarled, handing Ellery his keys and shoving him toward the car. "They're going to rip out your spleen in prison, asshole. They're going to dine on your guts while you watch."

Bridger hauled in a breath then, like he was going to need it to last him, and exploded up the stairs. "*I'm gonna fuckin' destroy you!*"

Jackson shoved Ellery in front of him, and together they sprinted toward the car.

Fish on the Run

ELLERY'S HEART thundered so hard in his ears he could have sworn he could barely hear, except Jackson was shouting "Start the car, asshole!" loud enough to shake the windows of the Honda, and he could hear *that* just fine.

"Why am I driving?" he panted.

Jackson ignored him. "Don't floor it. He's on foot, he's two floors up from his car—he can't catch us."

"Then why—"

Jackson fumbled for his phone, shouting, "*There*! Stop!"

Ellery hit the brakes with enough force to throw them both forward, but Jackson didn't complain. Instead, he hopped out of the car and ran around it, taking pictures, before something made him look up and he sprinted for the car.

Ellery looked in the rearview mirror, and just as Jackson hopped in and slammed the door, he saw Bridger bearing down with speed.

"*Go, go, go!*"

This time Ellery floored it.

"Toward 50, west," Jackson ordered. "Be ready to take the Business Loop split. It's right there!"

It was the least obvious direction to go, especially if they were going to the capitol, and it was also the quickest way to get in a place they could disappear.

"On it!" Ellery was good at driving just fast enough to make the green lights but not fast enough to trigger the yellow. He kept his head and drove with his usual precision, smiling a little when he flew through three lights in a row. Just as he was taking the hard right for the freeway, he saw a black SUV braking hard three lights back.

He closed his eyes and hoped.

"That was exciting. Why'd we do—"

"Why'd you call me stupid?" Jackson demanded.

"Why'd you get into a pissing match with a gorilla?" he demanded back. "Jesus *fuck*, what was the purpose of antagonizing him!"

"So he didn't go bother Toe Tag!" Jackson shot back. "If he was there to see his handiwork and maybe contaminate the body and destroy some more fucking evidence, anything that could distract him from that is a *good thing*!"

"Getting your face pounded in is *not* a good thing!" Ellery gripped the wheel hard enough to make his knuckles white, mostly in an effort not to flail.

"I didn't get my face pound—"

"You're *bleeding*, moron! I know you've got friends there, but is it really necessary to keep trying to go back to that fucking hospital?"

"Bleeding?"

Oh God, he had the balls to sound confused. "Your elbow, your lip, *another* cut under your eye. *Bleeding.*" The one from his fight with Connie Coulson *still* hadn't healed.

"Oh—oh, damn. Didn't see that." Jackson checked himself out with more irritation than pain. "Oh god*dammit*. On the fucking new upholstery?" His voice cracked with true distress.

Ellery gave a bitter laugh. "Really? He could have taken you apart, and that's what you're worried about?"

"This is the only new car I've ever owned. I've seen my own blood before!"

"Well I've seen too goddamned much of it!" He was shaking. His heart, his core, his stomach, all shaking. And Jackson didn't seem to see or notice or give a damn. Instead, he was rooting through the glove compartment, which he closed with a furious snap.

"Dammit. I haven't put in a first-aid kit yet! *Shit*!"

Ellery took the off-ramp by N Street and headed for Alhambra. "I think you're more worried about the goddamned upholstery than you are about the gorilla who almost killed you!"

Jackson looked at him as though he'd lost his mind. "What are you freaking out about? Jesus, I do that shit all the time. Do you think I come into office looking like hell just to dick with you?"

"*You said you did sudoku!*" Ellery shouted, out of patience. "You said it was the most boring job known to man! You said it was no big deal!"

"Well I *lied*," Jackson shouted back. "I lied because I was sad and scared and you were worried, and it...." He growled and got his voice back. "You know, if you think you can change who I am and what I do after one lousy fuck, we may as well stop fucking and just keep working together."

They were blocks away from the capitol, but Ellery saw an open parking spot on a side street and cut the car neatly to the left, dodging traffic as he went. He skidded into the spot with a screech of brand-new tires and brought them both up hard against their seat belts and then back again. It was a hundred degrees outside again, so he didn't turn the engine off, but he did put the car in Park so he could turn and have this fight out face-to-face.

"It was *not* a lousy fuck, you arrogant shit! It was a *superlative* fuck—it was *three* of them, four if you count the shower—and I'm *not* willing to let it end there because *you* had a chance encounter with a bad guy in a stairwell that stinks of piss and is now wearing a decent portion of your skin!"

"Well, I can't *not* do what I do!" Jackson flailed for a minute, and then he folded his hands under his arms and threw himself back against the seat. "I knew this was a bad idea."

"Oh no you didn't," Ellery snapped. "You knew this was a *wonderful* idea. *I* am the best thing to ever fucking happen to you, and I'm *not* trying to change you, you stupid asshole, I'm trying to *keep* you." Okay. *Now* he was out of wind. He turned around and leaned back against his seat. For a moment both of them scowled through the windshield, and then Ellery cut a sideways look at Jackson.

And saw that his eyes were shiny.

He was hurt.

Not just his skin, his everything.

Fuck.

Tentatively, Ellery reached out and traced a drop of blood under Jackson's cheekbone with a shaking thumb. He reached into his pocket with his other hand and pulled out a package of Kleenex and turned back. Jackson was still scowling out the window, and he made a grab for the tissue, but Ellery caught his hand.

"Let me. Please."

Jackson kept staring straight ahead, but he gave a small nod, and Ellery dumped some water on the tissue and started to clean his skin.

He finished the cheekbone and used a finger under Jackson's chin to get him to look Ellery in the eyes so he could clean the other wounds.

"You scared me," Ellery said quietly, working away. "You may be able to find bedmates by just shaking your ass, but I don't like enough men to want to sleep with them. I'm not ready to start looking again."

Jackson swallowed and nodded. "Don't assume I'm dead just because I'm down," he said roughly.

"Well, maybe don't antagonize someone who can kill you!" Ellery's stomach still shook. "I *like* you. Sometimes. Mostly. Sort of."

"Well, *that's* a ringing endorsement," Jackson said sourly. He took a quick check of his face in the mirror and then held his elbow up to check it out and sighed. "There's a grocery store in about two blocks. Let's go there and get some bandages. Here, give me the Kleenex and I'll try to keep the blood off my shirt."

"You are really fucking difficult, you know, that right?" Ellery asked, thinking the words were rhetorical.

"Which is an even *better* reason to not sleep with me again," Jackson said, but he didn't sound angry anymore, just resigned.

"It's a shitty reason not to sleep with you anymore," Ellery said, using some hand sanitizer and throwing the Kleenex in the fast-food bag that still held Jackson's little trash-made ping-pong balls. "Difficult means worth keeping."

Jackson snorted. "You're lying."

"No, I'm totally not. There's precedent." Ellery made his voice smug, his courtroom voice, the one that nobody bothered to contradict.

"You are such a dick," Jackson muttered, still gazing ahead. But his lips were quirking up and he no longer looked hurt, so Ellery was calling it a win.

Suddenly Jackson stiffened. "Did you see it?"

Ellery glanced out the window just in time to see a familiar squarish black SUV. "Is that him?"

"Yeah, probably. Think he's heading for the capitol?"

"Mm...." Ellery tried to get his head out of the Jackson space and back into the space where their lives were in danger. "I have no idea. I mean, yes, if our luck's against us, but think. Does he *really* want Chisholm to know his daughter is dead?"

"Obviously not," Jackson said thoughtfully. "Not if he went to all those lengths to hide who she is."

"Maybe he wants to see what Chisholm knows?" Ellery wasn't sure. Complete speculation wasn't his strongpoint.

"Let's go rattle their cages," Jackson said, an evil smile twisting his lips.

Ellery pulled the SUV into the grocery parking lot and grabbed Jackson's hand before he could get out. He wasn't gentle, in spite of the scrapes and bruises on the back. "Jackson, look at me."

Jackson faced him—and then rolled his eyes.

"Charming," Ellery muttered. "Go be a teenager on someone else's watch. I need a man today, sweet-shit."

"Sweet-shit?"

"Shut up. Look, we're going to go face Chisholm my way, okay? I want to make an appointment, greet him as a colleague. Hell, if the gods are fucking smiling, he'll think I'm as crooked as he is and offer a bribe, and *bam*! I've got a reason to subpoena shit he read in the fifth grade and we've got a case, okay?"

Jackson grunted. "Yeah, I've got it. I'm the gorilla now. I'll be your muscle, you'll be the brains."

"Not a gorilla," Ellery corrected grimly. "A tomcat. Try not to piss in the corners, tomcat, or we'll both have to live in the stink."

Jackson nodded once and then hopped out to go get his first-aid supplies. Ellery watched him go and hoped he didn't have to beat someone up in the middle of Safeway, because their day was complicated enough already.

UNLIKE THE hospital parking garage, which was full pretty much all the time, the paid garage by the capitol was only at about half capacity on Saturdays. On the one hand, it didn't say much for the dedication of the public servant, but on the other, it made it easier to pick a spot next to a nearly identical white Honda CR-V with dealer plates.

"Hunh," Jackson said as they hopped out of the car and into the sweat cauldron that was the parking garage.

"Hunh what?" Ellery was just relieved they weren't shouting anymore. He couldn't remember being as pissed off and *passionate* about anything in his entire life, but it wasn't a comfortable feeling.

"The dealer was right—it fits right in."

"Well, your brown Toyota was *old*. I can't believe you didn't get made all the time."

Jackson grunted again. "Liked that car." He strode quickly through the garage, and Ellery worked hard to keep up.

"Why *that* car?" Curiosity—so sue him.

"First thing I ever had that was *mine*."

Oh. "Oh." Ellery sighed and wondered if he could have a night to write up his homework on Jackson Rivers. It would be great if he had a brief to follow. *Has effectively raised self. Will not appreciate any direction. Lives simply—would rather have security than things. Is not afraid of pain or death. Terrified of losing family.*

He could see the notes, scrawled in his own hand, but even as he imagined what such a brief would look like, he loathed the thought of it. A legal brief wouldn't detail the way Jackson's skin felt under Ellery's palms, or the expression of hurt he took such pains to mask. It wouldn't document the tenderness in his eyes when he looked at an ugly, battered tomcat, or the patience he showed his neighbor with the good heart and the insensitive cultural vocabulary.

A legal brief wouldn't show the manic joy he wielded when confronting an enemy, or the rush of adrenaline that drove him as they eluded a pursuer.

There was a lot of Jackson that couldn't be taken down on paper, and Ellery couldn't reduce him to a set of notes.

And there was no reining him in, apparently. He charged down the street, heading for the front of the capitol building on Alhambra, and Ellery had to trot to tag him on the elbow.

"What?"

"Maybe not so much the frontal approach?"

Jackson stared at him. "Isn't that where visitors go in?"

"Yes, but look around you. There's extensive grounds. We don't *have* to run straight into Bridger like on the stairwell. Jesus, Jackson, a teeny bit of stealth?"

Jackson scowled, and pivoted on his heel, then took the first sidewalk he spotted, the one that wound through the rose gardens. Someone was setting up chairs for an event there—a wedding, if Ellery could judge from the crepe paper.

"Nice," he said randomly, and he returned Jackson's annoyed glare. "What? I said it was nice!"

Jackson grunted. "Yeah. It's nice."

"You don't like weddings?"

"I've only been to one. When Jade gets married, that'll be two. The kids grow up, maybe four. I'm just not that invested."

Ellery could keep up with his stride just fine. Keeping up with the way Jackson *thought* made his head hurt. "You don't think *you'll* ever be in one?"

"Are you *high*?" Jackson asked, wrinkling his nose.

"No."

"Have you met me?"

"I do believe we've fucked, yes."

"Then, Counselor, you need to go back and check your notes and see what in my history points to someone who is going to get married. Is it the zillion sex partners? How about the extensive scarring? Or being a needy, whiny little baby in the middle of the night? Maybe the history of being a human target? Oh, right, maybe it's my fucking *family*! Good God, man, you met my mother not eight hours ago. Use your fucking head. Who in their right mind is going to marry *me*?"

Ellery's face had gone cold, and he couldn't seem to find words.

"Jesus fuck," Jackson muttered, almost to himself. "That'll be a proposal. 'Hey, I'm irreparably damaged, and basically I'm a big emotional liability. Good luck with me. How about if I suck the life force right out of you? If you're lucky, I'll get shot at work, and maybe this time not sit like a useless lump of fucking flesh for a year.'"

Still muttering, he strode ahead, and Ellery stopped, just stopped, to soak in all of the things about Jackson Rivers that were *not* in the file.

But should have been.

He stared after Jackson, his heart frozen in his chest, before he caught Jackson looking behind him and giving a little sneer when he saw Ellery stunned by his words.

And that's when his heart started beating again.

Jackson expected it, clearly. Was probably even looking forward to the rejection. Oh hell, he was probably *happy* about it. Ellery walking away would just make his little world exactly like Jackson Rivers ordered things.

Ellery didn't live to make Jackson Rivers's life easy.

Better, maybe, but not easy.

With a few strides, he caught up to Jackson, shoulder-bumping him *hard* so he'd slow down.

"*What*?" Jackson demanded as they rounded the corner to the northeast entrance. "What was that for?"

"For trying to scare me off."

"I wasn't trying *shit*," Jackson snarled. "You can't expect anything more from me, can you? You said it yourself. I'm an alley cat—"

"I said a tomcat—"

"About the only thing I'm good for is picking through the trash and banging German shepherds. Walk the fuck away."

Irrationally, Ellery remembered Billy Bob sprawled on top of him that first morning, cuddling up to Jackson in bed when Jackson had been too out of his head to even know he was there.

"You fucking asshole. It's one thing to try to shove me away, but Jesus, give your cat more credit!"

Jackson paused halfway up the stairs and leveled him a look of such outrage he was practically cross-eyed with it. "My cat?" he stammered.

"I love that fucking cat," Ellery snarled. He came to the great doors and stood, waiting. "Now hurry—I have no idea what the hours are, or if our guy is still working or not."

Oh, he was working. They checked in with reception first and were directed up the elevator to the office floors. Ellery wasn't sure what Jackson thought, but for *him* it was always such an amazing thing to transition from the decorative museum-quality lower floor of the capitol building up to the purely functional office floors. He always thought it was a solid reminder that the people who wielded the most power were supposed to be the ones working hardest for it; he couldn't remember when the thought of graft or corruption had made him realize that sometimes it was exactly the opposite.

Shoulder to shoulder, the two of them strode down the corridor, keeping an eye on the placards on the doors until they found the one for G. Hallenbeck. Ellery made eye contact with Jackson as Jackson held the door for him, and he nodded.

Ellery was doing all the talking.

The receptionist was a surprisingly young woman, blonde, pretty, plump, with a picture of her smiling husband and pouting toddler on her desk. Ellery put on what he hoped was his best smile and was sort of depressed when she recoiled and eyed him suspiciously, like a housecat would eye a predator.

"Hello," he said, suddenly tongue-tied. "We, uh… we're looking for a Mr. Bill Chisholm—"

"He's real busy right now," she said, voice glacial.

"This is, unfortunately, important," Ellery said, matching her ice for ice.

"He's seeing a friend of his." She scowled, the implication being, of course, that Ellery would not ever be a friend of Bill Chisholm's.

"This could be very important to Mr. Chisholm," Ellery said and tried again for a charming smile.

Apparently he succeeded in the sort of smile that a snake would give a kitten.

Helplessly, he turned to Jackson with panic in his eyes.

And Jackson's own eyes went to half-mast. He thrust his hips out and slunk to her desk with enough testosterone in his swagger to make hair follicles abandon ship for miles. Oh dear God, Ellery remembered that smile on his face when they were in bed, and his groin ached—actually *ached*— while he watched Jackson turn sex appeal on like a faucet.

"Ms. Cochrane—Gloria," he said, dropping his eyes to her name placard. "I'm sorry. I know my partner here is a little scary. He is, in fact, a very good lawyer, and we're really worried about Mr. Chisholm's daughter. We were hoping he could give us some clues as to her whereabouts."

Gloria pressed her hand to her chest. "Oh, you know about Luanne? Why, the poor thing ran away a couple of months ago—she dropped out of college and her daddy got mad, and I guess they had a row. He's been frantic about finding her. That's who he's talking to right now, a policeman friend of his. Mr. Bridger said he didn't have any news, but Mr. Chisholm, he wanted to make sure."

Fuck.

Ellery and Jackson met eyes for a moment, and Ellery shook his head. No. No, they were not ready for this confrontation. He wouldn't take Chisholm to court with what they had—a hunch, a photo, and a dead body—and he wouldn't give an ADA this information yet in case that might tip his hand.

Jackson nodded and turned back to Gloria. "Hon, Mr. Bridger really does need his attention right now. Could you maybe pencil us in for Monday?"

"Yessir," she said, nodding. "That's really considerate of you. Can you and—"

"Make the appointment for Ellery Cramer, an attorney for Pfeist, Langdon, Harrelson & Cooper. I may or may not tag along."

"Absolutely," she confirmed. "I hope you two can find something on his daughter—he's absolutely distraught."

Jackson nodded, and for a moment both of them listened to the hum of voices coming from the closed office door behind Gloria. The conversation sounded intense but not finished.

"Ma'am, there is something you could help us with. We don't want to get Mr. Chisholm too excited in case this doesn't pan out, but you wouldn't happen to have a coffee cup or a napkin or something? We'd love to be able to produce something solid for him along the lines of DNA and evidence if we have to bother him."

Ellery tried not to roll his eyes. Yeah, it would be great to confirm it really was Chisholm's daughter, but Jesus, who was going to believe *that* pile of—

"Oh, yes!" she said, nodding like it made perfect sense. She reached into what must have been a trash can at her feet and, using a Kleenex, pulled out a Dr Pepper can. "This has to be his," she said, smiling fondly. "He's the only one in the office who drinks them. Says they taste better than coffee."

Jackson dimpled at her. "You are an angel," he said sincerely. "And so helpful. I do hope I can make it in with my friend here, Ms. Gloria. It would be a pleasure to talk with you again."

THEY EXITED casually and then strode down the halls like they owned them. By the time they hit the great doors at the northeast entrance, they were both hustling like bats out of hell, and Jackson did not need to be told twice that they needed to wend their way through topiaries and rosebushes in an effort not to stand out.

Ellery knew *he* was holding his breath until they reached the car in the parking garage, but he hadn't been sure *Jackson* was until he turned on the ignition, backed the car out, and began to ease it through the garage.

"Oh my—"

"Sh!" Jackson hissed. "I don't want to fucking jinx it."

They didn't talk again until they got to J Street.

"Back to the hospital?" Ellery asked, and Jackson nodded.

"I can make this run. I'll drop you off at my place and you can drive home."

Ellery fought the temptation to bang his head against the dashboard. "No, no—stop by my place after the hospital and I can get another change of clothes."

"Impose much?" Jackson muttered, but he didn't look annoyed when he said it. Ellery took that as a sign.

"Only when I'm wanted," he said, keeping the words casual.

Jackson cut his eyes sideways and then looked back at the road.

And sighed.

"I want you," he admitted grudgingly. "Wish I didn't. Do."

Ellery took his life in both hands and brushed up against Jackson's knee. "Foolish wish," he said softly. "We have such a short time on the planet, Jackson. Why waste it wishing you didn't want something that's good for you?"

"Why waste your time wanting *anything* to do with me?" Jackson countered bitterly. "It's like you're breaking the rules of the space-time continuum or something."

"Someday I'll explain it to you," Ellery said, crossing his eyes at the thought. "When I'm sure you'll use your powers for good."

"Moron."

"Tomcat."

"Shut up."

"Make me."

"You'll shut up when you're sucking my di—"

"And only then." Ellery was looking forward to it more and more with every barb. "Are you hungry? I'm hungry again. Do you want to eat? Maybe someplace with salad this time? And tables?"

"After the hospital," Jackson said grimly. "I would really like to have this DNA sample by Monday."

"Can you get it that quickly?"

Unlike in the television shows, DNA testing often took months for results.

"Toe Tag knows a guy," Jackson told him. "And IDing a DB takes priority. I think we could make it happen."

Ellery nodded, liking that very much. "Yes. I have the feeling that saying 'We know where your daughter is' will have a lot more weight than 'Come look at this picture for us.'"

They both sobered.

"God," Jackson said after a moment. "I'm not sure how dirty this guy is or how bad a man he was to get where he is now, but I... I can't imagine how bad seeing that picture is going to be."

Ellery hadn't thought of that. Not yet.

Jackson was a better person than he was. The thought didn't surprise him as much as it irritated him. *Dammit*, why did he have to write himself off as lost, or damaged, or... what was it? A useless lump of flesh.

The thought made Ellery nauseous—and enraged him at the same time.

They'd been to the morgue that morning, and Ellery was taken back to those moments with Jade and Kaden in his office, when both of them remembered how Jackson had almost ended up there too.

Scars indeed. They must be some terrible, terrifying scars, because they were hurting Ellery eight years later, and he hadn't even been there when they'd been inflicted.

"You've been quiet." Jackson's voice as they pulled up in front of the hospital startled him.

"Thinking," he replied—yes, quietly.

"What about? The case?" Jackson pulled up to the ambulance bay and put the SUV into Park. "I'll be back in ten," he said without waiting for an answer. "If anyone gives you shit, tell them you're waiting for a pickup."

Ellery nodded, aware that his brows were knit and he probably looked anxious or worried, but unable to change it.

"Seriously!" Jackson tried to smile. "What's wrong?"

"Hurry back," Ellery said, nodding. "I'm hungry."

"Whatever."

Jackson trotted off, and Ellery was left trying to adjust his thinking to the idea of mortality and Jackson Rivers being old and bitter friends.

JACKSON WAS good to his word, and he took them to a bistro on J Street for food. Jackson was all for talking about the case, but Ellery was pretty much done with *that* subject.

"Well, what else do we have?" Jackson asked, frustrated.

"Place you most want to visit?" Ellery asked suddenly.

Jackson didn't even falter. "Sri Lanka. India. It's busy and amazing and rich and poor and just sort of a chaotic repository for human beings and their history. What about you?"

Like that, Ellery's worries faded. He remembered all of his assumptions about growing up and falling in love, and how *his* person would have to want to travel, and have to want adventure, and have to be self-sufficient and able to deal with new situations and new people.

"Anywhere," Ellery said, taking a bite of sausage and kraut. "I got to go to Germany and France in college, and I loved them, but Sri Lanka would be excellent too."

Jackson's rare untwisted grin made an appearance. "Yeah? You want to travel?"

"Oh yes. I mean, right now if I get a vacation it's back to Boston to see family, but I understand that family obligations can go screw themselves if I manage a long-term committed relationship. My sister's been using that to bait the hook for years."

Jackson half laughed. "Bait the hook?"

"Yeah. I mean, I get that I'm gay, but I'm still expected to produce grandchildren. Eileen has produced the requisite two, and Mother is apparently insufferably in her business, so now it's my turn. Getting to travel instead of going to see Mother during vacations is supposed to make that all better."

Jackson narrowed his eyes playfully. "I hate to ask, but if you get to take family vacations *without* your mother, how is she going to enjoy the benefits of grandkids?"

Ellery wrinkled his nose. "Well, I understand that *Mother* does most of the traveling in that case. I didn't say it was a perfect system."

Jackson's chuckle echoed off the artfully waxed concrete of the bistro's floor and the bare boards of the interior. "I guess you work with what you have."

"*Exactly!*" Ellery said, suddenly so excited about this new relationship that he wanted to sing it to the stars. "And when you've got as much to work with as we have, you enjoy your job."

Jackson pulled up short and stared at him. "Oh my God. Stop drinking beer."

"Water, Jackson. You took the order. Now hurry up and finish. We've got stuff to do tonight." Ellery wasn't talking about writing briefs, but Jackson's no-nonsense nod told him that was what Jackson *thought* he was talking about.

Well, wasn't *he* in for a surprise.

Fish in His Own Skin

JACKSON DIDN'T want to think about the Monday interview with Chisholm, and he didn't want to think about how long Kaden and Rhonda were going to have to be in protective custody.

He didn't want to think about Jade sleeping with his neighbor or the fact that the hamburger in the morgue was connected to the time *he* was almost the hamburger in the morgue.

And he didn't want to think about Ellery and the challenge in his brown eyes whenever he looked at Jackson, and how he expected normal and Jackson could only offer himself, Jackson Rivers, bisexual freak of fucking nature.

He pulled up in front of his house and saw Jade's car behind Mike's truck, and Ellery's car in the front of the driveway. With a growl, he parked the SUV in front of the lawn and looked at Ellery expectantly.

"So, uh, see you—"

"Get mad if you finish that sentence," Ellery said smoothly. "Just keep your car here, and tomorrow I'll go home and change clothes, do laundry, and let you think about how much you miss me. But not tonight."

With that he hopped out, his briefcase in hand, and shut the door.

Jackson growled and banged his head on the steering wheel—and then turned the car off and followed him, clicking the alarm as he went. Ellery was waiting patiently at the door, and Jackson fumbled with his keys to let them in—and Billy Bob too, who was crouching in the bushes, growling and twitching his tail.

Unlike the day before, nobody had left their fingerprints on Jackson's home while they'd been gone.

Jackson could still *smell* his and Ellery's sex, and he was trying to process exactly how he felt about that when Ellery shut the door with a little unnecessary force and pinned Jackson to the wall with his slender body.

"Uh, Ellery?" The painted wall felt cool along his cheek, but Ellery's body was throwing off heat, and his erection pushed solidly against Jackson's backside.

Ellery's response was a long, slow lick on the shell of Jackson's ear. "I dare you," he whispered. "Say it. Tell me to go one more time. Tell me this won't work, or you're too damaged, or you don't want me." Ellery ground up against him harder, and the pit of Jackson's stomach, and his groin, and his thighs, and, heaven help him, his *asshole*, all gave a giant throb of arousal. "Say it," Ellery ordered, shoving his hands under Jackson's shirt.

"I... oh God." Wicked, angry fingers pinched his nipples, soft, and then hard, and then soft again. Ellery's lips moved from grazing his ear to the side of his neck, and Jackson tilted his head to give him access. Oh Lord, Ellery's touch, his body, his voice—all of it combined to *own* Jackson, to control him with his own insatiable need.

"Say it," whispered Ellery against his shoulder. He moved a hand to yank at Jackson's polo shirt, and his tongue stroked a line along fabric and skin. "Tell me you don't want me. You don't want this. *Say it!*" He bit *hard* at the join of neck and shoulder, and Jackson humped up against his own goddamned wall, whimpering with desire.

"Please," he whispered.

Ellery reached up and grabbed his hair, pulling his head back and arching his body, ass out. "Please what?" he taunted, running his hand down Jackson's spine and along his ribs. "'Please leave, Ellery'? 'Go do your laundry and forget about me, Ellery'? Please *what?*" He punctuated that last with a fumbling hand at Jackson's belt, and Jackson's knees actually went weak. Ellery was going to take him *here*? Against the wall in his hallway? *Here*?

"Please...." He was looking up at the ceiling—he should have been begging God for the strength to say no. Instead he was bending his knees, adjusting his stance, pushing back against Ellery's groin, because Ellery's cock was in there, behind his belt and his slacks and his boxers, and so help him, Jackson wanted it.

With a jangle, Ellery pulled Jackson's jeans down, leaving his ass exposed and sticking out. He kissed a gentle line down his back through his shirt, between his shoulder blades, down the tender indentation at the waist, and then, oh Lord, down his crease.

Before Jackson could even groan, Ellery had parted his asscheeks and licked a solid line from his balls to his taint, crouched behind Jackson like a beggar.

Jackson buried his face against the meat of his arm and howled, and Ellery *really* went to work on that rim job. Oh God, his tongue, aggressive and knowing, licked, tasted, penetrated, and Jackson could only gasp.

"Ellery, oh God—"

"Have you figured it out yet?" Ellery asked, reaching between Jackson's thighs to fondle his balls. He tugged gently as Jackson shuddered, and then he gave Jackson's aching cock one hard, merciless stroke. "What you're asking for?"

"Ellery… please…." Jackson's voice sounded weak in his own ears, and he almost hated himself for how much he loved this, *craved* it, wanted this possession and this hard, brutal fuck.

"Please?" Ellery mocked, standing up. Loudly he slapped his hands on either side of Jackson's hands while he ground his still-clothed body against Jackson's ass. "I'll tell you what. You stand here and think about what you want, and I'm going to go get what you really fucking need."

And then he was gone, shedding clothes and shoes down the hall as he went, and Jackson was left face against the wall, ass out and dripping with spit, while he wondered what was keeping him there. All he had to do was pull his hands away and go down the hall, ravage Ellery's mouth in a kiss before he took him, spread him, and fucked him, just thrust and pounded and—

Oh God. He was humping his own goddamned wall and Ellery was already back in the doorway, naked, his cock rampant and engorged, bobbing in front of him, covered in a condom and lube.

This time when Ellery shoved up against Jackson's ass, his cock slid between Jackson's cheeks and nudged his wet, stretched hole.

Jackson whimpered.

"Jackson," Ellery graveled in his ear. "Have you thought about what you want?"

And Jackson only had room in him for honesty.

"You," he whispered, greedy. "You inside me. That's what I want. Please."

Ellery fumbled between his cheeks for a moment, and then he thrust inside.

Jackson howled, biting a bruise on his bicep and still thrusting back against the stretch and the ache and the burn.

"Oh… oh… *yes!*" Ellery had him by the hair again, and the sting of Jackson's strands caught in that long-fingered fist kept him arched and needy and unable to move. Ellery shoved his cock all the way to the root, and Jackson craved him, needed movement, and all he could do was suck in his stomach and wiggle his ass and plead for more in breathless pants.

"Please…," he begged. "Please…. God, Ellery, fuck me. I need you. I need you so bad."

Ellery pulled back and rocked forward, grunting in pleasure, and Jackson wanted to weep with it. He was helpless, pinned against the wall by his own choice, forced to take Ellery's cock, his caresses, his pleasure, and he wanted it, wanted more, wanted to be fucked until his ass bruised, wanted to be owned.

Ellery didn't disappoint him.

"Fucking try to blow me off," he muttered, throwing his hips forward. "Send me away… you *need* me!"

"I need you," Jackson half sobbed.

"You fucking need me!"

"I need you!" he shouted. "I fucking need you!"

"You wanted me to leave!"

Oh God. "Please don't leave," Jackson begged. "Please… just fuck me… fuck me… fuck me… and fucking stay…."

"Oh God yes!" Ellery's voice broke then, and apparently so did his control, because his thrusts grew frantic, frenzied, and he pulled one of Jackson's hands from the wall, leaving Jackson mashed up, hardly able to breathe. Ellery shoved the hand toward Jackson's own prick and muttered, "Stroke it. C'mon, Jackson, come. I need to feel you come. I need to know you want it. Want me."

Augh! *Yes!* Jackson wrapped his fingers around his cock and took advantage of the fact that Ellery had let go of his hair and he could move. He dropped his head and thrust out his ass and stroked himself, squeezing and jacking as fast as he could.

"I want you!" he moaned. "Oh God, don't stop moving. Want you! Just you! C'mon, Ellery, *fuck me!*"

Wham, wham, wham! Every hard stroke sent Jackson against the wall with enough force to rattle the pictures in their frames, and Jackson's frantic jerking off became one hard squeeze. Then Ellery bit him again, hard—hard enough to bruise the back of his neck—and the pain, that did it, sent him over, hot, silky, spurting over his own hand as Ellery screamed loud enough to ring in his ear and rutted inside Jackson's ass, twitching as he filled the condom.

Jackson could feel the heat against his insides, and for the first time in his life, he wished for a clear test, wished they could get rid of the rubber and he could feel Ellery's spend boiling inside him.

For a moment both of them were tense with the rictus of orgasm, and then Ellery sagged against him. "Bedroom," he whispered. "Now."

Jackson, ever fastidious, tried. "I should wash the—"

"Now, Jackson. I need you to kiss me and tell me that was okay."

Jackson didn't want to lose Ellery's cock in his body, but he did turn just enough to catch his lips in an awkward kiss. "That was okay," he whispered. "Thank you. That was more than okay. That was…."

"What you needed," Ellery murmured, sounding comforted.

"Yeah."

They stumbled to the bedroom, picking up clothes and shoes as they went. Ellery dropped his bundle right inside the door, next to the hamper, and Jackson thought, *Fuck it!* and just added them all. They'd do laundry in the morning. It was obvious Ellery wanted to stay, and Jackson—Jackson ached. From the backs of his thighs to his stretched asshole to his heart.

He'd worked for so long not to get attached, secure in the knowledge that being attached meant having your heart ripped out. Jade and Kaden and Rhonda were his home. They were the only ones who had never betrayed him or left him. He didn't have to worry what he said in front of them, and they knew all his secrets. For nearly twenty years, that had been his touchstone. Even before the working undercover—and Patrick Hanover—no relationship had ever been as important as the family he'd clung to when nobody else gave a shit.

But now someone else gave a shit.

Jackson wasn't entirely sure what to do with that. He'd tried to get rid of Ellery, but that thing they'd just done—that had all the earmarks of someone *not* ready to leave. That thing—that was *real*. That was a priority relationship sort of real.

How was he supposed to manage that?

He picked up the extra clothes from the floor and then turned reluctantly toward where Ellery was stretched out on the bed.

"I turned on the air conditioner," Ellery said, propping his chin on his palm. "It gets *hot* in here!"

Jackson nodded. He sheened with sweat, and even though the light was off and the drape was over the sliding glass door, he could tell Ellery was the same.

"Not really in a cuddling sort of place," he warned.

"No cuddles, then." Ellery smiled, all teeth. "Come here and talk to me."

"We keep playing this game!"

Ellery nodded. "And we keep getting better. Think about it. Right now we know that we need to show each other our favorite movies, we both have a borderline unhealthy attachment to our families, and we could definitely take a vacation together in the future. That's more than some people know after months of dating."

"We also know that Jackson is a needy, whiny baby," Jackson muttered, hating himself, "and that he apparently likes to bottom."

"So is Ellery." He dimpled. "And he *loves* to bottom." His smile faded. "But he's also usually a selfish bastard, and if he sees a chance to give something—something needed—he's going to do that and feel good about himself."

Reluctantly Jackson let a smile twist his lips. "You feel pretty good about yourself, do you?"

Ellery patted the bed. "Come here," he ordered softly. "Come here and talk to me. We're going to think of not-awful things right now and touch each other really, really gently. And we're going to pretend you have some hope that when Kaden is out of danger and your family is safe, you and me can be a thing."

Jackson sighed, and a part of him gave in. He threw himself across the bed and let the overhead fan do its best to dry the sweat on his skin.

"We're a thing," he admitted reluctantly. "I mean, you're going to have to go home sometime—"

"I'll come back," Ellery promised readily.

Jackson scowled at him. "Until the day that you don't. I'm not stupid, I know how this works."

"Jackson—"

"But, you know, until that happens, I'll stop trying to make you go."

Ellery sighed and reached out hesitantly and started pushing Jackson's thick, curly blond hair back from his forehead. "That's acceptable," he said humbly. "But I mean, you're right. I've seen your mother—not met, really, but—"

"It was a mercy," Jackson said darkly.

"So I gather. But can you tell me in actual words what makes *you* so reluctant to start a relationship? I mean, I can hazard lots of guesses, and they might even all be right. But I want to hear you say it."

"Why?"

"Because words are my business, Jackson. Arguing is my business. When it's just a big silent wall, it's hard to fight. When you break it down to words…."

Against his better judgment, Jackson felt hope. "You're a defense attorney. I get it. Ellery Cramer, defend our life!"

Ellery's smile glinted in the dim little room. "I fully intend to," he said. He brushed his fingertips against Jackson's cheek, and the air conditioner kicked on. Both of them shivered, and Ellery dropped his arm and lay down parallel to Jackson, so they were face-to-face and could talk.

"I don't really know how to do this unscripted," Jackson warned.

Ellery touched his face again and then walked his fingers down Jackson's shoulder. "Okay. So let me do what I do best."

"Talk?"

Ellery finished up his finger walk with a kiss so gentle, Jackson's skin puckered with the chill of the touch. "Bingo." He kissed again, and again, teasingly but not quite hard enough to arouse, and Jackson found himself giving in to the moment, relaxing into the mattress and simply allowing himself to be touched.

Ellery's lips skated his bullet scars, and his tongue traced the edges of each one. Jackson grunted and breathed deeply, fighting not to shake him off. Lots of people had touched the scars—one freaky chick had even gotten off on them—but this was different. This was *accepting* the scars, and Jackson wasn't sure he could endure it.

"Talk to me," Ellery whispered.

"You keep telling me that, but I don't know what—"

"Okay. When did you know you were bi?"

Jackson thought about it, smiled. "Jade and I… we'd been together for about four years. We sort of knew… you know. Not lasting forever. I asked her who she'd want to date if she wasn't dating me. She told me… who was it? Tomas Serrano. Yeah. He was cute. Big puppy-dog eyes, full lips. One of those kids who could grow a mustache in the tenth grade and just sort of let it go all chia beard?"

"Not in prep school, but go on."

Jackson laughed, thinking that was probably true, and Ellery kept up his gentle, seemingly random touches on Jackson's back, his neck, his backside, his thighs.

"Anyway, I thought about Tomas and how he looked on the soccer field without his shirt, and how he was really sort of a gentle guy when we went to a shitty school, and I thought, 'Yeah.'"

"Did you tell Jade?" Ellery asked, sounding genuinely curious.

"Of course." Jackson shifted so he could look Ellery in the eyes. "Yeah. I didn't keep secrets from her *or* Kaden. Jade was sort of hurt at first. I told K that it was just like seeing a pretty girl. I wasn't going to cheat on her just because Tomas turned my key too. K smoothed it over, and Jade and I...."

He smiled. This memory was sweet.

"You've got to finish that sentence."

"Well, we sort of got Tomas alone one day and asked him which one of us he wanted to kiss."

Ellery sucked in a breath. "You're killing me."

"He'd never been kissed before," Jackson said, remembering the wide-eyed curiosity. "Jade went first and...." Jackson grunted, pushing himself against the bed. "Mm. Hot."

"And...." Ellery's voice sounded strained.

"My turn, and Jade had gone in sort of fast and hard, so I just leaned forward, about an inch away, and told him to put his hands on my shoulders." He could still see the bright eyes, feel Tomas's almost panicked breaths against his mouth, smell his sweat and the wildflowers that grew behind the portable buildings. "And suddenly he's going for it, pushing me up against the wall, sticking his tongue down my throat and grinding up against me." The memory made him hard. "Jade moved in behind him and nibbled on his ear and his neck and then reached down his pants, and we... we just *got off*, all wearing clothes and shit. I mean, you know. Adolescent and clumsy—but *damn*."

"Hot," Ellery croaked, and Jackson glanced at him slyly, running a finger down the delineated line of his chest, down his pectoral, along his flank, tracking the indentation of his waist. He got to Ellery's hip and kept tracing that line, across his hip bones and to his groin, then up his hardening cock. Ellery breathed deeply, oozing some pre, and Jackson caught it with his finger, bringing it up to his lips and sucking, hard.

"Hot," he agreed throatily.

Ellery groaned and rolled to his stomach so they were shoulder to shoulder. "Stop seducing me," he scolded, burying his face in the covers. "I'm looking for experiences here."

"Well," Jackson said, feeling sexy and sassy and in control for the first time all day, "that was quite an experience."

"What happened?" Ellery asked. "After?"

Jackson grunted and turned his face away. "Tomas... well, he was so embarrassed the next day he couldn't talk to either of us. And Jade, she... she told me that we'd seen the end coming, and maybe I should go see if girls were really what I wanted. I mean, they *were*. It just depended on the person, you know?"

Ellery gave a bemused chuckle. "Uh, no. When I was fifteen, I took a psychology elective—"

"Because prep school—"

"Damned straight. Anyway, so, they got to the Kinsey scale, and there was this girl I was friends with—"

"Name?" Jackson asked, knowing where this was probably going.

Ellery buried his head in his own shoulder. "I don't remember!" he wailed. "Because I am a *terrible person*."

Jackson laughed outright and told him to go on with his story.

"Anyway," Ellery continued when he'd recovered from his bout of social conscience, "this girl, whatever her name was, had been hanging out with me and being my very best friend and I had no idea—"

"None?"

"Swear to God, none. And the Kinsey scale came up, and we had to do an assessment test, and of course we were supposed to keep the answers private, but everybody was bragging about how the *whole class* was a solid zero—"

"Statistically improbable," Jackson said dryly.

Ellery cast him a foul-tempered look. "The whole way we look at the scale is statistically improbable—like the whole world is *mostly* heteronormative, with only a small percentage of gay or bisexual people? Do you *know* what the odds of that are?"

Jackson rolled his eyes. "The same as the odds of most of the people claiming they're straight when they're really bi? Yeah, I get it."

Ellery's lower lip formed *the* most adorable little pout when he was miffed. "You say that like it's common knowledge," he grumbled. "I thought I was the only one who thought that."

"Nope," Jackson said, reaching up to tap Ellery's lip back in. Ellery stuck out his tongue to tease his finger, and Jackson snatched it back. "Not the only one. Most of the guys I've slept with have believed the same thing, because they've known about the girls. And the other way around, actually. It's a thing. Now are you going to finish telling me about breaking this poor girl's heart?"

"She got off lucky," Ellery said. He rolled to his side, propping up his head again, and Jackson mirrored the pose. A part of him remembered that he and Jade had been doing the same thing less than a week ago, but that didn't seem as important as this did. That had felt like old friends parting. They'd see each other again and still be friends.

This felt like something else. Something bigger.

It was intimate and painful, and he studied Ellery's face in the falling darkness, almost eagerly. The bony jaw, the dark and probing eyes, the hair that fell across his brow when it wasn't slicked back.

His heart was an Etch A Sketch, and every turn of their conversation inscribed another line, another detail in the chambers within.

He almost couldn't breathe with the urgency of each new moment, the two of them sharing stories and breath.

"Lucky how?" Jackson asked so the story didn't go away.

"Well, everyone was lying about being a zero, and she came and said, 'I'm a zero, Ellery—are you one too?'"

Jackson grimaced. The impersonation hadn't been flattering. "And...."

"And I said, 'I'm a five, Clarissa—' *Clarissa*! *That* was her name! Anyway, 'I'm a five, Clarissa, but that's okay, I think your brother is hot!'"

"No!"

"I swear. I just hated everybody lying—I mean, I knew some of those boys had checked me out. There's eye contact. You know. And I thought that in twenty years, when we all showed up with our significant others, *I* didn't want a soul there to think I was a liar or a hypocrite or any of the other bullshit, you know?"

Jackson shook his head. "See, I just figured that if I wasn't sleeping with someone, it wasn't any of their fucking business."

"Yeah. I get it. Sexual politics—not your thing."

"No, it's not that, it's just personal. I was a big advocate for gay rights—even on the force when it could have been a big deal—because, yeah. Hypocrite thing. But I didn't put on my rainbow T-shirt and parade because… because just like the government should stay out of my sex drawer—"

"Condoms and lube. That's all you got, Jackson, I was just there."

"And porn."

"That must be on your computer."

Jackson laughed wickedly. "And yes, yes it is. Anyway, as I was saying…."

In those moments, as the shadows lowered and the air conditioner dusted their skin, they talked. Jackson could remember the name of every person he'd ever slept with, and it was quite a list, but he couldn't remember *ever* having a conversation like that one.

After an hour they got up, stretched, went to the bathroom, walking casually in their nakedness, and then came back to bed.

Jackson went first and was sitting on the bed and stretching when Ellery returned. For a breath, he paused, regarding Jackson from the doorway, the oddest smile on his face.

"What?" Jackson asked. "Ugly naked?" He crossed his arms in front of his scars, self-conscious for the first time in recent memory, but Ellery shook his head and walked gracefully to the bed.

"No," he said softly, bending down and putting his hands on Jackson's shoulders. "Beautiful naked."

Jackson raised his face and closed his eyes like a virgin sacrifice, of all things.

But when Ellery's mouth lowered to his, he felt blessed, and as they fell into the bed, the feeling grew stronger. Ellery rolled to his back this time, spread his legs, arched against Jackson in wordless need, and Jackson had always been good at giving.

He slid the condom on and sank into Ellery's body like it was home, and Ellery tilted his head back, closing his eyes and gasping like Jackson's cock invading his flesh was the sweetest thing he could beg for.

That moment froze, maybe for both of them, and Jackson held his breath, wanting that picture of Ellery locked behind his eyes forever. He was beautiful and strong and elegant and brilliant, and he was giving himself to Jackson of his own free will.

When Jackson started to move again, thrusting gentle and slow, Ellery smiled, and his eyes fluttered open.

"Fuck me, Jackson. Take me fucking hard. I want to remember your cock in my ass for *years*."

"*Yessss….*"

He wanted that too.

THERE WAS a sharp rap on the door at eight in the morning—then five of them, no bullshit—and Jackson sighed, wiped the drool from his mouth, slid out from under Ellery's possessive arm at his waist, and hopped into his jeans.

The cat moved up from the foot of the bed to bogart Jackson's spot, and Ellery curved into him.

"If that's your mother," Ellery muttered, "tell her she can't have you."

"Not Celia." The five quick raps repeated, and Jackson started out of the room. "It's Jade. I've got shorts in the drawer—maybe grab those since your knapsack never made it into the bedroom."

"*Fuck…,*" Ellery mumbled, and Jackson hustled to the door.

Jade was on the other side, wearing a bathrobe and looking irritated.

"Again?" she demanded, sweeping inside with a ziplock baggie in her hand. "He's here *again*? I mean, I know you were curious, but you never sleep with them twice!"

"We were checking each other out for a while," Jackson defended, turning to watch as Jade pulled out the coffee and started scooping it into the baggie. "What makes you think it's going to go away after a couple of days?"

"We?" Jade turned to him with narrowed eyes. "I knew *you*, but I had no idea *he* crushed on anybody. I didn't know snakes crushed."

"Be nice," Jackson snapped, voice flinty.

"Okay, okay!" Jade held out her hands. "Fine. You're a thing now. It'll be painful when you break it off, but—"

"We're completely ignoring the fact that you're sleeping with Mike now?" Jackson asked, because… dude. This was her second night too, and apparently now Jackson's coffee was fair game.

Jade turned away and mumbled, "You, uh, just woke up. Here. I'll make you guys some coffee of your own."

"Human of you," Jackson said dryly. "And appreciated. You hated Mike. You said he was a—"

"Sh!" She flailed coffee grounds everywhere and turned toward him in earnest desperation. "Don't *say it*. He might hear, and he'll get his feelings hurt! You *know* he means well!"

Jackson sauntered into the kitchen, turned a chair around, and straddled it. "*I* do—in fact, I've been trying to get *you* to see it for years. I just don't know when it became so obvious to *you*."

Jade harrumphed and made his coffee, then bagged her own grounds and cleaned off the counter. She turned to Jackson and leaned back, playing with the tattered tie of her violet chenille robe.

"He's sweet," she said unexpectedly. "And yeah, some of the shit that comes out of his mouth is just… fucking crazy. But he came to help my brother out, no questions asked. And I went in to check on Denny and the station and… we just started talking. And it hit me. My family, you—we mean a lot to him. And, you know, he's not *that* old." She nodded like this was something everybody should be aware of.

"Forty-five," Jackson said dryly. "Yeah. I get it. He's young at heart."

"He is!" Jade defended with sudden passion. "He's young at heart. And…." She bit her lip. "He's kind, Jackson. Which is why you two get along, I guess. But he's… he's just… he *worships* me. And you and me, we grew up together, and you weren't ever going to do that."

Jackson bit his lip and remembered… everything, from the night before. *Worship*. Was that how Jackson felt about Ellery? Was it the other way around?

"No," he said, the word punctuated by Ellery's voice down the hall.

"Do I smell coffee?" he called.

"Yes, yes, you do!" Jade called back. "And you need to get your skinny uptight butt in here, because I didn't just come in to steal your coffee!"

Jackson looked at her in surprise. "Why—what's doin'?"

Ellery padded down the hall and stopped in the doorway, hair rumpled, wearing Jackson's sleep shorts and nothing else. Jackson just looked his fill enjoying the pale skin and the clean lines of someone fit but not muscular and good-looking without being pretty.

"Yeah, both of you," Jade said. She turned back to gather three cups and set them on the counter. "Leonard Pfeist called me up—I guess he's been trying to get hold of you too, Cramer, but you maybe forgot to—"

Ellery grimaced, leaning against the doorframe. "I kind of turned my phone to vibrate and then—"

"Was it in your pants pocket?" Jackson asked. "Because I think I shoved them—"

"In the hamper. Yeah." They smiled shyly at each other. "We were otherwise engaged."

"I'm going to hurl." Jade went to the fridge and pulled out milk, and Billy Bob padded through the kitchen to wend about her ankles. She poured a dollop in his food bowl, because any more would make him sick, and then stood up and glared at the coffee machine for not dripping faster. "Anyway, Ellery's office got broken into. I mean, the *whole* office got broken into, but Ellery's in particular. It was completely destroyed. They were looking for something in particular, and Pfeist wanted to make sure you had copies on the company server—"

"I do!" Ellery said, sounding alarmed.

"Good, because—"

"Well, of everything except—" Ellery's gaze sought Jackson out. "Your file, Jackson."

"The one you made a zillion hard copies of?" Jackson asked, because damn, that had been good thinking.

"Exactly. Damn!"

"So you're covered?" Jade looked from one to the other.

"Yeah," Ellery said, dragging his hand through his hair. "But that's worrisome. I mean, we must be getting *really* close if—" A car backfire from outside startled him, and he glared at the door like it had done it on purpose.

Jackson's heart stalled even as he leapt out of his chair. "Jade! Get down!"

Jade had grown up in the hood in the nineties, and he knew she fucking *would*, but Ellery—oh *fuck*!

Jackson hit the doorway just as shots started to sweep the duplex and Mike's dog went apeshit.

"*Ellery!*"

He stared at Jackson in surprise and horror as Jackson threw himself through the doorway in a full-body tackle meant to get them both down.

Jackson was in midair when the bullet caught him, the velocity hurling him against the doorframe, and that was when he blacked out.

Fish Under Pressure

THE SHOOTING stopped but the dog kept barking, and Ellery tried to jumpstart his brain.

Jackson.

He'd managed to bring Ellery down as he'd fallen, throwing him back against the far wall of the hallway before his trajectory changed.

Ellery was spattered in blood.

"Jackson?" he asked, suddenly afraid. He'd *seen* Luanne Chisholm. For real. Touching distance away. He didn't want to touch Jackson's body if it had been destroyed by violence. He didn't want to think about the human who had lain next to him the night before, spilling secrets, laughing with surprising shyness, becoming more important to Ellery with every breath.

So certain Ellery would leave.

"Jackson?" he said again, pulling himself up and leaning over the still form. Jackson's shoulder and the meat of his arm were a mess— blood and flesh and bone and Ellery couldn't look at it.

But then the owner of that mess moaned, and Ellery raised a shaky hand to the hair that covered Jackson's eyes.

"I've been *shot*," Jackson slurred. "Mother*fucker.*"

"*Jackson*!" Jade shrilled from across the kitchen. "Oh my God—"

"Make her stop." Jackson moaned. "God, Ellery, make her stop."

"Jackson—dammit, you can't—" She was hitting those pitches that only terrified women could hit, and Ellery needed quiet, just some motherfucking *quiet* so he could think! God, just think!

"Jade!" Ellery barked, his courtroom voice coming from a place that he hadn't known existed. "Call an ambulance. Check on Mike. And for *fuck's* sake, shut that dog up!"

"Oh my God!" Jade pulled herself up and looked despairingly at the kitchen floor. Bullets had spattered the refrigerator and the cupboards, leaving food and cereal and broken glass strewn like child's toys. She looked at her bare feet and moaned, and then screamed.

"Billy!"

Ellery's heart fell to his feet. "I'll call the ambulance," he said, holding his face by Jackson's. "I'll get help."

"Fine." Jackson took a deep, painful breath but didn't try to move. "Could you find my fucking cat?" His voice broke. "God, Ellery, I really love that fuckin' cat."

"Yeah. Yeah, I'll find the fucking cat."

But Jade was sobbing in the mess on the floor, and Ellery wasn't going to throw hope that way. He was going to save all his hope for the ambulance and some help, and Jackson maybe not bleeding out on the floor of his own home.

APPARENTLY WHEN your house got shot up in a normally peaceful neighborhood, you didn't have to call an ambulance or the cops. Mike came storming over first, and then the police came in, and then the ambulance.

Mike was sweeping the floor so Jade could walk through the kitchen while the police came and talked to her—and Ellery tried to doctor Jackson's goddamned cat.

Billy Bob hadn't been shot; he'd been *crushed* under what used to be the toaster oven on top of the refrigerator. While the EMTs worked on stabilizing Jackson so they could roll him onto the gurney, Ellery grabbed an old tablecloth from the upended drawer of linens and wrapped the wailing, spitting animal tightly in a bundle.

The cat was the best part of the clusterfuck in the kitchen.

The cops and Jade were shouting at each other. The mostly male, all-white group of policemen were telling her to stop being hysterical and asking if she was on drugs and if maybe one of her friends had done this because she was sleeping with a white guy—pretty much all at the same time.

Jade was shouting at the cops that *they* should know who fucking did this because they were all dirty fucking assholes and they'd been trying to kill her family for years. When Ellery saw eyes narrow and faces harden, he thought he needed to pull a Jackson.

"Enough!" he barked, surprised when both sides calmed the fuck down. He approached Jade slowly with a whining, panting Billy Bob.

"Look, you and Mike need to take him to the vet's. His back leg is a fucking disaster, but he might live. When Jackson comes to—"

Jackson screamed. Ellery looked over his shoulder and saw that the EMTs had just shifted him to the backboard and were moving it to the gurney, and the sounds he was making... *oh God.*

Jade burst into tears. Ellery couldn't blame her—but he couldn't join her either. Instead he locked his jaw and shut his eyes, fucking *willing* himself not to lose it. "When Jackson comes to," he tried again, his voice ripping a hole in his chest, "he's going to want his ugly motherfucking ass-buggering tomcat to be okay, do you hear me?"

Jade stared him, her mouth liquid and chin shaking, and Mike wrapped an arm around her shoulders. He was wearing his boxer shorts and a tank tee, and iron-gray hair peeped out at his neck and along the sides of his chest. In a way he looked pathetic, skinny legged, knobby kneed, scared, and sad, but in another way, Ellery could see it now. He'd cleared a path so Jade could walk, he'd stopped her crying, and now he put his other arm out and nodded for the cat.

Fucking capable. Sometimes capable just trumped young and pretty because it fucking did.

"I'll take him," Mike said calmly. He looked up at the police. "You all took my statement, right? If it's okay, I'll get the lady out of your hair and you can talk to the nice lawyer fella. He'll know what's doing."

The cops exchanged glances, and Ellery could see them thinking it: Was it more worth it to get Jade out of their hair or pay her back for being a flaming hysterical bitch to their faces?

But Mike's good-natured practicality won out, and Ellery thought that he'd welcome this man at a gay pride parade any day.

Billy Bob howled as Ellery turned him over, and he took a deep breath and stroked the spot between the cat's ears for a moment. "I'll make sure he knows you're okay," he whispered.

Then he looked at the policemen around him. "I'm an attorney for Pfeist, Langdon, Harrelson & Cooper," he said clearly. "I think this attack is directly related to a case Rivers and I are investigating. Once the ambulance clears out, I can get you the make and model of the SUV that the shots came from, and I can give you a name. You're not going to like it, but I can give you a *fucking* name." Behind him he heard the lock of gurney wheels and the EMTs starting out the door. "But first—give me a minute."

The cops parted like the goddamned Red Sea, and thanks to Mike and the broom and dustpan, Ellery could walk through the fine layer of debris on the floor and follow the gurney out.

"Wait!" he called before they shoved Jackson in. His voice cracked and he hated it, but he couldn't change it.

Jackson was hooked up to an IV, hopefully of pain meds, and he was still awake. Loopy, but awake.

"Jackson!" Ellery said, coming up to the side that *wasn't* a mess of pressure bandages and gauze. "Jackson, can you hear me?"

"Lawyer," Jackson said, a loose smirk twisting his mouth. "Hot, but has a stick. You know. In his ass."

"That wasn't a stick," Ellery said, trying not to weep with relief.

Jackson laughed, low and filthy. "Nope. Not a stick." He took a breath and tried to focus. "How's Jade? And Mike? And my...." His voice hitched.

"They're fine." Ellery petted his good hand, not caring about EMTs or policemen or anything else. "We're taking the cat to the vet, Jade and Mike are fine, and I think the German shepherd has laryngitis."

Jackson smiled and then gasped, his face white and taut. "I'll be in the fucking hospital," he muttered. "God. God. Don't tell Kaden I ended up back in the hospital. He's still pissed from last time."

Ellery nodded and forced words past his swollen throat. "Yeah, well, I'm pissed now. You just piss *everyone* off, don't you?"

Jackson's face relaxed, and he looked mildly stoned again. "Yup. I'll be pissing you off until you lose that stick." He laughed then, and Ellery backed up and let the EMTs do their job.

"Where are you taking him?" he asked.

"Mercy San Juan unless he's got a place he already goes."

"Davis Med Center," Ellery said, thinking they'd be pissed if Jackson ended up somewhere different. "They all know him there."

The EMT was a stocky, ruddy guy in his thirties. "Sucks to be *that* guy," he said, and Ellery was forced to nod.

"I think he'd agree."

ELLERY DIDN'T recognize this set of police officers, and he wondered if they would have given Jackson shit too.

He *did* give them the license plate of the black Dodge Durango, and told them about the backfiring and how that SUV had tried to run them down once already, and had been seen—driven by Scott Bridger—more than once the day before.

"You have evidence against Officer Bridger?"

Ellery nodded. "Jackson collected it yesterday." He closed his eyes and thought. "He took fingerprint pictures and pictures of the license plate, which he sent to the secretary at our law firm. She ran the plates and probably filed the evidence."

The officer looked at his legal pad. "Pfeist, Langdon, Harrelson & Cooper, right? Will she be there when we call, or should we wait until tomorrow?"

Ellery's jaw hardened. "Well, if you hadn't been dicks to her about seeing if Jackson was all right, you could have asked her ten minutes ago. She just left with her boyfriend to see after the goddamned cat."

The cop—Officer Kryzynski—took a deep breath and let it out.

"Why didn't anybody tell us that?" he asked, voice tight.

"You were bullying her," Ellery shot back. "Was it because she's black? Because she's female? I have no idea, but you weren't giving her a chance to speak in complete sentences."

"We were—"

"You asked her if she was on drugs. The woman was standing barefoot in a destroyed kitchen and you asked her if she was on drugs."

"She was hysterical!"

"*So. Was. I.*" Ellery glared at young, blond, broad-faced Officer Kryzynski. "Do you not get it? She doesn't trust you right now because none of the policemen around her have proved trustworthy. The guy in the ambulance has been shot by cops before—and he *was* one. A good one. And he got partnered with a dirty cop in a shitty situation, and your brotherhood hasn't made his life easy. And if *my* house had been shot up, you people would have let me have a fucking Valium before questioning, do you know why?"

Kryzynski shook his head. "Enlighten me."

"Because I'm a white man who lives on American River Drive."

The officer's eyebrows shot up—light blond over piercing blue eyes. On any other day, Ellery would have enjoyed his square-jawed American-boy face. But today he wanted to punch it. "So what are you doing *here*?"

"Sleeping with my boyfriend," Ellery snarled. "Are you going to call me hysterical now? Does that make everything fit?"

Kryzynski swallowed angrily. "You are making an awful lot of goddamned assumptions about us—"

"I am," Ellery agreed. "And they might even be wrong. But I'm not going to know that if I don't trust you, am I? You started out not trusting *us* because Jade was a black woman in a bathrobe in Jackson's kitchen. I can either not trust *you* because you're all white cops, or I can give you my evidence and trust that you're not all *crooked* white cops. So what's it going to be? Are you going to betray my fucking trust?"

The young officer shook his head. "No. But we need that evidence."

"Well, I'll ask her to send it to you. Give me your e-mail address— fuck. I need to get my phone."

His feet were raw and hot on the front carpet, and he realized the driveway was already cooking. He must have burned the soles of his feet when he'd been talking to Jackson on the sidewalk. God. God, what a fucking day.

It got worse. He got back into the house and stepped over the bloody detritus on the carpet and tried not to weep, thinking, *My phone. Jackson sent me all the info—I just need my phone.* He was in the middle of rooting through the hamper for the slacks that held his phone when he glanced up at the table with the charger.

And realized that Jackson's phone, which had sat squarely on the bedstand in the charging station since the night before, was gone.

Ellery blinked. It had been there that morning when he'd gotten up smelling like sex and like Jackson. Now it was gone.

Breathing deeply in outrage, Ellery found his phone and started an e-mail. He was still tapping madly as he strode barefooted onto the front lawn.

Officer Kryzynski was waiting there for him, an expectant smile on his face. "So, do you need my e-mail?" he asked.

"Yup."

Ellery tapped it in—next to twenty of his best and highest-placed contacts, along with his mother. "So, you ready?" he asked, voice hard.

"Hey, I won't get to look at it until this afternoon," the officer said, shrugging.

Ellery hit Send. "Well, all of the other people I sent it to are going to see it bright and early in the morning."

"What happened to trust?" The surprise on his face could have been faked—and so could the hurt—but Ellery didn't give a shit.

"Trust disappeared when one of *your men* stole Jackson's phone. Do I know which one? No. So guess what?"

Kryzynski sighed and rubbed his forehead. "We're all dirty again," he said softly.

"Get your shitty fucking ass off Jackson's front lawn."

The man turned to Ellery, his face eyes narrow and flinty. "My name is Sean Kryzynski," he said, voice strong. "And you're going to see that name on the arrest report for Scott Bridger, and I'll make sure I'm involved in the investigation of who killed Collin Miles—"

"It *wasn't* Kaden Cameron," Ellery snapped.

Kryzynski shook his head. "You know, *that* I could have figured out for myself."

EIGHT HOURS later, Jackson was out of surgery, and Ellery sat next to his bed, writing acres of case theory and briefs and documenting the holy hell out of the past three days.

He wasn't taking any chances.

He was sending the entire lot of it to everybody he'd ever worked with or known. His first boyfriend, who now worked civil suits for a giant corporation, was getting a copy of this criminal brief.

Fuck discretion. If Ellery was gunned down in a pool of blood to cook on the fucking asphalt, he wanted *someone* to know who might be responsible.

And if Jackson died and Ellery lost his fucking nut, he wanted a credible defense if he did something unthinkable.

He'd left the house cleanup to Mike and Jade while the CSIs were still counting shells, but he felt like a coward for doing it. He just kept thinking that he couldn't look at Jackson's blood—*couldn't look at Jackson's blood*—when he didn't know how Jackson *was*.

Instead of staying there in the wreckage, harassing the scientists, he'd driven home to shower and change. He very carefully didn't think about the bullet hole that ran from his car's trunk to the engine—which was now making funny sounds.

He couldn't get through the rest of this day with Jackson's blood on him. He just fucking couldn't.

It hadn't mattered. Jackson was still in surgery when he arrived at the hospital, and for an eternity—maybe two or three eternities—he sat staring blankly at his phone, wondering who to text. Every fifteen minutes it was Jade—*No news*. Every minute after that, he called up his mother's number... and then didn't know what to say.

When the doctor came into the waiting room to say that Jackson was out of surgery and had been moved to ICU, Ellery actually saw spots in front of his eyes. Oh God. He should have called someone. Not for Jackson—for *him*. He nodded at the doctor and wiped his face with hands that shook.

"When can we... I... can I sit in his room until he wakes up?"

"Are you family?" the doctor asked, but not as though this were a sticking point.

"I'm the boyfriend," Ellery said. And if Jackson didn't like it, fuck him. He'd have to wake up to dispute it, and Ellery could argue him back under the anesthesia if that happened.

So Ellery gained access to Jackson's ICU unit. Then he texted Jade, opened his laptop, and tuned out everything else besides Jackson's heartbeat monitor and writing a fucking creditable account of how he came to be sitting next to a hospital bed, trying not to cry with relief. The account was important. He was going to have to leave Jackson's hospital room at some point, and he wanted to ask for protection. Paperwork, dammit. Paperwork mattered.

He got a call about two hours after he'd arrived at the hospital. He had to make a decision. The cat could have his leg amputated or he'd need to be put down, what was it going to be?

"Lose the leg," he told the vet dispassionately. "That animal will still be fucking German shepherds on three legs."

"Uh, about that," the vet replied. "We suggest neutering an animal who is not going to be used for breeding."

"Is that safe?" Ellery asked, wondering when the sex police had gotten into animal husbandry.

"We won't do it *now*," she said seriously. "But he's going to be here for at least two weeks under care. If you give authorization, we can have him neutered before he goes home."

Ellery hadn't known Billy Bob's actual vet. He'd had Mike and Jade take him to the first place he could find on his phone and told them to claim him as the owner. He was officially in charge of Billy Bob, and yes, he was being asked to make this decision.

Ellery thought about where Billy Bob and Jackson would be living until the house got fixed up.

"Balls off," he said, his tone short. "Cut them off. He'll probably still molest the German shepherd, but maybe he'll stay away from the lions at the zoo."

And that was it. That was the last decision he was capable of making. His head ached from details, from hunger, from goddamned *worry*, and he had nothing left. With a growl, he slammed his laptop shut and set it on the end table next to his sublimely uncomfortable hospital chair. He looked to his left, where Jackson lay, face white, breathing even, machines beeping ceaselessly in their effort to tell the world he was still alive.

Ellery was the only one who heard.

He'd thought he was okay with Jade and Mike's decision to stay and clean up Jackson's home. Jade had been nearly hysterical about Jackson, but she wasn't going to do any better in the hospital, and what they were doing seemed to be based on the desperate assumption that he was going to be okay. Ellery could understand that, especially for Jade. He was going to be okay—he *had* to be okay—so she was going to see about a place to come home to. That was her job. Both of them were being practical in a way Ellery wasn't sure he could be, and he admired them for it.

He admired them more when they walked quietly into the room, carrying bags of food and a giant soda.

Ellery stared at the white bag emblazoned with the familiar sandwich shop logo swinging from Mike's hand, and almost cried.

"Thank you," he said, wondering how he'd managed to function so long without food.

"Turkey, avo, and bacon," Jade said practically. "With a large root beer—that's your usual, right?"

Ellery nodded even though he usually went for Diet Coke, and took the bag, tearing into it without ceremony. Oh God, sustenance. It was amazing how much more *doable* the world was if you weren't starving.

Between mouthfuls of sandwich and soda, Ellery caught up on the state of the house—and he caught them up on the state of Jackson.

"The refrigerator is shot," Jade told him soberly. "And most of his dishes are gone. There's been some structural damage to the corner posts, and it needs a shit-ton of spackle and drywall and stucco to be sound. We had PG&E come out and turn off the electricity on that side of the building until we saw what wires were hit, and the air-conditioning unit might be unsalvageable. We're talking a month, maybe, in the heat of the summer, until we can get it back to spec."

"Well, he'll be spending at least a week of that in here," Ellery told her after swallowing the last bite. "Maybe three. They had to reconstruct the bone, and he's going to need X-rays again to make sure they pulled all the fragments. Lots of PT after this one—it's gonna be ugly."

"Well, I guess he'll be at my place," she said, sighing. "I was gonna turn in the lease and just take care of Kaden's house, but—"

"Turn it in," Ellery said, looking at Jackson. "My place is huge; he can stay there. His cat can piss on everything and I'll hire another maid. Don't sweat it."

"He's gonna *what*?"

Ellery jerked his attention to her outraged surprise. "You didn't see that coming?"

"From *Jackson*? One-night stand *Jackson*?"

"I got two," Ellery said, looking at that pale form on the bed. "I'm taking it as a sign."

"Yeah, you do that. I'll keep the fucking lease." Jade snorted. "Nobody gets romantic like that after two nights."

Ellery smiled at her, hoping his mouth and chin were firm. "I'm a lawyer, darling. I don't have a drop of romance in my soul."

THEY STAYED for a few after that, talking quietly and watching Jackson sleep. When they left, exhausted and sad, Ellery told them he'd be going home shortly. He fell asleep, head back against the seat, until a tall nurse with light brown skin and dark freckles under his eyes tsked at him and chivvied him to a cot.

Ellery lay down and wrapped the thin blanket over his shoulders. "Thank you." He kept his voice down to respect the night shift. It was hard—the room itself had muted light, but he could still see the brightness of the corridor outside and hear the activity that signified hospital life at all hours.

"You're welcome, sweetness," the man said, with enough camp in his voice to make Ellery smile. He'd worked hard not to ever lisp or swish, but he admired men who just did not give a shit. "It's too bad Kaden and Rhonda couldn't be here. But I'm glad he doesn't have to be alone."

Ellery squinted at him in the light. "Are you Dave or Alex?"

"I'm Dave, and pleased to meet you. Are you the nice man who bought us a new car four days ago?"

"How on earth did you know that?" he asked, laughing.

"It was a guess. Your man here got... soft when he said someone was taking care of it. He didn't know it, of course, but we've known Jackson for a while. We had hopes for him."

"Yeah?"

"Oh yeah. I mean, he makes a big show getting his freak on with anything that moves. Probably had fun doing it. But he's a deeper man than that, you know?"

"I think so," Ellery confided, and then he yawned. "Wake me up if he starts... twitching," he said. "I...."

"I'd have nightmares too," Dave told him, his bitterness unmistakable. "I have nightmares now, and I've *never* been shot."

Ellery shuddered. "Is why I didn't go home," he confessed, eyes closed. "I keep seeing it in my head."

Dave touched his forehead gently, like a friend. "Sleep, baby," he said, and it was like witchcraft, because Ellery did.

WHEN HE woke up again, it was morning, and Jackson was awake too, studying him from the hospital bed.

"You slept here," Jackson said as Ellery swung his legs around the cot.

"Jade and Mike offered," Ellery said defensively. "But they were trying to clean up your house."

"D'oh!" Jackson's pained noise reminded Ellery that he'd lost the only home he had. Even when he could move back in, how was he going to sleep there, wondering where the bullet holes were? "How's my fucking cat?"

"Alive, but he's going to be hobbling around on three legs. I hope that's okay."

Jackson's chuckle sounded stoned. "He'll still be able to fuck Mike's dog."

Ellery didn't tell him about the neutering procedure. That would just be too painful. "Sure," he soothed. "How're you doing? Do you need any more drugs?"

Jackson let out a groan. "Why'd you stay the night?" He wrinkled his nose, his green eyes going slightly crossed. "Wait. This is the third night we've slept together. Is that fair? I didn't get a say in this one."

"Are you kidding?" Ellery asked, standing and stretching. "When I'm sitting by your hospital bed, it counts as a fucking week."

"Nobody tells me the rules." Jackson might have been trying to pout then, but his face wasn't capable of subtlety with this much medication. "Was it my imagination, or did Dave come in and change my catheter? Because that was a violation."

"Thankfully I slept through that," Ellery said fervently. "I was given a choice, you know. Doctor, lawyer, or businessman. I barely made it through anatomy. Fucking frog."

"Yeah," Jackson said knowingly. "But was the frog a Kinsey six, that's what I want to know."

Ellery chuckled. "You're fun this high," he said, not able to help himself. "Is there any way we can just do this with alcohol and not bullets and anesthesia?" He finished his stretches and plopped down by Jackson's bed. Jackson's good arm was stuffed full of needles and tubes, but he twitched his fingers anyway, and Ellery slid his hand between the bars of the bed and held his fingertips.

"We can knock back some whiskey when I get out," Jackson slurred. "And then we can go find Bill Chisholm and shove a Scott Bridger up his ass." He giggled quietly to himself, and Ellery let him fade into sleep.

He stayed there, though, holding his fingertips and not thinking of much at all. It was hard to think when he had so much anger building in his chest. It didn't stay there. It suffused his body, blending into his arms, his legs, his neck, until he was vibrating with it—not just strong but *transcendent* with holy fucking anger.

What was it Hamlet had said? Now I can drink hot blood!

Fuck whiskey. Ellery Cramer wanted himself a goblet full of bloody retribution, and he needed a way to get it.

He was wondering how long he could hold the balance—tenderness with Jackson or the need to go wreak vengeance—when the familiar tread of practical low-heeled women's pumps echoed in the room.

His eyes popped fully open, and he stared at the doorway. She didn't *look* like a hallucination. She made average height look regal, and her hair had never been anything but deep chestnut brown. If Clairol stopped making that color, she'd probably bankrupt the company, but at least Ellery knew it was her. Intelligent brown eyes made up with thick kohl, lipstick bright red, a sleeveless white shell and a summer-weight cardigan, a black skirt, hose, and yes, businesswomen's pumps.

She must have travelled all night, but she looked like she'd stepped right out of her stylist's office, and Ellery was, as always, reluctantly impressed.

"Hello, Mother," he said, fingers tightening on Jackson's in spite of himself. "What in the f—hell are you doing here?"

She clipped in crisply and remained standing by his chair. "Well, Ellery, you've sent me half-a-dozen files in the last two days, all of them involving dirty cops and shooting people and all with the heading *For Safety* on the top. Did you think I wouldn't worry?"

"You weren't supposed to *worry*," Ellery said, pushing himself up. She waved him down, and he stayed. "You were supposed to *stay put* and, you know, knock mountains over if I got hurt."

"Well, apparently it was a near thing!" she said, her voice pitching just enough to let him know she really *had* been worried. "When I called your office, they said you were here. For a moment I thought you were injured, and then the woman said no, you were here visiting your boyfriend." She wrinkled her nose. "Your *boyfriend* got shot?"

"Shoving me down on the ground," Ellery confirmed, and just saying it opened a hole in his chest he'd been trying to close.

"So, he *is* your boyfriend?" She sounded like this was the most important thing in the entire situation.

"Sh!" Ellery glared at her. "If he hears you, he'll rip the tubes out of his arms just to run the fuck away." He looked at Jackson and smiled bitterly. "We're trying to ease him into the idea. I think it was sort of growing on him."

She nodded as though that made perfect sense. "Very well. So, what are you doing here?"

That threw Ellery for a loop. He looked left and then right and then at Jackson and then at her. "Letting him know he's not alone?"

"Well, he's not anymore," she said, setting her handbag down and pulling out her laptop. "And if you *really* cared about him, I'd expect more carnage by now."

Ellery found a smile stretching his cheeks. He released Jackson's fingers and stood, bending over to kiss Jackson's cheek. "Don't worry," he said softly. "I'll be back."

"Check on my cat," Jackson muttered.

"Of course."

Poor Billy Bob. He was going to miss his balls.

"I've got an appointment with Bill Chisholm in"—he looked at his watch—"two hours. If you'll excuse me, Mother, I need to arrange for some backup."

"Backup?" she asked, looking up from her e-mail.

"If I get shot, the only other person to take care of the damned cat has a German shepherd with hurt feelings. He needs me in his life." Traveled all night to walk into his boyfriend's hospital room and urge Ellery to go be a shark. "Just like I need you," he said graciously. She turned her cheek for a kiss, and he gave it with his whole heart.

"Mother?"

"Yes?"

"There are two nurses who are going to come in. Their names are Dave and Alex. Treat them like royalty, okay?"

"Of course, dear."

"And Jackson's ex-girlfriend and his neighbor are going to come in here too, and—"

"Royalty, yes. I understand. I'll cater the event. No worries. Now go bring back someone's head on the front of your Lexus for Mommy, okay?" She batted her eyelashes and he grinned, showing all his teeth.

"It'll fit with the bullet holes through the trunk," he told her. The car had run and the windows hadn't been busted—the bullet holes had been the last priority.

"You *are* going to get those fixed, aren't you?" she asked, as though he'd messed up his room.

"Of course, Mother. But I've got some shit to clean up first." He whirled on his heel then and left, because he wanted one of his best suits on, and a bloodred tie. Armor was armor, and hopefully he wasn't going to need Kevlar.

God love his mother. He really had learned from the very fuckin' best.

Fishes and Sharks

JACKSON REMEMBERED Ellery's kiss on the cheek—uncharacteristically sweet for both of them—but he didn't wake up again for another two hours.

When he did, it was because two women were fighting over him, which was an... unusual feeling to say the least.

"And I'm saying"—Jade's voice rang with irritated authority—"that I don't know you, and I'm not leaving him alone with you!"

"That's acceptable," said someone he didn't know. "However, before you stay here, I insist you wash your hands. You've been chain-smoking, and the smell is offensive."

"I'll tell you what's offensive, you—"

"She's right, Jade," Jackson mumbled. "I can smell it from here. You were supposed to be quitting."

He'd quit, she was quitting, all the time she was quitting—they'd promised her mother.

"Yeah, well, every time I get close, some asshole gets *shot*!"

Jade loomed over his bed, and he squinted. "You look like hell," he said clearly. "Go home."

"I thought you loved me," she said through a watery smile.

"Forever. Where's Mike?"

"Keeping my brother's business afloat. Fixing your house. Saving the goddamned world."

Jackson half laughed. "Look who *you* landed. An upper-fixer."

Her smile firmed. "Yeah. And you landed the original son of a—"

"Be nice."

She let out a breath and tilted her head back. "I just wanted to make sure you were okay," she said plaintively. "Ellery had to go... take a meeting or something—"

Jackson fought hard against the drugs—even managed to sit up halfway. "He had to what? Oh, fucking *ouch*! Mother*fucker*. Someone get this shit off of—"

"Please lie back down." That voice—regal, icy, irrefutable. "You have several bandages in place, and you're *bleeding through them*."

Jackson fell back down because he had to—*not* because she told him to. "Ellery is *where*?" he demanded. "Don't you get it? The guy who took out my house was circling that place like a shark around blood yesterday!" Or was it the day before yesterday? Fuck… was it Monday? "He's going to get *hurt*—I'm stuck in this fucking bed, and he's going to get—"

"Nonsense."

The woman stood up and sort of… *imposed* herself into Jade's place. She was barely taller than Jade, with dark brown hair and familiar, fine brown eyes. Her face was lined, not heavily, just enough to show she was old enough to have no fucks left to give about anyone's opinion.

But her hand on Jackson's forehead was warm, dry, and soothing. "He said he was calling for backup. He's a very bright man, my son. I don't think he'd leave this up to chance."

Jackson looked at her, aching. "We were in my *house*," he told her, trying to make her understand. "The man who shot us is a *cop*. Don't you get it? There *is no safe*."

"I don't believe that," said Ellery's mother. "And neither does he. And like it or not, young man, you're out of the game. Yes, if it was just a flesh wound, you could probably rip your painkillers out like a cowboy and go be his backup. But it's not. And you can't. And you're just going to have to trust him."

Jackson growled at her. He didn't *think* he had, but her eyes got big, and he figured he *must* have actually made that sound he'd been feeling.

"Oh no," Jade said, hand on her hip. "Jackson doesn't trust."

"Well," Ellery's mother replied, her composure slipping back on like a mantle of gold, "he's going to have to learn to. Weren't you going to wash your hands? I've ordered lunch—it should be delivered shortly. There's plenty for everybody."

Jade's eyes slid to Jackson's, and he would have shrugged if he could have moved at all. "Yeah. Sure. What're we having?"

"You'll see when you wash your hands. I have breath mints when you get back."

Jade made it a big deal—swayed her hips, growled a little—but she left.

Jackson wanted to shake his head. Well, yeah. Princess Bee, meet Queen Bee. Now go wash up, we're having dinner.

"I don't know how you can just sit there," he said, surprising himself. He couldn't keep looking at her. Her eyes were too much like Ellery's. He managed to turn his head enough that he didn't have to, and didn't have to remember that tender kiss on the cheek, or the fact that Ellery had slept there when he didn't need to, or...

Or the night before.

When Jackson had talked to another human being like they might have a future together that would make the past worth sharing.

"He's in danger," Jackson said at last, hopelessly. The window overlooked the parking garage, and he stared at it as it baked under the August sun. "How could you just... I can't *protect* him from here."

"That's amazingly sweet," Ellery's mother said, sounding amused.

"I am *not* sweet—ow! *Ow! Ow! Ow! Ow!*" Because he'd jerked, surprised at the idea of being sweet, and pulled something not meant to be pulled. He took a breath, and then another, and it turned into a sob. Oh God, his meds must be wearing...

Ah....

Very slowly, he turned his head and saw that Ellery's mother was pushing the red button on his morphine drip, and he smiled dopily at her.

"You're not supposed to do that," he said, knowing his eyes were at half-mast and not caring.

"Darling, what use is being shot if you're not stoned to the fucking gills?"

There was something very *wrong* with this woman. Something *amok.* But Jackson was out of pain and—

"Ellery...," he mumbled. "Don't let him get shot."

She stood over his bed and smoothed back his hair, much like her son had. "Sweet," she said, as though he'd argued with her. "My family doesn't much *do* sweetness. I think this is a good trait in someone marrying in."

"You're evil," he said. "Pure Satan." And then he giggled, because hey! Who *didn't* need six or eight doses of morphine at the same time? "No bullets for Ellery."

"Darling," she purred, "why should you get all the fun?"

"Wha's your name?" It seemed like he needed a better one than Satan.

"Taylor," she told him, raising a sculpted eyebrow.

"Imma call you Moostifer. Boosimer. *Lucy in the Satan tree with diamonds!*"

She laughed then, and her image went all red with little horns and a pointed tail and a goatee.

Then it split into a thousand different pictures of Ellery's mother, Lucy Satan, laughing her ass off.

And *then* he fell asleep.

When he woke up, evening was lowering. Lucy Satan was stretched out daintily, dozing on a cot, her ankles crossed above her unshod feet and three or four pillows under her head.

Alex was fixing Jackson's medication.

"Whoo boy," Alex said, seeing him waking up. "Someone sure did want you out of it. I don't even think you can *reach* the button."

"It's *her*," Jackson said sourly. "Lucy Satan. She's evil."

"Mrs. Cramer? She's an *angel*!" Alex laughed at him. "She ordered a little catered lunch in here, invited me and Dave and any friends. Called in Jade and your neighbor guy who calls me Light Loafers and then tells me I'm doing a damned fine job and he doesn't want anyone else working on you but me and Dave."

Jackson grimaced. "That's Mike. He's, uh—"

"A good guy without a computer. I get it," Alex said dryly. "So, you're awake. How's your shoulder feeling?"

"I have a shoulder?" As far as Jackson knew, he didn't have toes either.

"That's what we want to hear," Alex laughed. He sobered quickly, though. "Jackson, man, what in the hell are you doing in here?"

Jackson sighed. "Worrying," he said at last.

"About your friend? The one who was here all last night?"

"Yeah."

"Well, don't. He called his mother there about an hour ago. They talked for a long time, and when he was done, *that's* when she asked for a cot. I guess it's about ten o'clock in Boston, so maybe she was wiped out."

Or maybe she wasn't worrying anymore.

Well, there you go. Lucy Satan had a heart.

Jackson's shoulder gave a throb, and he blamed her. "She's evil," he told Alex seriously. "And I *hate* getting shot."

"Well, next time, duck faster."

Duck faster. That was funny. He laughed himself to sleep.

When he woke up again, Ellery was there. He was covered in scratches and wearing a pair of Jackson's sweats and an old, well-laundered academy T-shirt. Jackson's clothes. Jackson's shoulder gave a throb, and he forced himself to ignore it.

This was a story he needed to hear.

In the Home Pond

ELLERY CALLED Kryzynski on his way home, and the nice policeman offered to meet him in front of the capitol building at a quarter to ten.

Ellery told him to wait until ten fifteen, past the rose gardens, where the topiaries cast the most shade.

He needed time to change, for one, and the less time before the meeting, the more time he didn't have to worry about getting shot.

He wondered if Jackson had Kevlar he could wear. Probably—not that it had helped him in his own home—but Ellery wasn't going to ask for it now. If he couldn't walk into the state capitol without Kevlar, he really needed to find himself another job.

In another country.

He got home, changed into his olive suit and good wingtips, and then parked in the paid garage and walked down L Street to the capitol block. He remembered the conversation he and Jackson had two days before, and for some reason, that made it worse. Jackson, who didn't believe in marriage and would probably have applauded the Kevlar, had been shot in his own kitchen.

Jackson, who seemed to be paying for the sins of every corrupt cop in Sacramento, had gone down getting Ellery out of the way because *Ellery* didn't know enough to get down in a firefight.

Ellery had a continuous loop in his mind of Jackson's two expressions: terrified, in flight, tackling Ellery and getting thrown across the hallway… and soft. Shy. Telling Ellery his sex secrets, teasing Ellery gently about his own.

As he walked briskly, he found his chest getting tight, breath harsh and panting in his ears.

God*dammit*, he was angry.

"Hey, Counselor," Sean Kryzynski said, catching him in the shadows by the southwest entrance. He was wearing a sport coat and jeans, much like Jackson did for work, and Ellery had to swallow against how much he wanted Jackson there for backup instead.

"Officer," he said, nodding. "You wearing your Kevlar?"

Kryzynski looked at him sharply. "You expecting this to be—"

"Fuck!"

Ellery heard the backfire first and pulled Sean into the shade between two trees. "Did you hear that?" he asked, not sure if it was his heart beating fast or his active imagination.

"Yeah, that Durango had a—" Sean stared at him, apparently remembering Ellery's statement from the day before. "Holy shit."

Ellery spotted the black Dodge heading for the parking garage and gave thanks. "Ten minutes to the meeting," he said, looking at his watch. "Ready to sprint in your dress shoes, Officer? Because if we don't get to Chisholm first, Bridger might just win a free pass."

"Can he do that?" Kryzynski asked. "I mean, we have evidence on him. We have the photos, we've subpoenaed his phone records, and…." Kryzynski looked around as though they were standing in the precinct house and not in a secluded, shaded area surrounded by topiary. "And that blue wall you were bitching about isn't as strong as you think it is. People found out that Jackson got shot again, and I've gotten a lot of meaningful looks and promises to talk later. What went on with your— partner? Colleague—?"

"Boyfriend," Ellery said shortly, because he'd said it the day before, and he'd be damned if he wasn't going to make that fly now.

"*That* is a damned shame," Kryzynski muttered.

Ellery looked him up and down and rolled his eyes. "You need ten years and a fuckton of bullet scars to compete, junior," he said, not even surprised that Kryzynski was gay.

"I'll work on the years, but I'm not crazy about the mileage. Anyway, Miles is dead. Nobody's forgotten that. And there's only a few quiet whispers about going after Kaden Cameron—and that is damned strange. No. There are enough clean cops downtown who do *not* want to see your guy go under that I'm starting to wonder how he got blindsided in the first place."

"Bill Chisholm," Ellery said grimly. "That's all you need to know."

"And he's our saving grace?"

Ellery closed his eyes and thought about his mother, thought about Jade and Kaden and Jackson, and about everything he believed about family. "He will be, if only we can tell him the truth. Come on."

"Act casual?"

Ellery shot him a look Jackson would have been proud of. "You can act however you want. Just watch my fucking back."

They walked briskly, like they had business, and Ellery had to give young Kryzynski credit. He kept his eyes moving and his posture loose. Anybody looking at him would peg him for law enforcement, same as Ellery had pegged Jackson.

Which was good.

If they were going to outface Bridger, he might think twice about shooting a badge.

Of course, Collin Miles had thought the badge kept him safe too.

Into the lobby to check in. Kryzynski had to show his badge to pass his guns through security, and Ellery had a moment to think that Jackson hadn't carried a gun two days ago. He had one stashed in the glove compartment, but he didn't carry.

For a guy who looked as badass as Jackson Rivers, he walked around as open and vulnerable as the next guy on the street.

Ellery's fury burned a little brighter. Bridger had been in this same building, his gun probably showing in his shoulder holster, and he had walked out to kill. All Jackson had was what he grew up with—his street smarts and his damned near indomitable heart.

When Ellery and Kryzynski resumed their shoulder-to-shoulder stride through the corridors to the elevators, he felt translucent with anger, like flame.

Which may have saved their lives. They both heard clattering and someone yelling at the security guards to move faster—but Ellery didn't really believe Bridger could have parked and run that fast until they were in the elevator and the doors closed just as Bridger came into view, puffing, blowing, but sprinting toward their car.

Ellery glared at him, daring him to open fire here, in the capitol building, where three innocent civilians shared the car with them, and Bridger stumbled back in shock.

The doors closed completely, and they could hear him pounding on them as the car started to rise.

"Jesus," Kryzynski swore. "Stay in the elevator or run for the stairs?"

Ellery's heart pounded and he remembered Jackson's encounter in the stairwell. "Either one's a death trap," he said, swallowing but keeping his face impassive. "Did he look well to you?"

"Heavens, no," said a well-coifed woman in a black business suit. "He looked like he was going to have a heart attack right there."

Ellery nodded grimly at her, offering a tight smile. "Me too. I think—"

The elevator opened on the second floor, and everybody looked at him and Kryzynski.

"Go!" snapped Ellery. "Jesus, fucking hurry!" The baffled workers scurried out of the lift, and Kryzynski hammered the Door Close button in the faces of the people waiting to go up.

Kryzynski laughed in the sudden silence. "I hope you don't have any political aspirations, Counselor, because I think you just pissed off a senator."

Oh Lord. "My mother would be so proud," he muttered. Then he brightened. "But if you manage to shoot Bridger and tie him to the hood of my car, she might forgive me!"

There was a grim nod, and Kryzynski pulled out his phone. As the elevator doors opened, he was calling for backup from the active force, and some of Ellery's fear receded. Yes. They were on the side of the law—and that had meant something his entire life. There was no reason for that to change now.

The corridor seemed especially long, but he and Kryzynski clipped down it at a fair pace. The clatter from the stairwell didn't surprise either of them, though, and Ellery swung inside Chisholm's office just as Kryzynski drew his weapon and slammed the door shut behind him.

Gloria looked up from her desk in surprise. "Oh, Mr. Cramer!" she said, sounding dismayed. "Mr. Chisholm is here, but I was just going to call to reschedule your appointment." She looked around as though Jackson would suddenly appear. "Did you bring your friend?"

On the other side of the door, Sean Kryzynski, off-duty cop, started shouting at Bridger, his superior officer, to stand down.

Ellery was fucking done. "Bill Chisholm!" he yelled. "Bill Chisholm! I know where your daughter is!"

Gloria gasped, and behind her, the closed office door that he and Jackson had run up against opened. In the corridor, Ellery could hear security and what sounded like a doozy of a confrontation—but so far, no gunshots.

"My daughter?"

Ellery looked up toward Chisholm's office door and got a glimpse of their savior and the guy behind Scott Bridger—all rolled into one.

Middle-aged, with a roll around the middle and a ruddy, puffy face. Not enough exercise, too much red meat and wine—but not obviously evil. He had whitish receding hair and tiny eyes, too small to even see what color they were.

But not the devil.

Ellery reminded himself of that as he pulled out his phone.

"This," he said, holding it up, "is a rendering of her taking a picture of a crime scene Scott Bridger staged hours before her death."

Gloria and Chisholm both gasped, and Ellery looked those tiny eyes dead-on. "Do you want to see what she looked like in the morgue? Because if you want to know what I think happened, you need to have security arrest Scott Bridger now, and have them on the lookout for his accomplice."

"Is Owens here?" Chisholm asked, looking numb. "Bridger usually leaves him in the car."

Oh—*that* explained how he got there so fast. He must have been dropped off while his buddy parked. *D'oh!*

"You're dodging the point, Mr. Chisholm. Do you want to know what happened?"

Suddenly Chisholm's ruddy complexion went gray and his lips went a little blue. "Yes," he whispered.

Crooked lawyer? Yes. Corrupt politician? Probably.

But Ellery knew he was—had put money on him being—a father first.

Even Jackson's mom had been worried about her son.

"Gloria," Chisholm rasped, "do me a favor and call security. Tell them to take Bridger into custody and let Mr.—"

"Kryzynski," Ellery supplied quickly. He looked apologetically at Gloria. "Mr. Rivers is in the hospital," he said. "Because your boss's friend shot him."

She gasped, and Chisholm backed up and gestured to let Ellery in.

"Call them, Gloria!" he snapped, and then Ellery was beyond the gate and facing the lion himself.

Chisholm's stride was still purposeful as he walked into the office space and behind his desk. Ellery had a moment to look around—plain carpet, old if quality furniture, and walls with framed prints. Not original and not soothing, but personal. They must have pleased Chisholm and nobody else. On his desk were pictures of his wife, son, and daughter.

Ellery recognized a sweet-faced blonde version of the girl in the pixel rendering—and the meat in the morgue. She'd been beautiful at nine, and twelve, and fifteen. After that her smile soured and she stopped wearing her hair in a ponytail or a braid, going through several incarnations before turning it goth black.

She must have left home before she dyed it pink.

But Chisholm was sitting behind his desk, his tiny eyes narrowed flatly, and Ellery became acutely conscious of the fact that if he didn't make his case here, in this room, he was going to be lucky to get out of the capitol alive.

"Would you like me to tell you what I think happened?" Ellery asked, breaking the congealed silence.

"I want to know about my daughter," Chisholm growled, a bulldog or even a snake, but something tortured and mean.

"No," Ellery told him, "you want to know why you shouldn't let Bridger go and kill me. And my friends. And Kaden Cameron and his family. And Jackson Rivers, whom you tried to kill once already."

Chisholm's head jerked back, and he looked genuinely confused. "Jackson Rivers? What in the hell does he have to do with this? Did he kill her—was it revenge?"

All of that anger burning cold, white, and hot in the core of Ellery's being, and it fountained through him, a geyser of incandescent rage. "*I have had enough!*" Ellery shouted, pounding Chisholm's desk with both fists. "You will sit there and you will listen as I spill out the story of how you fucked up your life and destroyed your daughter—and you will sit there and listen—"

"You can't talk to me like that!" Chisholm bellowed, standing and waving, so much bluster, and Ellery's compassion, his plan, evaporated.

With shaking fingers, he called up that terrible picture, the one that Jackson had snapped while Ellery had been vomiting in the trash can. He enlarged it, focused it on the face of what had once been a pretty girl.

"*Look at that!*" He shoved the screen in Chisholm's face, screaming loudly enough to spit. "Look at it. And listen."

"Oh God." Chisholm sank down slowly into his office chair, hand in front of his face. "Lulu-belle. Baby… oh God…."

"It wasn't supposed to be like this, was it?" Ellery's chin and his voice were shaking, but he just kept talking. "It wasn't supposed to happen. You were an ADA, and you didn't set the world on fire. Nobody cared about Bill Chisholm, honest lawyer, fighting the good fight. You just kept putting away junkies and petty thieves, and your world never changed. Your family wasn't safer, and they weren't any richer, and you… you were trapped. You had two kids and a wife who thought being married to a lawyer would be more glamorous than this, right? And then you had this… this kid stumble into your lap. He had a line on crooked cops, and his IA liaison was incompetent and earnest and well-meaning. You set up a sting operation, you and a few underlings, and before you know it you've got… everything. You followed Hanover *everywhere*. You know where he took his money, where he traded his drugs. You know—"

"Everything," Chisholm muttered, choked. "Yeah."

Ellery found strength, thinking about how brave Jackson had been walking into a snake pit with a wire taped to his underwear. "So you decide to take over Hanover's operation. It's so easy. First you hire a recruit to fill the void. You met him your last year in the service, right?"

Chisholm nodded, lost in that terrible picture. Ellery let it sit, let it mesmerize him, let it pulp his insides, turn him to hamburger, because it was no more than he deserved. "You're very smart. I did one tour. Bridger did two."

"Yeah. Happens. Guys get tight. I get it. So you wanted to take over the operation, but Hanover was losing his shit, and Jackson was a fucking wreck. You couldn't keep him going in on a wire, he was going to get busted, and Bridger wasn't out of the academy yet. So you… now here's where I'm cloudy." Ellery let out a humorless laugh. "It's been an intense four days, you know. But don't worry. I left the notes in the files—if my mother hasn't figured it out, one of my partners will. But you managed to hire a sniper, someone from Hanover's past, if I have my guess, and he took out your loose ends."

Chisholm grunted, but he wasn't going to spill the secret if Ellery didn't know it, and it was too late to go back and tie up this loose end now.

"But it doesn't matter. Hanover's dead, Jackson is rebuilding his life one blood cell at a time, and you? You install Bridger in Hanover's place. Within a year, you've got enough of a side business to fund your bid as Hallenbeck's aide. And life is good. Life is *great*. No more criminals, no more shitty cases. Hours are long, yeah, but you get to take your kids on vacations, send them to college—that's all you ever wanted. Buy the wife a new car now and then, remodel the house. You didn't want the world, right? You just wanted to do for your family." Ellery tried to be snide here, but he didn't have it in him. That trapped feeling—he'd seen it enough times in the criminals he'd defended.

I had to, don't you see? My kids needed clothes. They needed a chance!

Wasn't legal. In Chisholm's case it wasn't defensible—but it wasn't monstrous. Not at first. Not until the blood began to spill.

Human. Just… human. Corrupt and fallible.

And fucked.

"My daughter?" Chisholm begged. "Lulu-belle?"

The pet name was going to break Ellery, damned if it wasn't. "She lost her way, didn't she? Ended up on the street, one of the junkies you used to put away. And you asked your friend Scott Bridger and his buddy Owens to look for her. Bridger put out some feelers, right? Knew the junkie haunts. Who to suss out. But in the meantime, Collin Miles went to Bess Carillo, who, against all common sense, was the *union lawyer* and not the liaison anymore. And Bess, she's still not great on figuring shit out. Collin Miles asks her if he's covered when he gives evidence against his partner, and she—she asks Bridger if maybe the boy is just deluded. Did he misunderstand something? Because God, this couldn't be happening again."

"Collin Miles?" Chisholm broke his terrified stare at his dead daughter. "What's this have to do with anything?"

"You knew," Ellery said, confirming by Chisholm's reaction, even if he had no evidence. "Well, that's handy. See, Bridger told you he was going to have to take out Miles—maybe even told you where. What he didn't tell you was that Luanne was there, probably waiting in the back of the gas station, and she saw Uncle Scott shoot down a cop."

"Oh my God," Chisholm said, voice cracking. "*Luanne!*"

"She was brave, your daughter," Ellery told him. "Because she took a picture and was probably going to send it to someone—just like I sent my files all over God and creation these last few days. But she didn't get a chance. Uncle Scott caught her, you know. He grabbed her phone and hey! Hello! He had the perfect crime-scene photo—didn't have to call in the forensics team after all." Ellery paused and shook his head. "Not bright, Uncle Scott. But pretty fucking brutal. Assembled the evidence, called the ambulances and his own buddies to come in and try to make things look kosher. And in the meantime he's got the girl—don't worry, guys, going to make sure she gets home okay. Just a junkie. It's all good."

"Oh God," Chisholm muttered, staring at the picture again. "Lulu—she knew him. She *knew* him." His voice rose, crackled, and pitched. "She *trusted him!*"

He broke down. Broke down into great gulping sobs.

Ellery walked to the door and peered outside and saw Kryzynski, eye blackened, shirt askew, talking pleasantly to Gloria.

"You have backup downstairs?" he asked, and Kryzynski nodded.

"Okay. We have enough to arrest Bridger and his friend, uh, Owens—"

"Tim Owens?" Kryzynski asked, horrified.

"Is there another cop named Owens that hangs out with Bridger?"

"No," Kryzynski said softly. "No. He's just… young. That's all. Young as Miles. I… you expect it to be the old guys, the guys who get tired."

Ellery looked at Chisholm, who was sobbing over the picture on Ellery's phone. "Some guys are born tired," he said. "Mr. Chisholm?"

Chisholm looked at him, face swollen, crumpled like toilet paper, destroyed.

"You can testify against Bridger and risk jail time for your own involvement. Or you can deny everything and risk him going free."

"Arrest me," Chisholm said, brittle as the cellophane around an empty carton of cigarettes. "Have Gloria call my lawyer and tell him to meet me downtown. My baby." He started to weep, soundlessly this time. "My baby."

Kryzynski got on his phone and called for backup, and Ellery watched as he cuffed Chisholm and walked him out of the office. Ellery grabbed his phone on the way out, exiting from that terrible testament to greed and corruption as quickly as he could.

THE REST of it seemed to take forever. Chisholm and Bridger were perp-walked across the capitol mall and taken away in police cars, and Ellery had a moment to realize that this was it. After the DA deposed him, he was out of this circle. All he had to do was deliver the evidence of the new case against Chisholm and Bridger and get Kaden released.

And maybe talk to the press a little too and turn public opinion in Kaden's favor.

He was waiting for Kryzynski to give him the all clear and escort him to his car, but that was taking a while. They were short one Dodge

Durango and one crooked cop. Ellery didn't like the thought of Owens out there. He'd been the one who killed Coulson and had tried to ram Ellery's car. A wingnut, a loose bullet, and a dangerous one at that, but Ellery couldn't just cool his heels in the lobby of the capitol building, smiling nervously at the lawyers, aides, and politicians walking in and out, until they found him.

When Kryzynski strode up to him, his relief almost gave him leave for a whole and unfettered smile.

"How you doing, flatfoot?" he asked, and Kryzynski blushed.

"I… uh. Crap. You know, I took the detective's exam, right? I think this right here might have just gotten me a chance—at twenty-six, which isn't bad."

"Congratulations," Ellery said dryly. "Can I go now?"

That young, fair face aged ten years. "Look, a couple of us are going to escort you. Don't make a thing of it. We'll escort you to the DA's office so you can give your official statement—you know the drill. But I don't want you unprotected until we get this guy in the hole, you hear me?"

Ellery sighed. "Yeah. Yeah. I really hope we find this guy, because I'm telling you, this has been the longest week of my life."

A week ago Jackson had been an unattainable sex symbol full of mystique and danger—and Ellery had thought wistfully that they would never touch.

Now they had touched, and Ellery hungered for another touch, and another, touches in peacetime, time to know each other better.

He really wanted to tell Jackson that their theories, half-articulated, not even fully researched, had been right. That they'd worked together successfully and not only cleared Kaden, but gotten to the bottom of Jackson's own trouble.

God help Ellery—he liked Kaden, but he *really* wanted to tell Jackson that his own mystery had been fully solved and that he could put it away now. Maybe the nightmares that shook him would ease just a little once he knew it hadn't been random—there had been a plan all along.

"Yeah," Kryzynski was saying into his radio as they cleared the steps. "We're coming down the northeast stairs, heading toward the garden. SWAT teams, are you in place? We want an escort across the street and…." He continued on, cop-speak, and Ellery wondered when had he gotten a radio? And in charge of the op? Ellery was reluctantly impressed. Not enough to give young Sean a second look, but impressed.

And then panicked.

A radio!

"Are you crazy?" he hissed as they cleared the stairs and set off down the garden walks. "We are dealing with *policemen* here. Do you not think they have *police scanners* in place?"

Kryzynski gave him a look of blank surprise.

And Ellery heard the backfire of a large vehicle.

And then, in a hellish parody of the previous morning, another good-looking man leaped on him and threw him to the ground.

Or, in this case, the rosebushes. Just as all hell broke loose.

Fish in a New Pond

JACKSON LISTENED to Ellery's story with increasing agitation. Part of it was the pain—he *needed* his fucking morphine—but part of it was....

"You... you just walked in there?" he said for the thousandth time.

"I had backup," Ellery said, Popsicle cool.

"Yeah, some young cop who's apparently hitting on you." Ugh. Jackson needed to not be in a relationship if it meant he felt like *this* when his lover got hit on. He did *not* like this roiling in his stomach, oh no, he did not.

"You've slept with half the city," Ellery said flatly. "And most of them would jump back in bed with you again—*with* their significant others. So just let me have one guy crushing on me, and deal."

Jackson jerked his head and tried not to howl, but Ellery saw through it anyway.

"You need medicine!" he gasped, and, *thank fuck*, pushed the call button for the nurse.

"Well done," Jackson said, scowling. "Your mother just pushed the morphine button until I passed out."

"I can *do* that?"

Jackson could see it—a little bit of power went a long way with this one. "No. It's illegal. She should be imprisoned."

Ellery pushed the red button once and looked at him. "How much does it hurt?"

Like the hounds of hell are gnashing my bones and tissue and skin between dull bovine teeth. "Not as much as my burning curiosity," Jackson muttered. "So you heard the backfire, and your new boyfriend jumped you in public—"

"And shoved me into the rosebushes." Ellery gestured to the scratches all over his face, hands, and arms.

Jackson winced, which, he thought, made him a really decent human being.

"You're laughing at me, aren't you?" Ellery demanded.

"No," Jackson said sincerely. "I am currently in so much fucking pain, I wouldn't wish bloodshed on another human being."

"I *knew it!*" Ellery hit the red button again, and this time Jackson felt it: the soothing colors of morphine-dendrite interaction bubbling through his blood like a psychotropic rainbow of pain relief.

"But I want to know what happened!" Jackson whined. "You can't make me sleep again, Ellery, the story's not done!"

Ellery laughed and stayed standing over his bed. Then he sobered, because the news was obviously bad. "They lost him. I've seen his picture—average height, brown hair, slightly large nose, lantern jaw. He was the cop who took your phone after you'd been shot." Ellery's jaw clenched. "They found the Durango about two blocks down after the shooting, but he was long gone." Ellery's face closed down—he was hiding something—but before Jackson could ask, Ellery spoke up again. "He knows where you live, and your contacts. I had Jade go through your provider and try to cancel service and erase your chip, but I don't know. He might have a real weapon there."

Jackson grunted. "Do we even know who he was?"

"Owens? We know he was a cop. Apparently he was Bridger's shadow since his own academy days—I don't know why. Bridger hasn't gotten that far in the confession, but it's coming. We took the death penalty off the table in exchange for full cooperation."

"I don't understand," Jackson said, trying to get this really complex idea out when his brain was wrapped in tissue paper and gauze. "Why do bad guys risk their life with every bad thing they do and then weenie out with the death penalty. Do they think it can't happen unless their hands are cuffed?"

"I wish I knew," Ellery said, sighing. Even in Jackson's rainbow-tinted euphoria, he could see the exhaustion tightening the corners of Ellery's eyes. "I just know he's out and he's dangerous, and I'm not going to rest easy until he's caught."

"Fuck." God, every now and then the universe threw in a little kick in the nads to remind you that life was fucking random. "Who killed Luanne?" he asked.

"That was entirely Bridger, may God damn him to hell." Ellery's voice throbbed with passion. "And by the way, we have a case for murder for hire for the guy who shot you eight years ag—"

"Drop it," Jackson said flatly. He had to fight to stay awake, but he wanted to be absolutely clear on this. "If it was murder for hire, it wasn't personal. Let's keep it that way."

"It was personal to me," Ellery said softly, stroking his cheek with one finger.

Jackson leaned into the touch shamelessly, hoping that when he could stop pumping morphine, he'd have his control over his emotions back. "I can't believe you just strolled in there like... like some sort of superhero and got him to break."

Ellery grimaced. "Chisholm was easy. He didn't think he was a bad guy. The guys who know they're bad guys, they're hard to break because they have no fucks to give. But Chisholm, he just... kept sliding down that slope, telling himself it was for his children."

And like that, Jackson could feel for the guy who'd fucked him over. He'd seen what was in the morgue, and it had hurt his heart. He couldn't imagine what it would be like if it was someone he knew—

Ellery.

He closed his eyes against the sudden surge of pain, of imagination, of retroactive fear. "Next time," he said, hating his wobbly voice and the drugs and the throbbing of his entire body underneath, "next time, you don't go there without me."

Ellery cupped his cheek. "That's a promise."

"Fuck promises," Jackson muttered. "That's me telling you how it's going to be."

"Sure," Ellery agreed. "You do that." Then he bent down and whispered, "Right up until it's my turn to top again."

Oh God. "Hatechu," he mumbled, and then he was out.

HE HAD one more surgery to remove bone fragments and add pins, and he was transferred out of ICU a couple of days later.

Ellery visited during the evenings after that, and he would report on the progress of the case. The day they finally finished taking Bridger's deposition, he came in white-faced and cold with fury and simply sat losing a game of chess for an hour before he spoke.

When he did speak, what he said was startling. "You're good."

"Good with what?" Jackson asked. He'd lost interest in the game forty-five minutes ago—he was just recovering, for Christ's sakes, and wasn't ready to "people."

"A good person." Broodily, Ellery shoved a pawn aside, then put it back and moved his bishop. Jackson thought he should do something with that opening, but fuck him if he could figure out what.

"You too," Jackson said. He meant it—so many times Ellery could have bailed, and he hadn't. So many times he could have left Jackson's family—or Jackson—in the wind, and he'd been faithful to the end.

"Don't give me credit here for anything but self-interest." Ellery pushed his queen over with a controlled movement.

"I don't know what you got out of this whole thing but a freeloading roommate and a cat that is probably pissing in your house!" Jackson grumbled. Ellery hadn't said anything, but Jackson couldn't imagine ol' Billy Bob in such a nice place without exacting a little damage. Jackson could only think of those perfect carpets, the lovely hardwood, and weep.

"The freeloading roommate and perfectly well-behaved cat are my blank check," Ellery snapped. "Don't you get it? I did all this to impress *you*!"

Jackson blinked slowly. It was true, they'd cut back on his meds a bit since those first two days, but he still spent a good portion of his conscious hours stoned. He wasn't sure he was processing things the way he should.

"Mission. Accomplished." He blinked again and squinted at Ellery, feeling owlish. "This was a bad thing?"

Ellery shook his head. "He's a bad man, Jackson. I should have been in it to get the bad man."

Jackson grunted. "I wasn't in it to get the bad man," he reminded, voice soft. "I was in it to save my brother. To protect my family. Sorry. Self-interest abounds here. We're both fuckers."

Ellery's laugh sounded a wee bit hysterical—but unforced. "Yeah. Yeah, okay. We're not Captain America. I get it."

"Even Captain America wanted something," Jackson told him. Yup, hospital cable had gotten way the hell better in the last eight years. "He wanted to not be powerless. He wanted to be able to change things himself. Still a decent guy. Motivated by self-interest."

"Ayn Rand was a prick," Ellery said viciously, standing up and doing that wandering thing. Jackson had to have help to go to the john—

and hell, that had been a cause for celebration. He yearned to wander around his kitchen again.

"I thought he was a she?"

"I read *The Fountainhead*—that philosophy was all about having a giant penis and fucking the world and then saying, 'Hey, look, world, you are forced to bear my brainchild, so boom! Suck it!' I stand by my epithet." Moodily he stretched his arms over his head, and Jackson tried to figure out what Ellery needed right here, right now.

"If we were at my house, I could blow you," he said pragmatically. That seemed to be what people needed when they were in this sort of mood.

"If we were at your house, there would be people coming in and trying to fix your air-conditioning unit."

"*Fuuuuck.*" Jackson couldn't help it. Irritability and cabin fever had officially set in. "Look, Ellery, I can't fix it. Bridger was a fucker, and no, I didn't know about it. I didn't know about Chisholm or realize Bess Carillo was sending more young men off to die—is anything happening to her, by the way?"

"No," Ellery said, disgusted. "The DA is ignoring that because they would have to get her disbarred and maybe press charges, so, you know. A warning. It's revolting."

"Fucking yes it is. But you're missing the point. We have a tiny bit of the world. Even Chisholm working for Hallenbeck—he had *finite power* to change the world. You either spend your time grabbing all the shit you can just for you, or you spend your time hoping you leave the world better than you found it. That doesn't mean you don't get good shit. It doesn't mean you don't deserve the good shit that you get. It just means that sometimes you walk away from the good shit to wade around in the muck and try to clean it up a little. And that's it. That's all I got. Some people got God—I've heard good things about the guy, but I don't know him personally. Some people got alcohol—they're fine as long as nobody gives them any goddamned guns. Some people got family, and those people I can get behind. But none of us—not you, or me, or hell, Kaden, who's the best man I know—can go out and change the fucking world without a lot of pain and suffering. So it's okay that's not how this started. What matters is that you ended it."

Great! One of the best speeches of his life! Two thumbs up! To punctuate it, he yawned.

And Ellery laughed. He stopped his wander and came to Jackson's bed. "*You*," he said, "get more interesting every time I talk to you."

"*You* get better-looking. I like your superpower best."

Because Ellery *did* look good. His hair had been pulled back from his face every day, perfect without fail, and his suits—all olive and navy, Jackson noticed—had been impeccable.

Someone, probably his mother, had given him a series of ties with Siamese cats on them. None of the cats had the same flair as Billy Bob, but every time Jackson saw a new tie, he smiled.

Ellery looked away, a faint crescent appearing at his cheek. "Mother is leaving tomorrow. She would like to speak with you again, without me, probably in the morning."

"If she tries to pay me to leave your scrawny ass alone, how much should I take?"

"My trust fund is pretty hefty. Start at the stars and see if she blinks."

Jackson laughed, partly because Ellery hadn't even rolled his eyes. "You sound pretty sure I wouldn't take the money," he teased.

"Oh, I know you'd take it. But your deal had nothing to do with me pursuing you, so you could take the money in good conscience and I could bugger you senseless once she left. It would be win-win, the scam of the century. Go for it."

Jackson winked. "I just might," he said with another yawn. He moved his body automatically to stretch, and once again the move left him breathless with pain. It was getting late anyway. Ellery had work at home, Jackson was sure. His eyes closed slowly and he blinked them open.

"Ellery?"

"Yeah?"

"How soon before Kaden gets out of protective custody?"

"I see the judge in two days." Ellery's voice dropped as though he were about to deliver bad news. "The department has been ugly about it, Jackson. They might end up guarded by marshals for another two weeks."

"Shouldn't that end after the arraignment?" Jackson asked. "That's only a few days."

Ellery nodded grimly. "We need to wait until it sinks in, Jackson. That Kaden *didn't* do it. That policemen *did* do it. Because right now there's an ugly street vibe, and until the reality hits, Kaden and his family aren't going to be safe in this city."

Jackson sighed. "I miss my family," he said nakedly. Jade and Mike had been by too, but Kaden, Rhonda, the kids—they were the core. The center. "But I'm glad you keep coming by." He was going to have nightmares this night, even with the morphine. Oh, God, *especially* with the morphine. And the pain under it. And knowing, seeing firsthand, what evil could do when it was riled. "Stay with me a little," he begged, hating himself. "After I go to sleep?"

Ellery nodded and swallowed. "I brought my briefcase," he said, and Jackson realized that was where he'd gotten the chess set. Well, detecting wasn't happening at the moment. "I'll work until it's time to go."

Jackson shut his eyes tight. "Thanks. Just… thanks."

Ellery brushed his lips against Jackson's cheek, and Jackson clung to that as he went under.

HE SLEPT badly. Alex and Dave came in twice during the early hours of the morning to make sure he wasn't pulling anything in his shoulder as he thrashed about. Alex ended up taking his break in Jackson's room, munching on a crappy sandwich and telling Jackson about the time he and Dave tried to have sex stoned and ended up needing a new DVD player. Jackson laughed at the story and tried really hard not to imagine the thing happening.

It didn't work.

He dreamed about the DVR growing a penis and having a really intense BDSM scene with his two favorite nurses, and woke up feeling a weird combination of disgust, embarrassment, and arousal.

Which didn't go away when he realized Ellery's mother was in the room.

"You're up?" she asked archly.

"Lucy Satan!" he said, because he liked the name.

"Certainly—but it might make family dinners difficult when you come to visit. You should probably stick to Taylor then."

Jackson blinked and hated everybody. "Your son has a crush on me," he explained patiently. "I have no idea how long this will last." He remembered his speech about self-interest the night before and felt perfectly vindicated in this next statement. "I will take full advantage of his delusion while I can, but don't worry. I'm an alley cat, Mrs. Satan. I'm not a keeper."

The woman had the nerve to laugh. "You're a *tom*cat, Mr. Rivers. Once a tomcat is fixed, he loses his urge to wander. Eventually he even stops pissing in all the corners. Believe me—you may be a fixer-upper, but once you are fixed, you *will* stop wandering."

Jackson swallowed, a little bit of fear in his stomach. "I don't want to be fixed," he said, trying not to panic about his balls in the middle of a purely theoretical discussion.

"Of course you do." She had been sitting on the couch while he slept, but now she stood and snapped her briefcase shut, then approached the bed. "I just came to thank you, Jackson."

"For almost getting Ellery killed?" Oh God. He was tired already.

"For giving him a chance to be great," she corrected, smiling slightly.

Oh fuck this. Fuck being fixed, and fuck being in a relationship, and *especially* fuck dealing with this scary woman.

"How much money would you give me to leave him alone?" Jackson asked, not sure if he was being facetious or not.

Lucy Satan's smile had an unusual number of teeth. "Far more than you're prepared to accept," she said coolly. "But I *will* buy you another car, once you're on your feet and your house is fixed. My son didn't have the heart to tell you that your old one—"

"It was *new*!" Jackson wailed.

"Your old new car was demolished in the drive-by." She shrugged. "But since you appear to be mostly healthy, I am taking my leave this afternoon." She took a few steps toward the door and then turned and pegged him to the bed with her poised regard.

"If I felt you were a danger to my son, Mr. Rivers, you never would have seen me. You never would have met me. You never would have known I was in Sacramento. And Ellery would never see you again. You may expect him this evening, after work, per usual. I suspect I shall see you this holiday season." She smiled regally. "A gift is customary, whether it's Christmas or Chanukah. I prefer silk and perfume, just as a general gesture. May you heal well by then, or the plane ride will be most uncomfortable."

And with that she was gone, and Jackson was left gaping.

He stayed that way until his next nap.

TWO WEEKS later he was *begging* to get out of the hospital, antsy as hell, irritable as *fuck*, and a miserable bastard to be around.

Ellery still came by a few hours every day, and the guy's company was… growing on him.

He supposed it would have to be. He had another month to go before his house was good, and Jade had sold her lease after Jackson's first week in the hospital. Jackson had asked her if she was sure about moving in with Mike so damned soon, and she told him that no, she would just be staying with Kaden and Rhonda while they caught up financially.

Then Mike told him that while there were workers in and out, he was converting one of the rooms to a strictly "Jade" room—a sewing machine, because she'd learned how to sew from her mother, and cupboards for fabric, and an extra bed for relatives.

"But Mike, what if it doesn't work—"

Mike had shrugged, winking. "It still makes me look like a catch, right?"

Well, yeah. Actually.

But Jackson wanted to get back to work. He could still work from a desk, right? He could run down stuff on the computer or help stake out a potential lead. He wasn't entirely helpless, right?

He just felt so helpless without a job, or a home, or Kaden to protect him.

He was two days away from medical clearance and had just finished a couple of laps around the long-term-care floor with his IV attached and his scrubs hanging low on his waist when he saw a big black man standing at the doorway to his room.

And he almost broke into tears.

Kaden's hug—careful of the healing, bandaged, casted shoulder and the IV with all the drugs—lasted a long, long time.

And then he parked his big body in Jackson's room and they had themselves a little chat.

About everything.

About three weeks in a small house up in the Northern California hills and homeschooling his kids. About how he'd worried the first time he and a marshal had gone into town for firewood, because he was pretty sure nobody there had ever seen black people, and how maybe that was true, but that didn't mean the rednecks were necessarily *bad* folks. Like Mike, he said. They said all the wrong things sometimes but still had good hearts.

About how he'd looked into how much money it would cost to live in a smaller place away from the city, away from the problems they'd known intimately since they were children.

"Not everybody's nice there," Jackson said, fearing what was coming next. He could see it—he could. "You have community ties here."

Kaden nodded, bobbing his head back and forth like he was weighing and measuring. Then:

"It's time for a change, Jackson. You and Jade, you both finally stopped screwing around with each other and are looking for somebody real."

"Hey, did Jade tell you about Ellery—?"

Kaden shrugged. "Yes. But no, that's not it. I'm saying we'll always be family, man. You will always be welcome to visit. We wouldn't have a place without a spare bedroom with your name on it, and one with Jade's name on it, and a gaming couch for when you're not there."

"But…." Jackson couldn't finish that sentence, because he felt like a child, lost and alone, hiding in his room and wishing his mother and her drugs and her john would just go the fuck away. He was a grown man, dammit! He swallowed. "Why? Why go now?"

Kaden shook his head. "Because two crooked cops came into my store, and one of them got blown away. And my employee and friend is dead. And a girl I only knew as a shadow got killed that same night. And I don't know if I can stay in my own goddamned service station ever again. I work two jobs down here. I could sell my house, my share in the service station, and go up in the hills and work one. I could see my kids for dinner every night. We've scoped out the schools—Rhonda can get a job anywhere. You know her—she's crazy good."

"But…." Interviewing. The one black woman in an all-white high school. Jackson just kept imagining throwing Rhonda into the high school in *Footloose*, and he was halfway to verbalizing that when he realized that he was being an ass about a world he was ignorant of.

But that Kaden had been living in for the better part of a month.

"How long?" he asked instead.

"Rhonda and I did the finances in this last week. We put a bid on a house while we were there, actually. We find out in two weeks. If it's accepted, we can be moved up before the kids miss more than a week in school, stay at a temp place, and be moved in by the end of September."

Jackson swallowed. "I can't coach River's soccer team this year," he mourned, remembering how much he loved that.

"They already started practices," Kaden said kindly. He nodded to a handmade card on the windowsill. "I see you got their good wishes."

Yeah. "So, I guess I don't even get to help move, huh?"

Kaden rolled his eyes. "Brother, all you have to do is sit in the shade and direct." And then Kaden's eyes grew bright, and his lower lip began to tremble. "After what you and that lawyer did for us, you get to come and be royalty, you hear me?"

Jackson's mouth twisted. "Self-interest, K," he said. "All the best stuff I do is because my life is better with my family in it."

He expected a hug then, but what he got was a glare. "Don't bullshit me, Jackson Rivers."

"What?" Jackson grimaced at him, hating that he couldn't twist and throw a pillow, not yet. "What do you mean, bullshit?"

"You, Mr. Cramer—you did this, you followed it through. You're good guys."

Jackson half laughed, half cried. "I'm not a good guy," he said, his voice a little broken. "I'm an asshole afraid of being alone."

Kaden stood and clasped Jackson's good hand in his. "Still bullshit," he said softly. "You're afraid of letting someone in who's not me or Rhonda or Jade. I'm not going to pretend I'm doing this for you—but maybe you letting someone in is the good that will come of it when I do."

Jackson finally got his hug, and then he was forced to just sit back and watch him go. Of course they'd see each other again, but his family was changing.

"I'm out of it for a little while and everybody gets delusions of grandeur," he said softly. But he didn't even have Billy Bob to give him the line back.

Ellery wasn't coming in that night—he'd already told Jackson he'd be working late so he could get Jackson situated the following afternoon. Jackson had that entire evening to sit back, stare at the television blindly, and wonder, *What next?* He was going to live in Ellery's house for a couple of weeks—how would that work?

How soon before Jackson crapped this thing up? How long before he turned what had been a distant workable relationship into a giant clusterfuck of emotion and recriminations? It had been a long time since he'd had a monogamous lover, but he seemed to remember that happening a lot.

But he couldn't bring all that up to Ellery when the guy came to pick him up in his recently repaired Lexus. For one thing, Jackson recognized the act of sacrificing your own schedule to help out somebody else, and he was humbled—and uncomfortable.

Of course, he was even more uncomfortable in the car back to Ellery's place, but that was mostly physical. He must have grunted one too many times, because Ellery finally burst out with, "Did you take the goddamned pain pill?"

"No. No, I didn't. Because I wanted to get the hell out of there, and I was afraid if I so much as looked at the oxy bottle, they'd make me shit in a bucket to prove I could."

Ellery half laughed. "Shit in a bucket?"

"You have no idea how much it comes up when you're in the hospital. God, what a nightmare."

"Well, let me get you a soda on the way home, and you can take your pain pill and be happy and stoned for the rest of the day." Ellery's dry humor was back in full force, and Jackson approved.

"That's sweet," he mumbled. "I don't want to take too many, though. You know—"

"Oh my God, do I. Chill out, Jackson. Take a Vicodin and take the edge off. If you become a junkie, I'll shove you in rehab and buy you a liver, but that's later and this is now!"

Jackson glared at him. "You are remarkably cavalier about my fucking health."

Ellery growled. "I'm going to slap you. Your health has been my only topic of conversation for the last three weeks. 'How's Jackson doing? Is he okay? What do you mean he's coming to your house? Wait, are you guys seeing each other? Is he ready for that? Because he could stay at my place *no strings attached*!'"

Jackson burst out laughing. "You are so making that up."

"I am not."

"You are too."

"No, I swear. That was actual text. I have the court reporter's notes." Jackson snorted. "You *lie!*"

"I'm a lawyer, that's my job, but not about this!"

They bickered as they got into the drive-through line and then on the rest of the way home. When they got to Ellery's house, Jackson stepped in, fully expecting to feel as comfortable as a farmer stepping off the tractor and into a five-star hotel.

What he was not expecting was the familiar smell of animal. Not cat pee, although clean litter was an undertone, just… furry mammal.

Followed by Billy Bob hobbling up to him, one powerful back leg making up for the loss of the other.

"Billy!" Oh Lord, his cat. Jackson's *cat* was there, and for some reason, of all the changes, of all of the big things walking over the threshold of Ellery Cramer's super awesome house in the super rich neighborhood might imply, having the damned cat made everything so very, very doable.

With a careful squat, he scooped Billy Bob up and then stood. Ellery caught his elbow as he was rising, and he grunted thanks, but mostly he was just worried about being nose to nose with his companion, the buddy who had seen a lot of people in and out of his bedroom but who had never left him alone.

The cat was already drooling when Jackson lifted him up. "Billy Bob," Jackson murmured. "Jesus, buddy, I'm glad to see you." He tapped Billy's bandage tentatively and realized that it was nearly plastered over with a tough wrapping. "And someone is taking very good care of you." He turned shining eyes to Ellery. "Thank you," he said gruffly. "I mean, you've been saving the world for the last month, and you've taken care of my damned cat. Thank you."

Ellery helped him to the couch and then sat next to him, scratching Billy Bob under the chin. "Is this all I had to do to impress you?" he said, smiling slightly. "I could have done without saving the world, frankly."

"I thought I told you—finite, tiny things," Jackson said. God, it wasn't the morphine. He could finally admit that. With the air of giving something up that he might never take back, he rested his head on Ellery's shoulder. "First you save my cat, tomorrow you save the city, maybe the day after, work on world peace."

Ellery wrapped a careful arm around his back and then leaned into the couch. Jackson felt the kiss on his hair, and for the first time in weeks, he wondered what it would be like to be intimate with someone again.

To be intimate with Ellery when all of the bandages were off and the pain pills were gone. Or even a little bit before.

"The cat I can do," Ellery said gruffly. "But I'd really rather just save you."

"I can save myself."

"Sure. Jackson, I, uh—I didn't want to mention this in the hospital, but, uh…."

Jackson saw it then and pretty much ignored whatever Ellery was saying. "Hey! What the hell happened to his balls!"

"That's what I was trying to tell you," Ellery said, wincing. "You understand—they said it was really the best thing for him since we didn't want to let him out—"

"You got him *fixed*!" Jackson wailed. Oh God! The betrayal! He looked at Billy Bob for recrimination, but the cat just purred some more and melted into his chest. "Billy! Speak to me, man! Are you going to be okay?"

Prrrr.

"Jackson, don't get hysterical—"

"But *why*!" Jackson demanded. "Why change things? Why risk who he is to fix what's not broken?"

"Because!" Ellery snapped—and pulled Jackson out of his cat-induced hysteria. "Because! He was breaking a little bit every day! Cats don't get mean when they've been fixed, Jackson. They don't *wander* when they're fixed. He was going to go away one day and never come back, and he doesn't even want to go outside now. They stay put when they're fixed. It's what they need!"

Jackson stared at him, absurdly hurt. "Is that what you want from *me*?" he asked. "Do you want *me* to be neutered? So I don't run away?"

Ellery squinted at him. "Okay, so oxy is not your drug, I can see that now. *No*. I don't want you neutered." Those two red crescents appeared at his pale cheeks, and Jackson felt a stirring at his stomach to know he could do that. "I like you *not* neutered, as a matter of fact," he said. "I like you very much *unneutered*." Ellery grimaced. "But I don't mind if you get fixed a little. I don't want to cut off your balls, Jackson. But I worry very much about what will happen if you decide to wander."

For a moment Jackson heard the words in his head. *I can't be fixed. I'll wander until I die.*

But Ellery's arm felt so warm around his shoulders.

Jade was falling in love with his neighbor.

Kaden and Rhonda were moving away.

Jackson's past had been put to bed—mostly—but a cold-eyed killer had his phone, and his contacts, and Jackson had to learn how to do his job all over again.

And a man he liked to kiss was offering him a place to sleep, and someone to bicker with, and a friend to eat meals with, and companionship—and sex. Definitely sex.

If only Jackson could hang around and not wander.

"If he's fixed, he won't wander?" Jackson asked cautiously.

"Not if he has a good home," Ellery said. "That's the way it should work."

Jackson nodded and rested his head against Ellery's chest a little. "He's got a lot of scars, you know."

"He's missing a leg, Jackson."

"I wasn't talking about the cat."

Ellery's sigh dusted his hair, but neither of them moved. "I was. But now I'm talking about you. I've seen your scars. I'll see your new ones. You don't wander away from home, and I won't change where it is."

"Kaden's moving."

Another sigh. "Yeah. Jade told me. She cried through lunch yesterday."

"Are you sure I can be fixed?" God, what if he wasn't? Ellery could walk into a lion's den armed with pictures and words—what if Ellery wasn't sure?

"I have faith if you do."

Jackson touched noses with Billy Bob and realized again how close his cat had been to not being. "Okay," he whispered. "Faith. I have some. But I also know that if I don't get back to work, you're going to need faith and a tranquilizing dart to keep me from going batshit crazy."

Ellery's sigh had a gearing-up quality this time. "Don't worry, Jackson—the firm needs you after your absence. And if they don't, I've got an idea too. And Owens is still out there, and Bridger hasn't named half the guys on his payroll, and—"

"Bad guys," Jackson said happily. "There's bad guys we can get."

"Yup. And then there's us."

Jackson smiled. "You're such a superhero."

"Shut up."

"Nope. That's not part of the fixer-upper package."

This time Ellery's kiss landed on his cheek, and Jackson turned his head just a little so he could taste it. Yeah. After a little more healing, he wanted more of that.

"As long as you admit you can be fixed," Ellery said against his mouth.

"Fixed creatures don't wander," Jackson breathed.

Neither would he.

Fish on a Mission

SCOTT BRIDGER had grown leaner in the past four weeks, and Ellery was glad for the bolts on the floor that held his leg and wrist chains. Jail had brought out the feral alien in him, and the veins and tendons in his neck and temples bulged with every snarled word.

"I told you," Bridger snapped, "I have *nothing* that you don't already have. You have his address—"

"A shitty apartment that hasn't been occupied in months." Ellery hated that—it suggested premeditation. "There wasn't even any furniture."

Bridger's aggressive bulldog stance retreated, even cowered. "That's... that's weird."

"You fucking think? All we know about this guy besides his old military file is what he looked like in his driver's license two years ago, but...." Ellery shook his head. This wasn't even his case. He wasn't planning on defending Bridger and certainly wasn't defending Owens. But Arizona had told him privately that the DA had turned the search for Owens over to the DOJ and was currently focused on prosecuting the men they had.

They had plenty of evidence to put Bridger and Chisholm away, and some of their more prominent flunkies as well. But Owens was gone. The chief of police had given a press conference calling him an underling, a perpetrator of petty crimes and one murder.

Jackson had taken one look at his police ID and told Ellery that he'd had plastic surgery, was wearing prosthetics between his gums and cheeks to change the shape of his face, and had subtly changed the color of his hair to a light brown from a much darker color.

And both of them had looked at each other grimly and swallowed.

There was something bigger going on here—something Chisholm and Bridger hadn't known about and Sacramento's criminal justice system was too preoccupied to pursue.

Looking at Bridger's face now, Ellery had that gangrenous feeling in his stomach all over again.

"Anything," Ellery said now, not too proud to beg. "Do you have anything that can help us get this guy? Remember, you just rolled over on him. He is out, and he's dirty, and if you could beat Luanne Chisholm to the bloody pile of meat I saw on a morgue slab, what could this guy do to you?"

Bridger blanched. "Hey, I knocked that girl out. She didn't know. I told her she was going to see her father and she…." His voice dropped. "She died happy. She never knew her Uncle Scott was a scumbag who…." He swallowed and pulled his armor on all over again. "Owens…." He closed his eyes. "I… I was beating the body because… because I didn't want anyone to know—you know this. And Owens watched me and…."

That quickly, the aggressive bulldog was completely gone.

"You gotta understand," he whispered. "I'm not like that. I did the things I did because… practical, you know? But Owens, he got off on it. He got…." His voice dropped to a whisper. "He got *hard*. I think he *came*, watching me do that to her." Bridger shuddered. "I mean, the guy came to my house for barbecues, hung out on my couch, but… until that night, I didn't know. And we were dirty. Dirty cops. Hookers, drugs— that's what dirty cops do. But I think there were more DBs than there should have been these last two years, you know?"

Ellery swallowed. "All female?"

Bridger shook his head. "Naw, but young. All young."

"White?" Ellery knew serial-killer profiles—who didn't watch TV?

"Pretty," Bridger said with a shrug. So ethnicity wasn't his profile. "Pretty and… dirty. Like us."

Oh God. Pretty junkies. Pretty sex workers. Young. He and Jackson, they had some work to do.

The guard came in then; Ellery's time was up.

"Hey, Cramer," Bridger said, some of the bulldog coming back. "You gonna give me anything—you know, for the info?"

Ellery nodded. "Yeah. I'm going to make sure you and Owens get homes in separate prisons, with lots of protective custody." He was trying to be a hardass.

Bridger almost cried. "Thanks, Cramer. That's fucking human of you. Thanks."

Ellery left the county lockup fighting the urge to vomit—and the burning need to shower. He needed to talk to Jackson. Jackson had a way of making these things human. They were still horrible, but Jackson didn't see monsters—unless he was dreaming.

Every night for the past week, Jackson had thrashed in his sleep. He'd calmed down with Ellery's quiet touch, but Ellery wanted… more.

He wanted to make all the monsters go away.

Stupid wish—Jackson's demons had been fully formed and full of flesh before Ellery arrived—but still. This was not going to make them rest any easier.

But Ellery keeping a secret might be the first thing to send Jackson running.

EVERY NIGHT for the past week, Ellery had gotten home and Jackson had been in the middle of trying to make dinner. It had been sweet but not perfect. Jackson could grill fish with one arm and toss a nonfigurative salad. He could make spaghetti, but he'd spilled some of the noodles, because Ellery had caught him trying to sweep the floor and scoop them up, his arm still dutifully taped in the sling.

It beat takeout, but Ellery would pick sex, even over home cooking, any day.

Jackson had been suspiciously finicky about sex.

It was like trying to pet a feral cat. Ellery would come up behind him while he was attempting a one-handed stir of mac and cheese, and Jackson would rub up against him for a moment and then dodge fluidly away. He would crawl into bed at night wincing in pain, but when Ellery suggested maybe a pain pill would be good, he'd grunt no and turn his head.

Ellery was wondering if he'd have to wait another six weeks for the cast and pins to come out before he'd get to touch him.

But driving home with that horrible fear in his stomach, that feeling of despair etched into his skin by Bridger's words….

He thought he was going to have to be the one to change. He called Jackson at the first stoplight. "I'm getting dinner," he said crisply.

"But—"

"You're supposed to be getting better and helping Crystal with her workload," he said, no bullshit in his voice. "Not playing maid. You suck at it. I'll be there with Thai food in an hour."

"I can't decide if I'm being rewarded or punished." Jackson's sourness had a decidedly wounded flavor.

"You're being taken care of," Ellery shot back. "Now have a snack, take a pain pill, and be prepared to listen to me bitch and moan about my day."

Jackson grunted. Ellery had very deliberately *not* talked about the worst parts of the deposition, just because they riled Jackson as much as they riled Ellery.

"Now *that's* what I'm talking about!" Jackson said after a moment. "I take it the relationship is back on?"

Ellery was so confused he almost missed his green light. When the honking behind him had stopped, he managed to talk again. "It was never *off*."

"Oh, it was. There was cuddling and shit, but it was all about 'Oh, poor Jackson. He's hurt. We have to be fucking gentle!' God. I can't even pay rent. Your mother bought me a fucking car, do you know that?"

"It arrived last night, Jackson. I was there." His mother had bought the exact same Honda, but she'd made this one silver.

"Jesus. Stop being so considerate of my fucking feelings. I was shot, not lobotomized."

Ellery took a deep breath and dodged a truck that was actively trying to kill him. "You ever think that maybe I just wanted to be... *gentle* with you?"

The puzzled silence on the other end of the phone told him that no, that thought had not occurred. "I'm sorry I've had to nap a lot," Jackson said contritely. "Or that I'm not... Captain America—"

"*You're* not Captain America? You *are* Captain America. God, you let that superhero thing go to your head. My lawyer powers are not bigger than your PI powers, and—augh! Traffic sucks in this city! Just shut up and let me bring you takeout!"

He hung up and swung into the parking lot of the Thai place on J Street, trying to lose some of his inarticulate irritation while he waited for food.

By the time he pulled up to his house, the pumpkin curry sending soothing waves of food-joy through the car, he thought he had a handle on what had happened.

Jackson was feeling helpless. Ellery had made him feel *more* helpless by protecting him. Oh holy Jesus, and Ellery thought *he* was the grown-up in relationships. He had nothing on a guy who'd had to fight for every scrap of affection he'd ever earned.

Jackson was sitting at the kitchen table, typing one-handed at his laptop while Billy Bob gazed at him affectionately from the table runner in front of him.

Ellery glared at the cat, and Billy Bob licked his whiskers back.

"You are not supposed to be there," he muttered, setting the takeout down. He scooped the cat up and set him on the floor. Billy Bob had the nerve to kick his single back foot at Ellery, and while the gesture was awkward, it was also unmistakable.

Fuck you, bub—I'm no more helpless than a hungry jaguar.

Jackson eyed him with unfriendly green eyes, hair falling forward over his forehead, jaw squared and ready to fight.

Ellery grabbed the back of the chair and jerked it around, the scraping sound on the tile echoing throughout the kitchen.

"What in the he—"

A kiss—hard and real, like that first time in Jackson's hall, fighting to top. Jackson returned it, biting his lip hard, pulling back and planting one hand on the back of Ellery's head and trapping him there.

Ellery gave back, taking charge, resting some of his weight on the table but using his other hand to burrow under Jackson's shirt. His left side was off-limits, but his right side was still sound, if a little thinner than it had been. Ellery grasped his bicep, kneaded his pec, skimmed fingernails across his nipple. Jackson tightened his hand in Ellery's hair, and he pulled back.

"What are we doing?" he rasped.

Ellery pinched his nipple hard enough to make him gasp and then sank to his knees.

The tile was hard, but Ellery ignored it and undid the fly of Jackson's cargo shorts. He tugged sharply, and Jackson pushed up, leaving himself bare-assed on the kitchen chair, his rampant erection thrusting out from the V of his hips and groin.

Ellery glared up at Jackson accusingly. "I have *missed* this!" And then he lowered his head and took Jackson's thrust inside his mouth.

Sweaty, yes—and musky. Salty and good. Ellery sucked hard and deep, feeling the head of that cock in the back of his throat, swallowing to keep from gagging, holding his breath for as long as he could, just to hold it all inside.

Jackson groaned and grasped his hair again, hauling him back so he could meet that furious pair of hot green eyes. "What are you doing?"

"No condoms." Ellery smiled through the glaze on his swollen lips. Jackson had told him that while healing, half-delirious with drugs and pain—he'd tested negative, he'd said. Ellery should be relieved, he'd said.

Ellery was more than relieved.

"I know that, but—"

Ellery didn't want to hear it. He wrapped his lips around that perfect fat and shiny cockhead and sucked him even deeper, satisfied on some visceral level to have Jackson's flesh in his mouth, against his palate and tongue. He pulled back, hollowing his cheeks, and sucked again, spurred on by Jackson's surprised grunts, his arousal, the frantic tugging in Ellery's hair.

God, Ellery was hard, thick and aching in his slacks, and he fumbled with his belt one-handed. He took Jackson down again, holding him there between his lips and teasing with his tongue so he could undress, shoving his pants and boxers down and grabbing himself as he grabbed Jackson. He let go with his mouth and caught his breath, flicking lips and tongue over the head while he stroked himself to the edge.

Then he really went to work.

Jackson's inarticulate grunts amped up, turned to frenzied cries, turned to Jackson gasping Ellery's name as his hips arched off the chair and he spurted, thick, salty, and clotted, into Ellery's mouth.

Ellery closed his eyes and swallowed, tasting it all, bitter, slimy, and animal.

He groaned, still hard, and Jackson pulled his hair again, lifting him up, up, until he stood in front of the kitchen chair with his dick at a ninety-degree angle, aimed at Jackson's mouth. Jackson stroked him, looking up into his eyes.

"Counselor, you've got my come on your mouth."

"Want some?"

Jackson's smile said filthy, sexy things about what he wanted.

"I'm going to suck you fucking dry."

His mouth, hot, slick, hard, closed over Ellery's cock, and Ellery tilted his head back and shuddered. Oh God, he was talented, taking Ellery down to the root, then pulling back, his tongue lashing around the head, probing the slit, his lips closing tightly over the edge of the bell.

Ellery groaned, and it was his turn to knot his fingers in Jackson's hair, but he couldn't make himself pull, couldn't make himself get rough. He had to settle for holding Jackson firmly and rocking his hips forward, letting Jackson swallow, then canting them back and letting him lick. Again, and again, his rhythm slow but intense, because Jackson's mouth was hard and tight.

And again, the climax building up from his shaking upper thighs to his—oh God! Balls! Jackson had let go of his cock and was fondling his balls while his mouth and tongue worked relentlessly, and Ellery's knees went weak. Oh God, oh hells, oh—"*Jackson*!" he gasped. "God! Just…."

Jackson let go of his balls and grasped his cock again, then did the unthinkable and let Ellery fall out of his mouth, barely balancing his head on a flat tongue.

He stroked Ellery hard and fast with his fist, his tongue tantalizing, scooping the pre from the slit, teasing the harp string underneath, while beating, beating, faster, faster—

"*Now!*" Ellery cried, and Jackson closed his eyes just as Ellery let loose, painting his face with thick white clots of come.

Ellery orgasmed until his knees threatened to collapse and he begged, "Enough!"

Jackson released him, keeping his eyes closed, and leaned his head against Ellery's hip while Ellery stroked his hair.

They were both sticky, covered in ejaculate, sweating from effort. Jackson used the hem of his shirt to wipe his eyes before he blinked owlishly through the come on his eyelashes.

Ellery's heart beat like a hummingbird's wings in his ears.

"Shower," he croaked, knowing that was hard for Jackson but not caring. For a week he'd listened to the damned stubborn man wrestle the waterproof sleeve over his shoulder, keeping his scabbing stitches dry. Jackson glared at him, but Ellery shook his head. "Get the fucking sleeve—I'll put it on. I want a shower with you, Jackson. I've been trying to be sensitive to you learning how to live with someone, but I'm done. Closeness. You and me. You need it as much as I do."

"Asshole," Jackson muttered.

In response, Ellery offered him a hand to lever up. Jackson took it. Ellery held on to him while he toed off his shoes, and then let go to pick up his clothes, and together they made their way to the bathroom.

Jackson was quiet during the shower, right up until Ellery started to soap his hair, and then he let out a groan that was positively hedonistic.

"So I'm handy to keep around." Ellery broke the silence.

"Yeah." Jackson leaned back a little, and Ellery finished rinsing so he could wrap an arm around his waist.

"So are you," he said in Jackson's ear.

"Prove it."

"After dinner."

Jackson had developed a smooth, almost birdlike way of moving as he'd healed, and he did that now, turning his head slowly sideways.

"Didn't we do this bass-ackwards?"

Ellery nodded and kissed his temple. "Yeah. Well, I need my investigator working on all cylinders for the after-dinner discussion."

Jackson sobered. "You certainly cleared out the main barrel."

"That's my job, Detective."

Foolishness, yes. But when they sat down, clean, cooler, in basketball shorts, ready to eat, Ellery was grateful for their foolishness.

The world was a scary and serious place sometimes. He and Jackson were going to need all of the playing, all of the lovemaking they could manage to deal with the work ahead.

AMY LANE is a mother of two college students, two grade-schoolers, and two small dogs. She is also a compulsive knitter who writes because she can't silence the voices in her head. She adores fur-babies, knitting socks, and hawt menz, and she dislikes moths, cat boxes, and knuckle-headed macspazzmatrons. She is rarely found cooking, cleaning, or doing domestic chores, but she has been known to knit up an emergency hat/blanket/pair of socks for any occasion whatsoever, or sometimes for no reason at all. Her award-winning writing has three flavors: twisty-purple alternative universe, angsty-orange contemporary, and sunshine-yellow happy. By necessity, she has learned to type like the wind. She's been married for twenty-plus years to her beloved Mate and still believes in Twu Wuv, with a capital Twu and a capital Wuv, and she doesn't see any reason at all for that to change.

Website: www.greenshill.com
Blog: www.writerslane.blogspot.com
E-mail: amylane@greenshill.com
Facebook: www.facebook.com/amy.lane.167
Twitter: @amymaclane

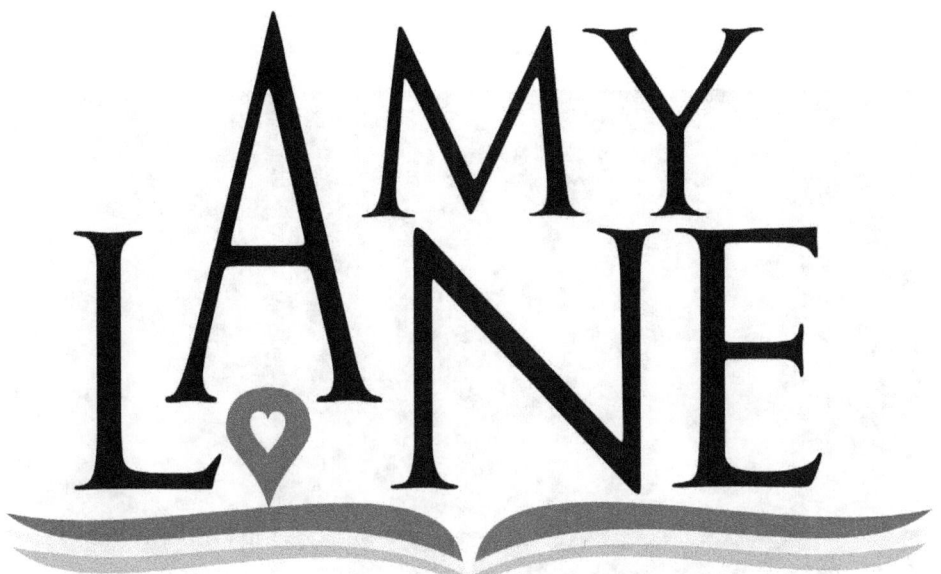

Choose your Lane to love!

Orange

Amy's

Dark Contemporary Romance

BEHIND
THE
CURTAIN

AMY LANE

Dawson Barnes recognizes his world is very small and very charmed. Running his community college theater like a petty god, he and his best friend, Benji know they'll succeed as stage techs after graduation. His father adores him, Benji would die for him, and Dawson never doubted the safety net of his family, even when life hit him below the belt.

But nothing prepared him for falling on Jared Emory's head.

Aloof dance superstar Jared is a sweet, vulnerable man and Dawson's life suits him like a fitted ballet slipper. They forge a long-distance romance from their love of the theater and the magic of Denny's. At first it's perfect: Dawson gets periodic visits and nookie from a gorgeous man who "gets" him—and Jared gets respite from the ultra-competitive world of dancing that almost consumed him.

That is until Jared shows up sick and desperate and Dawson finally sees the distance between them concealed painful things Jared kept inside. If he doesn't grow up—and fast—his "superstar" might not survive his own weaknesses. That would be a shame, because the real, fragile Jared that Dawson sees behind the curtain is the person he can see spending his life with.

www.dreamspinnerpress.com

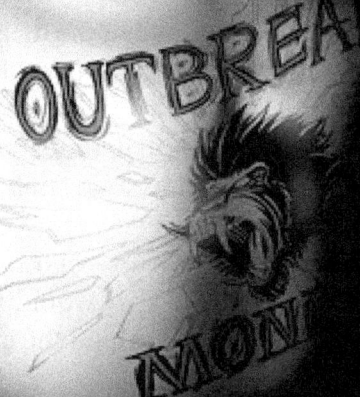

BENEATH THE STAIN

THE STAIN

OUTBREA

MON

AMY LANE

In a town as small as Tyson, CA, everybody knew the four brothers with the four different fathers—and their penchant for making good music when they weren't getting into trouble. For Mackey Sanders, playing in Outbreak Monkey with his brothers and their friends—especially Grant Adams—made Tyson bearable. But Grant has plans for getting Mackey and the Sanders boys out of Tyson, even if that means staying behind.

Between the heartbreak of leaving Grant and the terrifying, glamorous life of rock stardom, Mackey is adrift and sinking fast. When he's hit rock bottom, Trav Ford shows up, courtesy of their record company and a producer who wants to see what Mackey can do if he doesn't flame out first. But cleaning up his act means coming clean about Grant, and that's not easy to do or say. Mackey might make it with Trav's help—but Trav's not sure he's going to survive falling in love with Mackey.

Mackey James Sanders comes with a whole lot of messy, painful baggage, and law-and-order Trav doesn't do messy or painful. And just when Trav thinks they may have mastered every demon in Mackey's past, the biggest, baddest demon of all comes knocking.

www.dreamspinnerpress.com

Terrell Washington's childhood was a trifecta of suck: being black, gay, and poor in America has no upside. Terrell climbed his way out of the hood only to hit a glass ceiling and stop, frozen, a chain restaurant bartender with a journalism degree. His one bright spot is Colby Meyers, a coworker who has no fear, no inhibitions, and sees no boundaries. Terrell and Colby spend their summers at the river and their breaks on the back dock of Papiano's. As terrified as Terrell is of coming out, he's helpless to stay away from Colby's magnetic smile and contagious laughter.

But Colby is out of college now, and he has grand plans for the future—plans Terrell is sure will leave his scrawny black ass in the Sacramento dust until a breathless moment stolen from the chaos of the restaurant tells Terrell he might be wrong. When the moment is shattered by a mystery and an act of violence, Terrell and Colby are left with two puzzles: who killed their scumbag manager, and how to fit their own lives—the black and the white of them—into a single shining tomorrow.

www.dreamspinnerpress.com

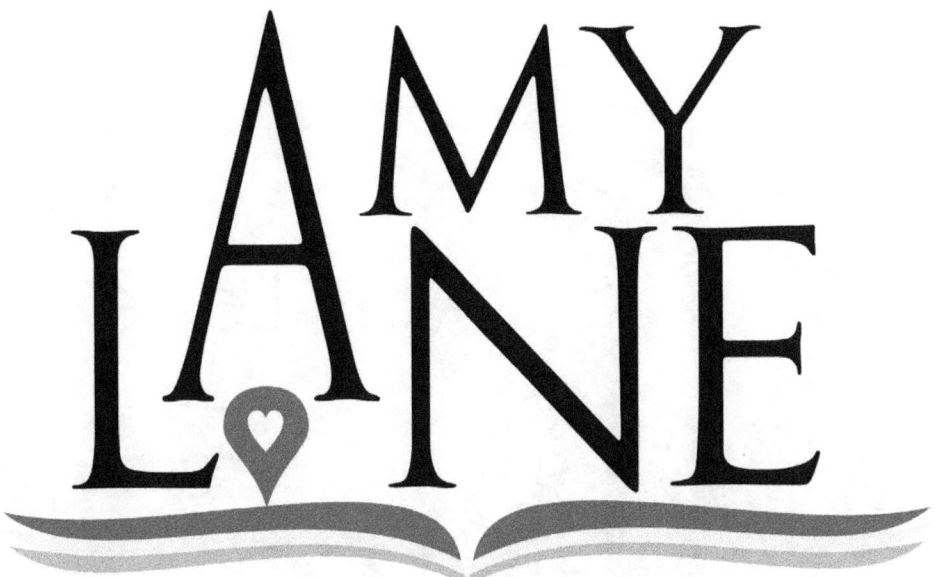

Choose your Lane to love!

Yellow

Amy's

Light Contemporary Romance

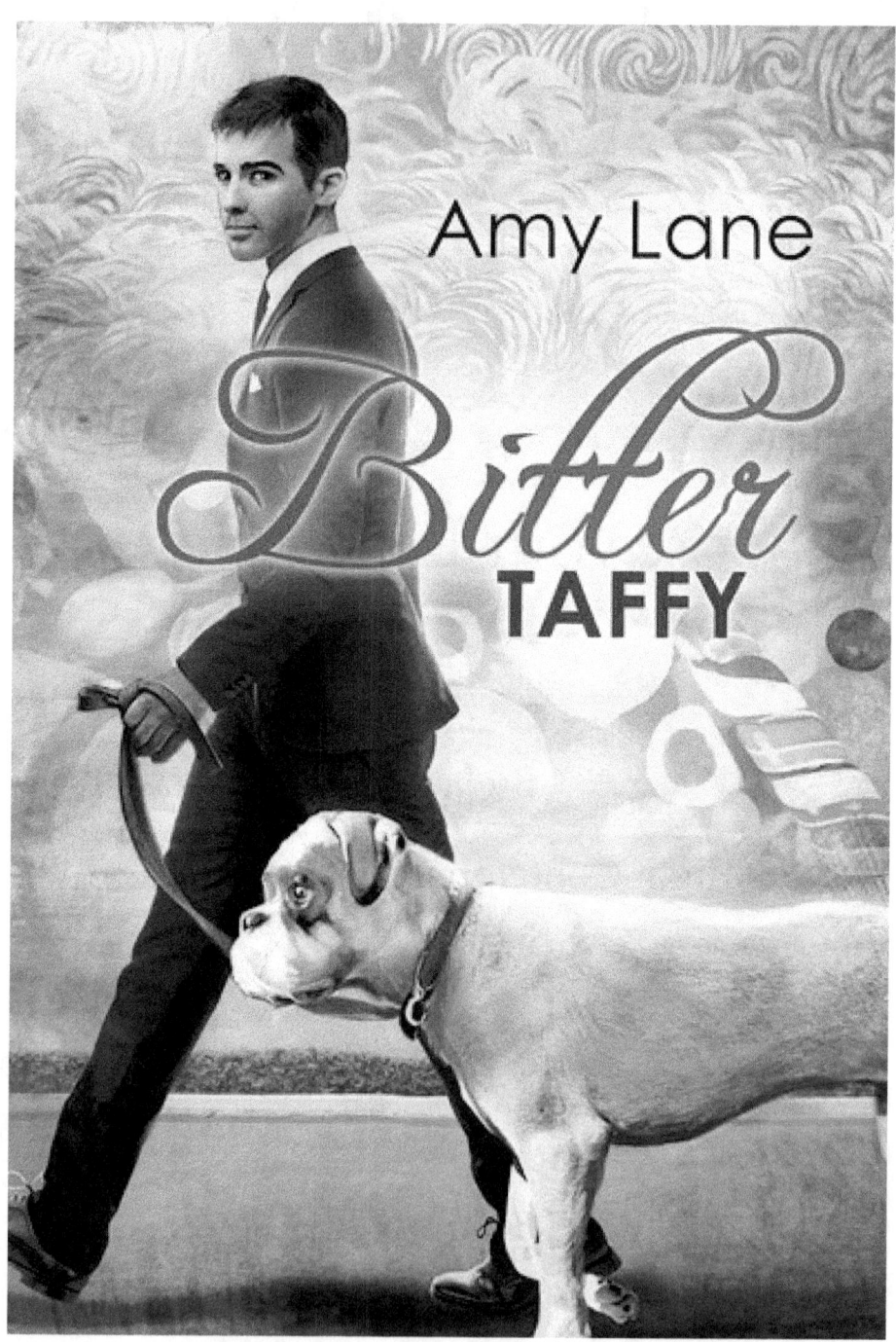

Amy Lane

Bitter
TAFFY

A Candy Man Book

Rico Gonzalves-Macias didn't expect to fall in love during his internship in New York—and he didn't expect the boss's son to out them both and get him fired either. When he returns to Sacramento stunned and heartbroken, he finds his cousin, Adam, and Adam's boyfriend, Finn, haven't just been house-sitting—they've made his once sterile apartment into a home.

When Adam gets him a job interview with the adorable, magnetic, practically perfect Derek Huston, Rico feels especially out of his depth. Derek makes it no secret that he wants Rico, but Rico is just starting to figure out that he's a beginner at the really important stuff and doesn't want to jump into anything with both feet.

Derek is a both-feet kind of guy. But he's also made mistakes of his own and doesn't want to pressure Rico into anything. Together they work to find a compromise between instant attraction and long-lasting love, and while they're working, Rico gets a primer in why family isn't always a bad idea. He needs to believe Derek can be his family before Derek's formidable patience runs out—because even a practically perfect boyfriend is capable of being hurt.

www.dreamspinnerpress.com

A Candy Man Book

Ezra Kellerman flew across country to see if he had another chance with the man he let slip through his fingers. He didn't. Rico has moved on, but he doesn't just leave his ex high and dry. Instead, Rico entrusts his family and friends with Ezra's care. Ezra, confused, hurt, and lost, clings to Rico's cousin and his boyfriend as the lifelines they are—but their friend Miguel is another story.

Miguel Rodriguez had great plans and ambition—but a hearty dose of real life crushed those flat. When Miguel finds himself partially in charge of the befuddled, dreamy, healing Ezra, he's pretty resentful at first. But Ezra's placid nature and sincere wonder at the simple life Miguel has taken for granted begin to soften Miguel's hardened shell. Miguel starts to notice that Ezra isn't just amazingly sweet—he's achingly beautiful as well. Suddenly Miguel is fending off every currently single man on the planet to give Ezra room to get over Rico—while fighting a burning suspicion that the best thing to help Ezra get over his broken heart is Miguel.

www.dreamspinnerpress.com